the Exception

usa today bestselling author
jenna hartley

Copyright © 2025 by Jenna Hartley.
All rights reserved.

No part of this publication may be reproduced, distributed, or transmitted in any form or by any electronic or mechanical means, including information storage and retrieval systems, without written permission from the author, except for the use of brief quotations embodied in a book review and certain other noncommercial uses permitted by copyright law.

This is a work of fiction. Names, characters, businesses, places, events, and incidents are either the products of the author's imagination or used in a fictitious manner. Any resemblance to actual persons, living or dead, or actual events is purely coincidental.

No generative artificial intelligence (AI) was used in the writing of this work. Without in any way limiting the author's exclusive rights under copyright, any use of this publication to "train" generative artificial intelligence (AI) technologies to generate text is expressly prohibited. The author reserves all rights to license uses of this work for generative AI training and development of machine learning language models.

Editing: Lisa A. Hollett
Cover: Qamber Designs

People who love you will love you exactly as you are.

jenna hartley

Content Warnings

This story contains explicit sexual content, profanity, and topics that may be sensitive to some readers.

For more detailed information, visit the QR code below.

CHAPTER ONE

Lily

"I have a favor to ask," my sister said as soon as I answered her call.

No "hello." No "how are you?" Or even "I miss you." Just… "I have a favor to ask."

I frowned and set down my scraper and respirator mask before taking a seat on the scaffolding. I didn't know why I was surprised. Honestly, I shouldn't have been. This was how it had been ever since Auntie Jackie had died. Ever since I'd inherited $100,000.

I wiped my forehead with the back of my sleeve. After spending a sleepless night adjusting countless buckets and tarps to prevent more water damage to the château from the rainstorm, I hadn't even bothered to put on a wig or apply my eyebrows or eyelashes.

Instead, I'd covered my bare scalp with a colorful scarf, as I often did when I was working. I didn't want to damage my wigs, and it wasn't good to wash them more than once every few weeks. Besides, I often got so sweaty while working that my scalp ended up getting irritated from the adhesive.

My sister was still talking, and I didn't know how much of the conversation I'd missed.

I cared about my family. I wanted to have a relationship with them. But it often felt so one-sided. If I was honest, it had for a long time. But my sudden windfall had magnified that. Sharpened it to the point of pain.

I'd always been the odd one out in my family. I was the only one of my four siblings who had left our small town in Montana. None of them had understood why I'd moved to LA to work as a personal assistant for a hotel mogul. They'd been even more baffled a year later when I'd sold nearly everything I'd owned and quit that stable, well-paying job to start a luxury-travel blog.

It had been a leap of faith to start *Gilded Lily*, but it had paid off. For the past two years, I'd gotten to travel the globe in style. My blog had millions of views every month, and I gave my honest opinion on everything from designer suitcases to accommodations.

When I was writing as Gilded Lily, my opinion mattered. People from all around the world listened. I'd never felt that way before—not with my family. Nor with anyone I'd dated in the past.

The only person who'd ever been supportive, who'd loved me unconditionally, was Auntie Jackie. Even now, even after she'd died, she was still trying to take care of me. I'd practically memorized the letter that had accompanied her will.

My dearest Liliana,

You and I have always shared a spirit of adventure. I know how practical you are, but you're a risk-taker too. I'm leaving you this money so you can take more risks. Use it to do something outlandish—something I'd approve of.

Live a big life. Keep chasing your wildest dreams. I'll be with you in spirit, every step of the way.

Remember, "The only limit in life is the one you set yourself."

*Love,
Auntie Jackie*

*My eyes stung with unshed tears, but I pushed them away. Crying was a waste of time and energy—both of which were currently in short supply.

I missed Auntie Jackie, but I was confident she'd approve of what I'd done with the money. I was definitely taking some big risks.

A year ago, I'd purchased the *Château de Bergeret* for $20,000. It had always been a dream of mine to own a boutique luxury hotel, and Auntie Jackie had given me the means to finally do so.

The château was a masterpiece, with distinctive French architecture and an impressive historical pedigree. It needed a lot of work, but it would all be worth it. Or at least, that's what I kept telling myself as I poured blood, sweat, tears, and all of my savings into this project.

"Are you still there?" Iris asked.

"Mm-hmm. Yep."

Needing to move, to do something, I climbed down from the scaffolding and passed beneath crumbling plaster, step-

---

* The quote "The only limit in life is the one you set yourself" has been attributed to Felix Baumgartner, an Austrian skydiver, daredevil, and BASE jumper.

over chipped tiles, trying not to let myself feel completely overwhelmed.

You couldn't ask for a more idyllic setting than *Le Jardin de France,* and I could imagine hosting weddings and so many wonderful events here. Elegantly dressed guests would cross the stone bridge via candlelight over the dry moat to reach the château. It was gorgeous. Majestic. Like something straight out of a fairy tale.

But lately, it felt like more of a nightmare.

There wasn't a part of the château that didn't need work, most of it major. Read: hella expensive. Masonry repair, landscaping, a new slate roof. But it was the interior that was truly a mess. Extensive water damage. Minimal furniture and most of it was old in a way that wasn't chic, would *never* be chic. Outdated plumbing and electrical.

Even though I was resourceful, and I'd been doing what I could between trips for my blog, I was out of my depth. And despite the experienced team I'd hired, progress was slow. At the rate things were going, I'd soon run out of money.

Right. Money. That was likely why my sister had called after all. She was still talking, and I was still drowning in my responsibilities, but Iris was my little sister. So, I tried to lend a supportive ear.

"Did she agree?" her husband, Dan, asked in the background.

"Agree to what?" I asked, hesitancy lining my tone.

She hushed him then asked, "You know how Dan and I are trying to buy that house?"

No. I didn't know that. But that was nothing new. My family acted like I lived on another planet just because I didn't live in Small Town, Montana, like the rest of them.

I sighed. I had a feeling I knew where this was headed, but I tried to give Iris the benefit of the doubt.

"That's great, Iris. Congrats." I peered around the foyer,

looking at all the work left to be done in just this one room. One of forty-five.

What was I thinking?

It had taken weeks to get even half the paint removed—years of white and cream layers applied over the château's beautiful *tuffeau* stone. I wanted to restore it to its natural finish, with just the original lime render on top.

"It is," she continued. "But we hit a snag with the financing."

"I'm sorry to hear that," I said, glancing at the time.

I needed to finish up here so I could check in with Luc before I had to leave for the airport. He was one of the qualified heritage artisans and a sort of project manager for when I had to be away. I also needed to pack.

"And I—*we*," Iris said, "were hoping you could loan us the money. We only need about $18,000, and we'll pay you back in a few months," she rushed to add.

Only eighteen grand? I wanted to laugh. She acted like it was nothing.

She planned to pay me back in a few months? Where was she magically going to get this $18,000? In such a short time frame?

I mean, shit. I could really use that kind of knowledge.

"Why not just wait a few months and pay it yourself?" I asked, trying to understand.

"Because the seller had several offers on the house, and we're lucky ours was accepted. If we can't get the money to make it happen, they'll move on to someone else."

"Did you ask Mom and Dad?"

"You and I both know they don't have that kind of money," she said.

And she thought I did? I wish!

"I'm sorry, Iris. I wish I could help, but I can't."

"Seriously, Lil? You can't even lend me ten grand?"

"No. I can't. I'm stretched thin as it is." And her attitude was pissing me off.

"Oh yeah." Her tone was full of skepticism. "It must be really hard—flying first class, staying in all those luxury hotels. You live in a freaking castle, for crying out loud."

My skin was hot. Tight. "First of all, traveling is my job. And I worked hard for those opportunities. My blog didn't just explode overnight. I had to cultivate those brand relationships."

"Whatever," she huffed. "God, you're so selfish."

Excuse me? I jerked my head back, feeling as if I'd been slapped.

Selfish? She was calling me selfish?

In the past, I would've brushed off her comment. I was used to my family's snide remarks. And maybe it was the exhaustion, the feeling of defeat weighing down on me after another intense rainstorm that had increased the damage to the château, but I couldn't just let it go. I couldn't.

"Maybe if you ever asked how I was or how the restoration was going, you'd know that I live in a tiny, outdated apartment in the basement of the château. I cook my meals on a hot plate. I don't even have hot water."

Nor did I have a shower; I had an old cast-iron tub. It was a far cry from the luxury experience I hoped to one day provide my guests. And every day, it felt as if that dream slipped a little further away.

"You only have yourself to blame. You were the one who decided to waste all that money on that stupid ruin," she sneered. "So don't complain about it now."

"I'm not complaining," I gritted out, trying not to lose my cool completely. But honestly, I'd had enough. This wasn't the first time my family had tried to guilt me into giving them some of my inheritance. I wasn't trying to be selfish, but the money simply wasn't there.

And even if it had been, I was under no obligation to give it to them. Nor did I care to, not when they acted like this. Self-centered. Demanding. Entitled.

"It sure sounds like you are," she said.

Enough. She had no right to lecture me about my choices. None of my family did. I was over it. Done.

Before I could think better of it or stop myself, I said, "I'm merely pointing out the fact that you don't seem to give a shit about me—none of you do—unless you need something."

"If that's how you feel, then never mind. I don't want your money anyway."

"Great!" I chirped.

"What? No, wait." Iris tried to backtrack. "I'm sorry. I didn't—"

Unbelievable. I scoffed. "Too late." I ended the call.

My hands were shaking, but damn, that felt good.

Fuck her. Actually, my whole family could go fuck themselves.

Just last week, my younger brother had called to ask for money to fix his car. Before that, it was my mom asking for help with a credit card bill. I was sick of everyone calling me for money. Simply expecting me to fork it over without even asking how I was.

Every day, I checked the dwindling savings in my bank account. And every day, I tried to figure out how the hell I was going to generate enough revenue to get me through such a massive restoration.

I was exhausted and overwhelmed. I couldn't continue to do it all—travel, maintain my blog, create content for my YouStream channel dedicated to the château restoration, actually restore the château. It was too much. Something had to give.

But did I ask them for help?

No. I knew I only had myself to rely on.

No bank wanted to lend me the money. And since I was a self-employed luxury-travel blogger, they'd deemed me and my project too much of a risk.

Fortunately, I'd done some research before signing the papers to accept ownership of the château. I'd received an affirmation from the French government that they'd help support the project. And they'd been true to their word. I'd received forty to sixty percent of the funding for various projects around the château, depending on the element of the property. It had to be heritage listed, and I had to use a qualified heritage architect and artisans. It didn't cover everything—far from it. But I would've had to stop long before now without that assistance.

Even so, I was struggling. We were still so early in the project because of the enormity of the scope of it, and any non-heritage elements like plumbing and electrical would need to be completely funded by me.

I kept applying for grants from cultural and heritage societies, prizes. Anything. I just kept hoping and brainstorming. And trying. I'd add even more advertising spots to my blog if I had to, as long as it wouldn't sacrifice the amazing community I'd cultivated.

As the French would say, *Quand le vin est tiré, il faut le boire.*

When the wine is poured, one must drink it. In other words, once the first step is taken, there's no going back.

And there was definitely no going back at this point. Not with my family or the château.

CHAPTER TWO

Graham

My assistant, Carson, poked his head inside the door to my office. "The board called an emergency meeting."

"What?" I asked, glancing up from my laptop. Surely I'd misheard. When I saw his expression, I realized he was serious. "Shit. When?"

"Ten minutes."

"We're supposed to be on the helicopter in ten."

He lifted a shoulder. "It sounds serious."

No shit. The board could call an emergency meeting at the request of two directors, but it rarely, if ever, happened. The fact that they'd called one now did not bode well.

"Did they say what it's about?"

He shook his head but stepped inside and closed the door softly behind him. "I don't know, but Donahue looked downright gleeful."

"Fuck." I turned toward the window and the view of the Los Angeles skyline.

Fred Donahue was one of the Huxley Grand board members—and a pain in the ass. He almost always opposed me. And ever since my biggest ally, Steve Harrel, had died, Fred had been even more determined to push his own agenda.

I pinched the bridge of my nose, wondering what he was up to this time. I had a few theories, but I didn't like any of them.

"Tell the pilot we'll be late—both of them." The helicopter was supposed to take us directly to the private airfield so we could leave for Mexico. There was nothing I hated more than being late. Well, being late and surprises.

"Yes, sir," he said. "Anything else?"

"Have my siblings been notified about the board meeting?" I asked, knowing that Carson would understand I was referring to both my actual siblings, Jasper and Sloan, as well as my cousins, Knox and Nate, who had always been more like siblings.

"Jasper's and Sloan's assistants are aware. I secured proxies from Knox and Nate, as they were both tied up."

"Good." I stood, gathering my laptop and shoving it and some papers into my bag. Very good. "And, Carson?"

"Yes?" He paused at the doorway and glanced back at me.

"Thank you."

He lifted his chin in acknowledgment then disappeared into the hallway. He was a good assistant, proficient. Quick. He didn't scare easily, like most of my previous assistants. All of them except one—Liliana.

I gnashed my teeth at the thought of her and her blog.

Liliana Fontaine. A great asset until she'd decided to start blogging about my company. I could admit that *maybe* there was some truth in her reviews. But I wished she'd come to me first, instead of sharing those thoughts with her millions of followers.

I squared my shoulders and smoothed down my tie. That wasn't what mattered right now. I pulled out my phone and texted Pierce, my lawyer and the closest thing I had to a best friend.

> Me: Running late. Board called emergency meeting.

Pierce: For what purpose?

> Me: To piss me off.

Pierce: Think there's going to be a vote?

> Me: Fuck if I know. With the way things have been going lately, it'll likely come down to the tie-breaker again.
>
> Me: Any progress with our plan to acquire additional shares?

Pierce: Still working on it.

SHIT. I HATED BEING IN A VULNERABLE POSITION.

According to the terms of my grandparents' will, all five of us had received an equal number of shares. Ten percent went to Knox, Nate, Sloan, Jasper, and me, so that the family continued to hold fifty percent of the company. But to pass anything, we needed at least fifty-one percent of the shares in favor. Now that Steve was gone, that was a much more difficult proposition.

Not only had his death left a huge void on the board, but his family had been forced to part with most of his shares to pay his medical bills. If I'd known, I would've settled the bills myself. Not to curry favor or increase my position, but because it would've been the right thing to do. Because he'd been a friend.

But I hadn't known. I hadn't realized how dire the situation was until it was too late.

I clenched and unclenched my fists. Now was not the time to dwell on that. I couldn't change the past; I needed to focus on the future. *My* future vision for the company.

Certain members of the board, led by Donahue, had been trying to oust me as CEO and replace me with someone outside the family. And I wasn't going to let it happen. My grandfather had entrusted the Huxley Grand empire to me, and I intended to hold on to it until I was ready to step down. And considering the fact that I was only forty-four, I had no intention of resigning any time soon.

I'd been running this company for the past fourteen years, but the brand was in my blood. I'd grown up hearing about the hotel business, about profit and loss statements, for as long as I could remember. And while, yes, thirty was a bit young to take over as CEO, I'd known the company—the industry—inside and out.

And my success as CEO proved it. I'd helped steer the company to greater wealth in more locations across the globe, while focusing on the luxury and sustainability our brand was known for. I'd increased profits. We consistently received the highest ratings of employee satisfaction in the entire hospitality industry. Probably in no small part because we paid the highest salaries, and we attracted the best, most diverse talent. Our company culture valued inclusion and innovation. This brand and what it stood for were my everything.

Donahue didn't understand. Could never understand.

He'd joined the board five years ago, and he'd had very distinct opinions about how things should be run. He came from an IT background, and he had a different mentality. He preferred to fail fast and break shit, whereas I was focused on maintaining the legacy and prestige of the brand.

I entered the conference room, and Donahue's attention snapped to me. I tried not to smirk. So maybe I *did* like surprises, so long as I wasn't on the receiving end.

"Graham?" Fred jerked his head back. "Aren't you supposed to be on a plane?"

"Helicopter, actually." I slid into my place at the head of the table. "But I would never miss a board meeting, let alone an emergency one."

His face reddened, and he opened his mouth. I braced myself for his tirade, but Danika placed her hand on his arm as if to soothe him. Silence him.

Mm. Interesting. I supposed that answered my question. Danika must be the other board member who'd called for an emergency meeting.

Carson switched on the projector, and I scanned the rest of the board members, trying to determine who else might be in on this little political maneuver. My younger brother Jasper appeared on the screen, his shirt unbuttoned and his hair wet. He'd flown to Mexico a week ago to finalize everything for our soft opening. Palm trees swayed in the background, and I tapped my fingers on my thigh beneath the table. He looked irresponsible. Like the billionaire playboy everyone expected. I knew that wasn't entirely fair or true, but he could *try* not to feed into their low expectations of him.

A minute later, our sister Sloan joined us. Her clothes were rumpled, and she was slightly out of breath. *Unprofessional.*

I needed to have a talk with the two of them. Because clearly, they didn't understand how precarious our current situation was. We were on the verge of a coup by the board.

But Jasper had been acting strangely ever since he'd gone

to London to stand in for Sloan while she'd taken her annual sailing trip. And Sloan had been floating on cloud fucking nine ever since she'd married Jackson. I was happy for her, truly. And I liked Jackson, respected him. But did they have to be so sickeningly in love?

Maybe I just didn't get it. Would never get it. Hell, I'd been told by women in the past that I was incapable of love. I hadn't wanted to listen, but when you heard something enough times, you tended to believe it.

"Everyone's here," I said, eager to end this farce of an "emergency" meeting. It was likely nothing more than a chance for Fred to stir up shit, as usual.

Fred stood, a sort of smug self-importance surrounding him and ballooning out. God, I couldn't wait to get out of here. "Thank you all for being here. I called this emergency board meeting because there's been a significant and sudden drop in our stock price."

I sat back in my chair. "Yes, it dropped, but it's not unprecedented. There was a scandal. We will weather it. And we will come out stronger."

I was trying to downplay the scandal, but it still rankled. Last year, allegations had been made that the brand wasn't taking the privacy and security of high-profile guests seriously enough. And rightly so. Paparazzi had slipped past security multiple times, as had someone who'd wanted to harm my sister, Sloan. The situation was now well in hand, thanks to her husband, Jackson.

Then we'd been the target of a sting operation to uncover escorts. Claims that Huxley employees had looked the other way. Or worse—actively recruited escorts to fill seats at our bars and clubs.

I'd been questioned about my knowledge, not that I'd known a damn thing about it. It had been a fucking mess, and it had shaken investor confidence. It had certainly made me question some things about how our locations were being run, and I'd kept a closer eye on operations ever since.

"Mm." Fred tilted his head, and I wanted to punch him in the face. "This was not a slight dip. It was a significant *plummet*. If we don't do something, and soon, it could go even lower."

Great. I just loved when members of the board resorted to scare tactics without considering the full picture. But if stock prices dipped low enough, they could force a vote to oust me as CEO.

"I understand that you're concerned. We're keeping an eye on it."

"Keeping an eye on it?" he spluttered. "So you want us to just sit here and watch as the company tanks." Fred flung the words at me. "Spend even more money on overpriced and ill-considered new developments? People are saying that the brand is outdated and elitist. That it's run by a cold, heartless billionaire."

I frowned. "Who's saying that?"

He pointed at the screen, where an image of me was displayed on the cover of a widely circulated, prestigious business magazine. In bold letters over the image were the words, "Cold. Heartless. Billionaire."

Fuck.

I needed to get my hands on a copy of that article.

Even so, my stomach clenched with dread, based on the title alone. The board had been on my ass for nearly a year, telling me to change my image. I hadn't heeded their warnings, instead brushing them off as over the top or ridiculous. Shouldn't my record as CEO of the Huxley empire speak for itself?

In the past, it had. But now that our stock price had dropped, I was in a weaker position. I needed extra shares to regain my footing. Before it was too late.

I remained silent, willing him to damn himself.

"What do you propose?" one of the other board members asked.

"A merger," Fred said, the word landing with a thud.

Several people gasped, but I was pissed. *A merger?* Was he crazy? And how long had he been planning this?

Despite my ire, I maintained a calm façade. Confident. Cool. In control.

"One dip in our stock, and you're talking merger?" I shook my head, and I was sure my expression was patronizing as fuck.

Because, seriously? That was his plan? A merger? That would likely send everyone into even more of a tailspin.

Though, I supposed Donahue had found another path to getting rid of me as CEO. Perhaps I'd underestimated him.

"Has someone approached you?" Sloan asked.

"Moretti."

Over my dead body, I nearly growled. But I didn't. Instead, I spun my grandfather's ring on my pinkie finger beneath the table and tried not to show how ruffled I truly was.

Moretti was a thug in a designer suit, and I wanted nothing to do with him. He'd been accused of multiple things, from bribery to assault, but he always seemed to get off. Regardless of his culpability, he was shady as fuck.

"Absolutely not," Jasper said. "No way."

"He's our biggest competitor. Our biggest threat," Fred continued, undeterred. A few people's heads bobbed in agreement. *Fuck me.*

"I think we should consider it," Danika chimed in. *Dear god.*

Between the two of them, they had twenty-five percent of the shares. That alone wasn't enough to push a merger through, but they could be persuasive. And after a series of recent missteps, I was on thin ice with the board. This latest article didn't help.

I might be the CEO, but with the way our company was structured, if it came to a vote and there was a tie, the fate of the company fell into the hands of one person. One law firm, actually. An independent third party that had been named in my grandparents' will and would vote only in the event of a tie.

And if they sided with the board, they could fire me. From my family's own damn company. I *needed* more shares. A majority of the shares.

"Just think of how it could enhance our reach geographically, as well as our market power," another board member said.

"What about cultural integration?" Jasper asked. "Employee retention?"

"I'm sure those details could be ironed out in negotiations." I wanted to punch the smug grin off Fred's face. I watched with horror as several others nodded their agreement.

Ironed out? This was a takeover attempt, and anyone who believed otherwise was deluding themselves.

"Moretti doesn't do friendly mergers," I bit out, wondering how long he had been planning this. "And if you're concerned about the brand's image, getting into bed with Moretti is not going to help."

Donahue shrugged, as if the entire fucking future of this company weren't on the line. "He wants to expand into the luxury segment, and he knows we're the best."

Of course he did. Because we were. Everyone knew that.

"Has there been a formal offer?" Sloan asked, and I was grateful my siblings were asking the questions I wanted to but wouldn't dare. I was afraid if I opened my mouth, all the thoughts I was trying to hold back would come spewing out.

The Huxley Grand empire had always been a family-owned brand. My grandparents had started the company sixty years ago, and my siblings and I had been carrying on their legacy since their deaths. We now had locations around the globe. And if I had my way, we'd be able to add decadent all-inclusive voyages on the world's finest luxury yachts to our impressive list of offerings.

Fred wore a thoughtful expression, as if he had all the time in the world. As if he were in fucking control. "No. He's merely expressed his interest."

Jacob Moretti was a liar and a thief who didn't know the meaning of the word "integrity." There was no way in hell I was getting into bed with him. No way I'd let him taint my grandparents' legacy.

I stood, beyond done with this conversation. "Until my attorney receives a formal expression of interest, there's nothing to discuss. Now, if you'll excuse me, I have a flight to catch."

Sloan's and Jasper's attention whipped to me. Jasper looked as if he might protest but then clamped his mouth shut. Sloan quirked an eyebrow but remained silent. They knew we'd discuss it when we were all together in Ixtapa.

Some of the fight seemed to go out of Fred, his earlier bluster fading at my seeming acquiescence. *Good.*

"Are you sure you should be leaving now?" Danika asked. "This stock situation is volatile, and I imagine a formal offer is forthcoming."

Mm. She was definitely in on it. But what did she stand to gain, besides the obvious?

"She's right," Donahue said, echoing her concern. Her fearmongering. "We'll want to move quickly if we receive an offer. Moretti isn't a patient man."

"We wouldn't want to seem desperate, would we?" Before

they could say anything else, I left the room without a backward glance.

After a relatively quick helicopter ride, Carson and I boarded my private jet. Pierce was already on board, enjoying a drink.

"I was just ambushed by the board." I removed my jacket and handed it to Tabitha, my preferred flight attendant from the Hartwell Agency, to hang before taking a seat. "They proposed a merger with Moretti."

Pierce winced. "How did Jasper and Sloan react?"

Carson excused himself to the private conference room to make some calls, likely knowing I needed some alone time with Pierce.

"They were both late to the call," I said. "Jasper looked like he was two margaritas into the day. And Sloan, like she'd just woken up from a nap." Which wasn't like her at all. Maybe it was jet lag?

"We can't all be perfect like you," Pierce teased.

I leaned back in my chair and stared at the ceiling of the plane. I was far from perfect, and sometimes it was exhausting that everyone held me to that standard.

"Not everyone thinks I'm perfect," I said. "In fact, apparently many people view me as a cold, heartless billionaire."

He cringed then reached into his satchel. "I assume you're referring to this." He placed a copy of the magazine on my tray table, where it landed with a thud.

I quickly thumbed through the pages until I reached the article about me. I skimmed the words, my jaw clenching so hard I thought I might crack a molar.

What. The. Fuck?

They were supposed to write a favorable article. Something to make me seem, I don't know, relatable. Instead, I turned the pages with a growing sense of dread. Quotes from an ex-girlfriend. A former board member. Anonymous sources that all made me look like the coldhearted bastard everyone believed me to be. Greedy. Aloof. Out of touch.

"Fuck." I dragged a hand through my curls, tugging. "Fuck!" I said again, more loudly this time.

Yes, I sometimes struggled to connect to people. But I'd thought the interview had gone well. Had I completely misread the situation, or was the magazine intentionally skewing my image?

"It's not ideal," Pierce said. *Understatement of the century.* "But we can fix it."

"How?" I asked. "The board has been looking for an excuse to oust me from my position as CEO. And this—" I picked up the magazine and waved it in the air. "This. With the way things are going lately, this could be my undoing."

"Anyone who really knows you, knows this isn't you."

I tossed the magazine aside then blew out a breath and pushed back against the seat. I drummed my fingers on the armrests.

"Graham. Come on. It's one article."

"One in a series. There was the *Vogue* one last month. And the—"

"Yes, but you can still turn this around. I wish you'd allow me to make your charity donations public. You give a ton of your fortune to environmental and animal welfare causes. People would eat that shit up."

It wasn't the first time we'd had this conversation. "I'd rather make it more about the causes than myself." It was why I always insisted on donating anonymously.

"That's just it. If you donated publicly, you would not only raise awareness for the causes that are important to you. But your generosity might encourage other high-net-worth individuals to donate more of their wealth as well."

"Not likely." I scoffed. "Most of them are trying to evade

taxes. They're not just going to give money away from the goodness of their hearts."

"That's probably what a lot of people think about you."

I grumbled at that.

"Okay. If you don't like that idea, then let them see you with Queen V and Prince Albert. Who doesn't love dogs? Or hell, you could just tell the story of how you rescued them. Or we could have someone interview you in your rooftop garden. Or with your family."

I gnashed my teeth. "That's *private*."

"Whether you like it or not, you're in the public eye. You can't expect to change people's opinions unless you show them who you really are."

I sighed, weary of this conversation. "I've successfully led this company for the past fourteen years. Shouldn't my record speak for itself?"

I leaned forward, resting my elbows on my knees. Pierce was the fixer, and we needed to fix this. Before I lost control of the company I loved, the legacy my grandparents had built and entrusted to me. *Fuck.*

"Look, I get that it frustrates you that they focus on personal drama, but that's what sells. It's what humanizes people. Most people who read that magazine can't imagine being a billionaire or running a luxury hotel empire. But they understand emotion. They are driven by it."

"They are idiots. And my personal life isn't up for consumption."

"It doesn't have to be," Pierce said. "Not all of it. But give them something to show your softer side. Hell, if they spoke to Brooklyn for even five minutes, they'd see how caring you are."

"No." My voice boomed through the cabin. My niece had to be protected at all costs. She already had to contend with the fact that her dad—my cousin Nate—was a famous actor/producer. And her new stepmom was a famous Olympian.

"It was just an example," Pierce said. "I wasn't actually suggesting it. I know better than that. But at this point, you're going to have to do something drastic. Something that will put the board at ease and show the world that you're not the man they claim you are."

He arched one eyebrow, and I could read so much into that one simple gesture. Because there was only one thing I could think of that would accomplish all of that.

I met his eyes, mindful of my words with Tabitha and Carson on board. "Are you suggesting what I think you are?"

Pierce inclined his head, and I let out a heavy sigh. Had it truly come to this?

"Sometimes you have to do the wrong thing for the right reason. I thought you were an expert at that." He gave me a pointed look that I ignored.

I hated to admit it, but I was feeling a bit desperate. And I no longer had the luxury of ruling out any ideas, even marriage. I might not have a formal merger offer in hand, but Moretti wasn't fucking around. When he set his sights on a company, he would do whatever it took to make it his.

I understood why Pierce had suggested this. I could even see the benefit of such an arrangement. I just didn't know if I could go through with it. Or if I did, if I'd be convincing.

But even if I agreed, who the hell would I marry? It wasn't like I was in a relationship. I hadn't been for a while. At least, nothing that had been serious enough to remotely consider marriage.

"I still think there has to be another way." A plan that didn't involve a sham of a marriage to a woman I didn't care about.

I might be pissed about the article, but it irked me

because they weren't wrong. I was a cold, heartless billionaire. And a fake marriage wouldn't change that.

CHAPTER THREE

Lily

"Damn. They really are giving you the first-class treatment," Jo said as we settled into the plush cocoon that was our seats.

I'd flown from France to New York, where I'd met up with my best friend, Josephine. Now, we were on a flight to Ixtapa, Mexico, to stay at the new Huxley Grand location.

Jo often accompanied me when I traveled for my blog. She had a popular YouStream channel where she posted about her life in a farmhouse in upstate New York. We'd been roommates in college and had been friends ever since.

A flight attendant appeared with two flutes of complimentary champagne. *Good thing the Huxley is footing the bill.*

The Huxley Grand was typically more generous than other brands I worked with, but this seemed exorbitant, even for them. I had a large following and was sought-after by luxury-travel companies, but I'd never given the Huxley brand glowing reviews. I'd been complimentary but honest. If I had suggestions—and I often did—I didn't withhold them. I treated them just like any other brand; I had to. My integrity as a blogger was important to me. I knew how much my readers relied on me to give my honest opinion.

Jo gasped, then held up a pair of silk designer pajamas from the amenities kit. I laughed. I could only imagine what my family would have to say about our seating arrangement. I rolled my eyes. That wasn't my concern. And for right now, I needed to focus on this trip. On my blog.

Once the flight attendant was gone, Jo leaned in, resting her elbows on her thighs. "So, are you worried about seeing…" She gave me a meaningful look. "You know."

Graham.

My former boss and the CEO of the Huxley Grand empire.

I hadn't seen—or worked for—Graham in nearly two years. Despite the fact that I was no longer his personal assistant, I continued to follow him, and his company, in the news. I told myself it was merely idle curiosity, keeping tabs on the industry, but I knew there was more to it than that.

I had a feeling if anyone would've understood my need to see the château project come to fruition, it would be him. That or he'd tell me it was a bad investment. I cringed at the idea of hearing those words from Graham Mackenzie. He was a shrewd businessman, a visionary, even if he was often misunderstood.

"Nah. Graham never attends this type of thing. If anything, I'm concerned I'll run into his brother, Jasper. But I doubt he'll recognize or remember me." I gestured to my hair, knowing they wouldn't expect me to have longer, darker hair like my current wig.

Hell, Graham had probably forgotten all about me. And I doubted he'd ever heard of, much less read, my blog. He was too busy for something so trivial.

Even if he had somehow checked out *Gilded Lily*, I always concealed my true identity. And besides, everything I'd written was something I would've said to his face. Though he would've just argued with me about it anyway.

I smiled at the thought. As annoying as he could be at times, I liked that he challenged me and my opinions instead of dismissing them. He'd treated me with respect.

I shifted my champagne flute, taking some pictures before repositioning the cocktail napkin. I needed to get my head in gear. As tired as I was of juggling the restoration and traveling for my blog, I relied on the income from my site to cover my monthly expenses. I couldn't afford to screw this up.

And yet, I couldn't stop thinking about the château and how much work it needed. If I couldn't find a way to fund the necessary restorations... I blew out a breath. I'd done the math on the way to the airport, and I had *maybe* two months before I was out of money.

Jo slid my champagne flute closer. "Here. You look like you could use this."

"Thanks," I sighed and gulped some down. The champagne was refreshing and decadent, a welcome change from the water I typically consumed. Everything else was too expensive.

When my phone vibrated, I pulled it out of my purse and glanced at the screen.

> Aster: You didn't have to be such a jerk to Iris.

I FROWNED. OF COURSE, MY SISTER HAD TOLD EVERYONE ABOUT our argument. *Of course* my brother would take her side.

> Mom: You need to apologize to your sister.

JESUS. I TIGHTENED THE GRIP ON MY PHONE. WHAT WERE WE, five?

And why had my mom automatically taken my sister's side? Without even talking to me, no less. Didn't I deserve the benefit of the doubt? Or the chance to tell my side of the story?

It was disappointing. And yet, I wasn't all that surprised. It hurt to admit that to myself.

I ignored all the other texts and replied directly to my mom.

> Me: Why do I always have to be the one to apologize? I didn't do anything wrong.

> Mom: This never would've happened if you hadn't been so selfish.

WOW. EVEN FROM HUNDREDS OF MILES AWAY, HER WORDS HIT like a physical blow. *Selfish?* Auntie Jackie had left that money to me.

It had taken me far too long to realize that my family only called when they wanted something from me. Or maybe I just hadn't wanted to see the truth.

But now that I had, I couldn't unsee it. And even if I could've, I wasn't sure I wanted to.

I'd never been more grateful for the flight attendant to announce that we had to put our devices into airplane mode. *Gladly.* I chucked my phone into my bag with a huff.

"Lil?" Jo nudged me. "You okay?"

The crew fired up the engines and made the announcement that we were about to take off. So, I dropped my bag to the floor and secured my seat belt before leaning my head back against the headrest. I closed my eyes with a sigh. "I am so done with my family."

"Uh-oh. What happened this time?"

This time. Right. "My sister's mad that I won't loan her eighteen grand for a down payment on a house. And now, the rest of my family is ganging up on me."

Jo's jaw dropped. "You're kidding."

"I wish I were."

"You're not going to give it to her, right?"

I guffawed. "No."

My family was under the misguided impression that I was rolling in cash. But unless something changed—and fast—I might be forced to sell the château. Not that I was going to admit that to Jo. Thinking about my money woes was depressing, and I didn't want to ruin our trip.

She gave my hand a squeeze. "I'm sorry your family is so shitty."

I squeezed her hand back. "I'm grateful I have you."

I was done with my family. I had a feeling that if I didn't call them, they'd never call me. Unless it was to ask for money. I was over their drama and their demands. If they wanted to have a relationship with me, they could start making more of an effort because I was sick of trying.

"You always have me." She patted my hand. "Plus, I found a steal of a deal on a flight to come visit. I hope it's okay, but I went ahead and bought the ticket."

"Really?" I perked up at that, and she nodded. "For when?"

She checked her phone then told me the dates. "Hopefully that works with your schedule."

I checked my calendar. "Yes. That's great. And you'll be there for the weekend of the *les Journées du patrimoine*."

Les Journées was a weekend event each year celebrating European heritage. Châteaux throughout the region, including mine, would open their majestic gates and invite visitors to experience these places and their heritage. It didn't matter that something was constantly under construction at the château; everyone wanted to see our progress.

And it was exciting. I loved being able to share the château with visitors. I loved hearing their feedback and excitement and gratitude for what we'd accomplished. It kept me going, even if organizing the event was a lot of work.

It required coordinating with the artisans for demonstrations, the local winery for tastings, and more. It was a huge opportunity but also a huge undertaking. It was my second year doing it, and I knew how much work it entailed. I had so much to organize, on top of everything else I was already doing.

"Why do you think I selected those dates?" She grinned. "You can put me to work."

Who needed family when I had a friend like her?

"I'd love that," I said. "But I can't ask you to do that."

"You're not asking. I'm offering." She nudged me. "Besides, it's not like you haven't helped me with a million projects around the homestead."

"Yeah, but I didn't do them because I expected something in return."

"I know." She made a silly face. "I want to help, and I want to see the progress in person."

"You mean you want to see Luc again," I teased.

She didn't rise to the bait, instead saying, "It's not completely altruistic. I mean…I get great views on my content, especially my YouStream channel, when I post about visiting the château."

I laughed. "Always happy to help. And, Jo?"

"Yeah?"

"Thank you."

"Of course. This trip helps me too. I need some fresh content. I've been running out of ideas for projects to do around the farm."

"I don't believe that for one minute."

She slumped in her chair. "I've almost finished all the major projects, and I'm afraid people will lose interest."

I tempered my teasing at the sight of her anxiety. "I often feel that pressure too. To keep people's interest. But you always come up with such creative content." I tapped a finger to my lips. "Maybe work in more of the other projects you do. Baking. You mill your own flour. Show that!"

"You really think people would be interested?"

"Heck yeah. And you have some retreats coming up, right?"

"Yeah. Sedona. South Africa. And Alaska. Though, I'm usually so busy running them that there's not enough time to focus on content. Even if there were, I want to make sure the attendees feel safe to share in such an intimate experience."

I could understand that. I'd attended one of her retreats, and it had been amazing. "You are great at creating an atmosphere where people feel free to be vulnerable. Actually, I was hoping that, one day, you'd lead a retreat at the château."

"Really?" she asked.

"Yeah. Maybe we could make it an annual thing. I want it to be a place for wellness. Luxury travel isn't just about expensive surroundings and sumptuous fabrics. It should be restorative for the mind, body, and spirit."

"Ooh. I love that."

We kept brainstorming until the captain announced that it was time for takeoff. As soon as the wheels left the ground, I was finally able to relax a little. I was still upset about my family's texts, but the fact that Josephine had booked a ticket and would be there to help with the *les Journées du patrimoine* was a huge relief.

When I yawned a third time, Jo inclined her head toward the end of our pod. "Why don't you close the curtains and rest."

I blew out a breath. I hadn't been sleeping well. The rainstorms always made me feel exhausted and defeated, magnifying the precarious state of the château.

I was stressed about money. About everything the château needed. The fact that my family was ganging up on me didn't help.

Auntie Jackie had given me that money. *Me* and no one else.

That was her decision. Just as it had been her money.

Hell, when she was alive, the rest of my family had never checked in on her. Never bothered to have any kind of relationship with her. They'd never cared about her until they'd found out about the money she'd left me. It was disgusting, and it made my heart ache.

I didn't want to think about it anymore. I didn't want to think about anything. So I pulled the complimentary silk sleep mask down over my eyes and reclined my seat into a bed, trying to enjoy this slice of luxury.

It was a far cry from the traveling I'd done as a child, which had been rare and consisted solely of road trips. All six of us crammed into a van that, more often than not, left us on the side of the road. And yet, that van was more reliable than my family. *What a depressing thought.*

"This is stunning," Jo said, taking it all in as she snapped a few pictures.

Lush tropical plants surrounded a grand entrance. And everything about the building spoke of the quiet elegance I'd come to expect from Graham and the Huxley brand.

"It is," I agreed, drawing closer to the interior courtyard where water cascaded off a fountain, light dappling the space between the wooden slats. "But it's also practical and sustainable. The water feature uses rainwater and helps regulate the temperature and humidity levels."

"Wow. That's cool. Plus, it's a nice way to welcome guests."

"Exactly," I said. The waterfall and walls cut down on noise and created a calming atmosphere to welcome guests.

I took a few pictures, wanting to capture it for my blog. Made a few notes in the app I used to prep my posts. But when I was finished, it wouldn't save. I frowned down at the screen, trying and failing to save again.

"Wow. Impressive. This was one of the last projects you worked on, right?"

I nodded. "It's designed by Atlas Blackwood."

Her eyes widened. "Holy shit. *The* Atlas Blackwood?"

"The one and only." Atlas was a famous architect known for his commitment to incorporating local materials and focusing on sustainability. When Graham had proposed Atlas to the board, they'd balked at the cost. Graham had had to fight them again and again—on that and other issues. But I'd secretly applauded him for his vision and his tenacity.

He might come across as cold and aloof at times, but I'd learned a lot from Graham during my time as his personal assistant. He'd been a fair and generous boss. And whenever I'd shown an interest in something, Graham hadn't hesitated to let me gain more experience.

Since I'd purchased the château, I often found myself

reflecting on his leadership. I'd asked myself countless times what he'd do if he were in my situation. And while he had more resources and family support at his disposal, his work ethic and determination helped me stay focused. Helped me stay motivated even when I felt like giving up.

After I'd told the front desk I was Gilded Lily, Jo and I were escorted to our suite. I peppered Jo with more facts about the hotel and its design. The building was nestled into a dramatic cliffside that overlooked the ocean. And the finishes—from the tile to the faucets—were all locally sourced or made by local artisans.

"I'm going to start getting ready for the welcome party," I called out from my bedroom.

I was still anxious about the château and my dwindling savings. But tonight, that didn't matter. Tonight, I was Gilded Lily, successful luxury-travel blogger.

I dressed and put on my makeup, then finished my look with a dark brown wig that was one of my favorites. Long and wavy, it was probably the closest to my natural hair, at least, what it used to look like before I'd lost all of it.

"I love that one," Jo said, catching sight of me in the mirror as I finished applying my eyelashes.

"Francine?" I patted my head with a smile. "She's my favorite."

I named all of my wigs. And after having alopecia for sixteen years, I'd tried all sorts of kinds. Different colors of hair. Different styles and lengths. It was fun to be able to change my look with my mood, and it helped ease some of the grief from my hair loss.

When I'd worked for Graham, I'd been in my lob era. And I'd worn a shoulder-length wig in a much lighter color. More of a golden-blond with highlights.

"They all look amazing on you." She grinned.

I thanked her, and then we headed out to the courtyard

where the event was taking place. Musicians played a lively tune, and I smiled as a gentle breeze flirted with the hem of my dress. We grabbed some drinks, and while I was comparing notes with another travel blogger about the best airlines for international travel, Jo got pulled into another conversation. We found ourselves on opposite sides of the courtyard.

Someone else asked me a question, and I got caught up in what I was saying about the size of some of the first-class seats. When my hand connected with a firm body, I startled.

"I'm so sorry." I turned to apologize, but my eyes widened as I took in the man I'd struck.

Graham?

"Liliana," he rasped. He leaned in, close enough for me to smell crisp cedar, another earthy, woodsy scent that I couldn't pinpoint, and notes of lavender. "Or does everyone call you Lily now? Because of your blog."

I was so surprised by his words that I stumbled back a step. I nearly collided with a passing waiter but luckily sidestepped him and his tray. "Sorry." I cringed, just trying to get out of the way before I injured anyone else. "Sorry."

I wobbled on my feet, my cheeks heating with embarrassment. *Oh god. Could this get any worse?*

Before I realized what was happening, my heel caught in one of the grooves between the stones. I windmilled my arms, but I was falling backward. I reached out for something, anything.

Graham was already stretching his arms toward me. My eyes widened, and I latched on to his lapels. But it was too late. I'd already gained too much momentum. And then he was coming with me.

The impact of the water was a shock to my system, cold against my heated skin. I pushed to the surface, spluttering as soon as my head was above water. Graham bobbed to the top, slicking his hair away from his face.

His thick curls were coiled even tighter from the water. Despite the fact that he'd just fallen into a pool, he looked every inch the billionaire CEO he was. Powerful. In control. Determination oozing from his pores.

He scanned me, and my skin warmed beneath his perusal. I was pinned in place by those intelligent green eyes, unable to turn or even breathe.

My heart raced, and I felt off-kilter from all the adrenaline suddenly flooding my veins. At least, that's what I told myself it was.

"Oh my god. I'm so…" I lifted my hand as if to smooth down his waterlogged tie. His bespoke suit clung to his muscles in a way that had my mouth going dry. "So." I shook my head in disbelief. "Sorry." I placed my hand on his lapel, as if that could somehow fix this.

He glanced down at my hand and then met my eyes once more. "Liliana." He placed his hand over mine, and I tried to ignore the frisson his touch sent through me. *That was new.*

Or maybe it was just that he'd so rarely touched me in the past. But now that he was, it was all I could think about. The way his larger hand enveloped my smaller one. The way his long, elegant fingers curved over mine. The rough calluses on his palms.

A camera flashed, and I winced at the brightness. It was then I realized everyone was staring at us; some of them even had their phones out, cameras pointed at us and filming. I gently patted my head, relieved my wig was still in place. *Thank god.*

I gritted my teeth and waded over to my purse, snatching it from the pool. And then I made my way to the stairs, trying to ignore the way everyone watched us.

Graham swore under his breath, something about how I was such a menace.

"How is this my fault?" I muttered, careful to keep my voice low.

He gave me a look as if to say, "Of course it's your fault."

I tried not to glower at him, but it was difficult. "You startled me. I can't help it that my shoe got caught."

"Not the most sensible footwear." He tilted his head to indicate the shoes that I was now holding in my hand. Strappy heels that were sexy and fun. "Maybe you should reconsider your shoe choice."

"Maybe you should reconsider your word choice," I spat back.

We hadn't seen each other in two years. But less than five minutes in, and we were already arguing. *Typical.*

"What are you even doing here?" I hissed under my breath.

Graham rarely attended events like this, leaving them to his brother, Jasper. Graham abhorred small talk, and these events were a waste of time, in his opinion. Yet he was here. And now that I thought about it, he didn't seem all that surprised to see me.

"Last I checked, I run this hotel." He kept his voice low, the water sloshing around us as we climbed the pool stairs. "And I was coming to say hello before you dragged me into the pool."

I lifted my chin, ignoring everyone around us. Unwilling to rise to his bait.

Graham yanked a towel from a cart beside the pool. "Here."

"Thank you," I huffed, taking it from him with more force than was necessary.

Graham leaned in. "People are watching," he said in a low

voice. Then louder, for the benefit of our audience, he said, "We're fine. Please, enjoy yourselves."

The musicians had resumed playing, and everyone seemed to have returned to their previous conversations. Regardless of whether that was true, that's what I was telling myself. Because Graham was right; I could still feel everyone's eyes on us. I was drenched and humiliated, and I just wanted to hide in my room and pretend this had never happened.

Josephine and a hotel employee rushed over as Graham was toweling himself off. "Oh my god. Lily, are you okay?"

I nodded. Just embarrassed and ready to get the hell out of here.

She rocked from one foot to the other, glancing at Graham's back and then to me. Her eyes went wide, and she mouthed, "OMG!"

"I'm going to head back to the room," I said.

"I'll go with you." She moved to set down her drink.

"No. No." I hugged myself. "Enjoy the party. I'll catch up with you later." She looked uncertain, so I nudged her, smiling brightly in an effort to convince her. "Have fun. And you better not come back early. At least, not on my account."

"Okay. Okay." She huffed, but she said the words with a smile. "Text if you need *anything*. Promise?"

"Promise."

She hesitated and then, finally satisfied by whatever she saw in my expression, she returned to the party.

I clutched at my purse, filled with a deepening sense of dread. I pulled out my phone, and the screen was black. "*Merde.*" Destroyed. Along with a ton of images I'd snapped of the hotel earlier for content, content I had planned for the château. I sagged, realizing that I'd never gotten the chance to upload them.

Graham wrung out some water from his jacket. "You can get a new one." It was said in such a callous, offhand tone that it pissed me off.

I glowered at him, my earlier concern replaced with anger. "No. I can't."

I couldn't just blow money on a new phone, but he wouldn't understand that. And even if I could, it still wouldn't solve the issue of my unsaved content. *Fuck.*

I brushed past Graham as I strode toward the building, still clutching the towel to my chest with one hand.

He easily caught up to me and grabbed my wrist, his hold light but authoritative. "Liliana, wait. You're bleeding." I followed his gaze down to my ankle, and sure enough, there was blood.

"I'm fine." I tried to shake off his hold. "It's a scratch."

"Allow me to help you." He held my wrist and my attention, lowering his voice as he added, "I insist."

"Always have to cover your ass, right?" I quipped. "I'm not going to sue you," I said as we headed toward the lobby. "If that's what you're worried about."

"You're my guest. Let me take care of you."

Why did my mind immediately jump to an image of him saying that in a completely different context? One with fewer clothes.

Did I hit my head on the way into the pool? I must have. That was the only rational explanation for the direction my thoughts had taken.

"I—" I opened my mouth as if to protest then my shoulders slumped, sensing that I was going to lose this fight. The idea of letting someone, anyone, take care of me was foreign. And especially someone like Graham. I mean, hell, I used to take care of *his* needs.

No. No. No. Not like that. His professional needs.

I groaned, telling myself to get it together.

"Fine," I sighed.

His eyes flashed with something—an emotion I couldn't name. "Good."

CHAPTER FOUR

Graham

The door to my suite closed with a snick. Liliana clutched the towel tighter to her chest. Her long hair dripped on the floor, a soft patter against the Saltillo tiles, darkening their terra-cotta color to an even deeper shade. Yet she remained silent, watchful. *Beautiful.*

I pushed away the thought, though I'd always found her attractive. Smart. Inquisitive. Kind. Soulful. I'd just never allowed myself to dwell on those qualities because she'd been my employee.

She's not your employee anymore.

Argh. I gnashed my teeth, annoyed.

I didn't even know what I was doing, insisting she come back to my room. I should've taken her to the resort doctor, not my room. This was foolish, and yet I couldn't seem to make myself stop.

I told myself it was because we'd garnered enough attention and I'd wanted to escape. But I knew that wasn't the entire truth.

She sighed with a weariness that seemed to go bone-deep. "What do you want from me, Graham?"

"Answers," I said, my impatience growing the longer I stood there, water sliding down my face. My body.

It had been Jackson's idea to fly her out for the Ixtapa opening. Jackson's idea to give her the VIC, or very important client, experience after her less-than-positive reviews of various Huxley Grand locations, which had been seen by her millions of followers. She had more influence than I cared to admit.

But he was right. This was a chance to remind her of everything the Huxley Grand brand stood for. I didn't understand why she needed reminding. She knew what went into the brand better than most. She'd worked closely with me for a year. And she'd always been outstanding at her job. Even when she annoyed me. Even when she pushed. *Especially* when she pushed me.

People rarely questioned me, but Liliana hadn't been afraid to. And that was what I needed—to be challenged. It made me more creative and innovative, more alive. So for her to turn around and write less than favorable reviews of the Huxley Grand…

I tugged at the collar of my shirt. The material clung to me, adding to my irritation. It made me want to crawl out of my skin, so I stripped out of my jacket and flung it on the back of a chair.

"I've read some of your reviews about the Huxley brand."

She placed her hand on her throat, and I couldn't help but follow the movement. Admire the elegant curve of her neck and the way her delicate fingers brushed over her pulse point. Was it racing like mine?

What the fuck is wrong with you?

"Was there a question in there?" she asked.

It wasn't even the reviews that bugged me—though I wasn't pleased about them. It was the fact that it had taken me so long to discover that she was Gilded Lily. I'd started by checking Gilded Lily's information when she stayed at our hotels in the past. But we'd only ever provided free accommodations, meals, and transportation, so it had all been arranged for "Gilded Lily."

Then I'd combed through her blog and social media. She never showed her face in any of her posts. Never shared her name or any identifying details. And her blog had been protected by layers of cybersecurity that—for a while—had even me scratching my head in frustration.

But once I'd gotten in, I'd learned some interesting things about Liliana. She seemed to be traveling less than before. But her current address had been the biggest shock.

She owned a château. In France. And she was restoring it on her YouStream channel, which was dedicated to showing the trials and tribulations involved with owning an historic property. She treated it as a completely separate brand from her blog, and I found it interesting that she didn't try to leverage the more established brand of *Gilded Lily* like so many other influencers would.

I'd watched a few episodes, captivated by her. She was funny and down-to-earth, but she always found the bright side. Her optimism was almost as annoying as it was unrealistic.

I cleared my throat, thinking of the change I'd witnessed in her on her YouStream channel. The lightness I saw that was different from when she'd been my assistant. Seeing her now, though, she seemed withdrawn. Closed off. Tired.

Dark circles lined her eyes, and her arms were crossed over her chest. Because of me?

"Are your reviews based on something I did?" I hadn't even realized I was going to ask that until the words left my mouth.

That wasn't me. I didn't talk first and think later. But

something about Liliana had me doing all sorts of things that were out of character.

I tugged at my shirt, the wet material clinging to my skin. I felt as if I might explode if I didn't get it off soon. The temperature. The texture. It was all wrong.

She jerked her head back. "What? No. Why would you think that?"

Maybe, as my siblings would suggest, I was paranoid, cynical. Considering recent events—the escort scandal that had rocked stock prices and investor confidence, a disgruntled former employee who had threatened my sister—my vigilance felt justified.

I told myself I was asking for the brand. To protect the company. But I knew that wasn't completely true.

And the longer we stood there, the more my agitation grew. It felt as if my clothes were suffocating me. I couldn't think straight. My heart was racing.

I started unbuttoning my shirt, unable to handle the feel of it on my skin a second longer. It was heavy and cold, and I couldn't get it off fast enough. But I was so irritated, my fingers weren't working fast enough to loosen the buttons.

"I—" She frowned, her brows drawing tight. And then she seemed to snap into action. "Let me help you."

I couldn't push her away. Couldn't hide this. Couldn't think of anything but getting out of my wet shirt as quickly as possible.

Liliana unbuttoned my shirt with quickness and efficiency. When her hand lingered on the bare skin of my chest, I felt...remarkably calm. Or at least calmer than I had even a second before. It distracted me enough, momentarily, that I forgot about the grating sensation of the wet material on my skin. *Strange.*

As soon as she'd finished unbuttoning, I stripped it off and tossed it aside, feeling a little lighter. It flopped to the floor in a wet mess. I tore off my undershirt as well, and it hit the tiles with a smack.

"Thank you." I shuddered, grateful to be free. "Thanks." I felt as if I could breathe again.

I inhaled deeply and let it out slowly, trying to center myself. When I finally chanced a glance at Liliana, she didn't seem surprised or disgusted by my outburst. Her expression was quietly thoughtful. Concerned. And while I appreciated her assistance, I hated that she'd witnessed such a vulnerable moment.

Her dress continued to cling to her skin, and my eyes bounced from her thighs to her hips to her breasts. When I finally returned my attention to her face, I realized she was staring at my chest with a dazed expression. My body heated from the inside out, and I gritted my teeth. *Focus, Graham.*

"How did you..."

"You're sensitive to textures," she said, practically stripping the words from my mind. Responding as if the answer was that simple. As if it simply was—not bad or good. But part of me.

She was right; I was sensitive to textures. But most people didn't realize that. I didn't let them see it. See me.

But Liliana had.

She'd always been observant, often anticipating my needs when she'd been my personal assistant. And I was in awe of her now. Her ability to understand what I needed and spring into action without judgment.

"You looked as if you were on the verge of a panic attack if you didn't get that shirt off," she added.

I studied her once more and realized she was shivering. I turned away, heading for the closet to grab us each a robe. I needed to check on her cut as well.

"Here. You can change in the bathroom." I held out a robe

to her before wrapping mine around me and tying the belt firmly.

Liliana chewed on her bottom lip, and it was damn distracting. She'd always been distracting. Beautiful. Smart. Stubborn. Some things might have changed since the last time I'd seen her—but her beauty wasn't one of them.

"Thank you," she said, heading down the hall and closing the door softly behind her.

While she was gone, I stripped out of my pants and put on fresh clothes before heading back to the living room. *There.* That was better. I felt more in control again. A sensation that evaporated when Liliana emerged from the bathroom, her body encased in the robe.

It felt even more intimate. *Fuck.*

I'd been so good about avoiding these situations in the past. Situations where I was tempted to cross a line I shouldn't. Where it was easy to forget that she was off-limits.

Focus.

I grabbed the first aid kit from the kitchen, poured myself a glass of whiskey, and then offered her one as well. "Leave them by the sink," I said, gesturing to the wad of wet clothes in her hand. "Housekeeping will take care of it and return them to your room."

"Thank you."

"Please." I gestured to the couch opposite, taking her in. Her hair was darker, longer. Or maybe it just seemed that way because it was wet. "Take a seat."

She clutched her robe at the neck, holding it close as she sank down across from me. The coffee table separated us and our matching couches. I leaned forward, sliding her a glass of whiskey. My eyes caught on the vase of dahlias. The flowers were native to the region, and they were bursting with color. I thought of Gran, and I could hear her voice telling me that dahlias symbolized kindness, steadfastness, and creativity.

She used to send me messages with flowers and their meanings. When she was alive, it had always been our thing. Was she trying to tell me something now?

I held out my hand to Lily. "Let me see your ankle."

She opened her mouth as if to protest, but I cut her off. "I'm not going to bite." Unless she wanted me to. "I just want a closer look to see if we should call the resort doctor. Despite what your reviews might imply, I do take extreme pride to ensure every single guest is well cared for."

She frowned at me, but when I didn't relent, she finally lifted her foot with a resigned sigh. "I know you do, not that you typically give your guests this personal level of care."

I gently placed her foot on my thigh. "Then consider yourself the exception."

I grazed the skin of her ankle with my finger, nearly groaning at the softness of her skin. She inhaled sharply.

I stilled. "Did I hurt you?"

When I glanced up at her, she shook her head quickly. I studied her briefly before returning my attention to her ankle. "Looks like a superficial scrape," I continued, reaching for the hand sanitizer. I cleaned my hands then grabbed the foaming antiseptic for her. I pumped some on, waiting for it to finish cleaning the wound.

"I'm sorry about—" she spun her finger in the air "—the pool thing."

I grabbed a bandage from the kit and dabbed some ointment on it. "No need to apologize. It was an accident. I'm sorry if I implied otherwise."

I could tell she felt bad enough about it; I didn't want to make her feel worse. And I was kicking myself for being such a jerk earlier, but I'd been caught off guard.

I applied the bandage to her skin. "There. That should do it." I smoothed my hand down the top of her foot.

She lowered her foot to the floor. "Thank you." She cleared her throat. "I, um, you were really good at that."

"What? Basic first aid?" I joked.

"You have a kind bedside manner." She sounded surprised.

"A by-product of being the second eldest of five. I can't tell you how many times I bandaged up Nate or Jasper, even Sloan." Usually, my grandparents did that, but sometimes, if they were in a meeting or couldn't be interrupted, I took on that role.

She smiled. "Always taking care of everyone else. But who takes care of you?"

My skin prickled. "I can take care of myself."

"Even so..." She paused. "Are you okay?"

This conversation was getting too deep. Too personal. So I opted for humor. "Apart from the fact that I'm never going to hear the end of it from my family. Yes."

"I get that." She blew out a breath.

"You have a big family too, right?" I asked, though I knew the answer, thanks to my research. Perhaps she'd told me in the past, but I doubted it. When she'd worked for me, I'd rarely spoken to her about anything that didn't involve business. I was cordial to my employees, but I'd always preferred to maintain a professional distance.

"I'm one of four," she said. "And I've always been the oddball."

"Same," I confessed before I could stop myself.

"Yeah, but..." She chewed on her lip. "It's different."

Was it? I tilted my head, and she seemed to understand.

"Your family still respects you and what you do. Mine—" She shook her head and glanced at the ceiling. Then she drank deeply from her glass.

"Yours?"

She set her glass on the table. "It's not important."

I leaned forward, my arms resting on my thighs. She huffed, perhaps sensing my unspoken questions. My unwillingness to relent.

"I should get going," she said. "I'm sure you have more important things to do."

She wasn't wrong, and yet…nothing felt more important than this. "I haven't seen you in two years. Surely we can take some time to catch up. Tell me what's been going on with you. What you're working on."

She tilted her head. "You really want to know?"

I draped my arm over the back of the sofa. "I wouldn't have asked if I didn't."

"Okay." She took a deep breath. "Well. I'm restoring a French château in the Loire Valley."

"Sounds like a big project," I said, as if I hadn't spent way too much time watching her YouStream channel.

She blew out a breath, but she smiled when she spoke. "Like you wouldn't believe. It's as full of character as it is defects."

She was proud of what she was doing. As she should be. The scope of the project was incredible, especially for one person to manage.

The magnificent Loire Valley château was steeped in history. It had been constructed during the reign of Louis XVI just before the French Revolution, and it had only changed hands twice during the past 250 years. Thanks to a complicated system of inheritance laws, increasingly expensive maintenance, and lack of agreement and interest from the various family branches who had owned it, they'd finally decided to sell for the bargain price of $20,000.

I was almost jealous that I hadn't discovered the property and snatched it up myself.

"And what do you plan to do with it once you're finished?"

"*If* I finish." She stared into her glass, her face full of defeat. I'd seen that same expression many times when I'd looked at myself in the mirror.

"You will," I said. "I have no doubt." She'd always been persistent.

And perhaps she was more of a risk-taker than I'd given her credit for. I could respect someone who put it all on the line for a project they were passionate about.

She laughed, but it was humorless. "That makes one of us. Lately, I'm not so sure."

"A project like that takes time and patience."

"It definitely does."

We were quiet, sipping our drinks. Finally, she said, "I'm surprised you know about my blog."

"I make it my business to know what people are saying about my hotels."

She straightened, lifting her chin. Proud. Beautiful. Like a fucking queen. "Everything I've written is something I would've—and *have* said—to your face. While I was your assistant, I made suggestions." She crossed her arms over her chest. "You were just too," she huffed, "stubborn to listen to anyone else's opinion."

I gnashed my teeth. "Oh. Right. Because a twenty-seven-year-old assistant knows better than the CEO who's nearly double her age and has been running the company for over a decade."

Fuck. This was like my argument with the board all over again. Why did no one see or respect what I'd done for the company? I'd devoted fourteen years to running the empire, and that didn't account for all the years I'd worked for the brand before that, serving in nearly every role possible.

My grandparents had been firm believers in earning your place. And in addition to instilling a strong work ethic in their grandchildren, they'd wanted us to value and appreciate the role of each and every employee in the company. I wondered what they'd think if they could see me now. I wondered if they—like the board—would be questioning my competence. The idea that I might have somehow disappointed them pained me.

Liliana rolled her eyes. "You're not nearly double my age. You're fifteen years older than me."

"Close enough," I huffed. Fifteen years might as well be fifty in this case.

"And yes, I'm young. But that doesn't mean you should discount my opinion. If anything, I represent the next generation of guests." She sat back, crossing her legs and revealing more of that delicious, creamy skin. I no longer had to wonder if it was as smooth as it looked; I knew.

She made a good point, but I wasn't ready to concede. "Your generation is so damn entitled."

Why did I get off on arguing with her? Most people vexed me, but she... I swallowed hard. Liliana had always intrigued me.

She scoffed. "Interesting choice of words coming from a man who inherited generational wealth and has opportunities because of that and the fact that he's a white, cis-het man."

"Says the white, cis-het woman who owns a château."

Our eyes locked, and the tension pulled taut between us. It felt as if it were a rubber band ready to snap. Or maybe I was just ready to snap. First, the shit that Donahue had pulled with the board, Moretti's proposed "merger," the negative article, and now this?

She inched closer, full of fury and fire. "Fair point. But before I purchased the château, I worked my ass off, first as your assistant, and then later to build my blog. Not to mention everything I've done to restore the château. And I'm not going to stand here and let you undermine my hard work and success." Her eyes blazed with indignation. "I might not have the experience or education you do, but that doesn't mean I don't have something valuable to contribute."

Damn. That was… Seeing her claim ownership and take pride in her work reminded me of how I felt about the Huxley Grand. And I hated that I was making her feel like I was attacking her work, just like the board was attacking me.

It prompted me to say, "You're right. I wasn't trying to undermine your hard work."

Her shoulders dropped, some of the fight going out of her. "Thank you for saying that." She blew out a breath. "It's not like I need someone to undermine my work when I'm sabotaging all my efforts anyway."

I frowned. "What do you mean by that?" I asked, unable to stop myself.

"My phone." She massaged her temples. "It had all my photos and a list of content ideas and…" She glanced toward her purse, which was resting on a towel on the table, the contents laid out on top. "Maybe I could put it in some rice? Isn't that supposed to be a thing?"

"I'll have my staff bring some up." I texted my kitchen staff, wishing I'd thought of it sooner, but I'd been a little distracted. "Didn't you back up your photos? Save them to the cloud?"

She shook her head, her eyes watery. *Fuck. Don't cry. Please don't cry.*

"I was having issues with my service, and then I was so busy that I didn't get the chance to check if any of them uploaded after my arrival." She stood. "I should…" She hooked a thumb over her shoulder. "I should go. I have to—" She glanced around as if searching for something. Her movements were frantic, and I hated seeing her so unsettled.

I could understand that she was upset. Stressed. But this seemed beyond that. She'd handled numerous stressful situations while in my employ, and she'd never reacted like this.

I made a note to look into the service issues. I wanted my guests to feel like they could escape, but excellent Wi-Fi was a given at our hotels.

"Liliana." I grasped her wrist. "Stop. Wait here."

I went into the bathroom and returned with a box of tissues before handing her one.

"Thank you." She sniffled. "God, this is so embarrassing," she murmured. Or at least, that's what it sounded like.

"What's wrong? What's going on?" I asked, all thoughts of boundaries and propriety taking a back seat in the face of her distress. She had a problem, and I wanted to fix it.

"I—" Liliana's eyes darted about the room, never coming to rest. She hiccupped around a sob. "It's nothing."

"It doesn't seem like nothing." I lifted my arm, tempted to wrap it around her shoulder. To console her. The feeling was both foreign and natural.

I didn't comfort anyone except maybe my family or my dogs. And yet, I found myself wanting to do something to help Liliana.

I settled for placing my hand on hers. She startled, then relaxed. She peered up at me with tears in her eyes and racing down her cheeks, and she was still the most beautiful woman I'd ever seen. Her eyes were so blue. Blue like the navy of the Huxley brand logo. A warm, rich color that spoke of depth and intelligence. They were rimmed with dark black lashes, and I couldn't have looked away even if I'd wanted to.

I sat with her, wheels turning, chest aching at the sight of her distress.

"Tell me," I commanded, impatient to find a solution.

THE EXCEPTION

I kicked myself for being so brusque in my approach. Demanding, even. But putting people at ease had always been more Jasper's forte.

"Come on," I said more softly. "You can trust me." I lifted her chin, forcing her eyes to mine. Wanting her to hear the truth of my words and believe them.

She blinked back tears and peered up at me. Her expression gave the impression that she was seeing me for the first time. I reluctantly dropped my hand from her chin, feeling exposed.

She considered me, and I wondered if she was going to answer me. Finally, she said, "Between traveling for my blog and restoring the château, I'm beyond exhausted and overwhelmed. I used to love traveling. Part of me still does, but I need a break. But without the income from my blog, I'll never be able to renovate the château. Even with it, well…" She blew out a breath, her shoulders slumping.

She was right. I knew how costly a renovation like that could be. Even so, I hated seeing her so defeated.

"Maybe everyone's right," she continued. "Maybe I don't know what I'm doing and I should just give up and sell the château."

I gnashed my teeth. I knew what it was like to have to fight for your vision. It was part of the reason I was so determined to gain control of the board. I didn't want to have to answer to them ever again.

I couldn't help but draw some parallels between Liliana's situation and my own. I glanced at the dahlias, wondering why they'd stuck out to me. Why I'd thought of my gran. I saw flowers every day, and yet it wasn't until now, until I was with Lily, that I'd remembered my gran's coded messages.

My eyes lingered on the petals of the dahlias. *Kindness. Steadfastness. Creativity.*

I might not believe in fate, but this moment, this meeting, felt like the universe was trying to send me a message. And what I was about to propose was nothing short of creative.

"Maybe I can help," I said. "Maybe we could help each other."

CHAPTER FIVE

Lily

Help? How in the world was I going to help Graham?

His expression had turned contemplative, and I wanted to know what he was thinking. Part of me wanted to take back my confession, erase my moment of weakness when I'd told him the truth about the château and my blog. But another part of me felt such a profound sense of relief, of release.

Graham understood. And it was nice to know that I had someone like him—powerful, business-savvy—in my corner. Even if it was only temporary.

A knock at the door to his suite interrupted my thoughts. Graham was already on his feet, answering it and returning with a bowl.

"What's that?" I asked.

"Dry rice. For your phone." He went over to my phone and placed it in the bowl.

"Thank you," I said, though I wasn't sure if it would actually work. Like my efforts to save the château, it might be too little, too late.

He grunted, returning to the bar, pouring himself another

drink before holding up my almost-empty glass. I hesitated then said, "Okay. Maybe a little more." I held up my thumb and forefinger.

While his back was turned, I patted my hair, paranoid that my wig had moved out of place even though I knew it was unlikely. The wig was made to look natural and to allow me to do any number of activities, from dancing to swimming. I knew that. And I knew how well it could hold in place, but I still found myself checking it frequently.

I wasn't ready to feel completely naked before Graham. The fact that I was wearing nothing but a robe while he was dressed in slacks and a crisp button-down shirt was bad enough.

I wasn't sure I'd ever seen him in anything else. I wondered if that was exhausting. To always seem so put together. So on top of everything. If he wore his uniform like a shield, just as I wore my wig to cover my insecurities.

He placed our glasses on the coffee table and took a seat on the couch once more. "How much do you think you need for the renovation?"

I sank back down into the cushions, taking the glass in my hand. "My architect and I plan to do it in phases. Right now, we're working on getting the roof and stone facades restored." That had been a huge relief, even though it was far from finished. Once it was, though, the west wing would be watertight, and I'd finally be able to start on some of the interior projects.

"For that portion alone," I continued, "the estimated cost is one million euros. With a projected timeline of two years. Fortunately, the DRAC agreed to support sixty percent of that." The maximum amount of funding the *Direction régionale des affaires culturelles* could provide.

"And you pay the other forty percent?"

He acted as if €200,000 was no big deal. Though, I

supposed, to him—a man with billions in his bank account—it wasn't.

"Yes. For that phase of the works."

"And after that?" he asked.

"That's the million-dollar question, isn't it?"

I explained how the heritage funding worked and what it did and didn't include. I was overwhelmed just thinking about the scope of the project and the potential cost.

"If you had to guess…"

"I honestly don't have a clue. That's what makes this such a risk. There's extensive damage on the second floor. And that's what's obvious. There's just no way of knowing an accurate cost until we get someone in there. Then there are the furnishings, textiles, and amenities."

"Do you have a number for those?"

"Well…" I hedged. "I created several levels. A budget reno, a middle level, and a dream level."

"How much for the dream level?" he asked.

"If I had to guess…" I blew out a breath. "And bearing in mind that this could change based on whatever issues we find with the interior…twenty million," I finally said, knowing he wouldn't let it go.

It was a pie-in-the-sky dream renovation that would restore the château to her glory and modernize it for guests. It also, hopefully, gave me some padding in case something unexpected came up. Which, at the château, it always did. But the number made me sick to my stomach.

"How many rooms does it have?"

"Forty-five," I said. "Though not all of them will be guest rooms."

He let out a low whistle. "Quite expensive for a boutique hotel."

"It's worth it," I said, trying not to sound too defensive. "I've done the market research. I've done the math. As long as

I can get it up and running quickly, the investment will pay off. The location is great for a weekend getaway or a longer stay. It's nestled outside this small village in the Loire Valley about two hours from Paris, and it's idyllic. Perfect for weddings. And the type of clientele who will be attracted to it won't bat an eye at the cost-per-night."

An emotion passed through his eyes, something I couldn't name. Something like pride. Admiration. Respect.

Or maybe that's just what I wanted to see.

I broke eye contact, dropping my head. It was something I'd been guilty of in the past. Believing what I wanted about a situation with my family. With guys I'd dated. Imagining that their feelings were stronger than they were. That things were more serious.

I was done with that. Auntie Jackie had always said that people showed you who they were through their actions, not their words. She'd always shown me her love and support, as had Jo. The rest of my family, not so much.

"And what's the projected timeline until completion?"

I was surprised that he was so interested in my project, though I supposed I shouldn't have been. Graham loved the development phase.

"At this point, completely unknown." Despite the fact that I'd worked my ass off for the past year. That I'd invested my blood, sweat, tears, and my entire inheritance, plus most of my life savings, into the building, and I might never recoup it. My stomach churned. "Mostly because I don't have the necessary funds."

"I assume you've reached out to lenders?"

"Yes, but no one wants to take on the risk."

"Mm." He rubbed a hand over his jaw. "It is one hell of a risk. What made you decide to take on such an enormous project?"

"Owning a boutique hotel has always been a dream of

mine. It's why I got my degree in hospitality, why I worked for you, why I started my blog." I could feel my skin growing warm, but I kept talking, my words coming faster. "I know I'm young. I know I'm in over my head. But I'd rather risk everything than always wonder…what if?"

I recognized his expression as his deep-thinking mode. He was contemplating something, so I remained quiet, giving him the space to work out whatever it was. I knew Graham needed time to process his thoughts. He was conscious of his words and the way he wielded them. So I sipped my whiskey and curled into my robe.

Graham turned to me. "I could do it. I could take on the cost of the restoration."

My jaw dropped. Surely I'd misheard him. I'd assumed he was asking questions because he was curious. Not because he was considering investing. Or maybe he wasn't interested in investing. Maybe he wanted to acquire it.

"I appreciate the offer." More than he could ever know. "But I don't want to sell the château. I don't want the Huxley brand to take it over."

"I figured as much. And I wouldn't want you to relinquish it."

I frowned. "Then what do you want?"

There was no way Graham—or anyone in their right mind—would give up that kind of money without expecting something in return.

"Marry me."

"What?" I choked on my drink. "Are you okay?" Maybe I needed to call the resort doctor for him.

That was the last thing I would've expected him to say.

"It would be purely a business deal," he hastened to add, ignoring my question. "I'd be your silent investor. The money would go through a trust. And we would be married in name only."

I wasn't sure whether to be flattered or insulted.

Graham didn't do relationships. I'd never seen him date while I was working for him. And while, yes, he could be very secretive, I'd known his calendar back to front. I'd spent lots of time with him. Besides, if he had been dating someone, there was no way his family would've kept quiet about it.

I paused at the thought of Graham's family. Knox, Nate, Jasper, and Sloan. Knox and Nate were technically his cousins, but he'd always referred to them as his siblings. The five of them had always been close—raised by their grandparents after both sets of parents had perished in a tragic plane crash.

I liked them, respected them, especially Jasper and Sloan. I'd spent the most time with them, interfacing with them as Graham's assistant. My expression soured at the idea of deceiving them. Lying to everyone.

"Why?"

I could understand wanting to be a silent investor. It was the marriage component that made zero sense.

"You need money, and I need a wife."

That was cryptic. I mean...why did he *need* a wife?

"What would you get out of this? Out of marrying me?" I blurted, still in shock.

There had to be some catch. Some...*something*. What could he possibly stand to gain from marriage, let alone to someone like me?

Marriage to me wouldn't offer him more status, money, or power.

He dragged a hand through his hair, the waves springing back after he'd released them. "You know how the board is. They want stability."

"And you're willing to go through with a sham of a marriage to appease them? Seems a bit extreme."

No. There was something more. Something he wasn't telling me.

I thought through everything I'd seen about the Huxley Grand in the news. And then I remembered a recent article that had popped up on my news feed about a scandal within the Huxley brand.

"I'm sure your board isn't happy about the decline in stock prices either," I said, trying to put the pieces together.

He arched an eyebrow, indicating that I was on the right track.

"And I'm guessing they're looking for reasons to oust you from power, especially—" I screwed up my face in disgust, remembering one of the board members in particular. He was always sort of slimy. "Frank? No. Fred."

Graham narrowed his eyes at me, and I knew I was right. I was onto something.

He leaned back, crossing his ankle over his knee. "You're remarkably well-informed."

I lifted a shoulder. "I pay attention to the industry."

"The industry or me?" he challenged.

I rolled my eyes. "Don't flatter yourself." Though he was closer to the truth than I cared to admit.

"Have you seen my other recent press?" he asked. I shook my head. I'd been between trips and swamped at the château. "They're calling me a cold, heartless billionaire."

As much as he tried to pretend it didn't bother him, I could tell it did. *Interesting.*

"I thought you didn't care about other people's opinions." I was teasing. Sort of.

"I don't. But the board does. Our marriage would not only refocus everyone from the recent scandals and dips in stock prices but show the board I'm a family man looking toward the future."

Wow. He was serious. And he was talking about this as if

it were a done deal. I knew it was a common negotiation tactic, but still…

"This could benefit both of us," he said. "I'd provide my money and my expertise for the restoration. And you could help me show everyone that I'm capable of loving someone other than myself or the business."

"And how *exactly* would I do that?" I asked, genuinely curious.

"You could—" He shrugged, and I'd never seen him look so hesitant. It was honestly kind of cute, the way his cheeks flushed with color. "Give me pointers on how to be myself but show a softer side."

I furrowed my brow. *Interesting. Okay.*

I still wasn't sure what that would entail, but oddly enough, I was more concerned with what he'd want out of the château.

"I assume you'd want a small percentage of the château's revenue once it starts paying out."

"Naturally. Twenty-five percent is acceptable."

"Twenty-five?" I laughed. "You've got to be joking."

He narrowed his eyes at me. If he was trying to intimidate me, it wasn't going to work.

"We both know that ten percent is standard," I said.

"My standard is closer to twenty-five."

"Perhaps, but you're forgetting the fact that you'd be receiving an additional benefit from the deal. Ten."

"Twenty," he shot back.

"Twelve. Take it or leave it."

He considered it a moment. "Okay." He held out his hand, presumably to shake on it.

CHAPTER SIX

Lily

"Whoa. Whoa. Whoa." I held up my hands. "I'm not ready to agree to anything."

I didn't have enough details. We might agree on the percentage, but there was so much more at stake.

Never in a million years would I have expected Graham to propose something like this. And definitely not to me.

If anything, I'd prepared myself to have him question my reviews of his hotel chain. I'd imagined us arguing about them, him trying to persuade me to revise them. Not…ask me to be his wife.

Breathe, Lil. Breathe.

This was a lot to process. Marriage to Graham. Money for the restoration.

Being married to a handsome billionaire seemed a small price to pay in exchange for twenty million dollars to fund the château restoration.

Twenty. Million. Dollars.

Did he have any idea what I could do with that kind of money? Did I?

"This business arrangement," I asked. "How long would it need to last?"

"A year. Maybe two."

A breath gusted out of me. Wow. *Wow!*

"You'd have to give up your blog or focus on something other than luxury hotels. Maybe experiences? Or even luxury goods?"

If I had the money for the renovations, I wouldn't need the income from the blog. And if the renovations were moving forward at full speed, I'd definitely need to be more involved at the château. While I hated the idea of giving up something that I'd spent so much time and effort on, I knew something had to give.

I could find ways to recycle old content as well as focus more on luxury brands. It was an option I'd been considering anyway. If I wanted to go back to it in the future, I could.

"That's fine," I said. "I'd slowly transition to doing my château YouStream full time."

"Great. That's settled, then." *Typical Graham.* He was bulldozing right through each and every one of my objections. "And we could hire a project manager to help alleviate some of the stress there as well."

I frowned. "This project is my baby."

"I get that, but I would need you by my side for our relationship to seem credible. And with the right team in place and the resources, you wouldn't have to babysit the project as much."

Was I willing to sacrifice time at the château for Graham's infusion of cash? If I wanted to complete the restoration, I wasn't sure I had much of a choice. I was out of options, and what he was offering me...

Twenty million dollars.

My head spun. I couldn't believe we were even discussing this or that I was actually considering it.

Am I considering it?

Part of me certainly was. The chance to see the château restored to its full potential was irresistible.

But if I agreed to this… If I married Graham, I wanted to know that he'd treat me as an equal. That he'd respect me and not try to control me or try to take over my project and make it part of his brand.

"I'd still want to be involved with the château," I said. "Maybe we could agree to spend two weeks a month there."

"Two weeks?" he scoffed. His expression conveyed skepticism.

"What? We'd split our time between LA and the Loire Valley. My work requires me to be there in person. And I'd be giving you two weeks in LA or wherever you need us to be."

"Still…" He shook his head. "I can't just up and leave LA for two weeks every month."

"Why not?" I lifted my hands. "You have the money, and you're the boss. You can do whatever the fuck you want."

Something flared in his eyes. Anger?

"Actually, I can't. If I want to move, I have to get board approval."

"You're not moving. Not permanently."

"True," he said, seeming to mull it over.

"Besides, taking an interest in your wife's project would show that you're not as selfish as everyone thinks you are."

He hmphed.

"And it's not like it's a short flight." Another reason to stay longer. Jet lag was a bitch. And an eleven-hour flight was no joke.

"There's the time difference to consider," he mused. "I'd have to make sure my meetings could be organized around it."

I tried not to look too eager, but I was certainly hopeful. He was considering it instead of dismissing it outright.

"Besides," I continued. "Wouldn't it be nice to have a break from pretending for half of the month?"

The corner of his mouth tilted upward, the closest he'd come to a smile. "You make a good point. I'm confident we could find some sort of compromise, even if it's not quite two weeks," he said, easing some of my anxiety. "Perhaps ten days."

More time at the château was preferable, but I could work with ten days. The fact that he was willing to consider it showed how desperate he was to make this happen.

Why was he so desperate?

And why was I so eager to agree? Yes, I needed the money, but I was getting ahead of myself. There were so many unknowns. I'd spent a lot of time with Graham, but that was two years ago. People changed. He could've changed. And even if he hadn't, there were things about this arrangement that gave me pause.

I scrunched up my face. "I don't like the idea of lying to your family. Of accepting your money." It made me feel icky.

Was I truly no different from my selfish siblings? They wouldn't have hesitated to take Graham up on his offer. But the idea of accepting money to be someone's wife felt wrong. It wasn't like he didn't have the funds; it was the principle of it.

"Think of it like you're providing a service. I'm paying you to do a job."

"Right. To be your fake wife." I wasn't sure that was any better.

I still couldn't believe he was trying to convince me. This seemed so out of character for Graham. Which was exactly why I suspected there was more to it.

Graham wasn't risk-averse. Hell, he often pushed the

brand forward with his innovations and vision. But when it came to his personal life, something wasn't adding up about this.

"Paying you handsomely, I might add. I would personally cover any renovations of the château not covered by government funding, grants, or prizes. All the money would be put into a trust that would be at your disposal."

That seemed fair. More than fair.

As to any future operating costs, I supposed I'd cross that bridge if and when I came to it. Hopefully, the revenue from guests would more than cover those costs. But that seemed so far away at this point, it was laughable.

I tried to imagine myself married to Graham and failed. It seemed incomprehensible. Yes, he was attractive. But we'd only ever known each other in a professional context.

He'd never given any indication that he was attracted to me—or anyone, for that matter. I wasn't sure we could pull this off, even if he wanted to. And that was a big if.

The idea was so very tempting. Unrealistic, but tempting, nevertheless. I mean…to agree to a marriage of convenience to my former boss? It was crazy, right?

I was about to try to laugh it off as a joke, but he said, "I'm serious." He smoothed his hands down his thighs. "Think about it. You'd be able to restore the château to its full potential. No expense spared."

Maybe it was crazy. Maybe *I* was crazy for even entertaining the idea at all. Or maybe I was chasing my dreams, doing something "outlandish," as Auntie Jackie had advised?

"Why me?" I finally asked.

He held my gaze. "Because you're one of the few people I trust."

His admission sucked the air from the room. Graham's trust wasn't freely given.

"Despite what I said about the Huxley hotels on my blog?" I asked.

He blew out a breath. "Maybe even because of it. At least I know you'll always be honest with me."

"Okay, but what if you meet someone? What if *I* meet someone?" I asked, though it seemed unlikely.

I was already so busy with the restoration, and if Graham and I went through with this, I'd be even more so. Traveling back and forth, pretending to be his wife.

His nostrils flared. "This will never work unless you're one hundred percent on board. Completely loyal to me for the duration of the agreement."

The agreement. Not "our marriage."

"I am, and I would be. But still...two years is a long time to put our lives on hold. I'm almost thirty. I might want to get married for real someday. Have kids."

"You don't know if you want that?"

"It requires me meeting the right person first."

Not that I had time for that. Between traveling for my blog and now taking care of the château, I didn't have much of a personal life. I'd had a few flings over the years, but nothing serious. I hadn't had the time or energy for it.

And honestly, the idea of being vulnerable with someone about my alopecia was terrifying. If my family viewed me as a burden, how was I supposed to find a partner who wouldn't feel the same way? Who would embrace my beauty, baldness and all.

Graham grunted but said nothing. His lack of an answer was infuriating. As if he thought it was unimportant. A minor detail in the grand scheme of things.

"And what about sex?" I asked, when he still hadn't responded.

If he was shocked by my words, his expression didn't show it. In fact, he looked downright predatory.

"Is this you trying to negotiate that into the deal?" There was a teasing lilt to his voice.

I rolled my eyes. "This is me trying to point out the flaws in your plan."

He crossed his arms over his chest, and I tried to ignore the bulge of his biceps. If his schedule was the same as it had been two years ago—and knowing Graham, it was—he started every day with a workout, and it showed.

"If you're not interested, just say so."

"That's not—" I sighed and dropped my hand. "That's not what this is. I just…" I didn't even know what to say at this point.

I'd never known Graham to be impulsive. Decisive—yes. Once he made a decision, he was rarely swayed from it. But this was so out of the ordinary that I didn't know what to think.

"Do you honestly think we could be believable as a couple?" I asked. "Because we might know it's fake, but to our friends and family and everyone else, it would have to seem real."

"People will believe what they want to. Besides, it's not like we just met. We have history."

"Even so, we haven't seen each other in nearly two years. I used to work for you. That's sure to raise some eyebrows." I knew how careful Graham was about his reputation and that of the brand. He might think this was a good idea now, but there was no way he'd actually see this through.

"Marrying a *former* assistant would be nothing compared to what my siblings have done."

I frowned. "You mean Nate getting engaged to his daughter's nanny?" I'd definitely seen their pictures splashed across the magazines at the grocery store checkout.

"Nate. Knox. Sloan. They're all engaged or married to

former employees. And they all had a relationship while they were still in their employ."

"Now, Jasper I could imagine breaking the rules. But Knox and Sloan?"

A rare smile teased the corner of his lips, and I reveled in it. It was fleeting, but I could tell that despite his ire, he was happy for them.

I sipped my whiskey, tucking my feet beneath me. "This I've gotta hear."

"Knox's wife, Kendall, used to be his house sitter. And before that—" he leaned in "—she was his son's ex."

My eyes widened. "Really? Knox?" I couldn't believe it. I also couldn't believe Graham was telling me all this.

Graham nodded.

"Are he and Jude still on speaking terms?" I asked, imagining it would be difficult to move past something like that, despite how close they'd always seemed.

"It was rough for a bit. But now, they're better than ever."

"Wow." I shook my head. "And Sloan?"

"Married her former bodyguard. Though *technically*, he resigned before anything 'improper' happened."

Okay. So his family might not bat an eye at our previous relationship. But still, this was Graham we were talking about.

"Yeah, but they're not...you."

He furrowed his brow. "What does that mean?"

He was... I wasn't even sure how to describe Graham, other than to say that he'd always held himself to a higher standard than everyone else. Even though he wasn't the eldest of the five of them, he often acted as if he were.

"Just—" I huffed. "Nothing."

His frown deepened, and I wished I'd kept my mouth shut. I got the sense that I'd offended him.

"Are you concerned you won't be convincing?" he asked.

"You already offered me the part. Don't tell me you're now trying to get me to audition," I teased, desperate to lighten the moment.

"If we were auditioning for a role, we'd have to do a chemistry test." His eyes darkened as they lingered on my lips.

"Mm." I toyed with the belt of my robe. "And what do you know about chemistry tests?"

"Nate once told me that kissing Hollywood starlet Cece Golden is like kissing a dead fish."

I couldn't help it. I burst out laughing. "No." I covered my mouth with my hand, grateful he'd dispelled some of the tension growing between us.

He nodded, his expression solemn.

"Well, I can promise you that kissing me would not be like kissing a dead fish."

We'd inched closer, close enough that our thighs were touching. The heat of his skin seared me through the layers of fabric separating us. It was both too close and not enough.

He turned to face me, his stare intense, his eyes hooded. Apart from that moment in the pool—or whatever that was when I'd smoothed my hands down his lapels—we'd never been this close. I'd never... I could've never imagined what it would be like to be the sole focus of his attention. It was intoxicating.

"Is that a fact?" he goaded. Or at least, I thought he was. Sometimes he was impossible to read. Enigmatic. Infuriating.

And hot.

No, not hot. I was not attracted to Graham. I was confused. Agitated or...something.

His breath ghosted across my skin as he lifted his hand to cup my cheek. I was bathed in his scent, lost to the moment. To him.

"I—" I swallowed hard, my mind a blank. What was he asking about?

His lips moved closer to my mouth, and my heartbeat continued its ascent. He dragged his nose down my jawline, setting my body aflame. My body was shaking, vibrating.

Graham wanted to see if our fake marriage could be viable. Judging from my body's response to him, that wouldn't be a problem.

I exhaled a shaky breath and tried to recenter myself, even when it felt as if my world had tilted off its axis. Perhaps he wasn't such a cold, heartless billionaire after all.

CHAPTER SEVEN

Graham

"I, um—" Liliana pulled back and shook her head as if to clear it. "You've given me a lot to think about." She laid her hands in her lap, a prim position that did nothing to dispel the lustful thoughts racing through my mind. The taste of her lips. The feel of her skin. Using my hands and my mouth to explore every inch of her body until she was begging for mercy.

Jesus, Graham. Get control of yourself.

This was a business arrangement, nothing more. That was all I could offer, all it could ever be.

Before I'd realized what was happening, she'd stood, gathering her purse. "I'll, um—" She hooked her thumb over her shoulder.

"Sleep on it," I offered, wondering if she felt as off-balance as I did. "We can talk tomorrow."

"Yeah." She looked anywhere but at me. "Yes." She headed toward the bowl of rice where her phone was resting

"Leave it. It's not like your phone is going to work right now anyway. I'll have someone take a look at it and return it to you tomorrow."

"Thanks, but it's my problem. I'll figure it out."

I placed my hand over hers. "Let me help."

She appraised me. "If you're sure."

"Yes. Now, can I walk you back to your room?" I escorted her to the door, thinking some space might be a good thing. Perhaps she'd been right to pull away. If she hadn't... I shoved my hands in my pockets, unwilling to let myself consider what might've happened.

She shook her head. "Thanks, but I'm good." She hovered on the threshold. "Well, um—" She tucked her hair behind her ear. "Good night."

"Night."

She turned for the elevators, and I braced my shoulder on the doorframe, trying to rein myself in. *What the fuck are you doing?*

That had been so uncharacteristic. So unexpected and spontaneous. When I'd asked Lily to come back to my room, I'd planned on asking her about her reviews. Not proposing that she become my wife. But my gut had told me to ask her, and my gut was never wrong.

I sighed, watching as she disappeared into the elevator. Then, I closed the door to my suite before grabbing my computer to send a quick email to Carson with some instructions. With that finished, I debated my next steps. I spun my grandfather's ring on my pinkie finger, tempted to log on to the hotel's security system to track the cameras for Liliana.

What the hell was wrong with me? I buried my head in my hands.

I'd never been this...concerned about a woman who wasn't family. But something about Lily had me twisted up in knots. Or maybe it was just the situation.

I had a lot riding on this. It was an unorthodox solution, to be sure. But that was nothing new. I was used to devising creative solutions to complex problems. I had to in my line of work.

Based on everything she'd told me, and everything I'd researched online about her architect, the plans, and the area, I wasn't worried about my investment in the château. My gut told me it was a good bet, and my gut never steered me wrong.

As to my future wife, I supposed only time would tell. Fortunately, we were working with a strong foundation. We knew and respected each other. And our history would make our love story more believable. We definitely had chemistry—that wouldn't be a problem.

At least, I hoped it wouldn't. Judging by my body's reaction to her, I wasn't so sure.

I took a deep breath and straightened, a restless energy coursing through me. I tapped my fingers against my thigh, beating out a fast-paced rhythm. *Shower, right. I need to shower.*

I switched on the water, setting the temperature to warm. Steam billowed over the glass enclosure, and I stripped out of my clothes before stepping inside. I pumped some shampoo into my hand, the scent of lavender relaxing and familiar. It was the smell of home. Of my garden and memories of my grandmother. Of hard work, understanding, love.

It had been fourteen years since my grandparents' passing, and while their loss had become more bearable, I still missed them deeply. I missed my grandfather's steadying presence. His confidence and surety. I'd always looked to him for guidance and answers. And I'd always turned to my grandmother for her silent understanding.

And now, they were gone.

I inhaled slowly for a count of four and then exhaled on a long, slow breath as I pushed away the memories. I finished washing up and then dried myself before putting on a clean robe. There was a knock at the door—short and swift. Carson.

He'd been fast, or I'd been preoccupied.

I headed over and checked the peephole, then unlocked the door to let him in. "Any issues?"

Carson shook his head. "Two new phones, just as you requested."

I took the plain one from him. "Thank you."

I was about to slide it into my pocket when it started vibrating with unread notifications. I silenced it but quickly skimmed the family text thread where Jasper had kindly shared some pictures of me in the pool. I ignored them. I'd deal with the second phone once Carson was gone.

When I glanced up at Carson, his attention was on Liliana's pile of wet clothes, a curious expression on his face.

"Sorry. I—" His eyes darted between my robe and the bedroom door, which was closed. He lowered his voice. "I didn't realize you had company."

"I don't."

"Oh." He rocked on his heels. "Okay. I just assumed…"

He clearly had questions, but he was smart enough not to ask them. It was one of the things I valued most in him—or any assistant—apart from loyalty. Discretion.

"How'd the rest of the event go?" I asked.

"It was great," he said. "Everyone really seemed to enjoy themselves."

"Good."

"Did you want to make a statement about the party? Several guests captured photos and videos of the—" he cleared his throat "—incident. But Jackson and I already had them removed from the devices before they were returned to their owners."

Shit. I hadn't even considered that. I'd been so focused on Liliana, on my proposal, that I hadn't even stopped to think about how our fall into the pool might reflect badly on the hotel or overshadow the event and the opening. That was odd. I pushed away the thought, chalking it up to stress over my precarious situation with the board.

That said, the pool incident might not be such a bad thing. All our guests, including my siblings, had witnessed Lily and me together. Maybe we could spin this as part of our story.

"Good," I said, even more grateful for Carson and his foresight. "Thank you. I don't intend to remark on the event. But we'll need to have Liliana sign a statement detailing her version of events and releasing us from liability."

"Liliana," he mused. "The woman who fell into the pool. I got the impression you know her."

"She was my assistant two years ago."

He arched one eyebrow. It was subtle, but I'd still seen it. "She used to work for you?"

"Mm. You can deliver the statement to the presidential suite tomorrow morning, along with her new phone."

"Is there a certain time you'd like that taken care of by?" he asked, though I suspected that wasn't what he'd truly wanted to say.

"Before nine."

He made a note on his phone. "Will do. Anything else?"

I considered it briefly, then said, "Make sure the private jet is on standby. I might be heading back to LA early. If so, I'll also need an appointment at Cartier."

He arched an eyebrow in surprise, but he said nothing except, "Of course."

"Thank you, Carson. That will be all for now."

He let himself out.

In the short time we'd been talking, my family text thread had devolved even more. After Jasper had sent everyone a picture of me in the pool with Liliana, Knox and Nate had provided their own quips. Sloan had shared a GIF of some guy in historical clothing climbing out of a pond, and then they were taking a poll between me and some guys named Mr. Darcy and Anthony Bridgerton. I had no idea what they were talking about, but I rolled my eyes and ignored them. I had bigger things to focus on.

I was putting all the pieces into place to act on my plan, but it didn't feel real. Was I crazy to consider marrying Liliana? Or was it brilliant?

When the arrangement ended, I'd have accomplished all my goals and then some. Even so, I worried there was some angle I was missing. Something that would leave me vulnerable. I glanced at the clock and decided to text Pierce.

> Me: Can you come to my room? It's time-sensitive.

Less than five minutes later, I was letting Pierce in.

He gave my robe a pointed glance. "I'm not used to such casual attire for our meetings," he teased, following me over to the sofa. "What's going on?"

"How fast can you draft a prenup and get a marriage license in California?"

Despite Liliana's reservations, I was positive she would agree. How could she not, given the circumstances? She was desperate.

Was I a bad person for taking advantage of her situation? Maybe. Or maybe I was merely proposing a mutually beneficial arrangement. She didn't have to say yes.

He spluttered. Coughed. "Come again?"

In the past, I'd always been opposed to the idea of marriage. Mostly because I couldn't imagine anyone I'd want to spend my life with. I still couldn't, but Liliana and I would have a business agreement. A partnership founded on mutual goals. Of a limited duration.

I explained, and Pierce listened quietly, only occasionally interjecting. Finally, he said, "I know I suggested this—mostly as a joke. But as your lawyer, I feel compelled to point out the risks."

"I'm aware of the risks. But without risk, there is no reward."

And the potential reward was substantial. According to the terms of my grandfather's will, if I married by the age of forty-five, I'd receive an additional ten percent of the Huxley Grand shares. An equal percentage coming from all board members who weren't his blood relatives. If I didn't marry by the required age, I'd forfeit that advantage and have to find another way to gain the upper hand. Or otherwise continually be at the mercy of the board.

In the past, I'd had enough allies on the board. I hadn't wanted to sour those relationships by taking away their shares, nor had it been necessary to maintain the control I needed. But with Steve gone, and my inability to acquire a majority of the shares, that argument was less and less compelling.

"I get that, but if you're caught…" He blew out a breath. "You could not only lose the extra shares but your position as CEO. Hell, Graham." He leaned forward, resting his forearms on his thighs. "It's technically fraud. You could go to jail."

"It's not going to come to that."

"I hope not." He leaned back. "Do you trust Liliana?"

"I wouldn't have suggested it to her if I didn't."

"Wait." He paused, eyes flashing to mine. "What? You already talked to her about it?"

"Briefly," I said.

"Please tell me you had her sign an NDA." Concern lined his tone and his features. "Her old one expired last year. And unless you're suggesting that marriage is somehow a trade secret, it's not covered."

"She won't say anything. And even if she did, it sounds so outlandish, no one would believe her."

"Jesus, Graham." He groaned. "Are you even listening to yourself right now?"

"I can trust her," I gritted out, even though I knew he was right. NDAs were essential, especially with something as explosive as this.

"You better hope you're right."

Yes, marrying her would help me accomplish my goals. But I'd been driven by a deep and intense need to help her. Not that I was going to tell Pierce that. He'd only be more determined to talk me out of it.

"What about her blog? Her negative reviews on the Huxley properties?"

"It was never about the negative reviews, and you know it."

"You're telling me her reviews didn't bother you at all," he challenged.

"Honestly," I said in a calm tone, "I hated that part of me knew she was right. And I was fucking annoyed that I couldn't figure out her identity for the longest time."

"And now?" he asked.

"I admire her. I've always admired her, you know that."

The silence was so loud I could practically hear him thinking.

"Even so, I thought you were opposed to marriage, period."

"I am. *Was*. But that was because I thought it was forever." Because my wife would expect something I couldn't give— Vulnerability. Connection. Devotion. "This..." I sighed. "This would be a business arrangement." And I knew how to navigate those. Personal relationships, especially romantic ones, not so much.

Though there had been nothing businesslike about that

almost-kiss. The feel of her skin was still seared on my brain. It was as if there'd been this invisible thread tugging me toward her. Urging me to touch. Kiss. Claim.

I pushed away the thought, telling myself it was a good thing Liliana had pulled away. It wasn't like it meant anything.

"A business arrangement. Right." He scoffed, doing nothing to hide his skepticism.

So, I explained Lily's project and her proposal that we spend ten days a month at the château.

"I know I suggested it, but this all just seems so out of character. I mean, hell, you rarely date."

"I don't date." It was a pointless waste of time.

I detested small talk. And the women I'd dated in the past had always tried to change me and then been disappointed when they couldn't.

"Exactly," Pierce said. "And now you're going to ask everyone to believe you've suddenly had this huge change of heart? And right before your forty-fifth birthday. It looks suspicious."

No shit. I'd rarely dated anyone long enough to introduce them to my family. The few times I had, it had backfired. They'd been charmed by Nate. Enamored with Knox. Infatuated with Jasper. It had only served to magnify our differences and my shortcomings.

But I couldn't just stand by and do nothing. I'd exhausted all my other options.

"Wouldn't spending ten days with her every month in France help with that?" I pointed out.

"I mean…yeah. I guess."

I only had six months until my forty-fifth birthday. Yes, my marriage to Liliana would likely seem a little too convenient. But I was running out of time.

Hell, sometimes, I felt as if I were racing the clock. I was closing in on the age my dad had been when he'd died in a plane crash that had also claimed my mom's life as well as those of my aunt and uncle. It felt so long ago and yet as if it had happened just yesterday.

"Even so, you're going to need to do something more than that."

"Like what?" I asked.

"A honeymoon would definitely be a good start."

"Honeymoon?"

"It's this trip that newlyweds go on. Romantic. Alone. Lots of sex."

"I know what a honeymoon is, smartass."

"Good. Then you'll realize that a honeymoon would not only help cement the legitimacy of your story, it would give the two of you some time away from everyone else and all their questions."

He made a good point.

"What about the merger?" I asked. "I can't just leave in the midst of all this."

"Leave that to me. As soon as you're married, I'll get the ball rolling. I'm sure between Jasper, Sloan, and me, we can handle it."

I knew he was right, but I still found it difficult to step back. Even when I knew it was temporary. When I knew stepping back for the sake of a "honeymoon" would be in the best interest of the company in the long run.

"We could stay at the château. That's romantic, and Lily would be happy to go there sooner rather than later."

"Yes, but Graham—"

"Yeah?" I was only half paying attention, my mind already spinning with possibilities.

"If you want people to believe you're a man besotted with his new wife, then you need to take that time away from

THE EXCEPTION

work. Otherwise, it's just business as usual, and people won't think anything has changed."

I grimaced, realizing he was right. *Damn it.* "You make a good point. I just hope Sloan and Jasper will understand."

"You've never taken a vacation. I'd say it's long overdue."

"You're one to talk." Pierce was just as much of a workaholic as I was.

"Yeah. Yeah."

"Speaking of your siblings, don't you think they'll have doubts?"

I shrugged. "You know how my family is. They might be suspicious at first. But hopefully, they'll be so thrilled, they won't question it too much. And if they do, Lily and I will be sure to sell it."

"You better hope so," Pierce said in a dark tone. "Because if you do this and something goes awry, you'd want them to have plausible deniability."

Liliana too. It was part of the reason I hadn't told her my true motivations for this marriage proposal. I'd told her enough to make my reasons seem believable. She didn't need to know about the shares.

It was better for me. Better for both of us, really.

"I have a plan," I told him, trying to project certainty.

"You typically do. But despite your best efforts to plan for every outcome, human emotion is always unpredictable."

I wanted to roll my eyes. "Liliana knows what this is. And so do I."

"Okay." His tone betrayed his skepticism. "I hope you're right."

I frowned. "What are you not telling me? Are you concerned I won't be able to pull this off?"

His silence had my gut churning. If Pierce didn't think it was possible, then I wasn't sure it was worth the effort to try. He knew me better than almost anyone.

"I probably shouldn't tell you this. I've never told anyone this, and absolutely no one can know," Pierce said, and I arched my eyebrow, intrigued. "Nate and Emerson's engagement was fake at first. And they couldn't stand each other. But if they could convince everyone they were in love, so can you."

I remembered the tension between them. But also, the attraction. It had been obvious from the start. I'd always figured that was why they couldn't stand each other—because they couldn't have each other.

But a fake engagement? I would've believed it of Nate but not Emerson. Plus, Nate was an actor. He had lots of experience playing pretend. Whereas I... I blew out a breath. I hated small talk. I struggled with romantic relationships. And now, I was going to ask everyone to believe I was madly in love? With my former assistant?

Even so, I found myself asking, "You're serious?"

"One hundred percent." Pierce's expression didn't change. He wasn't joking. "And look how well that turned out."

I didn't ask for details, and he didn't offer any. Nate was happy, and that was all that mattered. He and Emerson were a good fit, and Emerson was great with Nate's daughter, Brooklyn. Nothing like his greedy ex-wife.

"I'm just relieved we're finally rid of Trinity."

"Thanks to you," Pierce said.

I shrugged. I was happy I could help in some small way.

Trinity had gotten what she deserved, and Nate no longer had to worry about her manipulative bullshit. Brooklyn—and Nate—had deserved so much better than that toxic, selfish woman.

"Whatever you decide—" Pierce clapped a hand on my shoulder "—I'll support you. Just remember, things don't always go according to plan."

CHAPTER EIGHT

Graham

When my alarm went off, I stretched and climbed out of bed. After Pierce had left, I'd stayed up most of the night poring over information Liliana had sent me about the château and the scope of the project. The likelihood of success. If I was going to put my money where my mouth was, I needed to do my due diligence first.

Twenty million wasn't an insubstantial amount by any means, but after reading through everything, I was confident I'd recoup my investment. As long as Lily had the right teams in place—both during the restoration and after—I had a feeling it would do quite well.

And she was smart. Business-savvy. I wanted to take some credit for that, but I knew a lot of it was just her. She'd seen so much during her travels for her blog; reading her posts, I could see how her experiences had honed her instincts.

I checked in with my dog sitter back in LA, pleased to see that she'd taken Prince Albert and Queen V for a walk and to a local dog park. There was an image of them with puppuccinos, and I thanked her before gently reminding her that too many treats were not good for their health.

I loved spoiling them, but I also wanted them to live long, healthy lives. Irish Wolfhounds had a relatively short life expectancy of only six to eight years, and they were my constant companions. Since this was such a short trip, I'd opted not to bring them with me. But I missed them and their calming presence.

My dogs had always been happy to see Lily in the past. Another tick in her favor.

My gut instinct had been to propose without fully considering the ramifications, but now that I'd done some research and spent some time in quiet contemplation, I felt even better about my decision.

Yes, the château restoration was a good investment, which was a relief. But marrying her had so many additional benefits.

We could easily come up with a backstory. I knew we could work well together, especially when united for a common goal. And she understood me. She would never... expect anything from me. At least not in the way of comfort or emotional support.

Which was why this plan with Liliana was perfect. She knew me, and she understood what this was.

I wouldn't have to worry about where we stood or how she felt about me. We were in a mutually beneficial relationship that wasn't about love or emotion. We were united in our sense of purpose. A sense of finality and rightness settled over me.

With my decision made, I pulled on some athletic shorts and switched on the TV. The hotel had a huge selection of on-demand workouts that could be done from the suite. It had been one of Jasper's ideas, and I was grateful not to have to use the fitness facility. As nice as our amenities were, I craved alone time to recharge. I was surrounded by people most of the day, and this gave me a chance to work out in private without interruptions, without feeling like I was being observed.

I scanned the newer options, many of them led by famous athletes like Nate's wife, Emerson. Her workouts were some of my favorites. She had a good energy—offering positive encouragement without being saccharine. And her exercises were intense.

But after scrolling through some of the options, I realized I wasn't in the mood to stay inside, not when I knew the rest of the day would likely be spent in meetings. I'd always felt the most restored and relaxed after spending time in nature, and I knew of a quiet, unmarked route that led through the trees.

As I walked down the dirt path with the ocean just beyond the trees, I could finally feel myself relax a little. Some of the tension left me, the ocean breeze cool and refreshing. But then I heard a strange noise that sounded almost like the labored clucking of a chicken.

I paused, listened. It definitely sounded like a chicken.

I searched for the source. It took a few tries, but I finally found a small chicken stuck in the brush, shaking and scared.

"Hey there, little lady," I said in a calm, gentle voice. "What are you doing? Are you lost?"

She had to be. The closest properties were miles away, and we didn't keep live chickens here. She didn't belong to anyone as far as I could tell.

I watched her for a few minutes. She seemed injured. She made a few clucking sounds, and when I crept closer, she fluttered her wings but didn't take flight.

I sighed. "Rescuing a chicken was not what I had in mind today." The chicken seemed to cluck pitifully in response. "But I can't just leave you here."

I removed my shirt and slowly inched closer to her.

"Come on. I'm going to wrap this around you and get you to safety." I did just that, cradling her against my chest in my shirt. She seemed to settle a little, and then I headed back to my room, garnering more than a few curious looks from my staff.

Once I'd returned to my room, I called down to the front desk and asked to be connected with our vet concierge. The vet concierge, like our pillow menu, had been another great idea from Jasper. He was always so attuned to the finer details of the guest experience.

He'd pitched the idea as something to cater to our guests who wanted to travel with their pets. I was all for it. Pets were family, and they should be treated as such.

The vet assured me that she'd come check on the chicken as soon as possible. Until then, she told me the chicken would be okay hanging out in the bathroom until she could get a crate sent up. And she suggested that I get her some scraps from the kitchen.

After I ended the call, I smoothed my hand over the chicken's head, determined to make sure she was okay. She purred, the sound full of contentedness. For now, I'd done everything I could, so I set her on the floor in a nest of towels and hopped in the shower. She stayed in her makeshift nest, and I was glad she was already more relaxed than when I'd found her.

I was toweling off when there was a knock at the door. I went to answer it, confident it was room service.

"That'll be breakfast," I said to the chicken, trying to reassure her.

Room service might have a universal key, but it wouldn't work on my door. Whenever I stayed anywhere, I rekeyed the system to ensure I was the only one who could get in or out of my room. It was a security precaution, but also, my brother Jasper had an annoying habit of turning up uninvited.

I checked the peephole, rolling my eyes when I saw Jasper standing in the hallway with the room service cart. I debated not answering, but then my stomach growled. Might as well get this over with. I sighed and opened the door, stepping aside for him to roll the cart inside.

"This is new," I said in a wry tone.

"Nothing I haven't done before." He removed the domed lid with a flourish.

When we were younger, my grandparents had made us work nearly every job at the hotel. From room service to housekeeping, we'd been expected to understand and appreciate everything that went into running a luxury hotel brand. There were definitely some jobs I was glad never to have to do again. Like customer service. I shuddered.

Jasper excelled at guest interaction, but I ran from it. I much preferred jobs that were repetitive and physically demanding—I was great at housekeeping or assisting the vast team of gardeners. I'd also enjoyed my time in the kitchens; it was a fast-paced environment with minimal conversation. The focus was on speed and efficiency while striving for excellence.

I assessed the tray, frowning at all the food. "I didn't order all this."

"I did." He took a bite of my toast. *Bastard.* "And Sloan and Jackson are planning to join us."

I grunted. *Great.*

He opened another lid. "What the hell is this?"

"I'll take that," I said, scooping up the plate and carrying it back to my bathroom. He followed me, gawking as I placed the kitchen scraps on the floor near the chicken.

"Why do you have a chicken in your bathroom? Never

mind." He waved a hand through the air. "I don't know why I asked. I'm just grateful it's not another rat."

"Hey." I scowled at him. "Rats are highly intelligent."

"You've been trying to tell me that since I was five, and I'm still not buying it."

When we were kids, I'd always rescued animals and nursed them back to health. I'd gotten to keep some, but it had been difficult with how often we moved around with my grandparents. And the fact that most of our luxury hotel guests wouldn't take kindly to discovering a pet rat.

I shrugged. "I guess I'm still hoping that, one day, you'll see the light."

"Hoping?" Jasper tilted his head, a quizzical expression on his face.

There was another knock. I went to the door to let in Jackson and Sloan. I greeted Sloan with a hug and a kiss to the cheek, and Jackson with a handshake.

"Heads up," Jasper said. "Graham has a chicken in his bathroom."

Jackson furrowed his brow. "A live one?"

Just then, the chicken clucked, as if to answer his question.

Jackson glanced to Sloan, and they shared a cryptic look. But then it was gone, and Sloan shook her head with a wry grin. "You've always had a soft spot for animals, especially strays."

Sloan took a seat, and we joined her at the table. It was then I realized all three of them were looking at me.

"So..." Sloan—like Jasper—wore an expectant expression. Jackson's face was unreadable, as always.

I picked up my fork and knife with a frown. I'd just wanted a quiet breakfast alone before my busy day. Was that really too much to ask?

My phone chimed, and I glanced at the screen.

> Liliana: Thank you for replacing my phone.

> Me: You're welcome.

Jasper leaned over, glancing at my screen. I held my phone to my chest. "Texting with Liliana?" He arched a brow. "Interesting."

"And none of your business." I hit the power screen on my phone, darkening it so he wouldn't see anything else. Sometimes it was easy to forget we were in our forties when he continued to act like my annoying little brother.

"I didn't realize the two of you stayed in touch," Sloan said.

Jasper and Jackson shared a look.

I remained silent. If we were going to go through with this, with getting married, I didn't want to say anything that might run contrary to the narrative Lily and I were going to have to sell.

After a beat, she gave up on waiting for an answer. I thought that was the end of it, but then Jasper said, "So about last night…" He cut into his eggs. "Did you push her into the pool? Or did she pull you in? I wasn't quite sure what happened."

He planted his chin on his palm and batted his eyes. Waiting. Wearing a fucking Cheshire smile. I barely resisted the urge to punch him.

"It was an accident. End of story." I buttered my toast, the piece he hadn't eaten.

"Regardless, you two certainly made quite the splash last night," Jasper joked.

I clenched my jaw, desperately trying not to let my

annoyance show. "Yes. You're very funny," I said in a droll tone.

He chuckled, crossing his ankle over his knee. "What was funny was your expression when you emerged from the pool."

Sloan looked as if she was trying not to laugh herself. "Come on, Jas," she chided. "Be nice."

"Are you okay?" Jackson asked.

"It's nice to know that someone in this family cares about me." I turned to him. "Thank you, Jackson. Yes. I'm fine."

"Of course we care about you," Jasper said around a mouthful of food.

"And Liliana?" Jackson's gaze was piercing.

"I asked the resort doctor to visit her this morning, just to be sure. And she's fine."

"*Yeah*, she is," Jasper said in a suggestive tone. "Is it just me, or did she get hotter since she quit working for Graham? Probably because she's no longer working for an evil overlord."

I tried to ignore his comment, though it still irked me. Jasper shouldn't be looking at Lily like that. She was *my* assistant. Former assistant. Whatever.

Get your shit together.

Or maybe I was pissed because he was right. She did look good. She always had, if I was honest. She was leaner, but her curves were still gorgeous. And the way her dress had clung to her after our fall into the pool had left little to the imagination. But the fact that Jasper had noticed… I took a bite of my eggs, but they went down like glass.

"When are we going to talk about the merger?" Sloan asked, and I was grateful for the subject change. "We need to find a way to regain the majority of the shares."

"I'm handling it."

"Thank fuck." Jasper turned to Sloan, his shoulders

relaxing. "See. I told you Graham would have a plan." He brushed his shoulder against mine, lowering his voice. "You going to do some digging? Go after Donahue? Make it personal?"

"Mm," I grunted, noncommittal. That was certainly one option. Hell, it'd be a lot easier than pretending to be married for the next two years. A lot cheaper too.

I typically preferred to use my hacking skills for good, though I had no hesitation in using them to scare off someone who dared to mess with my family. Even so, any leverage I found would only help in the short-term. Without permanent control of the board, it was an issue that could keep coming up again and again.

"Let me know how I can help," Jackson said.

He was a former Navy SEAL who'd worked in private security for the past decade before becoming our chief of security. He certainly had the skills—or the contacts—to assist. Hell, if I said the word, he probably knew someone who could make Donahue disappear permanently without a trace. Not that I'd ever do that.

"I appreciate it," I said to Jackson.

"Do you think you could find something on Donahue?" Sloan asked, worry creasing her brow. "Because without Steve in our corner, I'm afraid of what will happen if Fred forces this to a vote."

As was I. He and Danika were growing too powerful. Too fucking cocky. The other board members were easily swayed by their fear tactics.

I hated being in a vulnerable position. And I hated seeing my siblings worry about our future. As the eldest, the one in charge, it was my job to protect them and our legacy. Not just our legacy, but my grandparents' as well.

"You think Moretti's got something on Fred?" Jackson asked, draping his arm over the back of Sloan's chair. He skimmed her back with his fingers, gently reassuring her with his caress.

They were always touching. *Always.*

Is that what everyone would expect if I were married to Lily? Touching her didn't seem like much of a hardship. Though, I'd never want her to do something she wasn't comfortable with.

I wiped my mouth with my napkin and took a sip of my coffee, remembering that Jackson had asked me a question. "I'm wondering."

Jasper let out a low whistle. "Shit. I certainly wouldn't want to be on Moretti's bad side." I narrowed my eyes at him. "Or yours."

Satisfied, even though I knew he was teasing, I leaned back in my chair. "What do we know about him?"

"He's shady AF," Jasper said.

No shit.

"Keeps a low profile online," Jackson said. "Never married. Had a rough childhood but made something of himself. Really skyrocketed in the hospitality industry about fifteen years ago."

Damn. And this was why Jackson was so good at his job. He'd done some digging without even being asked.

My phone buzzed with a new text message from Pierce.

> Pierce: Check your email. Moretti's offer just came through.

I OPENED MY EMAIL, BUT THE OFFER ONLY PISSED ME OFF EVEN more. When I glanced up, Sloan and Jasper were just as absorbed in their phones. Jasper looked angry, and Sloan looked worried. It hardened my resolve.

"Find out everything you can about him," I said to Jackson.

"Consider it done," he said. "Though I'm surprised you're not taking this on yourself."

I'd kept tabs on Moretti in the past, but only the moves he made in the industry. As long as he'd stayed out of my business, I'd stayed out of his. But now that he'd made this personal, it was time to do some digging.

My mind whirled with possibilities and questions. Why was Fred so motivated to push Moretti's agenda? Had Moretti offered him some sort of incentive? Or perhaps issued a threat?

I was sick of dealing with the board's bullshit. And seeing the concern hanging over my siblings. If I had those shares, we'd never have to worry about losing control to the board again.

"I know you can handle it, and I have other business to attend to if we're going to stop this merger."

Like making sure everything was in place if I needed to pull the trigger on my plan to marry Liliana, because I was done with being at the whims of the board. Of letting Moretti and his cohorts pull the strings. I was sick of worrying about what would happen to my grandparents' legacy.

My siblings and I had had enough taken from us. I wanted to reclaim control, and if that meant going through with this sham of a marriage, so be it.

I wondered what my family would think if I married Lily. If the circumstances had been different, I would've tried to wait a few months to establish our relationship with our family and friends and make it seem more legitimate. But Moretti's formal offer had definitely accelerated the timeline.

My family would certainly be surprised by my sudden nuptials. But would they be supportive? Or would they question my relationship with Liliana? Suspect the truth behind our "whirlwind romance" and think it was motivated by my desire to secure the additional shares, unintentionally casting doubts among the board?

Hell, maybe they didn't *want* to know. Jasper had been so eager, so relieved, to hear that I was handling the situation with the merger, that he hadn't pushed for too many details. Now that I thought about it, neither had Sloan.

It didn't matter. I'd made my decision, and I was ready to see it through.

That said, I wasn't sure where Lily and I stood after last night. She hadn't said no, but she hadn't said yes either. Resolved, I tapped out a quick message.

> Me: Have dinner with me tonight.

CHAPTER NINE

Lily

Josephine glanced up from her spot on the couch. Her legs were curled beneath her as she edited some content for her blog. "Where are you off to, looking like that?"

We'd spent the morning enjoying a facial and a massage, which had given me a lot of quiet time to consider everything. Even when Jo and I had been lounging by the pool, creating content for my blog and her YouStream channel, my mind had been preoccupied with thoughts of Graham and his proposal. Almost twenty-four hours later, my head was still spinning.

Several unread text messages from my architect were sitting on my phone. Any time my phone buzzed, I jolted, worrying it was from him or one of my family members. I needed to respond to my architect, even if just to let him know I needed more time to decide on some of his requests regarding various restoration projects, but I kept delaying the inevitable. Because I knew what every text meant: more money.

"Lil?" Josephine asked.

"Dinner," I said, knowing she already had plans to meet

up with another content creator she'd been dying to collaborate with.

"*With…*"

"My old boss."

"Graham?" She practically choked on his name.

"Yes. It's not a big deal. Okay?"

"Mm." She gave me a once-over. "Then why are you dressed like *that?*"

I glanced down at my dress, smoothing my hands over the fabric. It was a gorgeous blue ombre maxi dress that hugged my curves. The top was low, nearly dipping down to my navel. I'd used a ton of fabric tape to make sure it stayed in place. And I'd paired it with a starfish necklace and earrings. I'd twisted my hair—Francine again but refreshed after our impromptu swim last night—back into a low, messy bun.

"Too much?" I asked, suddenly feeling self-conscious.

"Depends on your goals," she said, waggling her brows. "Is this a business meeting, or something else?" She gave me a meaningful look.

In truth, it was both. But I couldn't tell her that.

"Tell me honestly," she said, leaning in. "Do you have a crush on Graham? Because I always sort of suspected… And then last night…"

"I, uh…" *What am I supposed to say?*

She smirked. "Oh, come on. You can't tell me you aren't attracted to him. The man looks like he walked off the cover of a magazine. And the way you always talked about him, I just sort of assumed."

"Assumed what?" I asked, resisting the urge to cross my arms over my chest, though I didn't disagree. Graham was something. Dark, curly hair. Chiseled jawline. Full lips. And those enigmatic green eyes that made me want to squirm beneath his perusal even while they heated my skin.

That whole "chemistry test." Just thinking of it had my skin growing warm. And I'd definitely spent some quality time with my vibrator last night just so I could fall asleep.

"Assumed you were crushing on him. Hell, I wouldn't blame you. He's hot in that stern, dominating way. I mean…" She flopped back on the couch. "He seems so buttoned-up, but I bet he's a freak in the sheets."

"Okay." I rolled my eyes, tossing one of the throw pillows at her. "That's enough."

"Oh, come on." She caught it and sank down on the couch, clutching it to her chest. "You can't tell me you aren't dying to know if I'm right."

I barked out a laugh, though mostly it was to hide my discomfort. After what had happened last night, I had a feeling she was right. But I snapped my mouth shut.

"You sure you don't know? I mean…you didn't come back to the room until *really* late last night. And you were only wearing a robe."

"Because I fell into the pool," I protested. "And he offered to have my clothes laundered by the hotel staff."

"That's it?"

"Yes," I said. "That's it."

"So, if you didn't sleep with him…" She sounded disappointed. "Then what did happen?"

I lifted a shoulder as I finished putting on my heels, a pair of strappy gold sandals that I adored. I hadn't had an opportunity to wear them in a while since most of my days were spent in dusty overalls, work boots, and shirts dappled with paint. "We talked."

My eye snagged on the bandage on my ankle, and I stilled, remembering how Graham's hands had felt on my skin. His entire demeanor had softened, his touch gentle and caring. Lingering.

"Right." She crossed her arms over her chest, jolting me from the memory. "'Talked,'" she said, using air quotes.

My cheeks heated, and I felt as if she could read my thoughts. "We did!" I protested, perhaps a bit too ardently.

"For hours?" Her tone was rife with skepticism, as was her expression.

"We hadn't seen each other in two years. We had a lot to catch up on. And he had questions about my blog."

I was being intentionally vague. Jo was my best friend, but if Graham and I went through with our crazy plan, there was a lot on the line—twenty million dollars and the chance to make my dream a reality.

Her eyes widened. "Shit. He knows you're Gilded Lily? Was he pissed?"

I lifted a shoulder. "He wasn't pleased."

"But he still invited you to dinner tonight."

"Mm-hmm." I pulled out the compact mirror from my purse, busying myself with reapplying my lip gloss. "Do you think I should change?"

"You look hot," Jo said. "But I didn't have to tell you that. And no, I don't think you should change. Not unless you want to."

There was a knock at the door—short and authoritative. *Oh good. He's here.*

I took a deep breath and slid my hands down my dress. "Looks like it's too late to change even if I wanted to."

She headed for the door. "He's going to have a heart attack."

I felt like I might have one myself.

I told myself it was because my future hung on this dinner. But it was more than that. And after last night, I wasn't sure what to think. About his proposal. Our almost-kiss. This spontaneous dinner invitation. Any of it.

I knew what Graham's schedule was like. Hell, I'd been

responsible for managing it for a year. I knew he maximized his working hours for efficiency and productivity. He rarely did anything spontaneous, unless it was important. And this dinner—not to mention his marriage proposal—was nothing if not spontaneous.

I'd spent the past hour getting ready for it, and I still felt completely unprepared. Before I could back out or make up some excuse for not going, Jo answered the door.

Graham's deep voice reverberated through me from the hall as he introduced himself to her. And when he stepped into the suite, I stilled. Graham looked good. Too good.

My stomach fluttered, with nerves or excitement, I wasn't sure. Especially as he continued to study me. Judging from his reaction, he liked what he saw.

The air was charged with something, and I felt myself being pulled closer to him. Drawn to him. His eyes raked me from head to toe, lingering on the large swath of skin revealed by my dress. I could feel my skin heating, my blood whooshing in my ears.

"Are you ready?" he rasped.

I nodded and grabbed my clutch, wishing I could make my hands stop shaking. Graham placed a soft kiss to my cheek, and I felt frozen to the spot. I could feel Jo's eyes on us, watching curiously. I knew she had questions, and I couldn't blame her. If our roles were reversed, I'd definitely have questions.

I was grateful when Graham offered me his arm, giving me an escape. I looped my arm through his, grateful for his steadying presence.

"Have fun." Jo winked, and the door closed behind us.

"Thanks." I waved goodbye and let him guide me down the hall.

I kept my attention focused on the elevators, trying not to laugh when one of the employees stopped and gawked at him from the hallway. Behind her, another employee with a cart of food narrowly missed running into her coworker. They glanced at each other then started whispering, their attention on Graham.

Once they were out of earshot, I said, "You do realize that *everyone* will be talking about this, right?"

He glanced down at me, one eyebrow arched. "That was kind of the point."

Right. Of course. Graham never did anything without a game plan. I didn't know whether that made me feel better or worse.

When we arrived at one of the on-site restaurants, Azul, the hostess led us to a candlelit table overlooking the ocean. It was intimate. Romantic. *Definitely didn't feel like a business meeting.*

Right. All part of the show. I'd do well to remember that.

Graham pulled out my chair for me. I took in the view from our perch on the edge of the cliff, feeling as if I were balanced on my own precipice. I could keep trying to save the château on my own. Or I could marry Graham and restore it to its former glory.

Part of me cringed at the idea of marrying for money, even if we both knew this was a business transaction going in. The other part was just so exhausted. I knew I couldn't keep operating at the level I was. And if I wasn't careful, I'd lose everything.

"How's your ankle? Is it healing okay?" he asked.

"I...yeah." I pulled my lip between my teeth. "Thank you."

We ordered drinks and our meal, and then the waiter left. Graham's green eyes bored into mine, and I couldn't help but get a little lost in them. I'd always thought he was attractive, but something seemed different tonight. Or maybe I'd never felt the full focus of his attention. Not like this.

"How are you enjoying the resort?" he asked.

"I, um—" I tucked my hair behind my ear. "I didn't think you were interested in my feedback."

"Perhaps I should've been more open to your suggestions," he said, surprising me again. I'd seen him act like this in negotiations. Graham could definitely be charming when he wanted. "What you've accomplished with your blog is impressive."

I blinked a few times, completely shocked. Was he... complimenting me?

Yes, Graham could be charming, but he could also be relentless, committed to a course of action. But as tenacious as he could be, he was never ruthless or brutal. He was guided by a strong moral code, a deep sense of loyalty and duty. When he put his mind to something, he was determined to see it through.

"Thank you."

"That said, your blog could be a sticking point with my family, especially regarding—" he leaned in "—our story."

"Wow. Okay. So we're jumping straight to that."

He smoothed a hand down his tie. "What else would we be here to discuss?"

"I don't know." I glanced around the room. "We might just try to slow down. Treat it like a real date. See how things go before jumping into negotiations."

"Seems like a waste of time."

"Is foreplay a waste of time?" I arched a brow, wondering what had come over me. Why had I made an analogy to sex instead of a business meeting?

"Point taken." He cleared his throat, straightening his silverware so it was perfectly spaced. "So, how was your day?"

I bit back a smile. Graham wasn't typically one for small talk, but I appreciated that he was trying. "It was nice. And thank you for replacing my phone. You didn't have to do that, but I'm grateful."

This morning, a brand-new iPhone had been delivered to my suite. It was identical to my old one but with more storage. Even the case was the same, but it no longer had the smudge marks on it from that time I'd dropped it. And all the files had been restored, though I had no idea how he'd managed that.

"It was nothing."

"Well, it meant a lot to me," I said.

"Did you get to do much exploring today?"

"I checked out the spa. Lounged on the beach. You?"

"Mostly meetings."

I wasn't surprised, though the idea that he was missing out on such an incredible place saddened me. Not to mention the fact that he'd worked so hard on this location and he wasn't even getting to enjoy his accomplishment.

I searched for a more neutral topic. Something Graham would enjoy talking about. Something that would prompt him to give me more than just a single-word answer.

"Has Atlas Blackwood visited the hotel since it opened?" I didn't want to stick to "work" subjects, but I knew it was a safer place to start. It would help put us both at ease.

The waiter returned to the table with our meals. My dinner smelled delicious, but I could barely do more than pick at it while I listened to Graham talk about Atlas. For a fake date, I was surprisingly nervous. Maybe because I knew how much was riding on this. So, I sipped my wine, trying to balance my need to relax with my desire to remain clearheaded.

Eventually, Graham frowned at my plate. "Are you not enjoying your meal?"

"I—" I rolled my bottom lip between my teeth. The food, even what little of it I'd tasted, had been delicious. But I was so keyed up, I'd barely been able to enjoy it. "I am. I'm just... distracted."

Graham leaned forward, placing his hand over mine. My pulse kicked up a beat. Especially when he angled himself so our foreheads were almost kissing. Energy sizzled between us, and I tried to focus on his words instead of the way his large hand felt blanketing mine.

"If you're still interested in my offer, come to my room after dinner, and we'll talk. For now, let's try to enjoy our meal. Weren't you the one who suggested this was foreplay?"

Was it my imagination, or was his voice deeper? I was convinced I'd imagined it, but then I met his eyes. His drank me in, like I was something he wanted to devour.

"Isn't this cozy?" a man asked, snapping me out of the trance.

Graham's eyes remained on me, despite the interruption. I expected him to yank his hand back from mine, but if anything, he tightened his grip ever so slightly. I forced myself to keep my hand on the table despite my knee-jerk reaction to hide it.

"Hey, Jasper." I smiled at him, the motion feeling forced.

"Liliana," he said. "Nice to see you again."

I bobbed my head. "You too."

"Brother." Graham tilted his chin in acknowledgment, an unspoken look passing between them that I couldn't decipher.

Jasper glanced from Graham to me, curiosity lighting his features. Finally, he asked, "What do you think of the hotel, Liliana? I trust you're enjoying your stay."

"Yes." I swallowed, grateful for the change of topic. "Absolutely. It's a lovely property, and all the staff have been so wonderful." The words tumbled out of me, and I knew I needed to slow down.

"Good. I know you got to sample the pool last night, but

hopefully you've been enjoying some of our other amenities." He had a teasing glint in his eye, but I knew he meant no harm by it.

Before I could respond, Graham stood, folding his napkin and placing it in his chair. "Jasper." Graham grabbed him by the elbow. "A word."

I tried not to stare as Graham practically dragged his brother to the kitchen, disappearing briefly behind a door. I smoothed my hand over my napkin and picked at my meal, trying to ignore the curious looks of nearby diners.

A few minutes passed, and then Graham strode over to the table with a sense of confidence I envied. Everyone watched him—how could they not? He was enigmatic and exuded power as he sliced through the room with ease.

He skimmed his hand along the back of my chair, his touch a ghost on my skin that left goose bumps in its wake. This definitely felt more like foreplay than a business meeting. Especially when Graham leaned over, his breath tickling the shell of my ear as he rasped, "Sorry about that."

I shivered. "No problem. Everything okay?"

"Just Jasper being Jasper." He took his seat and picked up his fork and knife. We ate in silence, and I tried to come up with something to discuss. Something that wasn't related to his proposal or his job or anything else that might increase the tension already arcing between us.

"How is Jasper?" I finally asked, knowing how important Graham's brother was to him, even if Jasper annoyed him at times.

"Good." Graham set down his fork and took a sip of his wine. Even after all this time, his one-word responses could still catch me off guard.

Silence. Not awkward. But also not entirely comfortable. It was as if we were struggling to find our footing in this new dynamic. We were no longer boss and employee, and I wasn't quite sure what we were.

I studied him, trying to imagine what it would be like to pretend to be married to him.

"You're lucky to have such a supportive family who loves you." I only wished I had that kind of relationship with even one of my siblings.

I hadn't heard anything more from them since my mom's text that I was selfish and needed to apologize to my sister. And I hadn't reached out either. Nor did I intend to.

"I know the three of you didn't always agree on everything, but you have one another's backs. And while I have a team of kind, talented workers at the château…" I drew in a shaky breath, surprised that I was going to admit this. But I supposed if Graham could attempt to make small talk, then I could share something about myself. "It really all falls on me."

He placed his hand over mine again, and my skin zinged from that touch. "I know what that feels like. And if you agree to this, to my proposal, I promise you will have the support you need."

If Graham was trying to sell me on the idea, he was doing a good job. I'd been drowning in decisions and responsibility and debt, and he was offering a lifeline. He was offering something even more priceless—understanding.

I found myself wanting to share more moments like this with him. And it gave me hope that maybe this crazy idea could work.

CHAPTER TEN

Graham

"You want a drink?" I asked, kicking off my shoes as soon as the door to my suite had closed.

"I'm good. Thanks." Lily hovered by the door, shifting from one foot to the other as if she couldn't decide whether to stay or go.

Was she having second thoughts?

I couldn't think straight. She made me feel distracted—all the time, but especially in that dress. Before now, I'd only ever seen her in business clothes. Professional clothes. And this dress was anything but.

I cleared my throat. "Before we discuss this any further, I'll need you to sign an NDA."

"Oh, um, sure." She chewed on the inside of her cheek. "Do you have a pen?"

"I do." I tried to imagine myself saying those words in a different context, where she was my bride. There would be no wedding without an NDA. I grabbed it and a pen from the safe in the bedroom. "Take your time to look it over."

She quickly skimmed the contents and then affixed her name on the signature line with a swish.

"Any questions?"

"Nope. Looks pretty standard." She should know. She'd reviewed plenty of them while in my employ.

With that settled, I grabbed a deck of cards, opening it and relaxing at the feel of them in my hands. I sank down on the couch, setting the deck on the coffee table.

The chicken started clucking, and I did my best to ignore it, hoping Liliana would too.

"Do you know how to play gin rummy?" I asked, trying to lean into building a rapport outside of our past as employer/employee.

A crease formed between her brows. "Did you hear that?" She tilted her head. "Do you hear… Was that a dog? Or no." She shook her head. "A chicken?"

"It's nothing."

"No." She shook her head. "I swear I hear a chicken clucking. Like, in someone's room."

I stood, worried something was wrong with my chicken. Not *my* chicken. *The* chicken. She was not my pet, even if she had quite the delightful personality. And now that she was clean, you could see her gorgeous plumage.

"Where are you going?" she asked.

"There may or may not be a chicken in my room."

"What?" Lily squawked, following me. "Are you serious?"

"I found her on the beach this morning. The vet says her wing is damaged, but she should make a full recovery."

"But what's she doing here?"

"I'm just keeping her until the vet can find her a home."

"You're keeping her. Here?" She said the words slowly, as if she couldn't make sense of them.

"Yes. Temporarily."

When I glanced at her, she was watching me curiously. "Yes?" I asked.

"Nothing. I'm just surprised, that's all."

"Why?" I asked. "I rescued Prince Albert and Queen V."

"Yeah, but they're not a chicken."

I scratched under the chicken's chin. "Does that make her any less worthy?"

"No. Nope." Her voice sounded strange. When I met her eyes, they were shining.

I gave the chicken one last glance, made sure her food and water were full. And then I gestured toward the living room.

"Does she have a name?" Lily asked. "Your new roommate."

"She's not my new roommate. I'm not keeping her. So, no, she doesn't have a name."

"Mm." She tapped a finger to her lips. "I think we should call her Lady Lorraine."

I chuckled. "Lady Lorraine?"

She stilled.

"What?" I asked.

She turned to face me. "You just…you laughed. You never laugh."

I frowned. "I laugh."

"Not with me."

"It's not a done deal yet, but I suppose if you're going to be my wife, we should probably work on our rapport, as you suggested."

"Is that what this is?" She gestured to the cards and the couch. "Working on our rapport?"

"No." I sat on the couch and shuffled the cards. "Games and puzzles have always helped me relax."

"I know," she said softly. So softly, I almost missed it.

I was coming to realize just how closely she'd paid attention to me. Not just as her boss, but as a man. It honestly made me feel like shit. That she'd been so attentive and perceptive, and I… I swallowed hard. Sometimes, I felt as if I was only scratching the surface with her.

A game of cards was as good a way as any to get to know someone. I also hoped that playing cards would give me something to concentrate on besides the gorgeous woman across from me. When I'd first seen Lily in that dress, with its swirling blues and dangerously low neckline, my tongue had nearly fallen out of my damn mouth. Even now, I found it difficult not to stare.

And I hadn't been the only one. The entire restaurant had been captivated by her. Jasper too, even if his flirting seemed tamer than usual. Now that I thought about it, he'd been going out less lately too. I made a note to follow up with him. Because a quiet Jasper typically meant one thing—trouble.

Liliana kicked off her shoes and sat on the couch next to me. Not close enough so we were touching, but still closer than I'd expected. Her scent wafted over to me—sweet, floral, a little powdery, and full of energy.

Unable to help myself, I drew in a deep breath, eager to take another sniff. It reminded me of my garden in the summer, the blooms bursting with color and fragrance. It was both invigorating and relaxing, and I wanted more of it. More of her.

"Why Lady Lorraine?" I asked.

"Since you make a quiche Lorraine with eggs."

"Clever," I said before explaining the rules of gin rummy.

We began to play, and every so often, she'd ask questions about the rules or strategy. It was fun. Easy. Especially after she really started to get the hang of it.

I watched her out of the corner of my eye, amused by the way her tongue darted out of the side of her mouth when she was concentrating. I remembered her doing that when she'd worked for me. Now that we were spending time together, I remembered a lot of things about Lily. Things I'd tried to ignore in the past.

When she won a round, her whole face lit up in delight. She was beautiful. Captivating.

I gripped the edge of the couch, feeling light-headed. What was this sensation? What the hell was wrong with me?

I shook my head as if to clear it, remembering that she wasn't interested in me. Not really. She'd pulled back from our almost-kiss last night because she wanted my money. And that was fine, because we were both getting something out of this.

"Think you got the hang of it?" I asked.

She nodded, but then she flashed me a wicked grin. "Care to make it interesting?"

I wondered what she was envisioning. Was strip gin rummy a thing? I supposed it could be. I imagined winning hand after hand as Liliana had to strip off her clothes piece by piece.

Focus!

"What did you have in mind?" I asked.

"The winner of each round gets to make a suggestion for our arrangement."

Ah. So she wanted to use this as a negotiation. That suited my purposes. "Fine by me."

I focused on the cards and my opponent, trying not to let my surprise show when she said, "Gin."

We showed our hands, and she won the round.

"Go ahead," I said.

"If we're going to do this," she said, shuffling the cards, "I don't want to wait. The château is in a precarious position, and the sooner I can get the funding to secure it and start on the projects, the better."

Excellent. Moretti's formal offer had come with a deadline. We had thirty days to accept, or it would expire. The board was already champing at the bit.

"I agree, which is why I had my lawyer draw up a prenup."

Her eyes widened as I slid her the document, our game—or the pretense of it—forgotten. "I'll put ten million dollars into a trust designated for the *Château de Bergeret.* My contribution will be anonymous. As long as we make it to the two-year mark, the additional ten million is yours."

"That's fair. Thank you."

"The terms are laid out in full, including the fact that upon our divorce or in the event of my death, you will not be entitled to any of my property or anything relating to the Huxley brand."

"As it should be," she said, and something inside me relaxed. "The Huxley Grand is a family brand." I had to protect my family and the brand at all costs.

Women I'd dated in the past hadn't always been so... understanding of that fact. They often wanted to take advantage of my money or my brand. But I knew that wouldn't be the case with Lily. It just wasn't who she was.

"That said, I used to be your assistant. Getting married would be a major shift in our relationship dynamic. I would be your partner, not your employee. And I want to know that you'll respect me, even if you don't always agree with me."

"If you're my wife," I said, the word still foreign on my tongue, "of course I will respect you. I couldn't marry someone I didn't respect, even if this is fake."

Her expression was thoughtful, and then she nodded.

"I'm taking a huge risk," I said. "If the truth of our arrangement ever came out, my board would likely fire me, and I'd lose control of the company." Not to mention potentially facing charges for fraud. But I didn't mention that. The less Lily knew about the additional shares, the better. I wanted to reassure her, but I also wanted to make it clear the stakes were high for both of us.

"I understand." She turned to the next page, skimming the clause on fidelity. "Everything seems reasonable so far."

"Good. And this is strictly a business agreement."

"If you're worried about me falling in love with you," she chortled. "Don't."

Okay. I wasn't sure whether to be grateful or offended. But at least we were both on the same page. Her reasons for saying that didn't matter. Or at least, they shouldn't.

"I know you don't do relationships," she said, as if to soothe the sting of her earlier comment. "You're married to your job. And after being the caretaker for the château for the past year, I get it. Even if I do still hope to one day get married for real."

"Exactly," I said, grateful that she understood me, perhaps more than anyone I'd ever dated. "Assuming all other terms are to your liking, I'd like for us to get married in LA on Wednesday."

Her jaw dropped, and she gawked at me. "This coming Wednesday? As in, less than seventy-two hours?"

"Is that going to be a problem?"

She'd wanted to move fast, and I was completely on board. We needed to put things in place to protect the château's interior and make it watertight. And if she was legally my wife, I could obtain the additional ten percent of the shares. There was no reason to wait.

"I don't—" She swallowed hard. "Yes, this is a fake marriage, but shouldn't we at least try to make it seem real? I need some time to find a dress. To tell Josephine. Then there's the matter of our guests. A photographer." The words were coming out faster and faster, like a Ferris wheel spinning off its axis.

"I've taken care of everything from the venue to the legalities." Carson had already contacted the staff at the Huxley Grand LA. They were on standby to set up for an intimate and discreet wedding on my terrace, though I hadn't told him who it was for. And Pierce was handling the legal side of things. "My stylist will have dresses for you to choose from. All you have to do is show up."

I'd expected Liliana to be relieved or happy. Instead, she seemed almost disappointed. Or maybe she was trying to negotiate for more. Most people would.

"Wow. Okay." She blinked rapidly. "I'm not opposed to the idea of leaving, but what am I going to tell Josephine about my sudden departure?" Lily asked. "We planned to spend the week here together. I was really looking forward to hanging out with her, and I feel like a shitty friend ditching her."

I lifted a shoulder, admiring her loyalty to her friend even if it was contrary to my plans. "Tell her whatever you want. Or don't tell her anything. For now, the fewer people who know, the better."

"Yeah. I get that, but she's my best friend. I can't keep secrets from her."

"Does she know how dire your financial situation is?"

She wouldn't meet my gaze when she shook her head. "No."

"Then you do keep secrets from her."

She rolled her eyes. "Thanks, Graham. That makes me feel a hell of a lot better."

I couldn't imagine how much pressure Liliana had been under all these months. And she'd only had herself to rely on. But she'd trusted me with the truth of her situation. And now, she had me.

She'd always been loyal to me. A good assistant. We'd worked well together, especially navigating high-pressure situations. I could only hope those qualities would carry over to our marriage, even if it was all just for show.

Whether I wanted to admit it or not, I cared about her. You couldn't spend a year in close quarters, working together day in and day out, and not care about someone.

Yeah, but you don't feel the same way about Carson that you do about Liliana. I pushed away that thought.

"I wasn't trying to upset you," I said. "Merely pointing out—"

She held up a hand. "Stop. Just stop."

I shut my mouth, knowing that I was only digging a deeper hole.

Finally, she said, "I know you want this done quickly, and so do I. But a public engagement and wedding would add legitimacy to our story."

"Not necessarily. We can come up with some backstory about falling for each other while you worked for me but never acting on it. Then reconnecting and having a whirlwind romance."

"A whirlwind romance?" She gaped at me. "Two words I never thought I'd hear from your mouth."

I frowned. "I can be romantic."

"I sure hope so," she said. "Because if people are going to buy this story, we're going to have to really lean into it. Be a little…extra."

I frowned at the idea of making a fool of myself. At faking intimacy. But this was important. I'd find a way to make it work. I had to.

"What will you tell your family?" she asked. "You mentioned that my blog might be an issue."

"I'll figure out how to spin it."

It wasn't like my family would be upset that I was in a relationship with the author of *Gilded Lily*. But I wished I hadn't made such a big deal of finding out who the blogger was. It would affect the timeline of our story. It could affect my family's acceptance of the lies we were about to tell them.

It would be suspicious if we had been dating and I didn't know Lily was behind *Gilded Lily*. So, a whirlwind romance really was our only option.

"What about your family? Are they going to be a problem?"

An expression passed over her face, but it quickly cleared. "I hope this won't be a deal-breaker, but I'm not on speaking terms with my family."

Oh. I hadn't expected her to say that. I didn't know the circumstances, but if Lily didn't want to speak with her family, it must be serious. I wondered what had happened to fracture their relationship to the point that it was beyond repair, but I got the feeling she didn't want to talk about it.

So I asked the only question that truly mattered. "Are you okay?"

She lifted a shoulder but wouldn't meet my eyes. "Honestly, it was a long time coming, but it still hurts."

"You're not the first person who has cut ties with your family. I'm sorry that your relationship is strained, but it doesn't change anything—at least not for me. In fact, it makes things easier because it's fewer people we have to convince." And fewer people who would be disappointed when this was over.

"I hadn't thought of it like that. Honestly, I'm more concerned about how to sell this to Jo. She's always been able to see right through me." She considered it a moment then said, "Actually, no. You know what? That's one of my conditions. I want to be able to tell Jo the truth."

"No," I blurted. "Absolutely not."

Her eyes flashed with anger. "Tell me something, Graham. Does Pierce know?"

"Yes, but—"

She shook her head. "He's your best friend. Therefore, my best friend should get to know too. She would never tell anyone, and if anything, she'd be an asset to us."

"Pierce is my attorney."

"And Jo is my…" She seemed to debate the best word, finally settling on, "Adviser."

I held her gaze; she didn't blink. *Fuck me.* She wasn't going to back down, was she? But perhaps she was right—having her best friend on our side could help us sell our story.

"She'd have to sign an NDA," I said, even though I didn't like it. More people meant more chances for someone to slip and reveal the truth.

"No problem."

"And I want you to have a bodyguard," I said, not wanting to dwell on her friend. I hadn't agreed to anything—not yet. Lily scrunched up her face, so I added, "All my brothers' wives have one. Sloan has one."

"Do you have a bodyguard now? And don't think we're done talking about Jo." She wagged her finger at me. "You didn't agree to my condition."

I shoved my hands in my pockets. "I don't need one. I have a fifth-degree black belt." And I was a hacker, but I didn't tell her that. I could inflict a lot more destruction from behind my keyboard than she'd ever know.

"The bodyguard is nonnegotiable," I continued. "If you're vulnerable, I'm vulnerable. There are many people who would seek to harm you to get to me or my money."

She blew out a breath and sank back against the sofa. "Jeez. Are you trying to talk me out of this?"

"No." I picked up the cards and placed them back in the box. "I'm just trying to make sure you understand what it would mean to be married to me." After what had happened with Sloan, I wasn't taking any chances.

"Okay," Lily finally said.

"Okay to the bodyguard, or okay to the deal?" I asked.

"Okay to both, assuming you agree to my condition that I can tell Jo the truth. Otherwise, I walk."

I scoffed. "You'd walk away from twenty million dollars over that?"

She met my gaze. Hard. Unflinching. "Yeah. I would."

Well, shit. I believed her. And that only made me respect her even more.

I debated my options. While I didn't want to tell any more people than absolutely necessary, this was important to Lily. If she thought her friend's support would bolster the believability of our relationship, then so be it.

"You can tell her it's a business deal, but you are not to tell her anything about why I need a wife."

"Agreed." She stood, smoothing her palms down her skirt. "Unless there's anything else, I should get back to my room so I can pack and figure out what to tell Jo."

I pushed off the couch to join her, appreciating her efficiency and decisiveness. "Then we have a deal." I held out my hand.

She placed hers in mine, her skin roughened from hard work, her grip sure and steady. "Congratulations, Mr. Mackenzie. You've got yourself a fiancée."

CHAPTER ELEVEN

Lily

When we arrived on the tarmac at the private airport in LA the following afternoon, a set of matching Audi A8s were waiting for us, along with two drivers. I glanced at Graham as he held out his hand to assist me down the last few steps of the aircraft.

"Thank you." I tried not to think about the fact that I was touching him. And in less than forty-eight hours, I'd be married to him.

Married. To Graham.

I tried to tell myself it would all work out. Once we were married, I wouldn't have to worry about funding for the château. But the idea of walking down the aisle set my heart galloping.

Graham signaled to one of the drivers, and she stepped forward. "Lily, this is Willow. She'll be protecting you."

I was grateful I was wearing sunglasses so I could scan her surreptitiously. She was about six feet tall, built like a rugby player, and wearing the prettiest shade of pink lipstick I'd ever seen.

"Hi," I said, holding out my hand. "Nice to meet you, Willow."

"You too," she said then returned to the car to give Graham and me some privacy.

"I have some business to attend to, but I arranged for my stylist to meet you at my penthouse. Jay will help you prepare for everything we have coming up."

Graham's cryptic wording had me wondering if he was referring to our secret wedding or something more. I knew what Graham's calendar was like—or at least, what it had been like two years ago. And I didn't imagine that much had changed. He often attended events around the city for various charities. Events I'd now be expected to attend with him, as his wife.

Would people view me as a trophy wife? A gold digger?

The truth was far more salacious.

I wondered what people would think if they knew that Graham had given me twenty million dollars to pretend to be his wife and help him secure his legacy.

It still seemed like an extreme move on his part, but I knew he'd do anything to protect his family's brand.

I rested my sunglasses on top of my head. "Okay. Sure. Did you want to give me a new passcode?" I'd visited his penthouse a few times while I'd been in his employ. Each time, I'd needed a different eight-digit passcode.

He shook his head. "I upgraded my home security last year. All you have to do is place your thumb on the keypad, and the door will unlock."

"Wow. Okay." That was incredibly high-tech. And then I frowned. "Don't we need to program my prints?"

"It's already done."

"But—" My mouth opened and closed.

"Close your mouth, *mon petit poisson.*" Then he mumbled,

"Before I put it to good use." Or at least, that's what it sounded like.

Maybe I was imagining things because that certainly didn't seem like something Graham would say. And definitely not to me. I didn't know what to remark on first—the fact that he'd spoken French or that he'd called me his little fish.

I tried to ignore the heat coursing through me at his suggestion.

"Do you actually speak French?" I asked in French. "Or did you use an online translator?"

"My grandparents insisted that we all learn multiple languages so we could communicate in a global economy." His French was perfect.

"Smart. I knew you were fluent in Japanese and Spanish. I just didn't realize you were also fluent in other languages," I continued, enjoying the fact that we could converse in another language.

"Japanese, French, Spanish, and German."

"Holy shit," I said, finally returning to English. First, the black belt and now this? It made me realize that maybe I didn't know my future husband as well as I'd thought.

"Have you always been fluent in French?" he asked. "I don't remember seeing that listed on your résumé."

"I was always proficient. I took French classes through high school and college, but I wasn't fluent until more recently. After I started looking to purchase a château, I enrolled in a French language immersion course so I could converse with the architects and artisans."

He nodded, his expression thoughtful. *"Tant d'idiomes amusants."*

"Oui." The language certainly had some interesting idioms.

"One of my personal favorites is, *'Qui ne risque rien, n'a rien.'*"

He who risks nothing, has nothing.

That wasn't surprising.

"Back to the fingerprint thing," I said, trying to get us back on track. I remembered that we weren't alone, and I was fully aware that Willow and the team were just standing by, waiting for us. "How do you have my fingerprints?"

"They're in your file from your background check when you got the job at Huxley."

"Oh." Right. Of course. That made sense.

"Also…" He reached into his wallet and pulled out a black Amex with my name on it. "Feel free to charge whatever you need."

"Whatever I need?" I choked on the word, thinking that was incredibly broad.

"Anything you need." Was his voice deeper, or was I imagining it?

"That card has no spending limit." And he'd added me as an authorized user? When had he even done that?

"And…?" He arched one brow.

"And you're already giving me…" I glanced around, mindful of my word choice. "So much."

"I trust you," he said.

"But what if I take advantage of it?" I didn't intend to, but I'd never had such spending power at my fingertips. I'd never been handed his personal black Amex card, not even when I'd been working as his assistant.

"You won't," he said simply.

"But how do you *know?*" I asked, still in awe of the trust he was placing in me. I knew it wasn't something he gave but something that had to be earned.

"Because—" he stepped closer, tucking a wayward strand of my hair behind my ear "—I know you."

I was still thinking about what Graham had said when Willow pulled up to his penthouse an hour later. I'd enjoyed talking to her in the car and getting to know her, not that she'd volunteered much information about herself. I supposed it was a job hazard—or maybe a requirement—but it wasn't like I had previous experience to go on. I'd never had a bodyguard before. I appreciated that Graham took my safety seriously, even if it seemed unnecessary.

I pressed my palm to the keypad outside, still skeptical that the door would open. Willow had received the "all clear" from someone else with Hudson Security during the drive, so she didn't have to go in to secure the apartment ahead of me. The lock disengaged, and as soon as I opened the door, I heard the sound of panting and claws on tile before I saw them. Graham's beloved Irish Wolfhounds. His pride and joy.

"Prince Albert! Queen V!" I grinned, pleased when Prince Albert nudged my hand with his head, silently asking me to pet him. Queen V leaned against my side, her weight a steady comfort.

"Wow," Willow, aka "The Beast," said from behind me. "They're even bigger than I expected."

"But the sweetest," I said, still wondering about her code name. That's what I assumed it was after Pidgeon, one of the other guys from Hudson Security, had called her "The Beast." I bent forward and rubbed Prince Albert behind the ears. "Aren't you?"

A noise startled me, but I tried not to let it show. I hadn't slept well, and I was on edge from keeping this secret from my best friend. At least in the short-term. I'd bought myself some time to figure out what and how to tell her. But I needed to have a plan, because she was coming to LA soon.

Coming to LA to attend my surprise wedding she didn't know about. I wanted to bury my head in my hands. I was exhausted from thinking of all the ways my life was about to change. Was *already* changing.

"So." I turned to Willow, setting my purse on the counter. "Why do they call you The Beast?"

"That's classified." Her face didn't move, and I wondered if she was serious or messing with me.

"It's okay. I know you only just met me, but I *will* find out."

She said nothing, remaining motionless by the door. Was she just going to stand there? Wait for me to…I don't know what. Sneeze?

God. This was weird. Having a bodyguard was weird, but it was one of Graham's nonnegotiable conditions. So I supposed I'd better get used to it.

"So, how does this work?"

"Ma'am?"

I scrunched up my face. Willow couldn't be that much older than me. Ma'am was way too formal and stuffy. "My friends call me Lily."

"Hudson protocol dictates that I call the principal ma'am or Ms. Fontaine."

I wondered what my family would think of this. Even if I had been on speaking terms with them, it was probably better not to tell them. I didn't want them coming after Graham for his money. My family would look at Graham, and all they would see was what he could do for them.

Are you really all that different?

I wanted to believe I was. I considered the situation logically, reminding myself that Graham had been the one to approach me. He'd been the one to offer to fund the château. I hadn't asked; he'd suggested it.

"Principal?" I asked.

"Our term for the client. It's standard in the private security industry."

"And your protocol…"

"Is very clear."

I leaned my hip against the counter. "Even if I've given you permission to call me by my first name?"

"That's correct."

Alrighty, then.

"Can you tell me what else I can expect from our relationship?" I went to the pantry to get some treats for the dogs. They were easy to find—located in a labeled container, of course.

"The team and I have a suite down the hall. We'll coordinate your schedule ahead of time as much as possible. If you want to go somewhere, text me, and I'll be available."

"Like that?" I snapped my fingers.

"Pretty much," she said.

"Okay. Wow." She took my phone and programmed in her number before handing it back to me.

"Any recommendations I make are for your own safety. I am discreet and professional and will try to respect your wishes as much as possible, unless they contradict your safety."

"Got it," I said. "Do you speak French?"

"Oui, Mademoiselle Fontaine."

I asked her a few more questions, testing her range and fluency before finally saying, *"Très bien."*

That would certainly be useful when we spent time in the Loire Valley, and I was grateful that Graham had thought to request a bodyguard with that skill.

I thought back to my conversation with Graham at the airport. I didn't think we'd said anything incriminating. But now that I knew Willow spoke French, we'd need to be more careful.

My phone buzzed on the counter, an incoming call from

Jo. Willow told me to text if I needed anything before letting herself out.

I debated answering Jo's call, but I didn't know what to say. Last night, when I'd returned to our suite, I'd made sure that I looked a little disheveled. And then I'd told her that Graham wanted to spend more time with me, so he'd invited me to LA.

She'd been surprised but excited, especially when I'd mentioned that he was throwing a party and she was invited. That part was true, but it wasn't the whole truth. The party was our surprise wedding.

Jo followed up her call with a text.

> Jo: What am I supposed to wear to this party in LA? I don't have anything super fancy.

> Me: Don't worry. We'll go shopping when you get here.

My shoulders slumped. I hated that I was lying to my best friend. And I was going to have to fess up sooner rather than later, but I'd been stalling while I tried to figure out what the heck to say. But also, afraid she'd try to talk me out of it.

It was so strange to be back in Graham's penthouse. Strange, yet familiar. The living room was such a contrast, with the large panel of windows that opened to a huge terrace with an incredible garden. I wandered outside, stunned by the lushness and variety of it. Flowers. Vegetables. Fruits.

Every inch of space was maximized, but it wasn't crowded. It was impressive, and I wondered how big of a team of gardeners Graham had to manage this.

I lingered a moment longer before returning inside to explore some more. The furniture and decor were all very high-end but also comfortable, inviting. It was a bit like

Graham—it seemed moody and brooding at first, but once you got closer, you realized that there was so much more than what met the eye.

Details were scattered throughout, and I leaned in to inspect an antique key with a plaque. Apparently, it had once belonged to the former palace that had been converted into the Huxley Grand Abu Dhabi. Gold-framed black-and-white pictures hung on the wall. Images of Graham's family. His grandparents. A couple with three young children. I smiled as I studied the photo, easily selecting Graham as the grumpy-looking one with a mop of curly hair. *What a cutie.*

I continued down the hall to the guest room, smoothing my hand over the silky duvet. The room was so gorgeous. So opulent. It felt like staying at a luxury hotel, like one of the Huxley Grand locations.

And when I peeked my head in the bathroom, I smirked. The shower was stocked with Huxley Grand shampoos and conditioners. A Huxley Grand candle in the hotel's signature scent rested on the counter.

It was certainly a huge step up from my bathroom at the château. I smiled to myself, wondering how Graham would react to those conditions. I supposed if marriage was a compromise, we were both about to make some accommodations.

THE FOLLOWING DAY, JO ARRIVED IN LA. SHE'D CHECKED IN AT the Huxley Grand LA—courtesy of Graham. And I'd invited her over to his penthouse so I could break the news about my wedding.

"Wow. This place is insane," Jo said, taking it all in. Queen

V and Prince Albert trotted up to her, and she let them sniff her hand before petting them.

"Gorgeous, right?" I asked.

"Definitely. Not as cold as I'd expected. And these magnificent beasts—" She peered down at Queen V. "Aren't you a pretty girl? Yes, you are."

I laughed, though there was a nervous edge to it. We were off to a good start, but I had no idea what she was going to think of the fact that I was marrying Graham in less than twenty-four hours. I still wasn't quite sure what I thought of it myself.

"Have you been comfortable at the Huxley Grand LA? Is your room okay?"

"That hotel is incredible. And the service, ugh." She held a hand to her chest. "They gave me a suite. I'm being treated like a princess. If these are the perks of you dating Graham, then I am all for it."

That was a relief, even if I knew she was teasing. But I was grateful to Graham for treating my best friend so well.

"And how would you feel about me marrying him?" My heart was pounding.

"Sure." She lifted a shoulder. "If he makes you happy. I could see that one day."

"What about tomorrow?"

She furrowed her brow. "What about tomorrow? Did you want to do something? Graham has his party, but otherwise, I'm free."

"That's what I'm trying to tell you. I'm getting married tomorrow. That's what the party is—a small, intimate surprise wedding."

"Very funny," she said, opening the door to the terrace and stepping out onto it. She shielded her eyes from the sun, totally unaware that I wasn't joking.

"I'm serious, Jo." I closed the door behind us, grateful that

Willow was down the hall in her suite. I needed to ease Jo into this conversation, as much as I could anyway. And having my new bodyguard hovering was not going to help.

Jo turned to face me, her gaze searching mine. Whatever she saw there made her eyes widen in surprise. I could tell she had a million questions. She looked as if she might burst. So I was surprised when all she said was, "But you only just started dating."

Instead of telling her the truth, I said, "He asked me to marry him, and I agreed."

She sank down on one of the outdoor sofas, patting the space beside her. I joined her, hoping she would understand. Hoping she wouldn't judge me.

"Why?" she asked, and I could tell that she was genuinely trying to fathom where this was coming from. "And don't tell me you love him. I know you, Lil. You might admire and respect Graham, but you don't love him."

"Aren't admiration and respect a good foundation for marriage?" I asked, doing my best to avoid admitting the real reason.

She leveled me with a flat look. "And the real reason?"

"Why else?" I lifted my shoulder. "Money."

She jerked her head back. "For the château?" I nodded. "I knew it was bad, but I didn't realize the situation was so dire."

"It is," I said, dipping my head to my chest. It really was. I'd made the best decisions I could, but it was still embarrassing to admit that I needed help.

"Even so... To marry someone you don't even love. For money? That's not you."

There was no judgment in her tone, but her words still felt like a punch to the gut. A reality check. It wasn't me. Or at least, I didn't want to believe I was capable of using someone the way my family sought to use me.

"I'm running out of time and options, and Graham offered to help me save it."

"Mm. And what does he want in return?"

"A wife."

She narrowed her eyes at me. "Why?"

"He has his reasons."

"Um, I'm going to need a little more than that. You're planning to marry this guy. *Marry* him. That's a huge commitment."

"I know!" I blurted, then softened my tone. "I know."

"So, he wants…a wife," she said again. "But why does he need a wife so badly? And why you?"

"Why not me?" I asked, latching on to that as I hoped to bypass Graham's reasons for marriage.

She rolled her eyes. "Come on, Lil. It's me. You know I'm not going to tell anyone. I would never do that, even if I hadn't signed an NDA that all but promised my firstborn."

"I know you wouldn't, but I also signed an NDA."

"Jesus." She dragged a hand through her hair. "Who the hell even does that? Makes their future wife sign an NDA."

People with something to lose. Something to protect.

"Think of it more like a business arrangement. This is a marriage in name only. We're both getting something out of it."

"What are you going to tell your family?"

"Nothing. I'm done."

"Wow." She sank back in her chair. "You know what? Good for you." Her support made my actions feel justified. I was done with my family's bullshit, and I deserved better.

"Right? And maybe I should tell them—for the sake of my…" I cleared my throat.

"Business agreement?" she offered.

"Yeah, that." I swallowed hard at the reminder.

"But I don't want to. I feel like…" How did I explain this?

"I feel like they don't deserve to know anything about my life and my choices. Especially not if they're going to judge or mock me. But I also don't want it to come back to bite Graham in the ass."

"Do you think it would?" she asked, and I knew she was trying to understand. Working with the limited information I'd been able to tell her about the reasons for our marriage.

I tilted my head. "I mean, maybe?" It wasn't like I thought the board would dig into the details of our relationship. Why would they? "But I also worry that they'd try to come after Graham for his money."

"Bleh." She mimed gagging. Her face fell. "I'm sorry, Lil. That sucks. But also, I'm really proud of you for doing what's best for you."

I curled my fingers into the couch cushion. "What if marrying Graham is what's best for me? Will you still be supportive?"

"I'm not going to lie, I'm concerned. This is a lifetime commitment. Don't you want to say your vows to someone you love?"

"I mean, yes. Of course, I want to marry someone for love. And maybe I will someday."

"So..." She squinted, thinking. "This isn't a lifetime commitment?"

I tried to think of how to phrase it so as to protect Graham. Ultimately, I said, "I know I'm putting you in an awkward position, and I hate that I can't tell you everything, but I need you to trust me on this.

"I do trust you," she sighed. She placed her hand over mine. "I know you're desperate to save the château. And I can understand that. But are you sure you're okay with this?"

I appreciated her asking, but it wasn't like I had another choice. And I knew Graham was good to his word. "I'm sure."

She regarded me, perhaps searching for any hesitation or

reluctance on my part before she finally said, "Even so, you have to admit this is weird."

"He's a billionaire. Weird, eccentric behavior comes with the territory," I joked.

"I just have so many questions."

"I get it," I said. If our roles were reversed, I would too. I was just afraid I might not have the answers.

CHAPTER TWELVE

Graham

I glided my hand down the front of my shirt then centered my cuff links, a birthday gift from Knox. I was minutes away from meeting Lily at the altar. We were to be married in a simple ceremony on my rooftop terrace. It was going to be an informal—but well-documented—affair.

If I'd ever planned to marry for real, this was how I would've done it—small, simple, intimate. Though, I would've invited my siblings.

I frowned at the thought. Not inviting them felt like a mistake, but it also meant that nothing would stand in the way of my wedding Lily. I still didn't know how I was going to tell my family after the fact. Or how they'd react. Though, one thing was for certain; they were going to have a lot of questions.

I sighed.

Perhaps sensing my distress, Prince Albert nudged his head against my leg. I smoothed my hand over his fur, wondering where Queen V was. Probably with Lily. My dogs loved her, especially Queen V.

"Cold feet?" Pierce asked.

"I'm not getting any younger," I said, trying to remind myself of all the reasons I was doing this. "The sooner we're married, the sooner I control the board."

"I know I pushed for this, but we can find another way to get the shares."

"We've been trying everything we can think of for fifteen months. We're running out of time, and this is our best option." Our only option, really. Moretti's offer was like a ticking time bomb.

I avoided Pierce's reflection in the mirror where he stood behind me. Instead, I kept my eyes focused on my jacket, smoothing out invisible wrinkles. As far as I could tell, everything was falling into place.

"Why? Did Liliana say something to you?" I turned to face Pierce.

He'd visited Liliana at the penthouse yesterday to go over the remaining legal documents. Had she said something to him then? Expressed reservations? Had Josephine tried to talk her out of it?

I hadn't spent much time with Liliana since returning to LA, but I'd been swamped with meetings and calls and emails. She was often asleep when I returned home, and I knew she'd been busy with fittings and work obligations of her own.

So far, our engagement was barely affecting my life. If anything, it was better. Queen V and Prince Albert seemed to enjoy her company, and she'd sent me pictures from their walks. Otherwise, she mostly kept to her room and herself.

I hoped it would remain that way even after we were married. Not that I didn't like Liliana. But I couldn't let our fake relationship get in the way of my plans. As soon as I was in possession of those extra shares, I wanted to hit the ground running.

"No." Pierce blew out a breath. "She didn't say anything. I only hope you realize what you're getting into."

"With her?" I frowned.

"And the château. That's one hell of a project." He let out a low whistle. "And unlike your other projects, you won't have control over the château or the restoration. Liliana is running the show, and I hope she knows what she's doing. Otherwise, you can kiss your twenty-million-dollar investment goodbye."

Did I like the idea of giving up control? No. But I'd been thorough with my research, and I had faith in her.

"She does," I said, annoyed by his interference. I'd done my own due diligence. But I'd also listened to her plans, watched her videos. She had a vision, and she had the fortitude to see it through. Now, she'd have the money.

He fell silent, but I could feel the tension thickening in the room. Soon, you'd be able to cut it with a knife.

Finally, I asked, "What's this really about?" Pierce was one of the few people I trusted not to bullshit me.

He sighed, looked toward the ceiling as if seeing guidance. "I don't want you to do something you'll regret."

"And you think I'll regret marrying Lily."

I'd made my decision. Liliana was set to walk down the aisle in minutes. Now was not the time for second-guessing.

"Not necessarily." He shifted, shoving his hands into the pockets of his tux. "But I wouldn't be a very good friend if I didn't ask if you were sure."

"I'm sure."

I was so sick of letting the board run amok. I was done with veiled threats and fears. I'd done everything in my power to keep the company from falling into the hands of an idiot like Donahue. And there was no way in hell I was going to let him destroy everything my grandparents had worked for in a "merger."

I spun my grandfather's ring on my pinkie finger and stilled. *Pops.*

I wondered what he'd think of my solution. Would he find it clever, misguided, or downright deceptive?

Everything I'd done was to make them proud. To live up to their legacy. To try to be a worthy successor.

And this... I massaged my temples. A fake marriage. A sham. I swallowed hard. I didn't have to wonder what they'd think; I knew exactly how they'd feel about dishonesty and deception.

I didn't want to let Liliana down. I knew how much she had riding on our agreement. And I wasn't someone who went back on their word—not without good reason. But... My stomach churned. I also hated the idea of disappointing my grandparents. It didn't seem right to let Lily agree to this, especially without knowing the full story.

I dropped my head to my chest, eyeing the sunflower-and-fern combination of my boutonnière, wondering what Gran would've picked for my wedding flowers. Black dahlias for betrayal. Or perhaps snapdragons for deceit and grasping intentions.

"I think I need to talk to Liliana."

Pierce patted my shoulder. "I'll make sure Josephine is occupied."

I walked down the hall to the guest room, my shoes clicking against the floor. I took a deep breath and lifted my hand to knock. Lowered it. Sighed and lifted it again, rapping my knuckles against the door.

"Almost ready!" she called out.

"It's me, Graham. Can I come in?"

"I, um—" There was a pause. "Now?" she squeaked.

Her voice was much closer now, and I imagined her standing on the other side of the door. I wondered what her dress looked like. I wondered if she was as nervous as I was.

"Yes, now," I said, knowing this was a conversation that couldn't be avoided.

The door remained closed. "Is everything okay?"

I shoved my hands in my pockets and rocked on my heels. "Can I please just come in?"

"But it's bad luck for the groom to see the bride before the wedding."

I leaned closer, careful to keep my voice low. "Not sure that applies, given the circumstances."

"Fine," she huffed, and the door swung open.

It was as if someone had punched a hole in my chest. She was gorgeous. I lost the ability to speak. To breathe.

Her seductive curves were encased in white silk that hugged her like a second skin. The material draped over her breasts, dipping low and hanging on by two thin straps that looked as if they might snap at the slightest provocation.

"Envoûtante," I whispered, desperate to touch her but afraid to all the same. She didn't belong to me. She could never belong to me, and yet, she was absolutely bewitching. Enchanting.

Her cheeks pinkened, and she dipped her head, her hair falling forward and hiding her face from my view. When she glanced at me from beneath her lashes, the look was so fucking coy. So coquettish, my cock stirred in appreciation.

I closed the door before facing her once more.

"Is everything okay?" she asked, twisting her hands together.

More than okay. *No. Wait.* I shook my head as if to shake some sense into myself. I'd come here to talk to her about the wedding, and seeing her had made me forget all about it. *Shit.* This was bad. Really bad.

I took Lily's hand in mine and guided her over to the bench at the foot of the bed. I sank down onto it, and after a moment's hesitation, she took a seat next to me.

"I—" I released her hand and twisted my ring on my pinkie, torn between a loyalty to the past, what I'd always seen as my duty, and the future. Not just my own, but Lily's, my family's, and that of the entire Huxley Grand brand.

I dragged a hand through my hair, struggling to find the right words. Any words, really.

"Graham?" Her tone was gentle, but I sensed her uncertainty all the same.

"I haven't been completely honest with you." There. That was a start.

"Are you..." She lifted a shaky hand. "*Oh shit*. Are you calling off the wedding?"

I took her hand in mine. I rubbed my thumb over the back of her hand, soothed by the contact.

"I want you to know that this has nothing to do with you and everything to do with me." When she said nothing, I placed my finger beneath her chin, guiding her eyes to mine. "You believe me, right?"

"Oh my god." She gasped. "You are, aren't you?"

There were so many reasons for and against this marriage, and all of them were important. My family. The brand. Her château. My integrity.

I took a deep breath and released it slowly. This was my problem, not Lily's. Which was why I forced myself to say, "I am, but I'll still invest in the château as promised, assuming we can agree to a fifteen percent return."

She was quiet for a minute, and I would've paid anything to know what she was thinking.

"That's very generous of you."

My shoulders dropped. This was it. No wedding meant no shares. And the board might be able to push through the merger. The idea of letting Moretti gut my family's company was devastating.

"But why would you do that? Why would you ask me to

marry you and go through the trouble to arrange everything, only to pull out at the last minute?"

"Because it's not only dishonest, but it's disrespectful to my grandparents and the legacy they built."

She frowned. "No. There's something more to it. Something about this has never added up. What aren't you telling me?"

Damn. How did she see through me so clearly? Was I truly that obvious, or was she just that observant?

She waited silently, giving me the time and space to organize my thoughts. That was something I'd often appreciated about Lily. She didn't push me to answer. She didn't get impatient. She waited, allowing me the time I needed.

"I'm motivated to marry for all the reasons I mentioned previously. But there's another, even more compelling reason." I took a deep breath. "My grandfather's will contains a provision that I receive an additional ten percent of the board's shares if I marry by the age of forty-five."

She jerked her head back. "Is that even legal?"

"Unfortunately, yes." I'd had a team of lawyers comb over the documents, to no avail. "My grandparents could've made my accession to CEO conditional on marriage, and it still would've been enforceable."

"Wow." She grimaced. "Yeah. I guess it could be worse."

"True. And I get why they did it. But I also know that they wouldn't have wanted me to marry solely for the sake of the shares. My grandparents wanted me to marry so I'd have a life partner like they'd found in each other."

"That's sweet," she said, flipping her hand so that ours were clasped together. "And I can see why they'd want that for you. Why any grandparent would want that for their grandchild. They loved you a lot."

I nodded. I'd loved them. Respected them. Was this really

how I wanted to repay them for everything they'd done for me?

"Marrying to secure the shares feels underhanded and deceitful, and I'm sorry I let it get this far." Yes, I might cross some lines with my hacking, but it was always for the greater good. It was for justice.

I didn't want to disappoint my grandparents. I didn't want to hurt Lily. And if we went through with this, I *would* hurt Lily. She was too kind. Too good.

"Why didn't you tell me about this before?"

"I didn't want you roped into this mess. I wanted you to have plausible deniability if anyone asked. There's more than just control of the board riding on this. We've had a merger offer."

"Really? Who wants to merge?" She gave my hand a reassuring squeeze. "I mean...I understand if you can't—or don't want to—tell me."

"Jacob Moretti," I seethed.

Her jaw dropped. "Did you see what he did to the Loft chain? He'll gut the Huxley brand."

"Exactly." And why the board couldn't see that, I'd never know. Probably because they had their heads too far up their asses. Or they were more focused on filling their pockets than what was best for the company as a whole.

"So that's the real reason you wanted to get married," she said.

I nodded, and she seemed to mull it over. I had no idea what she was thinking, but I was glad I'd told her.

"From the stories I've heard of your grandfather, he was a trailblazer," Lily said. "He took risks. He didn't always do what was expected, and it brought him great success."

I'd never mentioned it, but that was one of the things I'd admired most about Pops. His willingness to shake things up —the industry, guest expectations, you name it.

"I'm guessing that's a big reason why he chose you as his successor. Because of your ability to take risks and think outside the box. To think for yourself."

It was easily one of the nicest things anyone had ever said to me. And she wasn't wrong. When my grandparents had sat me down to tell me they wanted to leave the hotel empire to me, they'd said something along those lines.

"So, while I understand that this—" she gestured between us "—probably wasn't their intent when writing that clause, I can't imagine they'd be happy with the idea of a merger either. Especially if they knew how Moretti operates."

"They wouldn't," I said darkly.

"We may not be in love, but that doesn't mean we can't form a successful partnership," she said, my hope rising with every word. "And, ultimately, isn't that what they wanted for you?"

When she put it that way... I nodded.

"Do Jasper or Sloan have a clause like this?"

"Just me." But they'd never struggled with relationships and expressing their feelings like I had. My grandparents had probably assumed they'd both marry without the need for an additional incentive.

"They put you in charge for a reason. So maybe, this arrangement isn't conventional or ordinary. But you've never been anything but extraordinary."

My chest warmed from her compliment. I didn't even know what to say. No one ever recognized me for what I did. It was always expectations and pressure. Not gratitude.

Finally, I settled on, "Thank you, Lil. I—" I cleared my throat. "That means a lot. Especially coming from you."

She tilted her head. "What does that mean?"

I debated whether to answer, then said, "You know. Because I used to be your evil overlord."

She laughed. "Evil overlord? Isn't that a touch dramatic?"

"Jasper's moniker for me." I shrugged, trying to downplay my reaction to the fact that Lily hadn't agreed that it was warranted. She hadn't chimed in with some less-than-flattering nickname of her own. "And you know Jasper. He's always had a flair for the dramatic."

"Yes, but still—" She furrowed her brow. "I always found you to be tough but fair."

"Thank you," I said, grateful that had been her perception of me. It made me realize how much I valued her respect, and I could only hope it was the same for others in my employ.

"Look, Graham. I can appreciate having morals and integrity. Hell, I admire you for it. But life is full of difficult choices. It isn't always black-and-white. There isn't always one correct answer. Sometimes, we have to be willing to live in the gray."

"Is that what this is?" I asked. "Living in the gray?" With me.

"I suppose so."

"We can call off the wedding right now. I will invest as promised."

"I know what this company means to you, and I'm not going to stand by and let Moretti ruin everything. We're getting married." She dipped her head. "If you still want to, that is."

"I…" I swallowed hard, choking back emotion. She was willing to do this, even knowing everything. Perhaps *because* she knew everything. "Yes. But are you sure this is what you want?" I couldn't resist saying it again. "I'm giving you an out."

Her eyes blazed with something—anger. Stubbornness. "Maybe I don't want an out."

"Most people would," I said. "Most people would take the money and run." But she hadn't. Not yet anyway.

"I'm not most people. And neither are you." She gave my hand a squeeze.

She was right. She wasn't like most people, and she definitely wasn't like any of the women I'd been with in the past.

"That said," she continued. "There can be no more secrets between us. I'm going into this with eyes wide open. But I expect that we'll discuss anything that could affect the agreement."

"No more secrets," I vowed.

I wondered if I should tell her about hacking her blog, but technically speaking, it didn't affect the agreement. I knew that was a flimsy excuse, that now would be the perfect time to tell her, but it was in the past. Before our agreement. Before…anything. What was done was done.

"You're sure?" I asked, needing the confirmation.

Her eyes never left mine. "Yes." She adjusted my boutonniere. "I know you, Graham. I see how hard you work. How much care and attention you put into every aspect of running the Huxley Grand. And I refuse to let a technicality stand in the way of your success."

So maybe this wasn't what my grandparents had envisioned for me, but marriage was a partnership. And that's what I'd proposed to Liliana. I couldn't offer love, but I could give her my loyalty.

CHAPTER THIRTEEN

Lily

When I reached the terrace, bouquet in hand, I froze. Even though it was a small wedding, it was still unnerving to have all eyes on me when the harpist started playing the wedding march. It was just Jo, Pierce, the harpist, an officiant, a photographer, and Graham. But it still felt…intense.

I took a deep breath and tried to calm my racing heart. I was going to do this. I was going to marry my billionaire ex-boss. And I was going to pretend to be in love with him. No big deal.

As I walked beneath large potted trees with white lights strung between them, I felt as if I'd been transported to the French countryside. It was magical and intimate, striking the perfect balance of relaxed elegance.

Finally, my eyes landed on Graham. He stood beneath an arch of sunflowers and roses. And even though I'd seen him minutes ago, I'd been so distracted by our conversation that I hadn't really gotten the chance to take him in. I did so now, grateful that it was expected that the bride would drink in her groom. And what a sight he was.

Graham wore a gorgeous bespoke three-piece black suit that brought out the green in his eyes. It showcased his shoulders, narrow waist, and powerful thighs. He looked... I swallowed hard. He looked like my husband.

Like my husband?

He gave me a subtle nod, and I told myself to move. To act natural.

The fact that he needed a wife to not only improve his reputation but secure more shares somehow made me feel better about the whole thing. Like I was actually contributing something of value to the arrangement and not just take-take-taking like my family.

And while I could've just taken his revised offer of the money for the restoration, I couldn't accept it in good conscience. Not when I knew he felt just as strongly about saving his family's company as I did the château. Not once I realized just how much was at stake.

Freaking Moretti.

He was an ass who gave me the creeps. Thankfully, I'd rarely interacted with him when I'd worked at the Huxley Grand—mostly at industry events. But the way his eyes had lingered on me had always made me uncomfortable. He was vicious and conniving, and if I could help Graham prevent a takeover, I was in.

I only wished Graham had told me sooner. But the fact that he'd been willing to call off the wedding showed me how honorable he was. How committed he was to doing the right thing, even at great cost to himself.

Graham and I both had powerful reasons for wanting this marriage. And while it might not be conventional, I had faith in us. In what we could accomplish together.

That thought propelled me to take the first step toward him. Then another. It just all seemed so surreal. A dream mixed with some weird alternate reality.

I tried to tell myself that the only reason he felt like my husband was because we were going through this charade of a wedding. It was my emotions from the day and the fact that I was dressed as a bride. But a deeper, knowing sense of myself recognized him as the man I was supposed to spend my life with.

Graham watched me as I proceeded up the aisle, and I ignored everyone else but him. For a moment, we were locked in time.

It didn't matter that I tried to ignore that feeling. That *knowing*. Tried to push it away. That niggling sense of rightness just kept at it. Kept telling me that he was it for me. He was my person.

Oh shit. I shoved that thought into a box, pushed it to the deep recesses of my mind.

"You look…" He shook his head, stepping closer. *"Tu es absolument magnifique."*

Magnificent. Stunning. Those were the words he'd used to describe me.

I smiled and dipped my head to smell my bouquet, pleased by the compliment, even if it was all part of the act. *"Merci."*

Oh god. This was it. We were really going to do this.

I handed off my bouquet to Jo, and I was so grateful she was here. Graham took my hands in his, and I tried to focus on the feel of his skin against mine. Tried to calm my breath and school my smile into something natural.

The officiant spoke about love and commitment, but I barely heard him over the thunder of my heartbeat in my ears. Graham gave my hands a squeeze, centering me. Bringing me back to the present. Reminding me that we were in this together. We were partners.

"And now for the vows. Who has the rings?" the officiant asked.

Right. The ring. I hadn't even considered the fact that I'd be wearing a wedding ring. I hadn't even worn an engagement ring since it had all happened so fast and we were trying to keep it a secret.

Pierce stepped forward and removed a box from his jacket pocket.

"Graham," the officiant said.

We'd agreed to write our own vows and to keep them short and sweet. Neither of us wanted to promise a lifetime of love, when we both knew that wasn't what this was.

Graham took the ring from Pierce, and it was the first time I'd seen it. As he slid the ring on my finger, I couldn't help but gasp. It was a gorgeous diamond set on a thin gold band. It was simple and elegant, and exactly what I would've picked for myself.

I tried not to gawk at the ring, but it was stunning. It had to be vintage. I resisted the urge to screw my eyes shut. I sincerely hoped it wasn't a family heirloom.

Graham gave my hand a squeeze. "I promise to be your partner, your friend, and your husband. You are my family. I will honor our vows," he said, giving me a meaningful look. "And I will protect you with all that I am as we honor the past, cherish the present, and preserve the future."

I smiled. It was honest and heartfelt. And the words fit our situation perfectly.

Pierce stepped forward and offered me a ring. I took it from him and slid the gold band on to Graham's finger. Damn. I hadn't expected the sight of him wearing a wedding band to be so hot. Why was that so hot?

"Liliana, now it's your turn," the officiant said.

I took a deep breath. "I promise to stand by your side through the trials of life. You are my partner and my equal. I will be loyal and faithful, grateful for the past and excited about the future."

There. Graham gave me a subtle nod of approval.

I met his eyes, and the enormity of what I'd just committed to started to sink in. I was his wife. He was my husband. We were married.

And yet, I didn't feel as terrified by the thought as I'd expected to. Because this wasn't a real marriage after all.

"I now pronounce you husband and wife. You may kiss," the officiant said.

Wait. What?

I tried not to let my panic show. Our first kiss was going to be in front of an audience? Why had I not considered this earlier?

Graham placed his hand on my lower back, pulling me into him. Everything about him was so intense, so consuming, that I couldn't look away.

He cupped my cheek, sliding his hand along my jaw. His eyes darted to my lips, and suddenly, everything felt too real. Like it wasn't all for show.

He leaned closer, and my mind short-circuited. It was like that night in Ixtapa all over again, but it felt as if we were on the precipice of something more. Something even bigger.

Just do it. Just kiss me.

The waiting was torture. It could've been an eternity that passed, but it was probably only seconds. Finally, my eyes fluttered closed as he slanted his mouth over mine. A sense of peace and rightness settled over me. Confirming my decision.

His tongue briefly delved between my lips, tentative. Exploring. And my body was on fire.

He gave my hip a squeeze, and I wanted him to do so much more than that. But the sound of applause put an end to the moment. He pulled away, and all I could do was stare back at him with a dazed expression.

Whoa.

"Lil." *Lil.* There it was—that nickname again. Full of ease and familiarity.

Graham held out his arm, and I slid my hand into the crook. He placed his hand over mine, and even that featherlight touch set me on fire.

"I have the pleasure of introducing Mr. and Mrs. Mackenzie," the officiant said.

Graham guided me down the aisle. "No going back now," he murmured, his words and closeness sending a shiver down my spine.

I wouldn't have wanted to even if I could.

"Newlyweds," called a woman in all black. She had a camera around her neck and had been taking photos the entire time. "Can I get you back out onto the terrace for photos?"

Graham placed his hand on the small of my back. "Absolutely."

Pierce and Jo remained inside, sipping on cocktails and canapés prepared by the private chef Graham had hired for the event. I wondered what they were talking about. I wondered if Pierce thought this whole plan was as crazy as it seemed.

I'd spoken with him some in the past, but our interactions had always been fairly limited. If he needed a meeting with Graham, I'd scheduled it. But more often than not, he contacted Graham directly.

"Right over here," the photographer said. "That's it." She positioned us just so before snapping a few shots.

"Bride, hand on groom's chest."

I lifted my hand, placing it over Graham's chest as she'd directed.

"Great. Now, relax and look into each other's eyes."

Relax. Right. It was kind of difficult to relax when Graham was touching me. My body felt like a live wire.

I peered up at Graham, studying the hint of a few freckles on the bridge of his nose. My body was still buzzing from our kiss. Did he feel it too?

He lifted my left hand, bringing the back of it to his mouth for a kiss. "You are a beautiful bride," he said in French.

"Thank you." I continued the conversation in French. "You look—" I swallowed hard. "Really nice."

"Jay always does a good job." He leaned his forehead against mine, and the photographer continued snapping away.

"That he does. Thank you for letting Jo get a dress too. And giving her the VIP treatment at the Huxley Grand."

"It's not a big deal."

"It is to me," I said softly.

He pressed a kiss to my forehead, lingering. In that heartbeat, it felt...real. His touch. His words. *Us.*

"I'm surprised," I said in French.

"By what?" he asked, continuing the conversation in French.

"I don't know. I guess I expected something more formal for our wedding."

"Are you disappointed?" he asked.

"Are you kidding? This is beautiful. It's everything I would've wanted for my wedding." It was like he'd taken my dream wedding Pinterest board and brought it to life.

Future me was fucked because I knew my future potential "real" wedding would have a hard time surpassing this one. The idea made me sad.

"Then what's wrong?" he asked, a crease forming between his brows.

"Nothing." I smiled brightly. "You're making all my dreams come true." It was true, if a bit cheesy, but weddings had the tendency to make me emotional.

"And you mine." His eyes lingered on mine a moment longer before he asked the photographer, "Did you get everything you needed?" putting an end to whatever that was.

"Yep," the photographer said, attention on the screen on the back of her camera. "I got some great shots."

"Excellent. Thank you." Graham turned to me. "Shall we?" He gestured inside, and I let him lead me through to the living area where Jo and Pierce were drinking and talking.

By the time we bid our friends goodbye, the candles were burning low. There'd been champagne and a decadent meal, a small wedding cake. I'd even caught Graham smiling a few times, though I figured it was mostly out of relief. We were married. He could claim the shares he needed.

Jo was last to leave, and when I walked her to the door, she gave me a big hug.

"Thanks for being here and supporting me. It means a lot," I said.

"Of course. I'll always be here for you. I trust that you're making the best decision for you, even if I don't fully understand it."

I tugged at the corner of my eye, trying not to cry. My family would never, *ever* say something like that. So full of understanding and acceptance. I hadn't talked to them since before I'd left for Ixtapa, and I didn't intend to any time soon. At least, not unless they apologized for their behavior.

It had taken me longer than I'd cared to admit that my relationship with my family was toxic. But I was done. I was done being belittled and manipulated. And it made me appreciate Jo even more. It meant the world to me that my friend believed in me, no matter what.

"Have fun tonight." She waggled her brows.

I rolled my eyes. "Goodnight." I practically shoved her toward the door. "Thank you again, Jo. Seriously."

She lifted a shoulder. "You'd do the same for me."

"I would. Absolutely." I'd do anything for my best friend, and I was glad she knew it.

I closed the door softly behind her, sagging against it with a smile on my face. What a day. What a week.

I took off my shoes, and they dangled from my fingers as I wound my way through the penthouse. Everything was immaculate once more—the staff had been very efficient at cleaning up. The only things that remained were the flower arrangements that had lined the dining table, but they'd been scattered throughout the penthouse.

The aisle, the arch, everything else had vanished. Almost as if it had never even happened. But the ring on my finger said otherwise.

How nice it would be to put the Huxley staff to work at the château. Projects that usually took weeks would be accomplished in hours.

Graham was nowhere to be seen, so I ventured down the hall toward his office. I rapped my knuckles lightly on the door before entering. "Hey."

"Hey." He lifted his head from his laptop. He'd removed his jacket and tie, and his hair was wild, as if he'd been running his fingers through it. "Did you need something?"

"I, um—" I gnawed my bottom lip. "I just wondered if you wanted to share a drink."

"I need to take care of some things before we leave for France."

Oh.

"Right." I hoped my face didn't show the warmth creeping across my cheeks and down my neck. "Of course. I get it. You're busy." *And this isn't a real marriage.*

He returned his attention to his screen, practically dismissing me. I slipped back out of his office, closing the door softly behind me.

Stupid. Stupid. Stupid. I padded down the hall to my bedroom, tossing my shoes on the carpet.

I didn't know why I was so surprised that he had immediately gone back to work. I guess I'd just hoped…

Hoped what? That he'd want to spend time together?

Yes, this was a business arrangement. A marriage in name only. He wanted something from me, and I needed something from him. But our relationship didn't always have to be solely about business, did it?

It was our wedding night. I was his *wife*. His fake wife, yes. But even so, I couldn't help but be a little disappointed at how quickly he'd gone back to business as usual.

He'd have drinks to celebrate closing a business deal, wouldn't he? Why should this be any different?

I huffed, annoyed with myself. It shouldn't matter. It *didn't* matter.

I reached for the zipper. I twisted and tried to turn the material, but it wouldn't budge. The more I tried, the more I resembled a dog chasing its tail. Until I was panting and my cheeks were red.

I huffed and headed back down the hall to Graham's office. I stood there trying to compose myself. Trying to work up the nerve to knock again.

"Yes?" he asked, irritation creeping into his tone.

I entered the room, noting the glass of whiskey beside him. So, he'd wanted a drink; he just didn't want to share one with me. *Awesome.*

I guessed now that the negotiations were over and the deal was done, he no longer felt the need to be charming. To pretend. At least, so long as we were alone.

"Can you help me with my dress?" I asked.

He stood and rounded the desk, stalking toward me like a panther. All sleek lines, power, and grace. He was elegant and intimidating—and hot.

"Spin."

I turned so my back was to him. He gripped the fabric and tugged the zipper down, the sound of the teeth hissing as he took it lower and lower still. One of the straps slipped from my shoulder, sliding down over my skin. I clutched the front of my dress to my chest so it wouldn't dip even lower.

Graham was silent, and a heavy tension filled the air. I could feel his eyes on my skin, perhaps noticing my lack of undergarments. Or maybe just aggravated by the interruption. Who knew. With him, it was often impossible to tell what he was thinking.

I felt the ghost of a whisper of his touch on my back, and then it was gone. He cleared his throat. "Need anything else?" The dark tone of his voice had my pulse quickening.

I paused, turning to find him watching me with something a lot like hunger.

I have to get out of here before I do something stupid.

"Nope!" I chirped, bolting for the door. "Thank you."

When I glanced back at him, he was leaning against his desk. I gripped the edge of the door for support, annoyed at the sight of his long, elegant fingers wrapped around his glass of whiskey. "Enjoy your drink."

He frowned, but I closed the door before he could say anything else. It was going to be a long, lonely two years of marriage.

CHAPTER FOURTEEN

Graham

Less than a week into our marriage, and we were about to put it to the test. We were going to break the news to my family at dinner on Knox's yacht, and I only hoped we could be convincing. If not, well, we'd be headed to France soon for our "honeymoon." Maybe that would be enough to show them this was real.

I pulled up to the marina and put the car in park. The scent of Lily's perfume was intoxicating, distracting, and I needed to get out of the car before I did something stupid like haul her into my lap and kiss her.

Lily had spent most of the drive peppering me with questions about my family, claiming it was things my wife would know if this were a real marriage. I wasn't sure if it was my imagination, but it felt like she had placed a heavy emphasis on the *real* marriage part.

Was something bothering her?

If it was, I wished she'd just come out and say it. I was observant, but I could be shit at reading between the lines when it came to emotional subtext. Especially in romantic relationships. Not that this was a real romantic relationship, but it was a pseudo one.

However, now wasn't the time. So, I switched off the engine and rounded the hood to open Lily's door.

"You ready?" I smoothed down my shirt as I scanned the gated parking lot for my family.

I held out my hand for Lily, sensing her nerves. This was our first major test as a couple, and I knew my family would have questions. Lily and I had done our best to prepare, and now it was showtime.

She placed her hand in mine, and her diamond glinted in the light. I admired her ring briefly before spinning it so the band was facing outward. I wanted to buy us a little more time to break the news on our terms.

Her nails were painted a pale pink, and I briefly imagined her fingers wrapped around my cock. I quickly pushed that thought aside, but it wasn't the first time I'd fantasized about Lily. God, our wedding had been fucking torture. That kiss had sparked something inside me, unleashing a wildfire of desire that was becoming more and more difficult to extinguish.

So when she'd come to my office to ask for my help with her dress… It had taken all my restraint—more than I'd even thought possible—to resist touching her.

"Graham?" she asked, making me realize I was still holding her hand. Still having completely inappropriate thoughts about my wife.

Right. She was nervous. She was looking to me for reassurance, and here I was, thinking about her hand around my cock. *I am such an ass.*

I cleared my throat and released her. "You look great, and you'll do fine."

And she did—look great. She'd opted for a flirty sundress

in a cheerful yellow that made her blue eyes glow. She looked like sunshine personified.

My eyes followed the line of her delicate collarbone. The swell of her breasts. Jay had done a great job styling her. She looked like the wife of a billionaire, but she also looked like herself.

"I hope you're right," she said, clutching her purse.

I ushered her toward Knox's yacht, a hand on the small of her back. "I usually am."

She elbowed me in the side. I glared at her, and she laughed. When she tried to do it again, I grabbed her arm, and she pretended to try to fight my hold. She was laughing harder now, and I was holding in a smile.

As we neared the yacht, someone called out, "Graham?"

I shaded my eyes from the sun and peered at the upper deck. Knox was standing at the railing, his arms wrapped around Kendall's waist. The sun made it difficult to see their expressions, so I waved up at them.

Knox disappeared briefly before reappearing at the gangplank. He smiled, his eyes full of questions. Fortunately, he was polite enough to keep them to himself—for now anyway. I wasn't sure I'd be so lucky when it came to my other siblings.

Because while Knox and Nate were technically my cousins, they'd always been more like brothers to me. When we were younger, Knox had always had my back. And as we'd grown and matured, he'd been a good sounding board. Calm. Patient. Full of wisdom.

Knox might no longer be involved in the day-to-day operations of running the Huxley Grand brand, but his accomplishments were no less impressive. And while I could never imagine doing anything but continuing my grandparents' legacy, I admired Knox and Nate for striking out on their own. For being successful business owners themselves —Knox as the owner of the LA Leatherbacks, the pro soccer team. And Nate not only owned his own production company, he was an award-winning actor and producer.

"Knox, this is Lily," I said. "Lily, Knox."

Knox tilted his head, a twinkle in his eye. "You look familiar. Have we met before?"

"I used to work for Graham."

"Ah." He lifted his chin. "That must be it. Welcome aboard. Would you like a drink?" He glanced over his shoulder at me. "Graham, help yourself to whatever you want."

I wandered over to the fridge and selected a beer from the offerings. Emerson's laughter floated to me from the upper deck, and I assumed she was up there with Kendall.

"Is everyone here?" I asked, feeling my nerves build. I could only imagine how stressed I would be to meet Lily's family. And while I hated that her relationship with them was strained, I was relieved I wouldn't have to go through that ordeal.

"We're just waiting for Jasper, Sloan, and Jackson," Knox said.

Sloan and Jackson lived in London, but they'd come to LA following the Ixtapa opening. Brooklyn had a school play that Sloan didn't want to miss, and our next board meeting was later this week. I figured this was as good a time as any to break the news of my marriage to Lily.

"What about Jude and Chrissy?" I asked.

He shook his head. "Ezra has an ear infection."

"I'm sorry to hear that. I was looking forward to seeing them."

"Is that Uncle Graham?" Brooklyn called, her feet pounding on the stairs as she raced down to join us.

"Hey, kiddo." I gave her a side hug. "Did you get taller?"

"Since the last time I saw you?" She peered up at me with skepticism. "I doubt it."

Even so, I couldn't resist leveling my hand on the top of her head and dragging it to my chest. She was definitely growing.

"I'm looking forward to your school play," I said while Knox and Lily continued their conversation.

"Thanks! We've been working really hard on it. When can I garden with you again? How are my tomatoes doing?"

Lily quirked an eyebrow but kept her attention on Knox.

"Hopefully soon. And they're looking good, but they miss you."

She smiled at that.

I loved that my niece was interested in gardening. Spending time in nature helped me feel more centered after a hectic day, helped me feel closer to Gran. I was grateful that Brooklyn was interested; it felt like I was passing on Gran's knowledge and, with it, the memory of her.

Brooklyn lowered her voice to a whisper, forcing me to lean down to hear her. "Uncle Graham, did you bring a date?" She glanced over my shoulder, and I knew she was referring to Lily.

I smirked. This kid. She was just as nosy as the rest of my family.

Before I could answer, Jasper was boarding the yacht, Sloan and Jackson on his heels. Brooklyn flung herself at Sloan, and Jackson looked as if he might pop a vein.

"Auntie Sloan!"

"B! I missed you." Sloan smiled, but she looked exhausted. Pale. I frowned.

"I missed you too."

Now that everyone was aboard, the crew prepared to cast off. With every rope they untied, loosening us from the dock,

THE EXCEPTION

I tried to remain calm. Tried to remember why I'd thought it would be a good idea to tell my family that I'd gotten married while we were trapped on a boat together.

It's just for a few hours, I reminded myself.

We were scheduled to return to the marina after sunset. I'd chosen this setting because it was private and it had a designated end time, thus limiting the number of questions they could ask—for now.

I took the stairs to the upper deck in search of Lily. My family could be a lot. Even though she'd met most of them on multiple occasions, this was different. She wasn't my assistant or my employee; we were married now. And I knew everyone had questions, even if they were keeping them to themselves for now.

"Hey." Lily's smile was tight as she peered up at me, wrapping her arm around my waist.

I hesitated a moment before draping my arm over her shoulder. That's what a husband would do, right? What a real couple would do. Touch.

More often than not, I was trying to restrain myself from touching her—at least when we were alone. Like the night of our wedding. I skimmed my fingers along her skin, still full of regrets.

When she'd invited me to have a drink with her, I'd wanted to say yes. But I'd known it was a bad idea. And then she'd asked for help with her dress. When I'd unzipped it to see her bare, smooth back and the strap falling off her shoulder, I'd nearly bent her over my desk and taken her in all the ways I'd been imagining.

I wanted to touch her so damn bad. And it was nice to be able to do what I actually wanted for once.

I caught a whiff of her floral scent. I closed my eyes, feeling calmed. Grounded. When I opened my eyes again, Kendall and Emerson were communicating without words.

Having some kind of telepathic conversation that only best friends could.

"The Leatherbacks are having a good season," I said to Kendall, mostly to preempt any questions they might have.

"They are." She beamed. "You missed a great game last week."

I attended every home game I could, though hockey was my favorite sport. I was a huge Hollywood Hawks fan.

It wasn't long before the marina was fading into the distance. The rest of my family found their way to the upper deck, and I tried to ignore their curious glances. Liliana fussed with her outfit, her hair, but she was doing great. I knew she was nervous, even if she wouldn't admit it. I gave her shoulder a quick squeeze, wanting to reassure her despite my own uncertainty.

"Since we're all here," I said, not wanting to put this off any longer. Hell, I had a feeling Kendall had already spotted my wedding band, judging from her widened eyes. Time was of the essence. "I have an announcement."

I gestured to one of the yacht staff. I'd spoken to her after we'd boarded and asked that she prepare some champagne. Everyone quieted, and I swallowed hard, trying not to lose my nerve. When it came to my family, I rarely was the center of attention. It made me uncomfortable, as if spiders were crawling over my skin.

"Ooh. Champagne," Jasper said, arching his brow, as she held out a tray of champagne flutes. "What are we celebrating?"

Liliana glanced to me, champagne flute in hand. I waited until everyone had been served then noticed that Sloan was empty-handed.

"My wife," I supplied, handing Sloan a flute of champagne, which she nearly dropped.

"Careful, *hayati*," Jackson said, his quick reflexes saving the day. He held her hand and took the glass from her. Jackson went to the mini fridge and filled an empty flute with sparkling water before handing it to Sloan.

"Excuse me. Your what?" Sloan asked, eyes bouncing between Lily and me, drink forgotten.

"This is a joke, right?" Jasper glanced to the others for reassurance.

Liliana was tense, and I held her close, hoping to reassure her. "Does this look like a joke?" I held up Liliana's left hand to display her wedding ring.

"Surprise!" Liliana said, her entire body rigid.

Everyone else was silent. Dumbfounded. Except perhaps Kendall, though she was obviously still reeling from my announcement.

Lily lowered her hand, and I wrapped my arm around her waist. Jasper was unusually quiet. Jackson was watching this all unfold with interest.

"Since when?" Nate asked.

"Earlier this week."

Sloan narrowed her eyes at me. I was afraid she could see right through me. Afraid she was going to call me out for my fake relationship.

"I don't get it," Brooklyn said, breaking the increasingly awkward silence. "Shouldn't we be happy for Uncle Graham?" She peered at everyone, and I'd never been more thankful for that kid.

"We are happy for Graham," Emerson said, placing her hand on Brooklyn's shoulder. "We're just surprised. That's all. Right?" She elbowed Nate.

He shook his head as if awakening from a stupor. "Right. Surprised."

That seemed to snap everyone out of it. Knox was the first to step forward and offer his congratulations. I breathed a sigh of relief as Nate and the others fell in line. Emerson and Kendall soon disappeared downstairs with Brooklyn, leaving Lily and me alone with my siblings.

"Congratulations." Jasper looked...dejected. I frowned, hating the idea that I'd somehow hurt my family, even if I knew I'd done this for them. For all of us.

CHAPTER FIFTEEN

Graham

Sloan's eyes welled up with tears, and she sniffled. Fuck me. Not only was my baby sister crying, but I was the cause of it. And that was completely unacceptable.

I didn't know what to say. I didn't know how to fix this. And so, I kept my mouth shut.

"I'm sorry, Lily." Sloan met her eyes, swiping away a tear. "I'm sure you're lovely. And if Graham has fallen for you, I know the rest of us will too. I just…" Sloan's breath hitched, and her attention swung back to me. "I can't believe you didn't invite me to your wedding. I know how excited you were to be a part of Jackson's and my celebration. Don't you think I'd want to be there for you?"

My heart dropped. *Shit.* When she put it that way…

Jasper crossed his arms over his chest, and even Jackson seemed pissed. *Fucking hell.*

My throat was thick with emotion, and I felt paralyzed. Liliana glanced up at me, panic in her eyes. But before I could say anything, Sloan was turning into Jackson, seeking comfort as she buried her face in his chest.

He soothed her, whispering words of comfort as he rubbed her back, his attention focused solely on her. Meanwhile, Jasper glared at me, and I couldn't help feeling like I'd fucked everything up, when I had just been trying to fix it.

"I hate that you're upset," Liliana said, dipping her head. "And I'm sure it feels like it happened quickly. But honestly, it was a bit of a whirlwind romance for us too." She patted my chest.

Damn. She was good. She'd jumped right in. Trying to smooth things over while still making me look good.

"And I hope that once you get to know me, you'll be happy for Graham. Because we're happy." She smiled, and it was bright and forced, even if I was the only one who could tell.

How dare my family make Lily feel like she'd done something wrong. They should be thanking her for saving the company—not that they knew about that. I gnashed my teeth.

Someone mumbled that they were happy for me. But for the moment, I ignored my family and turned to face Lily, brushing her hair away from her cheek. She'd agreed to be my wife, but she didn't deserve this.

"Lil, you don't have to apologize."

"I know." She chewed on her bottom lip, and I could see the worry in her eyes. "I do, but I wanted to explain."

"He's right," Jasper said. "And I'm sorry we aren't giving off the best impression right now. This has nothing to do with you and everything to do with Graham."

"Family is important," Knox said. "I'm sorry I didn't realize you were dating someone, let alone that it was serious."

"None of us did," Jasper chimed in, a bite to his tone. "When I saw them together at Azul, it certainly seemed like a date. But still…"

"I get that we're all busy," Nate said to me. "But you can come to us. We're here for you. Good or bad, we're here."

Now I really felt like an ass.

"Did you not want to tell us because Lily used to be your assistant?" Jasper asked me.

"You know we'd never judge you, right?" Knox chimed in.

There was a pang in my chest, and panic raced through my veins. They were my family. My everything. I needed to fix this. I would fix this.

Liliana gave me a reassuring squeeze. "I would never want to come between you, but I asked Graham to keep our relationship a secret since I used to be his assistant, and now, I run a successful luxury-travel blog. Until I was able to transition out of that space, I didn't want anyone to think I was biased."

I supposed I should be thankful we were getting this all out of the way right now. Liliana's blog. Her role as my former assistant. Our marriage.

"Is that why you wrote the less-than-stellar reviews about the Huxley brand?" Jasper asked. "So *Gilded Lily* wouldn't seem biased?"

"Wait…" Sloan furrowed her brow. "What?" Her eyes widened. "*You're* Gilded Lily?"

"Yeah." Lily cringed. "Guilty. And I'm sorry about the reviews. But I had to be honest."

"I don't care about the reviews—not like Graham does. *Did?*" Sloan furrowed her brows. "I mean, do I wish they were raving reviews? Of course. But I value honesty."

Lily relaxed, and Sloan turned to me, confusion marring her features. "I thought you didn't know who was behind the blog."

I was surprised Jackson hadn't told Sloan about my discovering Liliana was behind *Gilded Lily*. It only raised him in my esteem.

Realizing that Sloan was looking at me expectantly, I said, "I didn't. At least not at first." I hoped she'd leave it at that.

"So, she told you about it...after you were dating?" Sloan asked, unwilling to drop the matter.

Before I could formulate a response, Jasper chimed in. "They couldn't have been dating. Not for long." He frowned. "He referred to her as 'annoying,' the bane of his existence."

Fuck. Had it been too much to hope he'd forget about that conversation? Sloan hadn't been there—it had been a guys' poker night. But Nate, Knox, Jasper, and Jackson had all witnessed my frustration toward Lily. This was exactly what I'd been worried about with our timeline.

Lily's smile was tight. *Shit.*

"No. No." Jasper wagged a finger. "They must have started seeing each other after he hacked her blog and discovered her identity." *Jesus, Jasper. Thanks.*

I stilled, Liliana's attention whipping to me. *Oh shit.* That was one secret I'd hoped to keep.

Yes, we'd promised each other no more secrets, but I'd tried to tell myself that didn't apply retroactively. I was a fool. And thanks to my big-mouthed little brother, I was going to have to figure out how to spin this.

"You *hacked* my blog?" Lily ground out.

I didn't want to have this conversation in front of my family. Especially not with the way their attention kept whipping between us like cats at a tennis match.

"I was just looking for information—trying to find out who was behind it, *mon petit poisson.*"

She narrowed her eyes at me. I silently begged her to drop it. Finally, she arched a brow, and I took that as her acquiescence. I knew this conversation wasn't over, but I was grateful we'd tabled the issue until we no longer had an audience.

"His little *fish*?" Jasper whispered to Sloan, who merely shrugged. Oh god, I was never going to hear the end of it.

"I'm grateful to your blog for bringing us together," I said, silently begging Lily to play along.

"So you reconnected, and then what?" Sloan was like a lioness—focused, determined, going in for the kill.

I needed to get my family off the subject of our relationship timeline. I'd anticipated it would be an issue, but I hadn't expected them to interrogate us like this.

"Since I was traveling and living abroad, we started emailing and talking. Getting to know each other again," Liliana said.

"Graham? *Talking*?" Jasper chortled, crossing his arms over his chest.

"Right?" Liliana joined in, though it sounded forced. I didn't think my family would notice, but I did. "I think having a long-distance relationship gave us time to really get to know each other on a deeper level. Though I guess I should've said that *I* did most of the talking. But Graham's an incredible listener." She slid her hand down my arm, sending sparks skittering in its wake.

Sloan's expression softened. "He is."

"It's one of the things I love about Graham," Lily said. "He's observant and insightful and patient."

Did she truly feel that way? Or was she saying it all for the sake of my family? I wanted to believe it was the truth, but... I pushed away the thought. This was an act. She was playing the part.

Everyone seemed to relax a little, and I hoped that maybe, just maybe, they were beginning to buy it.

"And Graham, what is it that you love about Lily?" Jasper asked, grabbing the champagne bottle and refilling his glass before offering Lily some, then Sloan. Sloan refused, and my mind snagged on that.

Nate elbowed him and muttered, "Don't put him on the spot like that."

I turned to Lily, trying to focus on her and block out my family. I stared into her eyes, thinking about all the things I appreciated about her. Her loyalty. Her resilience. Her determination.

I lifted my hand to cup her cheek, pleased when she leaned into my touch. "I'm not sure I could name just one."

Unable to resist, I closed the distance between us, brushing my lips against hers in a silent apology. If Lily was surprised by my actions, she didn't show it. Instead, she melted into the kiss, even as brief—too brief—as it was. For the first time since we'd boarded Knox's yacht, I felt as if I could breathe again.

When I turned my attention back to Jasper, I realized that everyone had grown quiet. They'd been too busy watching Liliana and me. They were stunned.

I should've been pleased that my family seemed to be buying our love story, but I couldn't stop thinking about that kiss. The taste of sunshine and champagne on her lips, the scent of her floral perfume curling through the air, winding itself around me like a protective cocoon.

I couldn't tear my eyes away from Lily. She was all I could see. All I wanted to see.

Nate cleared his throat, and she finally glanced away.

"You mentioned you were doing the long-distance thing," Nate said. "So now that you're married, I assume you'll be moving to LA." His question was directed at Lily.

"Well…" She tucked her hair behind her ear, and I decided to field this one.

"We're actually going to be splitting our time between France and LA," I said.

"Splitting your time?" Jasper gaped at me. "And you didn't think to talk to us about this first?"

"Nothing will change. I will still attend all meetings. And I'll work with Carson to shift my schedule during the times that I'm in France."

Sloan held a hand to her stomach. "I think I'm going to be sick."

I knew it couldn't be motion sickness. Sloan was a keen sailor. Hell, she and Jackson had spent nearly two months exploring the Caribbean earlier this year. I often thought she was more at home on her sailboat than on land.

I frowned. Was she truly that upset?

She dashed to the nearest trash can and hurled into it. Jackson was at her side, offering her a towel and water.

"You okay?" Nate asked when she returned.

She nodded, but she was still pale.

"Should we turn back?" Knox asked. "Take you to a doctor?"

"No. No." Sloan shook her head. "It will pass."

"But you never get motion sickness," I said, unwilling to let it go.

She peered up at Jackson, her face full of such love and devotion. She placed her hand on his cheek, and the way the two of them looked at each other spoke of their deep affection. They silently communicated something.

"We weren't going to tell everyone yet since it's still early," Sloan said. "And not to steal the spotlight from Graham and Lily—"

"Steal away," I said. *Please.* Anything to divert everyone's attention from Lily and me.

"It's not motion sickness," Sloan continued. "It's morning sickness. I'm pregnant."

Nate's eyes widened, a tentative smile forming on his lips. "Really?"

Sloan nodded, biting back a smile of her own. My heart felt full to bursting. I was thrilled for her.

Jasper set down his glass and immediately gathered her into a hug. "I'm so happy for you."

I shook Jackson's hand, unable to keep the smile from my face. This was good news, the *best* news. "Congratulations."

I opened my arms, and Sloan stepped into them. I gave her a long hug, beyond happy for her. "You're going to be the best mom," I said, quiet enough for only her to hear.

"Thank you." Her throat was clogged with emotion, and I knew what she was thinking even if she wouldn't say it. She wished Gran and Pops could be here to see this.

It had been years since they'd passed, but with every milestone, every marriage or birth they missed, the loss felt fresh. I knew no one lived forever, but that didn't lessen the pain of missing them.

"How are you feeling?" I asked, concerned for her wellbeing. It didn't matter how old she was or the fact that she was married to an incredible man; Sloan would always be my baby sister. It was my job to look out for her.

"Good. I'm about ten weeks along, and the doctor says everything looks really good."

"I'm glad you're feeling well," Jasper chimed in. "But you'll tell us if you need anything, right? Shorter days. Less travel. Whatever. We'll make it happen."

"Thanks." Sloan leaned into him. "I will. But for now, I'm good."

I glanced to Jackson for confirmation. He gave a curt lift of his chin, indicating what she said was true. I had no doubts he'd take good care of my sister and their child.

"Are you going to find out if you're having a boy or a girl?" Lily asked, probably as relieved as I was to have everyone's attention off us.

After everything my family had said, Lily's attempt to engage with my siblings and celebrate Sloan's news showed me how gracious she truly was.

Sloan's news also helped me reframe and understand my sister's earlier response. Yes, she was understandably upset about my secret wedding. But I could see now that her pregnancy hormones might have caused her tears. It was a relief to think that maybe I hadn't fucked up as badly as I'd feared.

"We're going to wait until the birth."

"Wow." Lily shook her head. "I don't think I could do that."

Sloan laughed, and it was nice to see her making an effort to interact with Lily. I tried to have faith that, given time, she would welcome Lily with open arms.

"Graham definitely couldn't, so I guess you're a good match on that. I mean, assuming you want children. Sorry. I shouldn't have assumed…" Sloan trailed off.

"I mean, yeah, maybe someday." Lily gulped down the rest of her champagne.

Jasper clapped a hand on my shoulder. "Oh, I can't wait for that. Graham as a father. That will be the day."

"Why do you say that?" Lily asked, frowning.

Jasper scrunched up his face. "He's so particular. I don't think he could handle the unpredictability that comes with raising a child."

"And you could?" I shot back.

Jasper said nothing, but he looked almost pained. "Hey." I nudged him. "I'm sorry. I know how good you are with Brooklyn. And how you were with Jude when he was little."

"And with me," Sloan said, smiling.

"Thanks," Jasper said, but I couldn't shake the feeling that I'd upset him somehow. Not just with the wedding announcement and the secrets, but with my comment about being a parent.

"Looks like we have several things to celebrate," Knox said, his arm draped over Nate's shoulder. He was the peacemaker of the group, always smoothing things over. "Lily, welcome to the family. As you can see, we're a little crazy. Now, does anyone else have anything they want to share?"

Nate chuckled. "Don't you think we've had enough excitement for one evening?" But as he said that, the boat slowed and then came to an unexpected stop.

CHAPTER SIXTEEN

Lily

"I still can't believe Graham is married." Emerson shook her head. "Can you?" she asked Kendall.

We were sitting on the top deck of Knox's yacht, drinking and talking on one of the outdoor sofas. Everyone else was scattered throughout the space, though Knox had gone to speak with the captain to try to discover the reason the boat had stopped. The engine had cut off, so we remained in place, bobbing on the water.

Kendall smiled apologetically at me. "*Emerson*," she gritted out, "has a tendency to say whatever she thinks."

"Sorry." Emerson cringed. "I didn't mean to be insensitive. I'm just surprised. I think we all are."

"Knox swore he'd never marry again, and..." Kendall held up her hand, showcasing her ring. It was a huge emerald-cut diamond that shimmered and sparkled.

"True," Emerson said, admiring her own wedding ring, a stunning red diamond. "I guess you never know. And with Graham, it's hard to know." She laughed. "I think the longest conversation I've ever had with him, apart from pitching the in-room exercise content, was about the Huxley Grand Abu Dhabi."

"Oh, that location is amazing, isn't it?" I asked, latching on to the change of subject. My anger was simmering beneath the surface. And every time they mentioned Graham, it flared again. I still couldn't believe my husband had hacked my blog.

"It is. Have you stayed there?"

"Once with Graham. For work. He has the original key to the palace in his penthouse."

"Don't you mean your penthouse?" Emerson asked.

"Yes. Of course." I rushed to course correct. "I'm still getting used to the fact that it's my home too."

"When you said that you and Graham stayed at the Huxley Grand Abu Dhabi, were you together then?"

I shook my head, reminding myself that they'd gone off with Brooklyn and missed that part of the conversation. "Our relationship was never anything but professional while I worked for him." I wanted to make sure that distinction was made because it was important to me, but I knew it was even more so to Graham.

I clenched my fists so tight my nails dug into my palms. I might be pissed with him for hacking my blog. And keeping it a secret after we'd promised no more secrets. I sure as shit wasn't going to let that go without more of an explanation. But I also wasn't going to let my emotions stand in the way of twenty million dollars.

"So, when did things change?" Emerson asked, leaning in as if for a juicy morsel.

"Not until well after I stopped being his assistant."

"Come on, Lily," Emerson said. "You've gotta give us more than that. We just found out that Graham—a man who is locked up tighter than Fort Knox—is married. And has been in a secret relationship. I'm going to need to know more."

THE EXCEPTION

"Em." Kendall nudged her. "She didn't come here for an interrogation."

Emerson raised her hands in surrender. "You're right. I'm sorry. I should know better. I'm just so surprised. Aren't you?" She turned to Kendall.

"I'm just happy to have another fun new sister-in-law." She gave me a warm smile.

"Thanks," I said. I could imagine being friends with them, and it made me sad that this was only temporary. "Have either of you visited that location?"

The breeze toyed with Emerson's blond ponytail. "I went to Abu Dhabi with Nate and Brooklyn when he was filming a movie there."

"The new Meghan Hart adaptation?" I asked, eager to keep the conversation focused on her. When she nodded, I said, "I saw a preview for it recently. I can't wait to watch it."

"I'll be sure to put you and Graham on the guest list for the screening."

Oh, he'll love that. But if he wanted us to convince his family we were a happy couple in love, then he'd need to put in the work. I smirked at the idea of forcing him to sit through a romantic movie. He'd hate it.

And he'd deserve it after what he'd done.

"Thanks. That sounds amazing. Hopefully the timing will work out with our schedule."

"Yeah. Sounds like you two are going to be busy. I want to hear more about this French château you're restoring," Kendall said. "Does it have a winery? And when can we come visit?"

"No winery, but it's set on twenty-three hectares of land and has the most incredible *grand allée*. And maybe someday you can come visit, but I'd recommend waiting, as it doesn't have heating or air conditioning yet."

"Wow." Kendall's eyes widened. "Yeah. Maybe I'll wait."

We all laughed.

"If you're interested in the progress of the restoration, check out my YouStream channel."

"Oh, I definitely will!" Kendall said.

"I know I promised no more questions, but can I just ask one more thing about Graham?" Emerson asked, unwilling to let the matter go. Part of me understood. I'd want more details if I were them too. Even so, I dreaded their questions and hoped I could keep my answers straight. "I have to know —" She glanced at Kendall and chewed on her lip. "Did you always have a crush on him?"

I let out a surprised laugh, both in relief and at the question itself. "I mean…not at first. Yes, he's hot. But he can be a pain in the ass too." *There. Honesty.* I was trying to stick to the truth as much as possible.

And apparently Graham thought of me as "annoying" and the bane of his existence. So, in my mind, calling him a pain in the ass was pretty generous.

Emerson smirked. "Apparently that's a trait that runs in the male side of the family. Sloan is lovely."

I nodded, completely in agreement. Sloan was a badass. She didn't take shit from anyone—something I'd always respected about her.

Sloan may not have welcomed me with open arms, but she'd still been nice. And now that I knew she was pregnant, I gave her a pass. She'd just found out her brother had gotten married, and she was dealing with some serious hormones.

"Nate?" I asked, glancing over at him. The man had always seemed so charming. Hell, charisma radiated from him like a Hollywood spotlight.

"Total pain in the ass when I first started working for him as his daughter's nanny." Emerson's smile was wistful. "He's lucky I adore Brooklyn, because I almost quit several times."

I tried to imagine it. "That bad, huh?"

"Oh yeah. He had all these rules."

Rules, huh? Sounds like someone else I know.

"What changed?" I'd seen their images splashed on the tabloids and online blogs, but I'd never paid much attention. They might be celebrities, but I believed their private life should be private.

She smiled. "I always thought he was hot. But seeing the way he loved his daughter and would do anything for her…I was a goner."

"Plus, he serenaded you with Taylor Swift." Kendall nudged her. "And gave you your dream purse."

"That certainly didn't hurt." Emerson dipped her head, her hair falling over her cheeks.

"*And* he was your childhood celebrity crush."

Emerson's cheeks were rosy. "Okay. Enough about me." She glared at Kendall, but it was all in good fun.

"What about you and Knox?" I asked Kendall.

She dragged a hand through her hair. "He was a great boss, but crazy overprotective. Still is."

"He's mellowed some," Emerson said.

Kendall shot her a skeptical look. "Has he?"

I bit back a smile. "You two remind me of my best friend Josephine and me. You're lucky that you get to be family officially."

"Jasper's single." Emerson shrugged. "Maybe she and Jasper…"

"I'm not so sure about that," I hedged, thinking about her fling or whatever she and Luc had going on.

Besides, I'd hate to get Jo wrapped up in this mess. I didn't want to consider what would happen when it was over. I pushed away the thought. That was two years away. Two years of lying to Graham's family.

Would it be two years of him lying to me? My expression soured.

Emerson leaned in, keeping her voice low. "Graham always seems so grumpy. Does he wake up that way?"

I laughed, mostly to hide my discomfort. I honestly had no idea how to answer. Graham and I had been married a week, but we'd barely spent any time together. And we definitely hadn't slept together.

"Emerson!" Kendall chided. "Don't ask her that."

"Oh, come on. If she's going to be part of this family, she's going to have to get used to it."

Part of this family.

Graham's family had done more in a single evening to make me feel welcome and included than my husband had all week. I didn't know what I'd expected, but I'd hoped we'd share the occasional meal. Maybe hang out. Have a conversation. If anything, he seemed determined to put as much distance between us as possible. How did he expect us to act like a couple if we continued to live separate lives?

Not that I wanted to be attached at the hip. Not by any means. But if we were going to be believable as a happily married couple, we should probably get to know each other.

Well, I knew a lot about him. So maybe I was put out that he didn't seem willing to make an effort to know me. Hell, maybe he'd planned to just hack into everything else like he had my blog. And then he wouldn't ever have to spend time with me. He could simply analyze the data and make decisions.

The more I thought about it, the more my anger reignited.

It was such a controlling billionaire thing to do. And while I'd always suspected that Graham would go to great lengths to protect his brand and his family, he'd crossed the line. I mean, Jesus. It wasn't like one luxury-travel blogger was going to make or break an entire hotel empire. Did he truly feel that threatened by me?

I seethed. He'd invaded my privacy. He'd had no right to do that. I didn't care what his reasons were; I couldn't imagine anything justifying his actions.

"Well, gang," Knox said, interrupting my thoughts. When I glanced up, I realized that everyone had joined us, including Graham. "Looks like we're stuck here for the night. Something's wrapped around the propeller, and it will not budge."

Kendall got up to stand beside Knox, and he pressed a kiss to her forehead. He whispered something to her, but my eyes were on Graham. His jaw was clenched so tight, I thought it might crack.

"So, that's it?" Nate asked. "We have to stay here until someone can tow us back to shore?"

"Pretty much," Knox said, calm and collected. The opposite of how I felt.

"And how long will that be?" Jasper asked.

"Tomorrow morning. Maybe afternoon."

Nate's eyes widened. "We can't take the smaller boat back to the marina?"

"We're too far out to do so comfortably. Not to mention it would be a choppy ride, and I don't like the idea of leaving the crew shorthanded."

"This is crazy," Emerson said, dragging a hand through her hair. We were all digesting the news that we'd be staying on the boat overnight. Something none of us had planned for.

"This is awesome!" Brooklyn said. "It's like one big family sleepover! And it's not even Christmas!"

I smiled. Leave it to the twelve-year-old to look on the bright side.

"Oh yeah," she continued. "We could bring the beds out here and sleep all together."

"Fun idea, kiddo. But I don't think that's happening." Nate gave her shoulder a squeeze.

She pouted. "Then can I stay with Auntie Sloan in her cabin?"

Nate glanced to Sloan. "I'm not sure Auntie Sloan is feeling up to that."

"Oh." Brooklyn's face fell.

"But we can absolutely hang out together in the morning," Sloan said, stifling another yawn.

"What about a helicopter?" Emerson asked.

"Not enough room to land safely on the deck," Jackson said.

If it had been my own family, I would've swum ashore. But Graham's family was lovely, so maybe this wouldn't be that terrible.

Emerson and Kendall had been the most welcoming. Apart from Brooklyn, who'd already asked if she could call me Auntie Lily. That had been a punch to the gut.

Lying to Graham's family was bad enough, but lying to a child? To Brooklyn? I wasn't sure I'd ever despised myself as much as I had in that moment.

I knew his family still had questions about our relationship, and I didn't blame them. If I hadn't been so mad at Graham, I would've been grateful he had so many people in his life who loved him.

Even so, this time with his family was making me realize how woefully unprepared we were to present ourselves as besotted newlyweds. And I wondered what it would take for them to accept our relationship. There was a lot riding on it.

Graham knew the stakes as well as I did. Here I was, working my butt off to ingratiate myself to his family, only to discover that he'd hacked my blog? *Hacked.* My. Blog.

No more secrets, my ass.

I was still trying to wrap my head around that. Not only the fact that he'd done it, but he'd tried to make light of it.

What had he been trying to accomplish? He'd said he wanted to discover my identity, but seriously?

"The good news is that we have plenty of food and water. And the weather is fair," Jackson said, making me wonder just how much of the conversation I'd missed.

Sloan yawned again, and Kendall stood. "Why don't I show everyone to their rooms. For anyone who's not ready to go to bed yet, we'll have games and drinks."

Brooklyn shot up from her seat. "I want to stay up!"

"For a little bit," Emerson said.

"Em." Kendall chewed on her lip. "Why don't you and Nate take a twin cabin since it has a queen bed and the bunks."

Emerson stood. "Great. Thanks."

"Jasper, you'll have the other twin cabin."

He sliced a hand through the air. "That's fine."

"Sloan and Jackson can take the double."

"Come on, *hayati*," Jackson said, standing and holding out his hand for her.

I wondered what the nickname meant. I wasn't even sure I knew what language it was in, but it had to be better than *mon petit poisson*. I mean, seriously? The French had some *interesting* terms of endearment, but I didn't want to be referred to as a little fish.

Did Graham think I smelled bad?

That my actions were fishy?

Why did he continue to insist on calling me that? And especially in front of his family? It was mortifying. Not to mention ironic in light of the things I'd discovered about him lately—lying, scamming, fraud, secrets, hacking. I'd worked closely with the man for a year, but I was beginning to wonder if I knew my husband at all.

Sloan smiled and stood. "Good night." Everyone wished them goodnight, and she gave Brooklyn a hug before heading downstairs.

"And that leaves Lily and Graham. Come on." Kendall looped her arm through mine. "I'll take you to your cabin."

I followed her down the stairs. This whole excursion would've provided perfect material for my blog. My blog that had been hacked by my fake husband. I bit the inside of my cheek, desperate to hold back all the thoughts waiting to burst forth about my blog and Graham and everything else.

"And here you two are," Kendall said, opening the door to a guest room.

The cabin was beautiful and luxurious. My eyes scanned the wall of large windows, the small built-in desk and chair, the backlit headboard, finally landing on the bed. And then it registered—there was only one bed.

Merde.

CHAPTER SEVENTEEN

Lily

One bed. There's only one bed?
I glanced over my shoulder at Graham. The look of panic in his eyes mirrored my own.

"Is something wrong?" Kendall asked. "I mean...besides the obvious fact that we're stranded out here until someone can tow us in." She dropped her head in resignation. "I cannot believe the propeller is stuck."

Me either. But none of this was her fault, so I rushed to reassure her. "We're fine. And this is lovely." I elbowed Graham. Apart from the kiss on deck earlier, it was almost as if he just expected me to take the lead in every interaction with his family.

He grunted, then said, "Yes. Thank you."

Kendall left us to settle in. The door to the cabin shut with an audible click, and the space felt too small for the two of us. This was *so* not happening. We were not going to be trapped in a cabin on a boat with only one bed.

Graham walked toward the walls, feeling along them, searching for something. Meanwhile, I felt as if they were closing in on me.

"What are you doing?" I asked, unable to keep the bite from my tone. My anger needed an outlet. Otherwise, I might explode.

"Sometimes the rooms on a yacht have Pullman berths. They fold out from the wall like a Murphy bed."

I glanced around, looking for signs of a cavity in the wall. Something, anything, that might fold out and turn into another bed. But there was nothing. A small closet with hangers, and a door that led to a beautiful en suite bathroom.

"This is never going to work." I flopped down onto the mattress with a huff. There was a chair. A bed. And the floor.

But even more than our current predicament, I was referring to our relationship. To the way Graham continued to hold me at a distance both in private and in public. We were supposed to be married, for crying out loud. And he'd kept a huge fucking secret about something that affected me personally.

"I'll sleep on the floor."

"Great." I tossed him a pillow, not even bothering to argue. He'd offered; I was more than happy to take him up on it. Perhaps I was being childish, but I was angry. I didn't want to share the same room, let alone the same bed.

"Fantastic." He took it and dropped it on the carpet.

I grabbed a blanket and tossed it to him as well. "Here."

He grunted and added it to his pile. "If you have something to say, say it."

"I can't believe you hacked my blog. Why would you do that?"

"I needed to know who was behind it."

Seriously?

"Yes, seriously," he said, making me realize I'd voiced the question aloud. He just had to control everything, know everything, didn't he?

That answer wasn't good enough.

"Did you do anything...malicious?"

I hadn't noticed anything. But why would I? I hadn't realized someone had been able to hack my site, period. It made me feel exposed. I wanted to increase my cybersecurity.

"As I said, I was merely looking for information."

I searched for a robe, yanking it off the hook in the bathroom. "And did you find what you were looking for?"

He unbuttoned his shirt, smoothing it out before hanging it in the small closet that was hidden in a recess in the wall. "I found you, didn't I?"

How could he be so calm? I felt as if I was going to explode. And the fact that he was so, *so* unruffled was only adding to my irritation.

"Wait..." I stilled, putting the pieces together. "You knew in Ixtapa that I was Gilded Lily. Did you invite me there? Was it some sort of trap?"

He dragged a hand through his hair. "No. I just wanted to talk to you."

"You could've sent me an email. Called me on the phone. Texted." Any number of things, really.

"Would you have responded?" he asked.

"You never gave me the chance," I said, not sure how to answer. But this wasn't about me; this was about him. And I wasn't going to let him turn the conversation around on me. "Is this something you do often? Hack into websites?"

He was quiet for so long, I figured he wasn't going to answer. But then he said, "When necessary."

I narrowed my eyes. "Define necessary." Because I wasn't sure that discovering the identity of the blogger behind *Gilded Lily* was necessary, strictly speaking.

"To protect the people I love."

"Mm." I crossed my arms over my chest. "And you felt that you needed to violate my privacy to *protect the people you love.*" It seemed like a flimsy excuse to me. "Did you really feel that threatened by a few blog posts?"

"I don't think you realize the power you have as Gilded Lily."

Wow. Okay. Either I had more reach than I realized, or he was more paranoid than I'd ever considered.

"I would never abuse that power. I posted fair and honest reviews. I didn't lie. I didn't say anything malicious or untrue."

"I know." His expression was unreadable.

"Then why even do it?"

I stared at him, willing him to explain himself. For a man who valued privacy and discretion, he seemed to have very little regard for mine.

He said nothing. Finally, when I couldn't take it any longer, I threw my hands in the air and turned away. "You had no right to do that. None." I was beyond annoyed with his interference in my life and my business.

"I—" I heard the rustle of his slacks as he stepped closer. He placed his hand on my arm, gently turning me. "It was wrong." His gaze was locked on mine, the green the color of the wind-whipped ocean before a storm. Dark. Foreboding. "I'm sorry."

"But you'd still do it again. You don't regret it." He didn't even seem all that remorseful.

"I regret upsetting you."

"No," I gritted out. "You regret that you got caught."

He said nothing, but he didn't have to. I took that as his assent.

He'd claimed that he'd wanted to discover my identity, but his actions seemed extreme, even for him. Or maybe— I sighed. Maybe I didn't know him as well as I thought I did.

I'd always admired Graham's loyalty and ethics. But in the span of a week, I'd learned that he was willing to commit fraud with a fake marriage scam and hack into someone's website and god only knew what else.

Yes, I'd told him I'd be willing to exist in the gray with him. But he'd crossed the line.

It made me wonder what other lines he was willing to cross. Did he just think he was above the law? That he had so much money, the rules didn't apply?

I'd never gotten that impression from him. But tonight, I was seeing a whole different side to Graham, and I wasn't sure I liked it.

A darker thought occurred to me. If he ever got caught for trying to scam the board, what were the chances he'd take me down with him? The prospect had me feeling lightheaded, and his grip on me tightened.

"Were you ever going to tell me?"

"What was done was done. Telling you wasn't going to help anything."

So, basically never. He'd never intended to tell me.

I backed away from Graham, forcing him to release me. Was he even listening to himself? Did he really not see how wrong that was?

"You are unbelievable," I seethed. "You talk about Moretti as if he's the bad guy, but you're no better."

His eyes flashed with anger. "Keep your voice down."

"Why? Are you scared to ruin everyone's image of us as the perfect couple?" I lifted my chin, unwilling to back down. "Newlyweds who are madly in love? Because news flash...I don't think anyone's buying it."

I'd done my best all afternoon and evening, but it had been stressful. Not because of anything anyone had said, but everything they hadn't. Despite their initial shock, they'd all been so nice, so welcoming. Sloan had even taken me aside to apologize for her outburst. Graham's family's kindness only made me feel worse about the whole thing.

"What are you talking about?" he snapped.

"We're supposed to be partners, and you allowed me to be blindsided in front of your family. You mentioned that my blog would be an issue, but you let me think that was because of the reviews I'd posted. Not because you'd hacked *my* site and it would mess with the timing of our 'story.'"

I crossed my arms over my chest. "We're supposed to be a team, but if this is going to work, we have to be able to trust each other."

"I *do* trust you." His green eyes swirled with emotions, imploring me to listen.

"No. You don't." I shook my head. "If you did, you would've come clean about the hacking and trusted that I'd still have your back."

"And would you have?"

"Do I like being lied to? Absolutely not. But if you'd come to me with the truth earlier? If I'd found out from you—instead of from your family—like I did with the provision in your grandfather's will, I wouldn't have been nearly as upset."

He was quiet. Why wouldn't he say something?

"Do you even realize how humiliating that was?" I paused, trying to gauge his reaction. His calmness grated on me. It was probably a front—at least, that's what I was telling myself—but still. I was livid, and he was just standing there, taking it.

"I would've answered any questions you had," I continued. "Provided any information you wanted. All you had to do was ask." I couldn't help it. I couldn't stop myself. I was a runaway train of emotions, and it was full steam ahead. "Or maybe you were afraid to ask because you're afraid to let people in. To let them see you."

He narrowed his eyes at me. God, his silence was so infuriating!

And still, he said nothing.

THE EXCEPTION

I crossed my arms over my chest. "I felt like I was in a fishbowl all evening. Like they were watching our every move, every interaction, waiting to call us out on the lie."

"You're being paranoid."

"Yeah, well, you would know." I glared at him.

He furrowed his brow. "What's that supposed to mean?"

I sank down onto the bed, exhausted. Defeated. Why had I ever thought this was a good idea?

I twirled my wedding ring on my finger. Barely a week into this marriage, and everything already felt as if it were crumbling faster than the walls of my ancient château.

"What are we doing?" I asked, feeling as if I'd been hit over the head with an anvil. My head spun. I could go to jail for this fake marriage. And for what? Money?

My shoulders sagged. This wasn't me.

"We're working together to achieve our goals," he said.

"It doesn't feel like it," I muttered, feeling dejected and scared and angry and so many other emotions I couldn't even name.

He'd lied to me. And not about something small.

"This feels like a mistake."

"Because of one evening?" he asked, incredulous.

Because of everything.

But I didn't tell him that. I didn't tell him that I felt like I was using him, and he was lying to me. And at this rate, we were going to fail. He'd forfeit his company, and I'd lose the château.

We were supposed to be partners. Sure, we'd each agreed to this for our own reasons, but we were only going to succeed by working together. Not by keeping secrets from each other. I was hurt. And angry—at him and myself.

"I was out there busting my butt to sell our relationship to your family." *And* he was calling me his little fish. "You can't possibly think that throwing around a term of endearment"

—and a shitty one at that— "and one kiss would be enough to convince them, right?"

"Jesus, Lil." He threw his hands in the air. "What more do you want from me?" He lifted his chin, and I wanted to punch the imperious expression off his gorgeous face. "I had my stylist work with you to give you a whole new wardrobe. Moved you in to my penthouse. I gave you twenty million dollars for the château."

Wow. I was reeling from his statement. Wow. Wow. Wow.

Yes, he had done all those things, but I wasn't impressed by them. By money. It made me feel like a hypocrite to admit that when I'd accepted twenty million dollars from him for the restoration of the château, but it was true.

"I'm not even going to dive into everything wrong with that statement. But what do I want from you? I want you to respect my privacy. I want this to be the partnership I signed up for. I want you to promise you're not going to lie to me again."

"I won't. Lie, that is."

I narrowed my eyes at him, assessing him. "And my privacy? Are you going to respect it?"

He hesitated, tugging on his collar. "Yes."

I sighed. What good was Graham's word when he'd already broken it once before? "I'm not sure I can trust you."

"Then think about the château. Remember what's at stake."

"No. That's not good enough." As much as I loved the château, I said, "Nothing is worth more than my self-respect. And you promised—" I fought the urge to rage, to stomp my feet, to do…something. "You swore that we would be partners. You even said so in your wedding vows."

He dropped his head to his chest. Then he took a breath, straightened, and stepped closer. "I'm sorry." My expression must have betrayed my skepticism because he took my hands in his. "I am."

"I've always believed you were a man of your word. Honorable. Ethical. But in light of recent events, I'm questioning everything I thought I knew about you."

"Come on, Lil." He gave my hands a squeeze. "You know me. You do."

"I'm beginning to wonder if you actually let anyone see the real you. You keep secrets from your family, hold them at a distance."

"It's for their—"

"Own good. Right." I swallowed. "I can see that you believe that, but that's not your decision to make. Only Sloan can decide what's best for her. Only Nate can decide what's best for him. Only *I* can decide what's best for me."

Perhaps sensing I was on the edge, he asked, "And what is best for you?" I heard the hesitancy in his tone.

I inhaled slowly. It was so tempting to walk away. But then what would've been the point of it all? I wanted to save the château, and I truly believed Graham wanted to save the Huxley brand.

Before I could answer, he asked, "Do you realize how many people are relying on me?"

"Over 150,000."

"One hundred and seventy-five thousand people. One hundred and seventy-five *thousand*."

"That's a huge responsibility. I can only imagine the burden you feel, and I know you take their welfare seriously."

"It is. And then there's my family. We've been through a lot. All we have is one another. And I'm the one they look to when they have a problem or need reassurance."

"Why do you think that is?"

"Because I'm the strong, steady one. And they know I will do anything in my power to fix it." I didn't think that was the entire reason, but I didn't tell him that. This wasn't about what I'd observed; it was about what Graham believed.

"And who gives you strength? Who fixes your problems?"

He lifted a shoulder, trying to brush it off as if it didn't matter. But there was a sadness in his eyes, an air of loneliness that clung to him like a lion watching over his pride. Protective but alone.

And in that moment, I felt sorry for him. I was still angry, but I could also feel empathy.

I softened, but my anger still simmered beneath the surface. "How can you expect them to when you don't share anything with them? A relationship is a two-way street. You can't expect others to be open and vulnerable if you're closed off and secretive."

"I'm—" He dropped his head to his chest. "It's not like I want to be this way. I think—" He swallowed hard, his Adam's apple bobbing. "I think I just needed this to work so badly that I was scared to fuck it up. And ironically, I still ended up fucking things up."

I wasn't sure I'd ever seen him more vulnerable. And while I knew he was sincere, I also worried it was another attempt to manipulate me.

I felt my shoulders relax. Maybe this whole situation wasn't as hopeless as I'd feared.

"Then do something about it."

"Like what?" he asked, genuinely confused.

"Confide in your family. In me. Or, at the very least, stop avoiding me." When he opened his mouth to protest, I held up my hand. "You asked for my help. And if you want everyone to believe I'm your wife, you're going to have to start acting like a husband."

"I *am*." He dragged a hand through his hair. "I take care of you, provide for you."

Did he truly not understand? He'd been in relationships

in the past. Surely he understood how this worked. What it meant to be a couple.

"Graham." I leveled him with a look. "Do you think that's why Sloan and Jackson are together? Or Emerson and Nate?" When he remained silent, I nearly shouted, "No! They're in a relationship because they love each other. Have you ever watched them together?"

He furrowed his brow.

"Oh, come on. I'm sure you have. You're one of the most observant people I know. So, tell me what you notice."

"They smile at each other a lot," he said.

"Yes. Good." God, this was painful. Like pulling teeth. "What else?"

"They call each other 'babe' and 'baby' and '*mi Cielo.*'"

"And the name Jackson calls Sloan. Hay…"

"*Hayati.*"

"Yes." I snapped my fingers. "What does that mean?"

"'My life' in Arabic."

Swoon.

He gave me a pensive look but then asked, "What else?"

I narrowed my eyes at him, not ready to move on just yet. Not ready to concede the point. Perhaps I was being harsh, but if this was going to work, Graham needed to get on the same page with me. He needed to realize we were a team. And he needed to stop holding back.

"I get that you're not big on PDA or showing emotion, but you can try to act like you care about me. Like you're attracted to me. Otherwise, everyone is going to think it's strange that you're more affectionate with your dogs than your wife. Unless you really are the cold, heartless billionaire everyone claims you are."

He clenched his fists, and I sensed that I'd touched a nerve. Good! Maybe it would finally spur him into action.

"Is that what you think this is about?" His nostrils flared.

"You think—what? That I'm not attracted to you?" He stalked closer, and I held my ground. "That I don't care about you?" I could feel the anger radiating off him in waves.

"I don't know!" I threw my hands in the air, fed up with this conversation. With him. I needed space. "It's not like you ever give any indication of what you're thinking. I thought I knew you, could read you, but you keep shutting me out."

By the time I was done speaking, my heart was pounding. A muscle in his jaw twitched, and I could feel the tension building like a storm ready to unleash.

He stepped closer, and I took a few steps back. The air was charged—one spark and it would combust. His eyes were dark, hooded. I licked my lips, feeling hot. Too hot.

But he didn't stop. He kept pursuing me until my back collided with the wall. I let out a little squeak, feeling a bit like a mouse trapped by a cat. He was toying with me. Hunting me.

"Should I touch you?" He grabbed my hips roughly, and my breath caught, lips parting. I...liked it. Liked the harshness of his grip and the intensity of his gaze.

He gave my hips a squeeze, and I nearly moaned in appreciation. I wanted to push him away. I needed him even closer. I was angry. I was turned on. I wished my heart would stop beating so hard so I could think straight.

"Should I kiss you?" He leaned in, his breath fanning across my hair. He smelled of mint and whiskey, and for a split second, I forgot why I was mad. "Is that what you want?"

He dragged his nose along the shell of my ear. My knees weakened, my entire body aching for his touch, angling toward him like a flower seeking the sun.

"Would that make me seem like more of a real husband?" he taunted. "Would that make you happy?"

CHAPTER EIGHTEEN

Graham

God, she smelled so good. Earthy and wild like my garden—my favorite place in the world. I inhaled her scent, waiting for her to pull away. Hoping she wouldn't.

She was angry. Hurt. And so was I.

Her earlier words had echoed painful comments from my past. And more recently, the article that had given me that detested moniker. I wasn't cold—I was calculating. Shrewd not heartless. People didn't appreciate the difference.

I didn't want to be cold or heartless, but if that was how I came across, then so be it. It was the only way to protect myself. Protect the people I loved.

But with Lily, I felt anything but cold. In fact, my heart was pumping so hard, it felt like rocket fuel surged through my veins. I burned for her.

Her comments stung, but I knew deep down that she was right. I should've told her everything. I should've trusted her, but it wasn't something that came easily to me. I wasn't used to showing my emotions or even letting myself feel them. That wasn't what my family needed, what the brand needed.

They needed strength. Confidence. Control.

But Lily was pushing me to open up. To communicate more. And it made me feel vulnerable in such a way that left me exposed. Weak.

After my parents' death, I'd vowed to never let myself feel that way again. I'd never allow myself to love something so deeply that I could be hurt so intensely. So, I'd suppressed my emotions. I'd denied the existence of my heart. And I'd been good at it. So good that everyone now believed that's who I truly was.

"I want…" She let out a shaky breath. Her pupils were dark, almost black.

"Mm?" I hummed, soaking in the feel of her skin, the warmth of her closeness. I didn't want to think about the past; I wanted to focus on the future.

But Lily wasn't my future, as much as I might want her to be. Which was why I should stop, but I couldn't seem to make myself. I'd never felt so at war with myself. I'd never wanted someone so badly.

My wife was going to drive me mad.

"Is this what you want? What you need from me?" I pushed, unable to resist. My patience was unraveling by the second.

But then she placed her hands against my chest and shoved. Not hard, but hard enough to snap me out of it, to make me take a step back. "Oh, fuck off, Graham."

"You sure that's what you want?" I arched my brow, challenging her as I ran my hand up her thigh, unable to resist. I couldn't stop thinking of the feel of her skin—so silky. So smooth. I couldn't stop touching her. I didn't want to.

"Yes. No." She groaned, goose bumps forming beneath my hand. "I just… I want you to talk to me."

Based on her body's reactions to me, I got the feeling that wasn't all she wanted. I maintained eye contact, determined not to be the first to look away. But fuck me, she was something. Sassy and strong and beautiful. This wasn't just about the physical attraction—though my cock hardened at the sight of her. I respected Lily.

The entire time she'd worked for me, I'd always secretly wondered if her skin was as soft as I'd hoped. Her lips as welcoming as I'd dreamed. Her body as supple as I'd imagined.

And now, she was in my arms.

I hadn't even kissed her, but she was already so responsive. Eyes dilated, pupils blown wide. Lips wet and begging for mine. Her small hands clutching my shirt to keep me close.

"I'm talking to you now."

"Keep talking." Her voice was breathy with want.

"That's all you want me to do? Talk?" I skimmed my nose along the edge of her jaw until I reached her ear. "You don't want me to fuck you?" I whispered. "Make you scream my name with pleasure?" Instead of cursing me.

"But, but—" She sputtered. "I thought you didn't mix business with pleasure."

How could I resist when she looked like this? Sounded like this? Desperate and needy and so fucking pretty.

I dragged my thumb down her throat, settling on her pulse point. Her heart was beating quickly, its pace matching my own.

I met her eyes, watching her. Waiting. "Apparently, you're the exception."

She swallowed hard, mesmerizing me with the long column of her throat. I imagined sliding my cock into her mouth, watching her take me deep.

"Do you truly believe I'm not attracted to you?" I arched up against her, letting her feel how hard I was for her.

She gasped. "I—you… What?"

"Because I am. You make me feel desperate, Lil." I kissed

her collarbone, the words tumbling out of me. She wanted me to talk, and now I couldn't stop. "This—" I placed her hand over my heart then slid it down to rest on my erection "—this is what you do to me."

"I-I..." She let out a shaky breath, and I catalogued all her reactions. Memorizing them.

Skin flushed. Lips puffy and parted in anticipation. Her hand giving a gentle squeeze.

I groaned, silently encouraging her to do it again. To do *more*. So when she started exploring me over my pants, I couldn't help it. "Fuck. That feels amazing."

Something shifted in her gaze, enough for me to lean in and brush my lips against hers.

"Tell me to stop," I rasped against her lips. But she didn't.

Instead, the kiss quickly turned heated—tongues and lips and teeth. A battle. A dance.

She gasped, arching up into me, grinding against me. "I'm still mad at you."

Her words, like her movements, were hard, meant to punish. Instead of pushing her away, I held her closer, looking into her eyes, even as we continued writhing against each other still fully clothed.

"So, be mad at me. Punish me." I pressed into her, pulling her more fully to me. Letting her feel me. I was so hard, I ached. But god, was this hot. She was hot. "I'd deserve it."

"I—" Her eyes darkened. "Yes."

I slid my hand up to cup her breast, measuring her response. Her breast was full, heavy, practically overflowing my hand. She was perfect. She was mine.

I pushed away that possessive instinct from the less-developed caveman part of my brain. She wasn't mine. And this wouldn't last. It never did.

"This doesn't change anything," she panted, perhaps at

war with herself. She was right, but I still hated to hear her say it.

"Of course not," I said, surprised by how level my voice sounded, even as I kissed her neck, her collarbone.

She grabbed my belt and yanked on it, bringing my attention back to her face. "And if you *ever*—" She gave it a tug, moving me like a puppet on a string. Hell, that's how I felt with her. At her bidding. "—lie to me again, we're done."

"I would expect nothing less."

"Good." She kissed me. Hard.

I crushed my lips against hers, intoxicated by her scent. By the feel of her in my arms. This woman was going to be my undoing.

I let myself get carried away. Let myself just feel—my mind blissfully blank of anything but Liliana and her scent. The little moans she made. The way she shifted her hips, as if seeking release.

Fuck. She was perfect.

The kiss at our wedding had been a shock—intense despite how chaste it had been in comparison. And this one was just as electrifying. We might not have an audience like we had at our wedding, but I wanted her, and she wanted this. We both knew exactly what this was—mutual release. Nothing more.

I couldn't offer anything more.

She clawed at my shirt, releasing the buttons from their holes. I scrambled to untie the straps that caressed her shoulders. Our clothes came off in a frantic, desperate rush until I was naked, and she was left in only her underwear.

In that moment, I swear my soul left my body. She was… God, she was magnificent. I didn't have the words to describe her, so instead, I tried to show her.

I kissed every inch of bare skin I uncovered, marveling at the heavy fall of her breasts, the dusty-rose color of her nipples, the dip of her navel. She writhed and moaned beneath my hands, pushing her breasts into my hands. Begging for my touch.

Her skin was so smooth, my hands slid over it like the finest silk. It was the most pleasurable sensation. And I couldn't wait to see what was beneath her underwear. Though, judging from the sheer panel at the front, she was completely bare. *Oh god.*

"Is this what you wanted from me?" I taunted, sliding my hand over her smooth mound and rubbing her clit through the material. She shivered. "Is this what you need, *mon petit poisson?*"

"Sit down and shut up." She pushed my chest, and I fell back onto the bed.

I tried to hold back my smile, but holy fuck was that hot.

I watched her from my elbows with a heated gaze, waiting to see what she'd do next. No one told me what to do. But I was willing to give Lily all the control. Hell, if I were honest with myself, she already had so much power over me it was terrifying.

Lily stood there, hands on her hips, staring at me. Admiring me. *Me.*

She grabbed the belt from my pants and walked beside the bed. I remained silent, full of eager anticipation. Excitement. My desire barely restrained. What would she do next?

"Sit up." Her voice was commanding, sexy.

Okay. I'd play along. I did as she asked.

"Hands behind your back."

I arched my brow. She held her ground, and I respected her all the more for it. I groaned inwardly—this woman was going to drive me mad with lust.

I placed my hands behind my back, and she secured them in place. The belt was wrapped around my wrists, so it was snug but not tight. With some effort, I could've gotten out of it, but I didn't want to.

"Is that...is that okay?" she asked, her voice a whisper of silk against my skin, her hair tickling my chest. It was the first time all evening she'd sounded almost hesitant. I appreciated her concern. She was angry, but she'd still checked in with me.

"Yes," I said, scarcely able to speak. My cock was so hard, it felt as if I might explode if she didn't touch me. "Wha—"

She pressed her finger to my lips, and I could feel my pulse beating there where our skin met. "Did I give you permission to speak?"

I shook my head, entranced by this new, commanding side to Lily. Had she always been this bossy? Or did I bring that out in her? I wanted to believe it was the latter. I wanted to believe this was just for me. All for me.

I'd never been with a woman who'd tried to dominate me. Wouldn't have thought I'd ever feel safe enough to let go, to trust someone like that. And as much as I craved control, as much as I wanted to torture her like she was me, part of me also wanted to surrender. Wanted to let someone else call the shots for a change. Not just anyone else—Lily. Being in charge all the time was fucking exhausting.

She smoothed her hands over my shoulders, watching me as she adjusted the pressure of her hands so it was just right. Her eyes lingered on my skin. "I'm in charge now." The words were scarcely above a whisper, but she commanded my attention all the same. "Do you understand?" She held my gaze without flinching. Without backing down.

I nodded. I was willing to do or say anything, so long as she continued touching me.

She stood at the foot of the bed, just out of reach. I bit back a groan. God, this was torture.

"From now on, you will communicate with me. Confide in me."

"Yes, ma'am," I said in a teasing tone.

She narrowed her eyes at me. "I mean it, Graham."

"I know." I sobered, letting her see my sincerity. "So do I."

She held my gaze a moment, then her expression softened, and she seemed satisfied. "Good. Now, we're going to work on your communication skills."

I arched my brow, intrigued. My cock was practically leaking from the tip at this point, the belt biting into my wrists in a way that was almost pleasurable. Ordinarily, something like that might have triggered my senses to go wild, but I was so keyed up that I'd barely noticed it. Even now, it was a welcome distraction from my need to drive into her relentlessly over and over.

"Every time you follow instructions or communicate with me," she continued, "you'll get a reward."

"What kind of reward?" I asked, intrigued. Fuck me, I was dying to know what she had in mind. I would've never expected this from her. I would've never expected that I'd like it.

"You tell me. What do you want?" she asked.

"Kiss me," I demanded. When she didn't move, didn't speak, I added, "Please?"

"Where?" she asked, prolonging my torture. "Here?" She placed her finger to my lips.

I nodded. She leaned forward, allowing no part of her body to touch mine apart from where our lips met. Our tongues tangled, and I groaned, trying to break free from my restraints so I could touch her. My muscles jumped from the strength it took to hold myself back. To wait for her to make her move.

She leaned back with a dazed expression that mirrored how I felt. "Where else?"

"Everywhere," I said the word on a sigh.

Hands on her hips. Fucking glorious. "You'll have to be more specific."

"Shoulder." One word. That was the most I could manage. *Pathetic.*

She placed the tip of her finger on my shoulder, and even that minimal contact had my skin heating. "Here?"

I nodded again. Again, she descended, her lips touching my skin. Fuck, she was sexy in control like this.

"Tell me if you don't like something. Or if you need me to touch you a different way."

I blinked a few times, stunned. She was the first woman I'd been with who had noticed. Who not only cared about my comfort and needs but made it a point to make me feel comfortable to express them.

"Graham?" she prompted.

"Yeah," I rasped, my throat clogged with emotion. "Yes. I will."

"Good. Now, where else do you want me to kiss you?" she asked.

I wanted to tell her to kiss me anywhere and everywhere, I didn't fucking care. But I knew that wasn't going to get me what I wanted. Lily wanted me to be specific. She wanted me to show her that I was listening. That I could and would cooperate.

I absolutely could. Because she made me feel safe to express my needs. She made me believe that she would not only listen but care.

"My...nipple," I said, my eyes snagging on her nipples. I wanted to suck them into my mouth until I released them with a pop, watching them pebble and harden.

"Here?" she asked, trailing her nail around one of my nipples. My cock jerked in attention. I hadn't expected it to feel that good.

"Yes." All I could think about was kissing her. Using my lips and my tongue and my teeth to drive her as crazy as she was currently making me.

"I need to touch you." I strained against the belt, eager to break free.

"No." Her tone was calm, but the word cracked through the air like a whip. "You need to learn to sit back and let someone else be in control."

Was that what this was? A test in restraint? Her exerting her dominance over me?

Because if so, fuck me, I was in. I was totally fucking in. I could give up control if she would keep touching me.

"Can you do that?" she asked. I got the feeling she was asking about more than just in the bedroom. And while I didn't know if I could let her lead outside the bedroom, she made me want to try.

"I—" She was so distracting, so beautiful, she made it difficult to think straight. Especially when she dragged her finger down my chest. "Harder," I said, referring to the pressure.

She immediately adjusted her pressure as she continued her way down to my stomach. I swallowed hard. "I can try."

She sighed, but the curve of her lips told me she was being playful. "I suppose that's a start."

"Does that mean I get another reward?" I asked. God, I sounded so fucking eager it was pathetic. No better than Queen V and Prince Albert when they were begging for a treat.

"Where else do you want me to touch you?" she asked.

"Anywhere," I gusted out, my body on overdrive from her touch. *Oh god.* She used just the right amount of pressure so that I could lean into her touch instead of recoiling from it.

And something about being restrained, about her being in

control, had somehow dulled some of my sensitivity to textures. Or at least, that's how it felt.

She glared at me. *Right. Be specific.*

"My cock," I rasped, scarcely able to speak. "I want you to suck my cock."

She didn't even bat an eye at my request. She got on her knees on the floor before me. She looked like a fucking queen.

"How do you like it?" she asked.

"Lick the tip. Swirl your tongue around it."

"Like this?" She did as I asked—fucking perfect. And I damn near bolted off the bed.

"Yes," I hissed as she continued to lick and suck me. "Yes. *Fuck.*"

I could feel the orgasm building in my spine. I clutched the sheets behind my back. It was coming too fast. But then she gripped my base and held me firmly. My eyes nearly rolled back into my head, and I saw stars.

"You like that?" she asked.

"Yes," I groaned.

She held my base firmly while licking and sucking the tip of my cock. It was heaven and hell. I came so close to coming, but then her lips were gone. Her hand was stroking me and it felt good, but it wasn't her mouth. I *wanted* her mouth on me.

"Graham," she rasped. I swallowed hard at the sound of my name on her lips. Lips that had just been wrapped around my cock. She peered up at me from beneath her lashes. "Do you want me to keep sucking you off?"

"Yes. Please," I gritted out.

She pumped me, edging me as she licked my balls. *Oh god.*

"Do you promise to show some emotion in public?" Her breasts rubbed against my balls as she continued stroking me, occasionally dipping down to take my tip in her mouth and swirl her tongue around it. "I'm not asking for you to be vulnerable with everyone. I just need you to show up for me. To be my partner."

"I'll...try." I practically croaked out the word.

"No." She stood from the floor, her movements graceful and full of power as she dragged her fingers along my skin. She grasped my shoulders and straddled me. "That's not good enough. If you want to save your company, you have to."

"I'm not sure I can." *Show the emotion or save the company.* I'd spent so many years burying my feelings that I wasn't sure I could even find them anymore.

She grabbed the base of my cock, circling it tightly with her fingers. She continued to rock against me while maintaining that pressure at the base, making me both harder than ever and yet unable to find my release.

"I know you. You're one of the most stubborn and determined people I've ever met. If you want to do something, you will."

I watched Lily, waiting. Her eyes were full of fire, and she was a sight to behold. Determined. Beautiful. Strong.

"Please," she whispered. "Tell me you will."

In the past, I would've lashed out, pushed her even further away. But deep down, I knew she was right. And I knew I couldn't run from this—her. I didn't want to. She was my wife, and we were in this together. If anyone made me want to try, it was this woman.

"I will," I whispered back. "I will," I said again more loudly.

"Good." She released her hold on my cock and rocked against me. I forgot everything but the feel of her.

Unable to balance with my wrists bound, I growled my

frustration. "Untie me. *Please*," I tacked on. "I want to touch you."

She reached behind me and unhooked the belt, freeing my wrists. I immediately reached out for her, desperate to touch her. She gave a little squeak when I squeezed her ass.

"Graham." She narrowed her eyes at me.

"What?" I dragged my nose down her cheek. "I'm just practicing for when we're in public."

"We're not going to be naked in public."

"Mm. Perhaps not." But I hated feeling exposed. And baring myself emotionally felt almost worse than what I imagined it would be like to be naked in public.

I slid my hands up her back and into her hair. Before I could massage her scalp, she grabbed my wrists and pulled my hands so they were cupping her breasts.

"God, yes." She arched her back, her pussy sliding over my cock. "Please tell me you have a condom."

I squeezed my eyes shut, forcing myself to stop moving. "I don't."

"What about the bathroom? Do you think there's one in there?" she asked, clearly not getting the memo that we needed to stop. Soon, it would be too late for a condom.

"Unfortunately, this isn't the Huxley Grand," I lamented. "And I doubt there are complimentary intimacy kits in the bathroom."

"Technically, you are my husband. And by the terms of our agreement, I'm only allowed to have sex with you."

I chuckled. "Which section was that outlined in?"

She slapped my chest, and my dick twitched in response. She smirked. "Mm. You liked that."

"I—" Before I could answer, she ground against me again. *Fuck.* I gripped her hips. "Stop trying to distract me, wife."

"But it's so much fun, husband." There was a wicked gleam in her eyes.

"I, um—" I cleared my throat. "I've never had sex without a condom."

"Neither have I. Not that I've been with anyone in quite a while." I shouldn't have been as pleased by the thought as I was.

Was she suggesting what I thought she was? My dick twitched, and she groaned, grinding herself against me.

"I want you inside me," she whispered into my ear, still rocking against me. "I'm on birth control."

I couldn't believe what she was offering me. It wasn't something I took lightly, but the idea of fucking her bare was…oh god. I didn't know if I had it in me to resist.

"I want that too," I said, cupping the back of her neck. "But are you sure?"

"Yes," she said with zero hesitation.

Maybe I hadn't completely fucked up. If she was willing to honor me with her body, maybe I could earn her trust once more.

I gripped my cock at the base, positioning it at her entrance. "Last chance to back out."

"I don't want an out," she said, repeating the words she'd said to me on our wedding day. And then she sank down on me, and I let out a strangled cry. Oh god. My entire body quivered with delight. She felt so good, especially as she began to ride me, taking control anew.

"Fuck yes," I rasped, my hands on her breasts, her back, her ass. I slid my hand up her spine, gathering her hair and loosely wrapping it around my fist.

She slid her hands to my wrists, guiding my hands to her back. I leaned forward and kissed her neck, drinking her in. Then I worked my way down to her nipple, sucking it into my mouth, swirling my tongue around the tip until she was crying out.

"Keep going." I gave her ass a playful slap. "Don't you dare fucking stop."

She gripped my chin, hard. "If you can be this passionate, sensual man in private, then you can show some emotion in public." Her skin was flushed with color. She was mad. She was turned on. She was… Oh fuck. She was going to push me over the edge.

I felt everything all at once, and it was too much.

I rolled us so I was on top. I grabbed her hands, interlocking our fingers. She was giving me so much of herself, I found myself wanting to give her something in return. "Maybe I want everyone to believe I'm a cold, heartless billionaire."

She locked her legs around my hips, pulling me closer. Our movements were aggressive, angry even. "Why?"

I got the feeling that she was genuinely confused. And that she was trying to understand.

"Maybe it's because that's what I truly am." Sweat dripped down my forehead as I tried to hold back. Tried to wait for her to climax first.

I reached between us, teasing her clit with my thumb. I watched her expression, listened to the sounds she made, determined to learn what gave her pleasure. I ducked my head, sucking one nipple then the other between my lips. She writhed on the sheets, clawing my back with her nails. *Fuck,* that felt good. So good.

"You don't really believe that, do you?" She rocked so she was on top once more. She peered down at me from her position, her hair dusting my pecs, her glorious body on display for me.

I cupped her breasts, tweaking her nipples, hoping to distract her from her questions. She'd already broken through so many of my walls, I was afraid to let her in further. Afraid if I did, everything would come crashing down.

I covered her lips with mine, silencing her with my mouth, my hands, my cock. But she wouldn't let it go.

She met my eyes, the calm in the storm. Her body was slick with sweat, and the room echoed with the sounds of our pleasure. "Maybe it's not everyone else who needs convincing. It's you."

CHAPTER NINETEEN

Lily

Graham flipped me over so I was lying on my stomach. I wondered if he was trying to regain control after my comment. Control over me? Over himself? Maybe just over the situation.

And he was doing a good job of it—distracting me. Especially when he trailed his fingers down my back, eliciting a shudder.

I glanced at him over my shoulder, biting back a groan at the sight of him. God, he was sexy. A sculpted chest that would make an artist weep. A dark trail of hair that led to his long, proud cock.

He leaned forward, and with his hands resting on my hips, he asked, "Is this okay?"

"Yes." I wiggled my butt in invitation. I didn't want to go back to his cold façade, and I could tell that was what he was trying to do. He might be checking in with me, but he was also checking out. It was kind of fascinating to watch him battle himself.

He gripped my hips, my ass, giving it the most delicious squeeze. I knew this was a bad idea, but that was a problem for future me. Because if having sex got Graham to open up to me, even briefly, to communicate with me, then I wasn't sure I could regret it.

Graham lined himself up with my entrance, slowly sheathing himself inch by delicious inch. It was torture of the best kind. I moaned into the mattress, overwhelmed by the feel of having him so deep inside me.

I was still pissed. But currently, my brain was too overwhelmed with pleasure to think much beyond the present. Beyond the feel of the way our bodies were connected.

He grasped my hips and pulled me up so my ass was in the air, my cheek pressed to the bed. I closed my eyes, gasping at the new position, at the depth. It was so intense. Almost too intense.

"You okay?" he asked, checking in with me again.

I nodded.

"Lil?" he bit out, and I realized how much restraint it took to hold himself still. And yet he waited, seeking that verbal confirmation.

"Yes." I swallowed. "*Yes.* But I need you to move."

He gave my ass a squeeze and edged himself in a little deeper. I hadn't realized he wasn't fully seated until then. I sucked in a jagged breath at the sensation of fullness. I gripped the sheets, twisting the material in my fists, as if to gain purchase.

"Fuck. You're so tight." It sounded like it pained him. "You feel so fucking good."

"Look at you, using your words," I teased, wanting to get us back to that place where he was playful and engaged.

His hand gave a sharp crack as it hit my ass, scorching my skin. Pain and pleasure bloomed in the spot where he'd spanked me, and I closed my eyes as I tried to find my bearings. I'd never been spanked. Never even considered that it was something I might enjoy, let alone with my ex-boss.

I was supposed to be in control. I was the one making the demands, and yet, he'd completely flipped the script once again.

Up was down. Day was night. We might be moored on the yacht, but I felt lost at sea. Especially when he smoothed his hand over the skin, rubbing circles until the sensation faded. How could he shift so quickly from punishing to tender? How did he seem to anticipate exactly what I needed when I wasn't even sure what I wanted?

"Love your curves."

He did?

While I was still grappling with that revelation, he gripped my hip with one hand and smoothed the other up my spine. I felt his desire in every caress. I melted beneath his touch, my body going into overdrive. My pleasure building and building until I thought I might explode.

Oh god. I nearly whimpered at the sensations.

"Are you close?" he rasped, his control slipping. "Please tell me you're close, *mon bijou.*"

It was the sound of the French term for "my jewel" on his lips that nearly pushed me over the edge. "Yes." My voice was breathy. It didn't even sound like me.

"I can feel your pretty cunt squeezing my cock. God—" I moaned in response to his words. "You're so tight. So perfect."

He seemed to have no problem finding his words now. If only I could get him to communicate like this with me all the time. But then I imagined his deep, roughened voice whispering such naughty things to me over dinner with his family, and I nearly came on the spot.

"I'm almost there," I cried out. "But I want us to come together." I felt as if I were holding on for dear life as he pounded into me, chasing our mutual release.

"Partners," he said.

"Partners," I repeated, my mind freezing on that word even though my thoughts were barely coherent.

"Yes," he hissed. He moved harder and harder, faster, until I was completely untethered, the world spinning around me in a blur of stars and colors.

"Oh my fucking god," I cried out. "Oh…" I squeezed my eyes shut, everything going black as I was consumed with pleasure.

Graham convulsed, emptying himself into me until we were both panting and sated. He rested his cheek on my back, and I could feel his heart beating quickly, his cock twitching inside me. I wasn't sure I'd ever felt this close to anyone.

When he pulled out, he lifted one of my ass cheeks. I glanced at him over my shoulder, and he wore a dazed expression. "Fuck me. That's hot."

He dragged his fingers through the wetness seeping from me, our desire coating his digits. He lifted it to my lips. "Suck."

I held his gaze as I opened my mouth, pulling his fingers inside before licking them clean. He growled, and I wasn't sure I'd ever seen him look more…feral. It only made me realize just how wrong I'd been about Graham, the situation, myself, everything.

I am in so far over my head.

I ROLLED TO MY SIDE, FEELING A GENTLE ROCKING SENSATION as I woke, trying to remember where I was. In the past week, I'd jumped from France to Mexico and now to LA. It was disorienting, to say the least. Not to mention the drastic change in my circumstances.

Married. I was married to my billionaire ex-boss. And, unless last night was a dream—and part of me really hoped it was—I'd slept with my fake husband. My fake husband who was paying me to be his wife.

Way to go, Lil.

But god, was it good. I mean *really* good.

I kept my eyes screwed tightly shut, not ready to face reality. As far as I could tell, Graham was still in bed behind me. And, if I was lucky, he was still asleep.

I cracked one eye open, surveying our cabin. The sun peeked through the curtains, and I knew it was only a matter of time before he was awake. Hell, I was surprised he wasn't already up, showered, and dressed. He was typically an early riser.

Desperate to avoid what was likely to be an awkward conversation—at least for a little longer—I carefully scooted to the edge of the mattress. I made as little noise as possible, pushing out of bed and wrapping a robe around me.

Graham looked so peaceful—lying on his stomach, an arm thrown over his head. I wasn't sure I'd ever seen him more relaxed, and I softened. I wondered if he ever let himself put down all the heavy burdens he was carrying.

I let myself linger a moment longer, drinking in the sight of him. A wayward curl hung down his forehead, scruff lining his jaw. He shifted, and the sheet slid lower on his hips, giving me a tantalizing glimpse of his backside. I had to bite back a sigh. Last night had been fun, but it couldn't happen again.

I tiptoed to the bathroom, softly pulling the door closed behind me and locking it. I switched on the shower and waited for the water to heat. My body ached in all the right places, and while I longed to climb back into bed, to sink back down on him, to have him all to myself in the most intimate of ways, I knew it was a bad idea.

Once was a mistake. Twice was... Well. I shook my head, forcing away images of a repeat of last night, because it wasn't happening. Graham was like fire and ice. Either way, I was going to get burned.

I readjusted my wig and twisted it up beneath a shower cap I'd found beneath the sink. Luckily, I still had a few weeks before I'd need to remove it and give my scalp a chance to breathe.

I dropped my robe to the floor and climbed beneath the spray. I wanted to bury my face in my hands, but I couldn't mess up my makeup. Fortunately, I had a pencil to touch up my brows. But these lashes had to stay on until we got back to the penthouse.

I groaned. *What were you thinking, Lil?*

I wasn't sure whether it was my own inner voice asking me that or Jo's. Either way, my business arrangement was getting messy. *Too messy.*

And if there was one thing Graham hated, it was messes.

Which was why part of me was surprised that he'd let things go as far as he had. Was it really about wanting me? Or had he been trying to prove a point?

I sighed, bracing my hand on the cold wall of tile. My thoughts were a tangled mess. This wasn't supposed to happen. I wasn't supposed to have sex with my fake husband.

I needed to stop thinking about last night and figure out how to smooth things over with Graham. How to build on the progress we'd made with communication, but also, how to go back to how things had been—at least physically.

I rinsed and toweled off before wrapping myself in a robe. I debated texting Jo but decided against it. I'd gotten myself into this mess, and I'd get myself out of it.

Besides, she was in Sedona for her retreat. And I didn't

want to distract her focus from that. So, I finger-combed my wig to make sure it looked natural. My clothes were still discarded on the bedroom floor, and I tried to steel myself as I opened the door to the bedroom once more.

Graham was sitting at the table in a robe, his hair mussed. He assessed me over the top of his mug of coffee and arched one brow. "Morning."

God, I could get used to that gravelly morning voice. Waking up in bed with him after a night of amazing— *Nope. Stop.*

"Morning," I said, trying not to look as sheepish as I felt.

He slid a mug toward me. I tried to get a read on him, but he was just as closed off as before. It was almost as if last night had never happened. I wasn't sure whether that was a good thing or not, but it meant that all the progress we'd made was just…gone.

"I got you an oat latte," he said. "Everyone will eat breakfast together upstairs, unless you'd rather stay in and order a tray."

Tempting as it was to hide away in our cabin, I said, "We should probably make an appearance, don't you think?"

He assessed me. "Yes. We should."

"Thanks for the coffee." I picked it up, noting that he'd folded my clothes into a neat pile and set them on the end of the bed. A bed he'd made with the precision of one of the members of the housekeeping staff at the Huxley Grand.

I slid my free hand over the comforter, impressed by how smooth he'd gotten the material despite our nocturnal activities. "I'm impressed, husband."

"Why? Because I can make a bed?"

"Make a bed?" I scoffed. He was totally downplaying his skills. "This is expert-level bed-making. I'm not sure any of my exes even knew how to make a bed, period. Let alone how to make it look like a five-star hotel."

"Clearly, the men from your past were inferior."

"Clearly," I drawled. If only he knew. "If I were looking for a househusband, you'd definitely be a front-runner."

He stood, a menacing look in his eye. "A front-runner?"

"To be fair," I teased, "I'd have to evaluate your other skills."

What am I doing? This wasn't at all how I'd imagined this conversation in my head, but I supposed I should just be grateful that it wasn't awkward.

"I should hope last night would've dispelled any doubts as to my other *skills*." His tone was laced with an undercurrent of desire.

Is he... Was Graham flirting with me?

My body quivered with anticipation, my core heating, but I quickly shut it down. Trying to shut out the memories of last night, but it was damn near impossible. At some point in the night, Graham had woken me with his head between my thighs. It was like a fever dream, him pulling me on top of his face, eating me out until I came on his tongue. His body hovering over me, eyes locked on mine. His deliciously wicked words. *That mouth.* His fucking mouth.

Stop!

"Actually, I'm glad you brought up last night." I straightened, trying to seem confident and at ease when I felt anything but. "It was...fun," I said, finally settling on the word, even though it was woefully inadequate. "But we both know it can't happen again." There. I'd said it.

"I completely agree." Wow. He hadn't even missed a beat. Hadn't needed to consider it at all.

I jerked my head back. "You do?"

I wasn't sure why that surprised me. Or maybe that was disappointment I was feeling. I guessed, deep down, some small part of me had hoped that he'd try to fight me on it.

That he'd try to convince me it wasn't a big deal. That we should sleep together again.

But he hadn't.

My heart sank, wondering if he was filled with regret. No, Graham didn't do regrets or remorse.

We were in agreement. I should be happy about it. He was making this easy on me.

"Yes. We got carried away, but as you reminded me, I don't mix business with pleasure. This is a business agreement," he said, emphasizing the word business. "And there's a lot at stake."

"Exactly," I said, though the word sounded hollow to my ears.

This was for the best. At least, that's what I kept telling myself.

CHAPTER TWENTY

Graham

"Lil?" I called out from the foyer of my penthouse. "The car is almost here."

"I'll be ready in a sec!" she yelled from down the hall. "Promise."

I chuckled to myself. We'd survived the ordeal on Knox's yacht, and now we were attending a charity event with Nate and Emerson to benefit an LA animal shelter. It was a cause I was passionate about, but I didn't fucking want to go.

I wanted to stay home, drink my whiskey. And putter around in the garden with Brooklyn. But Lily and I were leaving for France soon, and this was a good opportunity to show off my wife.

I heard the click-clack of high heels, and then Lily emerged from her bedroom. *Fuck me.* My wife was stunning.

I drank in the sight of her. Those gold sandals that showed off her perfectly painted lilac toenails. A white dress clung to her curves, a cape draping over one shoulder. The other was bare. The cut was relatively modest, and she looked elegant, graceful, and refined.

I imagined the dress pooled on the floor at her feet.

Wondered what she was wearing beneath it. Wondered if she was naked like she had been on our wedding day.

Stop. Just stop.

We'd agreed this was just business despite our momentary lapse of judgment, and I needed to remember that. But every day I spent with Lily, every moment I spent in her presence, was like a cruel kind of torture. I wanted her, but I couldn't have her.

"Is this okay?" Her cheeks were the most alluring shade of pink. "I've never attended one of these events as a guest before."

"Yes," I choked out. *More than okay.*

She stepped closer, and I felt as if I might combust. It had been days since the incident on Knox's yacht, and I couldn't stop thinking about that night. Not just the sex, though that was definitely on my mind more often than not.

But also, the things she'd said to me. Even now, Lily's words continued to rattle around in my head. Her insinuation that *I* was the one who needed convincing that I wasn't cold and heartless.

She adjusted my bow tie then smoothed her hands down my lapels. "What are you going to do tonight?" Lily asked. Her touch made it difficult to think straight, let alone speak.

Was there something I was supposed to do tonight? Because all I wanted to do was stay home and lose myself in her.

I didn't want to show her off; I wanted to keep her to myself. And that was a problem. That was the whole point of this arrangement.

"Graham?" she prompted, and her commanding tone took me right back to *that* night. *Fuck.*

"Hm?" I asked, eager to do whatever she asked. Anything she asked.

"At the gala?" she added.

Right. The gala. I tried not to outwardly sigh.

"Make a spectacle by publicly donating a fuck-ton of money?" I asked, trying to will away my hard-on. Knowing that if she stepped even an inch closer, she'd feel how much I wanted her.

"Yes, *and...*" She tilted her head. "What else did you agree to do?"

Right. *That.* Fuck.

"Show some emotion," I said, trying not to groan. Of all days to have to show some fucking emotion.

"Exactly. You've got this." She gave my chest a pat. "It's the perfect event for you. I hear there will be animals there. Maybe they'll even have a chicken for you to cuddle." She winked then turned to walk off.

"Not so fast," I said, grabbing her wrist and spinning her back to face me. She hadn't expected that, and she almost twirled straight into me. "I have something for you."

"You do?" she asked, breathless.

I want her. I stared at her lips—pouty, pink, begging to be kissed. *Again and again and again.*

I released her and grabbed the velvet box from the coffee table. "For you."

She frowned down at the box. "What's this?"

"Open it and see," I said.

She opened the box and gasped. "Wow."

"They're French. From the same time period as your château."

"They..." Her eyes darted to mine. "What?"

"Try them on."

"I don't think my ears can handle the weight," she joked. Though, honestly, they had to be a bit heavy.

Each earring had a huge pear-shaped diamond encircled by smaller diamonds, which hung from a short diamond link that connected to a triangular-shaped stud. They were magnificent, a statement.

"You don't have to wear them if you don't want to. Or if they're not your style." I'd just wanted to do something nice for her. Surprise her. And I was fucking this all up.

"Are you kidding?" she asked. "They're incredible."

"Nate loaned them to me from his private collection."

Her eyes widened. "Are you serious?" She pushed the box back toward me. "I can't wear those. They're his mom's."

Nate's mom had collected rare jewelry. Knox had inherited a few pieces, but Nate had the bulk of it.

"God, I can't even imagine how much these earrings must be worth," she said. "Shouldn't they be in a museum or something?"

"Beautiful objects are meant to be enjoyed," I said, thinking of the art I'd inherited from my grandfather. "Besides, they're insured."

"Yeah, but they're one of a kind. Irreplaceable."

"*Things* can be replaced." I removed one earring from its spot, nestled on velvet. "People can't. And Nate's happy for you to enjoy them for the evening."

"Really?"

"Does that surprise you?"

"Yes. He barely even knows me."

"You're my wife, and I won these. For you."

"What do you mean, won them?" She narrowed her eyes.

"My brothers and I play a weekly game of poker. Jackson joins us when he's in town. Pierce sometimes too. We typically wager things or experiences, not money. Borrow jewelry or box seats to a big game or the chance to drive one of Jasper's classic cars."

"Huh." She tilted her head, a thoughtful expression on her face.

"What?" I asked.

"It's just hard for me to imagine having that kind of relationship with my siblings."

"I'm sorry that hasn't been your experience with your siblings, but you know mine are more than happy to welcome you to the family." At least they had been after they'd gotten past their initial shock that night on the yacht.

Since then, they'd invited us to so many dinners and events, I could barely keep up. And Kendall and Emerson had been eager to include Lily in their weekly yoga sessions, among other things. I was grateful to them for welcoming her into the fold.

Lily smiled, though it was tinged with sadness. "I feel bad, though. Knowing that I'm lying to your family."

"You're also helping them."

She scoffed, clearly doubtful.

"You're helping me," I said. "Fuck. You know how much I hate attending these events. Having you by my side will make it easier."

She arched a brow. "You don't usually admit stuff like that."

"I'm trying this new thing my brilliant wife told me about. It's called communication."

She laughed, seeming a little lighter.

"May I?" I asked, holding out the earring.

Lily turned so her back was to me, sliding her hair away from her ear. I placed the earring through the hole in her lobe then slid the back on. She shivered, and I moved to the next ear.

"Are you cold?" I asked. "Nervous?"

"A little," she said, and I wondered if she was both.

"Don't worry," I offered. "Most people will be too dazzled by Nate and Emerson to pay us much attention."

"Yeah, but we'll be seated with them. And didn't you say some of the board members will be there?"

THE EXCEPTION

"Mm-hmm." I guided her closer to the wall of windows overlooking my garden and the terrace, letting her see her reflection. "What do you think?"

"I think..." I could hear the smile in her voice. "That I look the part—wife of a billionaire."

"You look beautiful," I said, not sure why her words grated on me.

"Thank you." She met my eyes in our reflection in the glass. "You really think people will buy this? Us?" she asked.

"You did a good job with my family. And I promise to do a better job pretending tonight too."

"Good. I'd hate to have a repeat of what happened on Knox's yacht." Her eyes widened as soon as the words had left her mouth. Her honesty felt like a punch to the gut. "What I meant was—"

My phone buzzed. "Our driver is waiting downstairs."

"Right, um. Right." She seemed flustered, and my good mood evaporated with her words.

I'd hate to have a repeat of what happened on Knox's yacht.

Was she referring solely to our fight or also to what had come after? To the intense, passionate way we'd claimed each other? Fuck. My head was such a mess over this woman.

I usually had no problem sticking to my rules. And yet with Lily, I found myself wanting to break each and every one of them.

"OH FUCK." NATE TURNED AWAY FROM WHERE EMERSON stood across the room, a determined look on her face as she scanned the crowd for him.

I twisted my wedding ring on my finger. People were

everywhere. I hated attending these types of events, but Nate had always thrived in the spotlight. I envied him for it—for the way he so easily interacted with people in social settings. When I'd rather be anywhere else.

"What?" I asked as he grabbed my elbow and dragged me toward the bathroom. "What are you doing?"

"Quick. Hide."

I followed him, no questions asked. Had he spotted a fan he wanted to avoid? And where the hell was his bodyguard?

Nate pulled me around the corner, hiding us in an alcove. "Is she coming?"

"Who?" I asked.

"Emerson," he gritted out.

I peeked my head around the corner, feeling like we were fourteen again and not in our forties. "No. She got sucked into a conversation with someone."

"Good." He panted.

I turned to him, brow creased. "What's going on? Why are you hiding from your wife?"

"Because she wants to adopt another puppy."

"You just can't say no to her, can you?"

"It's not that." He glanced away briefly. "I've already arranged for us to adopt it, and I wanted it to be a surprise."

"Oh my god," I groaned under my breath. He was such a sap when it came to Emerson, but I was glad he was so happy. I thought back to what Pierce had told me about their relationship starting off as fake. I wondered what had changed. How they'd gone from dislike to disgustingly in love.

"Oh, come on," Nate said. "You'd do the same for Lily, wouldn't you?" He shook his head. "I don't even have to ask. You're splitting your time between LA and France. That says it all."

"I'm excited to see the château in person," I admitted.

"You've never visited?" He gawked at me. "I thought you'd been doing the long-distance thing."

Right. Shit.

"Yeah. We have, but we usually tried to split the distance."

"I bet that was exhausting."

I lifted a shoulder. "You know how it is to travel," I said, not wanting to outright lie any more than I already had.

"I can't believe how quickly everything is changing. Our family is growing."

I glanced back at Emerson, eyeing her flat stomach as she led Lily out to the dance floor. First Sloan was pregnant, now Emerson?

Nate elbowed me. "I was referring to you marrying Lily and my new dog."

"Right."

He clapped a hand on my shoulder and leaned in. "A word of advice from one married man to another."

"What's that?" I asked, following his gaze to where Emerson and Lily were on the dance floor. I'd never seen her let loose like this, have fun. A smile lit up her face, and she shook her ass in a way that was undeniably tantalizing.

"Women love the big, romantic gestures, but the small ones are just as important." He took a swig of whiskey. "Like dancing. I get the feeling Lily would love for you to ask her to dance."

"I don't dance." Correction—I hadn't in a very long time.

"But you will for her. Especially since I'm guessing she didn't get a first dance at your wedding."

Fuck. He was right. I really hoped he wasn't going to lecture me about not having family at the wedding.

"Look," he said. "I know I owe you for what you did—"

"You don't owe me anything," I said, though we both knew exactly what he was referring to. I'd never admit that my hacking had led his ex-wife to drop her custody battle and her demand for something she didn't deserve.

He held my attention, unwilling to let me look away. "I just wanted to say thank you. Will you let me thank you? You don't have to admit to anything," he huffed.

I nodded, swallowing back my emotions. "You know I'd do anything for Brooklyn. And you."

He draped his arm over my shoulder. "I know. But sometimes, you should let us return the favor. Let us be there for you. That's what family does."

I grunted my assent.

He chuckled. "And here I thought marriage might help you get in touch with your feelings," he teased.

"I may not wear my feelings on my sleeve like some people—" I gave him a meaningful look "—but that doesn't mean I'm not in touch with them."

"Touché." He tilted his glass at me before downing the rest. "I'm glad you found Lily. Em might be a pain in my ass at times, but I can't imagine my life without her."

"You should mention that in your next award acceptance speech," I deadpanned.

"Oh, I will. But more importantly, I tell her that every damn day."

I moved to leave, but he placed a hand on my shoulder, steadying me. "I know I'm being sappy, but fuck." He smoothed a hand over his hair. "It's the anniversary of…" He trailed off. We both knew exactly what today marked, even if we weren't willing to say it aloud.

The day his parents and mine had died in a plane crash. The day that had changed the entire trajectory of our family's lives.

"I know." My tone was solemn. As if I could forget.

"Come on," Nate said. "Let's go celebrate the fact that we're alive with the people we love."

Love. I was incapable of love. But Nate didn't seem to think so.

Was Lily right about me? Was I the one who needed to alter my thoughts?

The song changed, shifting to something slower. A man approached Lily, and I shoved my hands into my pockets, watching, waiting to see how she'd react. She was smiling, but it was tight, forced. And even after she shook her head, the man didn't budge. When he turned his head, I saw red.

Moretti.

First, he was trying to take my company, and now my wife?

I stalked over to them. "Lily." Her name came out as more of a snarl. I wrapped my arm around her waist. "Sorry for the delay. You good?"

She nodded.

"Moretti." I lifted my chin. "I see you've met my wife."

"Yes," he mused. "Congratulations. And I look forward to discussing the marriage of our two illustrious companies."

Fucking Moretti.

I ground my molars, but before I could say anything, Lily jumped in. "Graham, it's our song."

I peered down at her, trying not to let my confusion show. *Our song?* Her eyes sparkled, and I found myself nodding. "That's right. Dance with me."

I ignored Moretti completely, sweeping my wife onto the dance floor. She placed her hand in mine and rested the other on my shoulder. I slid my hand over her hip. She smelled fucking delicious. It calmed me, but I could still feel Moretti's eyes on us, watching us. I didn't like it.

"Graham," she said, placing her palm on my cheek and smiling up at me. "Relax."

"I. Can't," I gritted out.

She laughed as if I'd said the funniest thing in the world.

Then she leaned in, her lips grazing the shell of my ear. "Yes. You can."

"You're the one who told me to show some emotion." I spun her out before pulling her back into me, holding her even closer than before. I cupped her hand over my heart, our pelvises kissing.

"You were definitely showing some emotion. You looked like you were going to rip his head off." She arched her brow.

"He'd deserve it."

"Completely agree. I was two seconds away from kneeing him in the balls before you showed up."

"You were?" I asked.

"Fuck yeah. He wants to steal your company."

I didn't know why, but her words filled me with a sense of pride and satisfaction. It was nice to have someone in my corner, ready to leap to my defense.

"So, this is our song, huh?" I asked, finally calming down enough to listen to the lyrics. A man sang about loving all your imperfections and giving your all to a partner, and it was really quite soulful.

"I guess so." Lily grinned, and I spun her again. "Where'd you learn to dance like this?"

"Many years ago, when I was a kid, a princess and her family stayed at one of our hotels for the summer."

"Really?" she gasped. "Which one?"

"The Huxley Grand Luxembourg."

She leveled me with a look. "No. Which princess?"

I shook my head, my lips sealed. "Doesn't matter. The point is, she needed someone to practice dancing with, and my grandparents volunteered me."

She gaped at me. "You've danced with a princess? How am I supposed to compete with that?"

"There's no competition, *ma reine*." I took a step back, holding her hand and bowing slightly at the waist.

Her cheeks turned a beautiful shade of pink, like the peonies that blossomed in my garden in the spring and early summer. Oh, she liked that. She liked being called my queen, and I liked her reaction.

"Everyone's watching," she whispered, quivering in my arms.

I straightened and turned her so her back was to me. I wrapped her arms around my neck and cascaded my hands down her curves. I wouldn't allow myself to touch her when we were alone—she didn't want that. So, if this was my only chance, I was going to take full advantage of it.

I dipped my head, keeping my words low just for her. "Do you like that? Do you want them to watch?"

She sucked in a sharp breath, and I had a sudden vision of fucking her in front of a mirror. Her eyes locked on our reflection as I took my time to explore every inch of her. I bit back my groan.

"That's what you want, isn't it? You want them to watch us. To see us together. To *believe*." She kept her voice low, and it wove around me. Seductive. Alluring. "You're really good at pretending when you put your mind to it. Very convincing."

Convincing, right. I supposed I should be grateful Lily was pleased that I was playing the role of besotted husband. But that was the trouble, wasn't it? She didn't realize it wasn't *all* for show. She didn't realize how I felt about her. I wasn't sure I'd call it love, but it wasn't lust either. I couldn't stop thinking about her, and not just that night.

My mood soured, but I tried not to let it show. When the song changed to something more upbeat, I took the opportunity to excuse myself to get a drink.

As I sipped my whiskey and looked out over the room, I wondered what the hell was wrong with me. This was exactly what I'd wanted, wasn't it?

CHAPTER TWENTY-ONE

Lily

Graham stared up at the château, while Queen V and Prince Albert lumbered across the expansive lawn. I'd just finished giving him a tour of the grounds, the dry moat, and the château itself. After having been away for nearly two weeks, I felt as if I were viewing the project with fresh eyes.

Luc and the team had accomplished a lot while I'd been gone, but even so, I could only imagine how it appeared to Graham. Was he regretting his investment? Thinking the restoration was ill-fated?

So far, I'd done everything I could to live up to my end of the deal. Before leaving LA, we'd attended a charity function, and I was still thinking about it. Graham had done such a good job that night, even I'd been hard-pressed to remember it was all pretend. With his front brushing my back, his hands skimming my body… I shivered at the memory. At the way his deep voice had sounded when he'd called me his queen and asked if I liked being watched.

Holy hell.

I'd been ready to throw myself at him. To let him do whatever he wanted with me, right there, right then, regardless of who might be watching. Maybe even *because* they were watching.

What is wrong with me?

This was a fake marriage. My husband had hacked my blog. Though, some of my anger had since faded.

Graham was trying to make amends. He'd insisted on helping me beef up the cybersecurity on my blog and YouStream channel. He'd also had a team from Hudson Security install security cameras at the château, both for insurance purposes and to enable me to see what was going on.

And, okay, so I was attracted to him. I told myself that wasn't a bad thing. That spark made it easier to convince everyone else we were a happily married couple.

"You should be proud of yourself," Graham said.

I eyed him skeptically. Was he mocking me? I didn't think so. He sounded sincere.

"I mean it, Lil. What you've done is incredible. The scope of this project…" He shook his head, rubbing a hand over his mouth as he surveyed the château. "I don't think I fully comprehended it until I was standing here, seeing everything you've accomplished."

I wanted to bask in his praise, like a flower that finally felt the sun after a long, cold winter. It was so nice to have someone see what I'd done and appreciate it. Someone whose opinion I respected. Someone I admired.

My family—and most of the locals—might think I'd lost my mind, but Graham believed in me. And that meant more than… I sucked in a jagged breath. More than he could ever know.

I dipped my head, using my hair as a curtain. "Thanks." Needing to break the tension, I said, "You may not be as impressed when you see our accommodations."

The word brought to mind Knox's yacht and the night Graham and I had shared a bed. Since then, we'd returned to our separate rooms and separate beds at his penthouse. I knew it was for the best, but I still found myself wishing for a way back to that space. To that intimacy, communication, and connection.

We'd been so in sync.

I often fell asleep thinking of that night, remembering the way he'd touched me. Looked at me. As if I really were his jewel, as he'd called me in French. Something rare and precious that he wanted to protect.

He was still parsimonious with his words, reserved. But it felt as if he were thawing. Softening. He'd ask me questions about the château or my travels. My family and my dreams. And I'd ask him about his. It was nice.

I'd made several appearances at Graham's office, and we'd gone to lunch. But we'd also shared some dinners at home, alone. We'd even taken the dogs on walks together, and I knew he was trying. But every night, I'd returned to my bedroom, spending my nights alone.

I told myself it was for the best. I told myself this was what I'd wanted. And yet my body craved his touch.

Messy, I reminded myself. It was too messy, and there was too much riding on the success of our agreement.

"I was wondering about our living space," he mused, bringing me back to the present. "I noticed you left it off your tour."

I shrugged as if to say, "Guilty."

He gave my shoulder a playful shake. He'd been doing that more lately—touching me. At the gala. In the kitchen. Even now, when no one was watching. I didn't want to like it, but I did.

"Come on," he said. "It can't be that bad."

I rolled my lips between my teeth. "Mm-hmm."

It was probably even worse than whatever he'd imagined. And compared to his luxury LA penthouse, it was practically a shack in the woods. Yes, we were staying in part of the château, but it was still very rustic.

That said, it was one of the few parts of the château that was actually habitable. It had running water, was tucked out of the way of the construction, and was private.

"This way," I said, heading for the entrance to my living quarters.

I'd been meaning to do a video on it; it was one of my subscribers' most frequently asked questions. Apart from how much the restoration was going to cost. But that was anyone's guess.

Thanks to Graham's investment, though—that was what I'd decided to call it—I could move forward with a ton of projects I'd been putting off. I'd already spoken to my lead architect about them, and I couldn't wait to get back to work myself.

I opened the door to my apartment within the château. It was nestled in the basement, though you entered at ground level since it was located in the dry moat. I cringed, imagining Graham's reaction to the spartan accommodations.

The internet was spotty. The linens were old but soft and clean. And I hadn't put much effort into the decor—hadn't had the time or desire. Besides, this was just temporary.

One day, I'd move in to a larger, more modern apartment in the château. I'd have shutters that opened to a view of the gardens. A fully functioning kitchen, laundry room so I wouldn't have to venture into town every time I needed to wash clothes. Which, considering how hard construction was on mine, was often. I also envisioned a large, rainfall shower and—best of all—hot water.

But for now, I lived simply, and it suited my needs. At least, it had.

Now that Graham and I were married, now that I'd spent the past week at his penthouse, I worried he wouldn't be comfortable here. It was much smaller than his place, and I hadn't considered how intimate it would feel to share such a cozy space with him.

"Here's the kitchen and dining." I gestured to my basic food storage, mini fridge, and hot plate. There was a simple farm table with two chairs that I'd found in one of the château's rooms.

He surveyed the space but said nothing.

Queen V and Prince Albert sniffed around, exploring their new home. I'd gotten them new beds and toys. And I'd filled some bowls with food and water.

They were huge creatures, but they were known as gentle giants for a reason. They'd always been friendly and affectionate with me, and it was nice to have them here.

I gave Queen V a quick pat, glancing back at Graham over my shoulder. I watched him as he surveyed the space, trying to get a read on him.

"Moving on," I said, desperate to fill the uncomfortable silence. "Bathroom." It had an outdated toilet with the tank near the ceiling, a cast-iron claw-foot tub, and a sink. "No hot water," I said quickly, trying to gloss over that fact as I led him toward the bedroom. "And bedroom."

I spied some bras on the bed before shoving them into the dresser. My cheeks were on fire, and I couldn't look at him. Thank goodness my wigs were still hidden in my suitcase. If I'd realized I'd be having company, I would've taken more care to tidy before I'd left for Mexico.

As it was, the bed was sloppily made, and it was small. And old. It was definitely not as sexy or luxurious as Graham's penthouse or even the cabin we'd stayed in on Knox's yacht. My cheeks heated, remembering that night. Remembering the way Graham had touched me, caressed me. Looked at me.

His jaw hardened. "You've been living like this for the past year?"

I twisted my hands together, my earlier thoughts forgotten. "When I wasn't traveling for my blog, yes."

"What do you mean, there's no hot water? How do you keep clean? How do you wash your clothes?"

"Laundromat in town." I glanced away. "And I take a lot of cold showers. Well, baths, actually."

"Cold—" He opened his mouth, aghast. "You're kidding, right?"

"I wish I were." Though now that Graham was going to be living here with me in such close proximity, the cold baths seemed like more of a necessity. "Honestly, they're more like lukewarm. You can use the electric kettle to help warm the water, but it takes forever, so I only do it every so often."

He shook his head, and it sounded like he muttered, "Unacceptable."

"Look," I sighed, trying not to visibly flinch at his tone. "I'm sorry it's not up to your standards. I've had to prioritize projects, and this one was relatively low on the list."

"Not up to my standards?" he scoffed. "I couldn't give a shit about that. And I get having to prioritize projects, but Lil—" He turned to me, grasping my shoulders. "You're my wife. You have twenty million dollars at your disposal."

"For the restoration of the château. Not for my personal use."

"Honestly, I don't give a fuck what you use it for. But I do expect you to make your comfort a priority."

I crossed my arms over my chest. "You *expect*?"

"You know what I mean." He turned back to face me. "But yes, actually, I do insist that you do something about this." He gestured to the room.

"Because you're ashamed that I'm living in such squalor."

"No. Because you deserve better, and I have the means to give it to you."

I didn't know whether to be touched or insulted by his statement. Even so, fixing up my current living quarters seemed unnecessarily frivolous. "I don't want to spend a bunch of time and money fixing up an apartment that will eventually be converted into something else."

"It wouldn't have to take long, and the cost is irrelevant."

My frustration was mounting, my skin growing warm. "It matters to me."

He leaned in. "I think you forget who I am and what it means to be married to me."

Oh, I hadn't forgotten. Before we'd had it out on Knox's yacht, being married to Graham had meant silent dinners. Nights spent alone.

And while I didn't want to ruin our tentative peace, I also refused to revert to how things had been. I refused to let Graham call the shots. I refused to be a silent partner in this marriage.

"There's nothing money can't buy," he said.

I scoffed. "I suppose that's true. I mean, you bought a wife." I gestured to myself.

"And you sure as hell didn't come cheap."

I glared at him. "Ironic then, how cheap you just made me feel."

I spun away. Done with this conversation. With him.

Entitled. Elitist. Asshole.

"Lily, wait."

"Why?" I asked. "So you can insult me again?"

"I'm not—" He dragged a hand through his hair. "I wasn't trying to insult you. I realize now how it might have come across, but that's not how I meant it. And I'm sorry."

His earnest apology calmed some of my anger. Not completely, but enough to keep me from fleeing.

"What do you propose, then?" I asked.

"I'm not saying we should spend a lot. But a basic, functional kitchen and bathroom don't have to cost much. An upgraded bed." He cleared his throat. "Beds." He seemed to place extra emphasis on that final "s" and the fact that it was plural.

"I actually ordered a new mattress for you, but it won't be here for another week. And I ordered you some sheets from the Huxley Grand brand." Because I knew they were his favorite, and he slept better when he was comfortable.

"Thank you. That was very considerate. But what about you?"

I waved a hand through the air. "Don't worry about me."

"You're my wife. Of course I'm worried about you."

Because I was his obligation. Graham saw it as his duty to take care of me.

I shouldn't care. I should be grateful he was so generous. So considerate. Especially considering the fact that our marriage was fake. But somehow, it only made me feel worse.

"This isn't open for negotiation," he added.

"News flash, Graham," I said, crowding him. "That's not how a relationship works." I jabbed his chest.

He covered my hand with his, holding it to his heart instead. His eyes searched mine, and it felt as if he were seeking something from me. What? I didn't know. Because he didn't want a relationship, didn't want me. At least not in any capacity other than as his pretend wife.

His response had caught me off guard, but I was determined to stand my ground. "Don't you remember what we discussed?" I gave him a pointed look, referring to *that night* without actually mentioning it.

His eyes were hooded, and then he leaned in, his arm

brushing against mine as he said, "Oh, I remember *everything.*"

His breath was warm on my skin, and his nearness sent a riot of visions flitting through my mind. Memories of that night. My mouth went dry. So dry. I licked my lips, and his eyes tracked the movement.

"Then you'll recall that in this relationship, we are equals," I said, trying to stay on track.

He stepped closer, and my heart rate picked up. "As if I could forget."

I forced myself to snap out of this lust-induced haze, though my words came out with more of a bite than I'd intended. "Then start treating me like one."

"I—" He dropped my hand and pinched the bridge of his nose. "How is me looking out for you not treating you like an equal? Aren't people in a relationship supposed to support each other? Take care of each other?"

He seemed genuinely confused. And I had to admit, he made a good point. I just wasn't used to letting anyone take care of me.

My shoulders relaxed. "I mean, yes. But there's a way to discuss something without making demands."

"Okay. How about this? I would like to do a basic renovation of our living quarters to make them more comfortable. And the money for my proposed renovations to our living space wouldn't come from the restoration budget."

What?

"I—" I shook my head. "You've already done so much. I don't want you to have to do that."

"I understand, but you have to realize this is motivated by selfish reasons. We could hire a crew to do the work the next time we're in LA. It's not a big project. It shouldn't take long."

What he said made sense, but still… "I can't ask you to do that."

"You're not asking. I'm offering."

I hated the idea of him spending even more money, but I knew he wouldn't let this go. And if we were going to be spending a significant amount of time here over the next two years, it would be worth the investment.

"Okay," I finally relented. "Only because I want you to be comfortable while we're here. You know, given how extra your lifestyle is," I teased.

He narrowed his eyes at me, crowding me now. "Oh, I *see*. You think I'm what? Pampered? Spoiled?"

I lifted a shoulder, unable to hide my smirk. I was goading him. I wanted more of this light, playful banter with him.

He narrowed his eyes at me. He didn't have to say the words "take that back" for me to know that's what he was thinking.

"You're sure about the project?" he asked. "I don't want you to think I'm overstepping or being demanding."

"Are you ever not demanding?" I teased.

"I'm not the only one who likes control." He arched a brow in a sexy move that sent a wave of desire through my body. *Fuck me.*

How could he be both so…infuriating and so, so hot?

I smoothed my hand down my throat, my pulse fluttering beneath my fingertips. He closed the remaining distance between us, his cologne invading my senses. Making my heart beat faster as desire pumped through my veins. He lifted his hand as if to touch me, and I felt the ghost of his caress on my cheek.

For a moment, I thought he was going to kiss me. *Please kiss me.* My body was aching for his kiss, his touch.

But then Graham's phone rang, and I excused myself. After being gone for so long, I had a million things to catch up on. And while I should've been focused on everything I needed to accomplish before we had to return to LA in ten days, all I could think about was Graham. And that was exactly why it was a bad idea to mix business with pleasure.

CHAPTER TWENTY-TWO

Lily

"Hey, Luc," I said in French, waving as I approached. Queen V had tagged along, and Luc's eyes widened at the sight of my four-legged companion.

I'd spoken to him over the phone a few times while I'd been away, and he'd sent me updates with text and pictures. I appreciated all his help, and I knew he was probably wondering about my extended absence. Plus, I needed to introduce him and the crew to Graham and tell them about the team from Hudson Security that was going to conduct an audit of the château's security.

That had been Graham's idea, and I hadn't been opposed. In fact, it was a relief. Despite many well-posted "Private Property" signs, there'd been a few times in the past when someone had driven up to the château wanting a tour. Wanting to ask questions. I had enough people coming and going, and it was such a large property, that the idea of Hudson doing a security audit gave me some peace of mind that I hadn't realized had been lacking.

"Lily, hey." Luc kissed both my cheeks. "And who's this?" He peered down at my furry companion.

"This—" I patted her back "—is Queen V."

"Nice to meet you, Your Majesty." He held out his knuckles, allowing Queen V to sniff him before she nudged him, wanting him to pet her.

"Sorry I was away for longer than expected." Queen V explored the area, soon returning to my side.

"It's not a problem. Work has proceeded as planned."

"Yes. I can see." I peered up at the roof, shading my eyes from the sun. The stonemasons were busy measuring for the new cornerstones. "It looks great. Thank you for keeping me updated. I appreciate you taking over while I was gone."

"Absolutely."

The more I'd thought about it, the more I'd realized that Graham was right. I needed a project manager, especially now that I was going to be away so much. I couldn't think of someone better suited to the role than Luc. I only hoped he'd agree.

"Part of the reason I was gone so long was because I found a private investor for the château restoration."

"You did?" His eyes widened. I nodded. "That's great news, Lily."

"It is." I smiled, relief and excitement coursing through me. We could now save the château. "That said, I'm going to be traveling between here and the US, splitting my time every month."

"Oh." His face fell. "I'm sorry to hear that. I know how much you love working on the château, and the crew will miss you. I hope everything is okay."

I appreciated his saying that. The crew had become my friends, my family.

"I will miss being here every day, but my husband's business is in LA, and we agreed to split our time."

"Husband?" Luc jerked his head back. "I wasn't…"

"I'll introduce you later," I said, trying to gloss over any questions. "And since I can't be here all the time, I'd like for you to be my project manager. I want you to oversee everything and be my eyes and ears. I'm asking a lot, but I'm also offering you a raise."

"I'm invested in the success of the château, and I appreciate the trust you've placed in me. I'm honored." He held a hand to his chest. "I won't let you down."

"Thank you, Luc."

"Thank *you*." He gave me a hug. But then he froze, dropping his arms and stepping back from me.

I followed his gaze to where Graham was standing, a menacing look on his face and Prince Albert at his side. "Ah." I rushed over to Graham, eager to smooth out this misunderstanding. "Here he is now. Luc, this is my husband, Graham, and his…our other dog, Prince Albert. Graham, this is my site manager, Luc."

They shook hands, then Graham immediately wrapped his arm around my shoulder. *Possessive much?*

I wanted to laugh, but I was too busy delighting in his touch, trying to ignore my body's response to him and the way he'd claimed ownership of me. Why was that so hot?

"What are you doing out here?" I asked, finally taking in Graham's attire. He was wearing work clothes, and they looked worn-in, well-loved. I had no idea he even owned anything like that. "I thought you had meetings?"

"I cleared my schedule. The château is your project, but I want to help," he said in French. Judging from Luc's expression, Graham had risen a few notches in his esteem.

I wasn't sure Graham had ever cleared his schedule. Actually, that wasn't true. He'd done it once—for Brooklyn. He was so wrapped around his niece's finger. I loved it.

"Help how?" He'd already invested a shit-ton of money into it.

"With the garden. Stripping lead paint. Whatever. Put me to work."

Oh, I want to put you to work, all right.

Unfortunately, he didn't seem interested in *that*. It was like he had an off switch. Or maybe it hadn't been as enjoyable for him as it had been for me. That seemed impossible, but he'd been nothing but proper and polite since, and I was going to freaking explode.

"How would you have time for that?" I asked.

"You make time for what's important." He peered down at me with something like tenderness and respect. Was he saying *I* was important?

"Besides…" Graham nuzzled my hair, lowering his voice. Though it wasn't quite so low that Luc wouldn't pick up on what he said. "It is our honeymoon after all."

Honeymoon? I stilled. *Ah. Right.*

So much for thinking that he wanted to spend time with me for me. There was always a hidden agenda. Graham was always strategizing.

I mean, I applauded his dedication to making our fake marriage seem real. And I knew how difficult it must have been for him to step back and take time off, even if he was looking at the bigger picture. But this was the furthest thing from a honeymoon.

We might be staying at a romantic château, but our bed was falling apart. Forget sexy bikinis or lingerie, I was wearing work clothes that were caked in paint. And we were standing in the midst of a construction site.

Making time for what was important was probably code for keeping an eye on his investment.

"So, what's on schedule for today?" Graham asked, confirming my suspicions.

"Luc?" I asked, my smile tight.

"As you can see, we've got the stonemasons on the roof.

And I've got a team up on the first floor, working on removing the tiles so the cables can be installed. We need to remove all the original tiles and clean the edges so they can eventually be set back in place."

"Is there something I can help with?" Graham asked.

"Yes, but…" Luc glanced between us. "Shouldn't you be enjoying your honeymoon?"

I placed my hand on Graham's arm. "As long as we're together, we'll enjoy ourselves." I smiled up at him. "Isn't that right, *mon kinkajou*?"

Graham clenched his jaw at my term of endearment. I wanted to kiss him there just to see what he'd do. See how far I could push him.

We'd see how he liked being referred to as my kinkajou.

Luc merely shook his head. "Okay." He turned and headed for the door to the château, and we followed.

"Do you have an interest in restoration?" Luc asked Graham as we walked, the dogs trailing behind. They seemed happy in their new environment, and that was a relief. I knew how much they meant to Graham, and I cared about Prince Albert's and Queen V's welfare.

"Very much, yes."

I climbed the stairs to the first floor, greeting each of the crew members by name and introducing them to Graham. After Luc explained what needed to be done, Graham and I set to work with the team. I'd remove the tiles and take them to Graham. And he'd file the edges. It was exhausting and dirty work, and I was secretly curious how long he'd last.

After a few hours, he was still going strong. Making jokes with the crew in French, talking about construction techniques. Engaging with them. He was one of them.

"Having fun?" I teased, bringing him another bucket of tiles. His clothes and hair were covered in dust.

He'd always seemed like this buttoned-up billionaire who

didn't like to get his hands dirty. And now, he'd shown me a different side to him.

"Yes, actually. This task may be tedious, but I like working with my hands. And I enjoy the repetitive nature of it."

"In that case, we have many tasks around here that you will enjoy." I grinned, pleased at how seamlessly he'd slotted himself into my life here at the château. Maybe the novelty would wear off for him at some point, but for now, I was impressed. Relieved. Grateful.

I'd always known Graham was a hard worker, but I'd never seen him take on such a physical task. It was hot. *He* was hot—forearms flexing, dust flying. His face set in concentration. He looked up, and I ducked away, embarrassed that he'd caught me watching him.

On and on, it went. Removing tiles. Moving stacks of them. Dust and more dust.

My body was aching, but with the afternoon light quickly fading, the crew was wrapping up for the day. I wasn't sure I'd ever seen Graham so relaxed, so at peace as he'd been today. We finished and shared a beer, celebrating the completion of the project. They thanked Graham for his help, and we followed them down the stairs. I was covered in dust, and it was going to be a nightmare to clean this wig, but it was worth it.

After we returned to our apartment, we ate a simple meal on the stone bridge overlooking the dry moat. Queen V and Prince Albert rested at our feet. As I glanced out over the grounds and château, I was filled with a sense of contentment and ease. I'd missed this place, and it was bittersweet to be back, only to know we'd be leaving again so soon.

"Thanks for your help today," I said.

"It was fun."

"It was." I smiled. "I'm impressed."

"Why?" He furrowed his brow. "Because I pitched in?"

I lifted a shoulder. "I mean, honestly, yeah. I didn't realize you'd get into manual labor."

"Who do you think manages the garden at my penthouse?"

"A team of gardeners."

"When I have to be away, yes. But that garden is mine. My design. My plantings. My domain."

"Wow. I had no idea."

"My grandmother and I used to love to garden. She taught me so much about plants. About respecting our environment."

I'd noticed that he was passionate about the gardens and often knowledgeable about plants and their care and uses. Even when I'd been his assistant, he'd always pointed out various plants and told me interesting facts about them. Now, I realized it was his way of keeping his grandmother's memory alive.

"I'm guessing you have some ideas for the château's gardens," I said. When he nodded, I added, "I'd love to see them."

"I'd be happy to help. Tomorrow." He stretched his arms over his head with a groan, and I had to tear my eyes away from the sliver of abs he'd revealed with that movement. "I need a hot shower and a comfortable bed, but I'm not sure either of those is on offer," Graham said, setting down his wineglass. "Unless you were messing with me about the cold water."

"Just think of it like going to a health spa." I sipped my wine as I smoothed my hand down Queen V's back. "Isn't everyone always touting the benefits of cold plunges?"

"Since you're so keen to extol its virtues, maybe you should go first."

"Nah. Go ahead. You can use the kettle to heat the water if you want. I won't think less of you." I winked.

He chuckled. "Mm-hmm." He stood, inhaling slowly. "This is going to suck, isn't it?"

"Yep." I saluted him. "Get used to it."

He turned, his dark chuckle threading its way through the night air. It was chilly, and it would only get colder. Come morning, there'd likely be a thick layer of fog blanketing the grounds.

I lingered there a while longer then returned inside to wash the dishes. I grabbed my pajamas, dreading how long it was going to take to clean my wig. I only had a few that were similar enough in color and cut that maybe Graham wouldn't notice if they weren't exactly the same. Maybe I could buy a few cheap ones online and hide them under a baseball cap?

Or you could just tell him.

I could. But our relationship felt so fragile and new. We were still learning to trust each other, and revealing my hair loss required a level of vulnerability I wasn't quite prepared for. I was still recovering from the fact that Graham had hacked my blog. I wasn't ready to trust him with my alopecia.

Graham emerged from the bathroom, rubbing his arms with his hands in an effort to warm up. He was dressed in a dark-green Henley that brought out the color of his eyes. I dragged my eyes down his body to the gray sweatpants that hung low on his waist. Apart from his clothes today, I hadn't ever seen him in anything but a tux or a bespoke suit, even at the penthouse.

It was like he was an entirely different person. Relaxed. Casual. At ease.

Was it the clothes, or was it the environment? Hell, maybe it was the fact that he was taking a vacation for the first time, maybe ever. Though, considering the work he'd done today, it wasn't exactly restful. Even so, I could tell it had been restorative for him.

His eyes were brighter. His muscles looser. His smile came more easily.

"Well, that was invigorating," he said, his hair still wet.

"See." I grinned. "I knew you'd come to appreciate it." I gathered my clothes. "You done in there?"

"It's all yours."

"Great. Thanks."

I stepped inside the bathroom, and god, it smelled good in there. I closed the door and inhaled deeply, remembering the feel of his skin pressed against mine. The way it felt to be close to him.

I shivered, despite the fact that it was relatively warm. Graham must have turned on the space heater while he was bathing. And now, the room was nice and cozy.

I removed my robe and undressed, letting the tub fill. While it did, I washed my wig in the sink and hung it up to dry before climbing into the tub. When the water first hit my skin, it was a shock of cold, like always. Despite my haste, goose bumps still covered my body. Finally done, my hands shook as I grabbed a towel from the drying rack and wrapped it around me.

There. The worst was over.

I dressed and reapplied my eyebrows and eyelashes. God, this was going to get really old really fast. Then I pulled out my hair dryer, quickly drying and styling my wig. I only hoped the new wigs I'd ordered wouldn't be delayed like Graham's mattress. At this rate, we'd be lucky if it arrived before we returned to LA.

I squeezed my eyes shut. *Merde! The bed.*

We hadn't shared a bed since that night on Knox's yacht— and for good reason. But now, there was no avoiding it.

I sighed and stepped out of the bathroom. Queen V

immediately lifted her head, glanced at me, and then rested it on her paws again. Graham was sitting on one of the chairs, Prince Albert's head in his lap as he read a book. My heart pinched at the sight of them, and a sense of rightness and belonging settled over me.

"I'm going to bed," I said, ducking my head, suddenly overcome with shyness. "Join me when you're ready." Why did the last word come out higher, making it sound more like a question?

He appraised me over the top of his book. "Are you sure?"

No. "Yeah. I think we can handle sharing a bed until your new mattress arrives."

He tilted his head, assessing me, before returning his attention to the book. "I'll be there soon."

"Sure. Take your time." *I'll just be freaking out beneath the covers.* "I'm sure we're both so exhausted, we'll just pass out." *Shut up, Lil! Just shut up!*

I went to my room and checked my wig again in the mirror before climbing beneath the covers. I kept the small lamp on so Graham could find his way but turned and faced the wall, staring at the cracked plaster. My body was exhausted, but my mind was on overdrive. There was no way I was falling asleep now, even if I was tired.

A little while later, the mattress dipped, and the covers shifted as Graham slid into bed. He nudged me. "Sorry. Didn't mean to—"

I scooched closer to the edge. "No. It's fine. It's a small bed."

"I'd be surprised if it's even a full." He shifted, and it was impossible not to touch. "Did you use my body soap?" He sniffed.

Oh god. I was mortified. And I'd never been more thankful that he couldn't see my face.

"Did you just sniff me?" I teased, going on the defensive to hide how self-conscious I felt.

"*If* I did, it was only to confirm my theory." He sounded smug.

"Mm-hmm. Sure." I punched down my pillow—trying and failing to get comfortable. How the hell was I supposed to sleep when he was lying next to me? All I could think about was his smell. The heat radiating off him.

I moved again. Nothing felt right. Either his elbow was jabbing me, or I was about to fall off the bed.

"Jesus. Will you stop moving? Just—" He huffed. "Here."

I turned so I was facing him. *Big mistake.* He held out his arm, inviting me to lie on him. His hair was damp, and his expression was soft. How could I resist an invitation like that?

"I don't want you getting any ideas," I said, telling myself the same thing.

"Of course not." He looked almost offended. "Cuddling isn't in my vocabulary. This is strictly out of necessity. Otherwise, one or both of us will end up on the floor."

I hesitated a moment, holding his gaze. And then I lay down on his chest. Oh, it was heaven. He was warm and steady, and I relaxed at the sound of his heartbeat.

"Better?" he asked.

"Yes. But this isn't going to bother you? I mean…I know you're sensitive to textures. And I don't want to cause you irritation."

"Oh, I'm irritated all right," he muttered.

"I can—"

"No." He held me tighter to him. "Don't move. I prefer deep pressure, compression. Most of my issues with texture relate to how clothes and materials feel against my skin. Or if someone's touch is too light."

I'd noticed that he seemed to recoil from light pressure,

so I tried to avoid it. "Anything else?" I asked, wanting to understand. Wanting to make sure he was comfortable.

"Some foods can be an issue, but it also depends on my bandwidth. If I'm tired or overstimulated, things are more likely to bother me."

"I can understand that. Sometimes I get overstimulated when there's a lot of heavy machinery making noise on the property. But if there's something I can do…" I trailed off, not sure what else to say. Not wanting to make him uncomfortable. "Please tell me."

"Thanks," he said. "And thanks for listening without judgment."

I furrowed my brow. "Why would I judge you for something that's out of your control?"

"You'd be surprised," he said.

Understanding dawned on me. "Have other people judged you for your sensitivity to textures?"

He blew out a breath. "Yeah. So, I learned to hide it as much as I could. Otherwise, I risk being labeled as entitled or difficult."

I pushed up on my elbow, meeting his eyes. "That's shitty, and I'm sorry you've had to deal with that. But you don't have to hide it with me."

He was quiet a moment, then said, "Thank you," in a gruff voice.

"So, the cold bath…"

He blew out a breath. "Fucking sucked." He tucked his other arm beneath his head and stared up at the ceiling. "Jesus, Lil. How have you been living like this for all these months?"

I smoothed my hand up his chest and then back down again, mindful of the pressure I used. I observed his reactions, making sure that he still seemed relaxed. The fabric of his Henley was so soft, and I needed something to distract myself from his nearness.

"It helped that I moved here in the summer," I said. "And at first, it felt like one big adventure."

"And now?"

"It's become a race against the clock to save the château and its domain."

"Mm." His voice rumbled through his chest and into me. He slid his hand up and down my back. The motion was so natural. It felt nice. Like this was the way it was always supposed to be. "You've taken on a lot, but you have a good team."

"I do." I smiled, thinking of Luc and all the others. "Over the past year, they've become more like family."

"I can see that. Luc, in particular, is protective of you."

"He's just a friend," I said, surprised by how eager I was to reassure Graham. "Actually, I think he and Jo had a little something going on."

Graham chuckled, and I loved the sound of it, loved that I was the cause of it. "Interesting."

"Do you think Queen V and Prince Albert are adjusting okay?" I asked.

"They love it here. As do I."

"I'm glad," I said, my body relaxing at his admission. At his touch.

"Thank you for making them feel at home—buying treats and beds and food. And thank you for letting me be a part of this."

"Are you kidding? Thank you for making this possible." I would never be able to repay his generosity.

"My pleasure." He gave me a gentle squeeze.

Huddled beneath the blankets, ensconced in Graham's arms, I felt safe and protected. Cared for. *I could get used to this.*

CHAPTER TWENTY-THREE

Graham

Lily shifted, and I tried not to groan. My cock was already so hard it was painful. The cold bath hadn't helped. And lying in bed with Lily's soft, warm body pressed against mine certainly wasn't helping either.

We were barely a few weeks into married life, and I was tired of pretending. Tired of putting on this façade that I was unaffected by my wife, when everything she did set me ablaze. If I were honest with myself, it always had.

But Lily didn't want to mix business with pleasure—she'd made that very clear after what had happened on Knox's yacht. And at first, I'd agreed. I liked things neat and tidy, and having sex with my temporary wife was neither.

So, I'd continued on as if nothing had happened. Or I'd tried to.

It was easier to maintain my distance in LA, with all the distractions and the demands on my time. Where we could easily retreat to our separate rooms in my large penthouse. And I could jack off in my shower to thoughts of her. Something that had happened more often than I cared to admit.

But here, in the French countryside, everything was

different. Lily was different, and I could feel a shift in myself as well. I'd enjoyed the hard work and camaraderie. I'd enjoyed sharing a simple meal outside, with Prince Albert and Queen V at our feet. And as much as that ice bath had sucked, it was worth it if it meant I'd get to hold her in my arms.

So much for giving her space. All I wanted to do was keep her close.

I am so fucked.

I kept my hand on her back, despite my desire to explore her body. All the while, I answered her questions about my siblings. About my plans for the brand. My hopes for the future.

But mostly, I listened to her as she talked about her dreams for the château. I marveled at her vision and tenacity as she told me about the obstacles she'd faced every step of the restoration. And yet, despite everything she had on her plate, she'd put things in place for me and my dogs.

Eventually, her voice grew softer. Her thoughts more spaced out. I felt pleasant. Warm. Relaxed.

I wondered if this was how my grandparents felt when they were with each other. And I could understand even more why they'd wanted this for me. It was more than just companionship; it was…understanding. Working together toward a mutual purpose.

I pressed a kiss to Lily's hair, filled with gratitude. But instead of telling her everything I was feeling and thinking, I merely wished her sweet dreams before saying goodnight. *"Bonne nuit, mon petit poisson."*

She was quiet for so long, I figured she must have fallen asleep. But then she asked, "Why do you call me your little fish?"

"Because it bothers you," I said, almost as a reflex. My body was at ease after a day of manual labor. My mind was calm. Surprisingly, I just wanted to fall asleep with her in my arms.

She turned to me, eyes slits, suddenly much more awake than I'd expected. "I'm serious, Graham."

"What makes you think I'm not?" I was teasing, but I didn't let on. It was too fun to mess with her. I liked when she got all riled up.

Her breasts brushed against me, and I could think of nothing else. She straddled me, pinning me down. "Tell me."

All I could focus on was the feel of her body pressing me into the mattress. Her hands lightly gripping my wrists. Her breasts hovering over my face, barely concealed by her thin T-shirt, nipples begging to be worshipped.

Before I could stop myself, I arched my hips, letting her feel my desire. She gasped then narrowed her eyes at me.

"Don't try to distract me, husband."

"Why? Is it working?" I asked.

She ground down onto me, and we groaned in unison. "No."

"You sure about that, wife?" I asked, captivated by the sight of her. The feel of her.

She gnawed on her bottom lip. "I..." She gulped. "I don't know."

And yet she didn't stop. She kept at it, teasing herself, teasing both of us, as she rubbed along my cock. Driving me wild. Her breasts swaying beneath the shirt, taunting me. I wanted to see her. Taste her. Touch her.

"Maybe we should practice our communication skills," I suggested, hoping she'd pick up on what I meant.

She arched a brow. "We can do that outside the bedroom."

"We could..." I let that sentence trail off, giving her space to reconsider. "But I feel like talking now."

She considered it, a smile playing at her lips. "I'd hate to miss an opportunity to *practice*. What's on your mind?"

I loved seeing her like this—playful and unguarded.

"First, I'd have you sit on my face. I need to taste you," I said, and I wondered if she could hear the desperation in my voice. "Make you come."

"Graham," she groaned, but I sensed the hesitation on her lips. Even so, she whispered, "What else?"

The words continued spilling out of me, and I didn't try to stop them. "I know I shouldn't, but I want you. You drive me crazy with wanting you." I leaned up and kissed her collarbone, her shoulder, angry that there was any fabric between us. "I can think of little else."

"Look at you using your words," she teased, and I knew she was trying to deflect. Avoid answering. *Fuck that.*

"Should I keep going?" I asked. She hesitated. So I added, "Nothing has to change."

Because that's what she wanted. And even though I wanted all of her, I would gladly take anything she would give me.

"But you know it will. It will make an already messy situation even messier." She changed her angle, and we moved faster. Her eyes rolled back in her head.

Her mouth said one thing, but her body told an entirely different story.

"I. Don't." I flipped us so I was on top, taking advantage of her distracted state to take back control. "Fucking. Care."

Her eyes darkened, and I knew she was turned on. So I continued. I kissed her cheeks, her neck, everywhere I could easily reach.

"But you like things that are neat and tidy. You li—"

I silenced her with a kiss. "I like *you*."

She smiled, beaming up at me. "I like you too. I like you here, like this. But—"

Her words and the sweet way she looked at me sent a thrill through me. I kissed her again, harder this time. And she gave as good as she got, rolling us again so she was on top once more.

"We can't." She placed her palms to my chest, continuing to rock against me despite her protests. I wondered if she even realized she was doing it.

"Why not?" I asked, taking her left hand in mine and bringing it to my lips. I held her gaze as I kissed each of her fingers, lingering on her ring finger. Whether she knew it or not—admitted it or not—she was mine.

"You won't even give me a straight answer about your pet name for me. We're pretending to be married—"

"We *are* married," I said, smoothing my hands over her waist until I was grabbing her ass. *Oh fuck.* She was wearing these tiny lace panties beneath her T-shirt and nothing else. "We're not pretending."

God. She was perfect. And I wanted her.

"Fine," she huffed. "We're married for real. We're just pretending to be in love. Which is *why* this is messy. Adding sex to the mix is asking for trouble."

"We did it before." And I was going to come again if she didn't stop. Was she trying to drive me crazy?

Her eyes fluttered closed, and I couldn't decide if she wanted to throttle me or kiss me. "Yes, but that was…"

Don't you dare say it was a mistake. I gave her hips a gentle squeeze, her skin warm beneath mine. *Don't you dare.*

"A momentary lapse in judgment," she finished.

I relaxed, grateful she didn't view it as a mistake. A lapse in judgment—fine. I could work with that. But I didn't want to cause her regret.

"Then let's have another lapse in judgment." I smirked, hoping to lure her in like she had me.

She leaned forward, and the ends of her hair dusted my shirt. "Tell me why you call me your little fish, and I'll consider it."

I chuckled. *My wife.* She drove a hard bargain. And that's why we were such a great fit.

"Hm." I pretended to consider it, but I was more excited about the idea of driving her crazy. "Nope."

She slapped my chest and moved to climb off me. "You're terrible."

I didn't let her go far, turning toward her so we were spooning. My front was to her back, and she was trapped in my arms. "You love it."

I was so hard for her it hurt. There was no way she didn't feel it, feel me pressed against her ass.

She shivered then yawned. "Well—" She yawned again, and it was totally fake. Then she reached out to turn off the light. "Good night."

So that's how she was going to play it. The little tease.

I knew she wanted me. Just as she knew I wanted her.

I lay there a minute, trying to get my breath—and my body—under control. I remained still, willing myself to get it together.

And then I totally caved.

"You can pretend all you want, but I'd bet good money you're wet for me," I rasped, inhaling her scent. It mingled with mine, and it smelled like home.

"Shh," she whispered. "I'm sleeping."

My chest shook with laughter. "If you were sleeping, you wouldn't be talking."

She was quiet.

I slid my hand over her stomach, teasing the edge of her panties. "Let me make you feel good. No expectations."

She shifted a little, squirming. I smirked, encouraged.

"You know you want me to," I said, sliding my hand lower. She widened her legs, and I rested my hand over her mound. She didn't stop me, so I kept going. "You want me to tease your clit."

She whimpered, and I started massaging her clit through her underwear.

"You want me to bring you to the edge with my fingers. Building your pleasure slowly—" Her panties were soaked, and I let loose a groan. "Again and again until you scream my name."

Oh god. I needed that just as much as she did. Maybe more. And that was terrifying.

I'd never needed anyone.

"Yes." Her voice was shaky but clear. "Yes." She widened her legs, giving me more freedom to move.

I moved her panties to the side and slid my hand beneath them, using the pressure from the material to add to her pleasure.

"I'd put my hands and my mouth all over your body." Her hips started rocking, and every brush of her ass against my hard-on had me nearly exploding. "I'd make you come so hard and so many times that you forgot your name." I nipped her ear. But I'd make damn sure she'd never forget mine.

I kept that one hand working her clit, while I slid the other up to tease her breasts. I groaned. My god, her tits were glorious. Two full handfuls that were incredibly sensitive to touch.

I leaned my forehead against the back of her head, needing to be closer. Needing more.

If the way she widened her legs, parting her thighs for me, was any indication, she did too. I slid one finger inside her.

"And then, when you didn't think you could take any more, I'd have you sit on my cock."

She groaned, and I could tell she was close. Her body was squeezing me like a vise, and her movements were wild, desperate. I wanted to ruin this woman like she'd ruined me.

She placed her hand over mine, guiding me to the spot she wanted me most. "There." She let out a garbled sound.

Even now, she couldn't resist taking control. But I didn't mind. All I cared about was her pleasure.

"Tell me what you need."

"Faster. More pressure," she instructed between pants.

I'd planned to drag this out, to torture her, but instead, I did as she asked. And then she was coming, crying out as she fell over the edge. Falling apart in my arms.

"*Oui, mon ange,*" I said, coaxing every ounce of pleasure out of her. "*Voilà, c'est ça,*" I coaxed. *There you go. That's it.* I kissed her shoulder. "*Donne-toi à moi.*" Give yourself to me.

Her body relaxed in my arms, all the fight going out of her. She turned her head, kissing me. "*Merci.*"

"*Ton plaisir est ma recompense, Madame Mackenzie,*" I replied, letting her know that her pleasure was my reward.

Giving her pleasure brought me pleasure.

She reached back with her hand, wrapping it around my shaft over my pajama pants. It was so tempting to give in. It felt so good.

But I'd told Lily that I had no expectations, and I'd meant it. I didn't want her to think that everything about our relationship was transactional. So I grabbed her hand in mine and wrapped them both around her. "Sleep."

"But—"

"Shh," I hushed. "Good to sleep, *mon bijou.*" I kissed her hair and tried to will away my hard-on. "*Ton plaisir est tout ce dont j'ai besoin,*" I whispered. *Your pleasure is all I need.*

"You're late," Sloan said when I answered her call a few days later. "And—" She leaned forward, likely to get a better look at her screen. "You're a mess."

This was certainly a change. Usually, I was the one critiquing my siblings, not the other way around. I wondered if Sloan's shortness had something to do with pregnancy hormones, though I was smart enough to keep my mouth shut.

"I've been busy." I set my respirator aside and headed outside into the fresh air.

After we'd finished removing the tiles on the second floor, Lily was working on prepping a room for wallpaper, and I'd been tasked with removing lead paint from the front hall. It was tedious but satisfying. And it gave me time to think. About Lily, about her dreams for this place, about what I'd do with the garden if I were given free rein.

"Doing what?" Jasper asked. "And what are you wearing?" He frowned. "Is this some sort of kinky honeymoon role-play for you and Lily?"

I narrowed my eyes into slits.

"Okay. Okay." He held up his hands. "Forget I asked. But seriously, what are you wearing?"

"It's a paint suit." I removed the hood and ran a hand through my hair. "I've been stripping the lead paint off the ceiling in the main entry."

Jasper and Sloan blinked at me.

"What?" I barked.

"I never thought I'd see the day that Graham fell in love," Jasper said. "But it's happened."

"What does that have to do with paint stripping?"

Sloan smiled, resting a hand on her stomach. She'd gone back to London, the city's skyline glittering in the background. "Everything."

"How are you feeling?" I asked Sloan, eager for a change of subject. "How's my future niece or nephew?"

"They're great." She beamed. "I'm finally less nauseous. And baby is doing well."

"I'm glad," I said, feeling as if a weight had been lifted. Even so, I knew I'd be on edge until the baby was safely delivered.

"And Jasper?" I turned to him. "How's everything in LA? How are you?"

He froze as if surprised I'd asked, and I made a note to make more of an effort. To try to treat him as more of an equal. To communicate more, as Lily always suggested, and not just in the bedroom.

"It's...fine." He cleared his expression, reverting to something more neutral. "I can't believe you're not going stir-crazy. You've barely logged in to the company server."

I lifted a shoulder. "I'm on my honeymoon."

"Yeah, but..." He shook his head, his expression one of disbelief.

"I thought you'd be happy," I said, confused.

"I am. I'm just surprised, that's all," Jasper said.

"*Pleasantly* surprised," Sloan chimed in. "Though the board has been grumbling about your absence."

"What's new?" I asked. If I were there, they'd claim I wasn't a devoted husband. If I were gone, they'd whine that I didn't care about the company. There was no winning. "Fortunately, they no longer get a say in our lives."

"That's actually what we wanted to talk to you about," Sloan said, looking to Jasper. I wondered what was going on. What was I missing?

Maybe I should've checked in more frequently, but I was supposedly on my honeymoon. Okay, that was a lie. Now that I'd signed off, I was actually enjoying myself. I couldn't remember the last time I'd actually taken a break. Especially not to do something solely for pleasure.

I think I'd always clung so tightly to the reins because I feared that if I stepped back, everything would fall apart. But I should've had faith in my employees, in my family. I hired the best and paid them handsomely, and I needed to trust them to do their jobs.

My siblings were more than capable of running the company themselves. Something I'd only recently admitted to myself, thanks to Lily. Perhaps it was time to stop viewing them as my baby brother and sister in need of my protection and start seeing them as the capable, intelligent adults they were.

Instead of demanding answers, I waited for Jasper to speak. He sighed. "There have been rumors. Questions about your relationship with Lily."

I'd expected as much, but his tone gave me pause. "What kinds of rumors?"

"About an improper relationship. Reporters sniffing around."

"The fuck?"

"I want to loop Pierce in on this. We need to get our story straight before the next board meeting," Jasper said, sounding entirely too responsible. I was coming to realize that maybe I didn't give him enough credit.

"Pierce will tell you the same thing I will. There is no story." I gripped the phone tighter, wondering why this was the first I was hearing of it. "Lily and I reconnected long after her employment with the Huxley brand ended. We fell in love and got married."

Jasper and Sloan shared a look.

"Yeah," Jasper said. "You see…" He scrunched up his face. "That doesn't sound terribly romantic."

Maybe not, but those were the facts. "I don't need to

justify my relationship to them."

I was already calculating ways to take them down. Lily was my wife, and if they insinuated anything improper, anything that would hurt her or her reputation... I clenched my fists, seething. I would put their publications out of business faster than they could say "Lily."

Jasper rolled his eyes. "Here we go again."

"What?" I asked. What had I missed? I'd been so focused on protecting Lily that I hadn't paid enough attention to the conversation.

Sloan groaned. "This is just like the cold, heartless billionaire thing all over again."

"How?" I asked. "Doesn't my marriage prove that I'm warm and loving?" That was kind of the whole point. Well, that and securing the additional shares.

"You're telling us to feel a certain way without showing us why. It would be like saying Scrooge had suddenly decided to become generous and loving without showing us his donations or his visits with his family. Or his generosity toward Tiny Tim and his family," Jasper said.

"So now I'm Scrooge?" I dragged a hand through my hair. *Fuck me.*

"It was merely an example," Sloan said, as if she hadn't just called me a selfish, uncaring bastard. Was this truly what my siblings thought of me? "Jasper's merely trying to say that you can't just slap on a wedding ring and tell everyone you've changed. You have to *show* them."

"What do you want me to do?" I seethed, feeling attacked. "Fuck my wife on the conference table in front of the entire room?"

"Is that an option?" Jasper asked.

"No!" Sloan and I shouted in unison. I tried to take a deep breath, desperately resisting the urge to reach through the screen and strangle him. Thank fuck Lily was still inside the château. No way I wanted her hearing this conversation.

I dragged a hand through my hair, though it snagged on all the dirt caked in it. "I don't know what to tell you. I don't know how to prove that our relationship is real. I don't see why I should have to. Nobody questioned your marriage to Jackson, and it was fast."

"Graham." Sloan softened. "Jackson and I had history. And our marriage didn't have the ability to drastically reshape the company."

I sighed. *This again?* "She's my wife. And I prefer to keep my private life private."

"We get that," Jasper said. "But we're your family. You can't keep shutting us out."

Was that how they felt? Was that what they thought I was doing? Was I?

"Give us something to work with," Sloan said. "We know this is difficult for you, and we're willing to do the heavy lifting. But if we're going to present a united front to the board, you're going to have to give Jasper and me a little more to go on. Especially, if you want to dispel any doubts about the legitimacy of your relationship and put them to bed once and for all."

That was what I wanted, wasn't it? And I could see how patient my siblings were with me. How hard they were trying.

I thought about what Lily would do. Tie me up and make me use my words. I almost groaned aloud at that image, because god, I was so hard for her. All the fucking time.

We hadn't had sex again—yet. But it felt like we were working up to it. And honestly, waiting—painful as it was—was kind of fun.

I was a patient man. I'd play Lily's game. I'd work on my

communication skills every damn night if that's what she wanted.

"Graham?" Sloan prompted in a gentle tone.

I shook my head as if to clear it. "Right. Okay. What do you recommend?"

"Let's do a test run. Go over some of the questions they might ask you," Jasper said.

Sloan nodded. I grunted. That sounded like fucking torture.

"How long have you been together?" Jasper asked.

"Long enough." When he glared at me, I said, "It feels like forever and a moment."

Sloan wore a soft smile. Okay. Clearly a good answer. Vague but romantic. I'd try to stick to that.

Sloan asked another question, then another, alternating with Jasper as they continued their rapid-fire interrogation. Asking me about Lily's favorite color. The reason we were splitting our time between France and LA. On and on and fucking on it went.

I knew they were doing this to help me prepare, but I also suspected they were secretly curious about my relationship with Lily. My *feelings* for her.

"What do you love about Lily?" Sloan asked.

"Everything," I snapped, unable to take it anymore.

"Graham." Sloan narrowed her eyes at me, but I realized it was true.

Lily was smart and passionate and tenacious, and I admired her. There weren't many people I'd say that about, but that didn't mean I loved *her*. I couldn't. Could I?

"That answer isn't going to cut it," Sloan continued. "You have to know that."

"What I know—" I gnashed my teeth "—is that I'm married, and the board can't do jack shit about it." So what if there'd been rumors? Reporters? It wasn't ideal, but it would blow over.

"Actually..." Sloan grimaced. "They can. And they are."

I gripped the phone so hard I thought the screen might crack. "What are you talking about?"

"Some of the board members hired an attorney to contest the marriage provision of the will."

"Good luck to them. We all know that provision was valid."

"Yes, but we also know what they'll come after next." Jasper gave me a meaningful look.

Lily. My stomach clenched with dread, but I had to project strength. Certainty. My siblings looked to me for leadership and guidance, and I would not—could not—let them down.

If my siblings weren't convinced, the board wouldn't be either. I needed to put a stop to this now. If not for me, then for Lily. I refused to see her torn apart in the board's quest to take me out. It was not happening. I wouldn't allow it.

"Let them come," I said with more confidence than I felt. "I've got nothing to hide."

"Maybe not, but you need to be prepared. No one even knew you were dating Lily, let alone seriously. And now you're conveniently married six months before the deadline to inherit the shares. If we're asking these questions, everyone else is too."

"She's right," Jasper said. "You always talk about how important family is, but then you go off and get married in secret. It looks odd."

Ouch. I'd underestimated how upset my siblings would be about my surprise marriage. I felt bad, but I reminded myself that I was doing this for them. For my grandparents too. And now, for Lily and the château.

Sloan met my eyes, her expression solemn. "I know you

think you're the big brother and you have to do this all on your own, but you don't."

Did she know the truth about my marriage with Lily? If nothing else, she certainly had her suspicions.

"She's right," Jasper said. "We're a team."

I was tempted to confess, but I couldn't. I would never put my siblings in that position.

"And, Graham," Sloan said. "You know this has nothing to do with Lily, right? She's lovely. And if you're happy, we're happy. Yes, we're pushing you, but we see how much you care about Lily. I mean—" She blew out a breath. "The fact that you left LA. That you're shifting your schedule so dramatically every month so you can be with Lily at the château speaks volumes."

Spending time away from LA certainly hadn't been the hardship I'd feared. In fact, I found that the more time we spent at the château, the more I dreaded returning to LA. I was growing more invested—not just in the project, but in Lily.

We spent our days restoring the château, and I was constantly in awe of my wife. She always had dust in her hair and a smile on her face, and she was the most beautiful woman to me. Then, after a simple dinner on the stone bridge that spanned the dry moat, we'd go for walks through the grounds with Prince Albert and Queen V, brainstorming ideas for the gardens. We spent the nights in bed, talking as we held each other.

It was the first time in a long time that I could remember being content. I thought about Lily, and how it no longer felt like an act. It felt…real.

CHAPTER TWENTY-FOUR

Lily

"Hey." Graham linked his hand with mine. "I have something I want to show you."

"You do?" I asked, intrigued. "What is it?"

He'd been stripping paint again all day, while I'd been finalizing the preparations for *les Journées du patrimoine*. The culture festival would be here before we knew it, and I wanted it to be a successful and fun event—both for the château and for everyone who came to visit.

Plus, it was good to keep busy. Graham and I were headed back to LA tomorrow, and I was apprehensive. Both about leaving the château, though I knew it was in good hands with Luc and the artisans. But also because of what it would mean for Graham and me.

Back to work at the office for him, obviously. But would we go back to our separate rooms? Separate beds?

The new mattress had been delayed, so we'd continued to share our small, lumpy bed. It might not be the most comfortable, but I didn't mind because I liked sleeping in his arms. And he seemed to enjoy it too.

He was different here. Calmer. More relaxed. More approachable. I liked it. Liked him, and I didn't want this version of Graham to disappear when we left.

Queen V and Prince Albert tagged along as always, content to explore but careful to stay close. They were so sweet and mild-mannered, and I loved having them around. Growing up, I'd never had a pet. My parents had always joked that our house was already too much of a circus, and they were right. But I'd always, *always* wanted a dog.

Don't get too attached, I reminded myself.

This marriage. These dogs. Everything about it was temporary. And I was merely kidding myself if I believed otherwise.

Graham dragged my hand to his mouth, pressing a kiss to the back of it. He'd done that more lately—touched me. Linked his fingers with mine. Pressed kisses to my temple. Held me in bed at night.

"You okay?" he asked, brushing his thumb over my skin.

We'd spent so much time together that he knew how to read me. Then again, he'd always been very observant.

"Yeah." I brushed my hair away from my face. "Just tired. Lots to do before we leave."

"I know." He gave my hand a squeeze. "I don't want to leave either."

"You don't?" I asked. I'd suspected that he'd fallen for the château, but I found myself wishing he'd fall for me.

Which was silly.

Graham had always been very upfront about what this was—a business arrangement, nothing more. Wanting more would not only be greedy but foolish. And yet I couldn't help wishing for it anyway.

The more time I spent with Graham, the more I wondered how anyone could ever accuse him of being heartless. He was protective and loving. Thoughtful and generous. Or maybe that was the side he only shared with me.

I'd seen Graham Mackenzie the CEO in action countless times, and I felt privileged that he trusted me enough to show me his soft inner core. He was a lot like Queen V and Prince Albert in that way. At first glance, their large size made them seem imposing and threatening. But they were really so sweet and just wanted to be loved. Like Graham.

He shook his head. "I love it here."

The sincerity in his tone filled me with liquid warmth. I leaned my head against his shoulder, giving his arm a squeeze. "I'm so glad."

"And I've enjoyed my time off. But when we get back, it will no longer be our honeymoon. And I'll need to work."

"Right," I said. Everything was about to change, perhaps more than I'd even realized.

"Plus—" He wore a pinched expression, and I tried to brace myself for whatever was coming. "The board is being a pain in the ass."

"About the luxury yacht line?"

"Among other things." He was being cryptic, and I didn't like it. Already, I could feel a change in him, as if he was rebuilding his shields to prepare to be Graham Mackenzie, CEO. And not the man I was coming to know and love.

"I'm a good listener," I said, giving him a gentle nudge.

"I know. And it's something I probably should've mentioned sooner, but I didn't want to ruin our time together."

I was immediately on alert, my body stiffening. "What's wrong?"

We continued walking, following one of our familiar routes through the grounds. "Talk of the merger has been tabled for now."

"That's a good thing." I peered up at him and shielded my eyes from the late afternoon sun. "Isn't it?"

"It is."

"Then what's wrong?"

"Several members of the board hired a lawyer to contest the validity of the marriage clause in my grandfather's will."

I frowned. "Based on everything you've told me, that sounds like a waste of time and money." Though, wouldn't that be a kicker. I wondered how quickly Graham would try to divorce me if that were the case.

Neither of us had mentioned our relationship's expiration date lately, but it still loomed in my mind.

"Agreed," he said, his tone giving zero indication of his thoughts. "But there's more."

I waited, giving him space to work out what he wanted to say. Though I remained on edge the entire time.

"There are questions about our relationship."

"What kinds of questions?" I paused, coming to a stop in the middle of a copse of trees.

He slowed. "Accusations that we had an inappropriate relationship while you were my employee."

I peered up at him. The fading sun cast him in a golden glow that made him seem almost otherworldly. With the magnificent château rising up behind him, he looked like he'd stepped out of the pages of time. My every fantasy come to life.

If only we could just stay here.

But that wasn't part of the deal. And I had a role to play.

"And here I figured everyone would accuse me of being a gold digger," I teased, though I knew people were likely saying just that. "Now they'll also think I slept my way to the top."

"Lil." He took my hands in his. "I will do everything in my power to protect you. You know that, right?"

I nodded. I did know that. Regardless of how Graham might feel about me, it was in his best interest to protect me and our story.

"What can I do to help?" I asked.

"I talked to Pierce, and he suggested that we do a couple of interviews. Try to head off some of the rumors."

I sighed, both at what that would mean for me and for Graham. Graham never did well in formal interviews. He always came off as stiff, elitist, cold. He needed a different format. Something more casual. Something that would allow him to relax. To be himself and forget about the audience. A plan took shape in my mind.

But first, I had something I needed to tell him. If we were going to be interviewed, if people were digging into our relationship, into me, he deserved to hear about my alopecia from me. But even more than that, I found myself wanting to tell him the truth.

It had been exhausting—having to make sure my hair and eyebrows and lashes were perfect, even while I was working on the construction site.

"There's something you should know," I said, nerves knotting my belly. I worried about his reaction. I hated that I cared so much.

He paused. "Is everything okay?"

"Yeah." I blew out a breath. "I probably should've mentioned this before, but it didn't seem relevant to our agreement."

"And it does now?" he asked.

"It does, but also, I'm tired of keeping this secret." There was a tense, pregnant pause. And then I said, "I have alopecia." I pointed to my head. "This is a wig. I lost most of my hair before I was thirteen, and I've worn wigs ever since. I don't have any body hair, including eyebrows or eyelashes. I have to apply them."

He was quiet. Contemplative. And then he stepped closer. "I don't know much about alopecia. Is it painful?"

"Only when people bully you for something you have no control over. When you're teased. Called everything from 'a freak of nature' to the 'hairless wonder,'" I said, trying not to let the memories affect me. When I looked at him, he was glowering. "But physically, no. It doesn't hurt."

He narrowed his eyes, a muscle in his jaw popping. "Names. I need their names."

"Graham." I placed my hand on his chest, feeling the raw strength beneath my palm. His muscles were clenched as if he were bracing for a fight—as if he'd fight the world for me. "They were stupid kids. It doesn't matter." Though, it wasn't just stupid kids; it had been my siblings too. Some of the guys I'd dated hadn't been much better.

"It does, and you know it. Words have power. And the things they said to you—" He shook his head, disappointment radiating off of him in waves. "Anyone would be affected by that."

I swallowed past the lump in my throat. Graham had understood and validated my feelings more than anyone else ever had, even my parents. Most of the time it had felt as if I were a burden. Or that they didn't understand me or know how to deal with me.

In the beginning, trying to determine the cause of my hair loss had been time-consuming and expensive. Then, once we'd discovered it was alopecia, someone had suggested wigs. Wigs weren't cheap, nor were the creams and medicines we'd used to try to regrow my hair, to no avail.

My siblings had been brutal. Even if they weren't mocking me, they always seemed to resent me for getting so much attention from Mom and Dad. It wasn't like I'd asked for the attention. Or that I *wanted* the hair loss.

But Graham had been kind. Caring. Sympathetic.

For a man who had been labeled as cold and heartless, he was anything but. At least, not with me. He was warm and understanding. Accepting. No one had believed me, stepped up for me, until Graham.

"I don't want to dwell on the past," I finally said. "I just thought I should mention it because it might come up."

His body was still coiled tight with tension, so I placed my hand on his arm. "Thank you for wanting to defend me. No one..." I swallowed, shoving back the feeling of tears. "Well, you're the first to...besides Jo anyway."

"What about your family?" he asked.

I shook my head. And that reminder only reaffirmed my decision to cut them out of my life. Maybe one day we could try to have a relationship again, though things would have to change drastically. Because I was done letting them walk all over me. Letting them treat me the way they had.

It hurt to admit that, but it also felt freeing.

I was creating my own family. With Luc and the artisans. With the community around me. With Jo and even with Graham—at least for now.

He gnashed his teeth. "I'm sorry, Lil." He pulled me to him, hugging me. "That's shitty. But now you have me, and I won't let anyone hurt you."

My tears—like my voice—were muffled by his chest. "Thank you."

He held me as long as I needed, giving me space and compassion and support. I'd never felt so...loved. Not that he loved me, but I felt it all the same. Finally, reluctantly, I pulled back.

"I'm honored that you told me." He cupped my cheek. "That you trust me."

Okay. Seriously? This was the kind of reaction I'd always dreamed of. We'd see if he still felt the same when he saw my bald head, but I was melting at his sincerity and concern—for me.

"Thank you for making it easy to tell you." God, it was such a relief to finally share this huge thing with him.

"You must save a ton of money on hair removal and hair care."

I laughed. Leave it to the businessman to consider the financial implications of my condition. "You'd think that, but buying high-quality eyelashes and wigs gets expensive. Well, not this wig." I flicked my hair aside. "It's relatively cheap, all things considered."

Plus, there was the cost of creams to keep the skin of my head from drying out. Kits to make my eyebrows look realistic. Scarves and hats…

He slipped his hand into mine. Warm. Comforting. "Will you show me sometime?" he asked as we resumed walking. "Only if you feel comfortable."

I nodded, surprised by how readily I'd agreed. But also… not.

"So I had an idea. About how to work on our image as a couple."

"Yeah?"

"Yeah." I grinned. "What if you joined me on-screen in some of my videos. Just casually drop in every so often. You wouldn't even have to talk. Just let the viewer see us together."

He pursed his lips. "Are you sure that's a good idea?"

"Why not? I think you'd do great in an informal setting like that."

"No." He shook his head. "I meant for your channel. I don't want to jeopardize your content."

I melted a little at his thoughtfulness. "Are you kidding? My viewers would love you. You're like a modern Mr. Darcy, strolling across the grounds of a majestic château. Ooh." I snapped. "Do you think you'd be willing to stand in a pond in a white shirt?"

"What?"

"Never mind." I smiled, amused by his expression and this conversation. Though, damn, my viewers would lose their shit if I staged something like that.

That said, I wasn't sure I wanted to share Graham with the rest of the world. I knew it was in our best interest, but I liked that I got to have him all to myself when we were at the château.

We continued walking, meandering among the old trees. Hands intertwined, heart full. The leaves crunched beneath our feet, a squirrel scurrying up a nearby trunk.

"Who is this Mr. Darcy?" Graham asked. "This is the second time I've heard his name. First Sloan, and now you. Should I be jealous?"

"He's only every woman's fantasy."

He growled, pulling me into him. "Why is my wife fantasizing about another man?"

I was both turned on and amused, and I didn't know whether to laugh or moan at the feeling of his body pressing into mine. He was hard and strong, and I closed my eyes, overwhelmed by the sensations. We hadn't had sex again—yet. But Graham had pleasured me almost every night, only letting me return the favor every so often when I insisted.

I didn't know why I'd been holding out on having sex. If I admitted it to myself, I did know. But I hadn't been willing to admit it to myself.

Sex complicated things. I was trying to keep some distance between us. I'd promised myself—and Graham—that I wouldn't fall in love with him. And here I was, doing just that.

How could I not? Graham made it so easy to fall for him. The man was thoughtful and nurturing. He'd taken it upon himself to heat up my bath every night with the electric kettle. He supported my dreams and valued my opinions, often listening to me talk about the château for hours. And after his reaction to my alopecia, I didn't want to hold back anymore.

He spun me so my back was to a tree, his arms caging me in. "Liliana." His nostrils flared. "Answer me."

I debated toying with him a little longer, just to see what he'd do. Or maybe he was messing with me. Because who hadn't heard of *Pride and Prejudice*?

"You're a lot like him, you know. Tall, brooding—"

He narrowed his eyes at me. "Where can I find this Mr. Darcy?"

I started laughing.

"Liliana." He collared my throat, and everything reduced down to that pulse point. To that point of contact.

I could barely focus on anything but him, but I wanted to tease him a little more. "Have you seriously never read *Pride and Prejudice*?"

"What does that have to do with anything?"

"Fitzwilliam Darcy and Elizabeth Bennet? One of the greatest love stories of all time."

He pulled a face, his hand resting over my erratic pulse. "I was always more into chess and gardening. I don't have much time for pleasure reading, and I'm pretty sure that book wouldn't make the cut." Spoken with such disdain.

"It should," I said, swallowing, feeling his hand move because of it. His eyes darted there then back to mine. "It really should. And gah. *ACOTAR* and *Outlander* and *Fourth Wing* too. Epic love stories, and the heroes…" I sighed.

"Why look to fiction when there are epic love stories that exist in real life?" He slid his hand down my throat, smoothing over my breast.

"Such as…"

"My grandparents, for one."

"Mm," I said. "Okay. Unfortunately, I never met them." Though I had heard stories of their legendary love.

"Prince Albert and Queen Victoria."

"Your dogs?" I laughed, but it quickly turned into a gasp when he lightly pinched my nipple.

"No. Their namesakes. Their deep commitment and abiding love were admirable. They were all about family and duty."

My lips curled into a smile. That was really sweet, actually. I'd never known the true reason behind their names, but I'd certainly heard rumors during my time at Huxley.

He tilted his head. "Why do you seem surprised?"

"I'm not, but I know some people who would be."

He frowned. "What does that mean?"

"You know what a Prince Albert piercing is, right?"

He stared at me, aghast. "You thought I named my Irish Wolfhound after a dick piercing?"

"*I* didn't. But, yeah—" I lifted a shoulder. "Others do." When I'd been working at the Huxley Grand, it had been a joke among the employees.

"And I suppose they think the V in Queen V is for vagina?"

"Vulva, actually."

He grumbled, and I couldn't help but laugh.

"You know," I said, grabbing his collar and pulling his lips down until they hovered over mine. "I never would've guessed you were such a hopeless romantic."

"And I never would've guessed you had such a dirty mind."

I tugged so his ear was close to my lips. "Read some of my favorite books, and then you'll understand."

His eyes narrowed into slits. "I don't like the idea of you thinking of other men—fictional or otherwise."

I started backing away toward the château, raising a brow. "Then I suggest you give me something better to think about."

His eyes darkened. "Is that a challenge?"

I smirked and lifted a shoulder. And then I turned and walked away, my core heating at the determined expression on his face.

CHAPTER TWENTY-FIVE

Lily

"Let me grab my camera gear, and then we can get started."

"Now?" Graham balked.

"Unless you have somewhere better to be?"

"I definitely have something I'd rather be doing." He gave me a pointed look.

"Mm." I bit my lower lip. "Tempting."

He took a step forward, and I held up a hand as if to stop him. "Nope. I know what you're trying to do."

"And what's that, Mrs. Mackenzie?" He took another step closer. His chest met my palm, easing against my resistance.

"Distract me."

He closed the distance, and my hands rested on his chest. "Is it working?" He dipped, pressing his lips to the skin behind my ear, a featherlight touch that set my body ablaze.

"I—" I cleared my throat. "I, uh..." I clutched his shirt in my fists, trying to concentrate. Focus.

Focus, Lil!

My phone buzzed in my pocket, and I straightened and

took a step back. "Okay." I patted his chest. "That's enough—for now. You're not getting out of this."

He arched one eyebrow as if to say, "You sure?"

I planted my hands on my hips and narrowed my eyes at him in response. Hoping the gesture conveyed that I was sure. Even when my body was screaming in protest at the loss of his touch.

"No rest for the wicked." He adjusted himself. "I'll go change, and then we can get started."

I smoothed my hand down his chest, unable to resist touching him. "You look great. Relaxed. At home. The more comfortable you are, the more it will reflect on-camera."

"But I'm CEO of one of the most lucrative luxury hotel chains on the planet."

"And everyone knows that. They see you in suits all the time. But they don't get to see you like this."

I only hoped that I'd get to see Graham like this after we returned to LA. I knew things would change. Of course they would. He'd go back to working full time, and we'd go back to attending public events. But I hoped we'd still be as vulnerable and authentic with each other.

"Are you sure this is a good idea?" he asked, showing a rare hesitance. Was he nervous?

I placed my hand over his heart. "Do you trust me?"

He brought my hand to his lips, pressing a kiss to my palm. "Of course."

"Then trust me on this."

He blew out a breath. "Okay. Let's get this over with."

"That's the spirit," I teased and ducked inside. I checked my phone, frowning at a new message from my mom.

Over the past few weeks, I'd ignored countless texts from my family. Their anger had since cooled, turned into apologies. A thinly veiled attempt to manipulate me into giving my sister the money.

Sometimes I wished I could go back to *before*. To when my family hadn't been jealous and resentful. To when they'd viewed me as an oddity instead of a piggy bank that they tried to guilt into giving them money.

I deleted the text and grabbed my gear. As soon as I returned, Graham took my camera bag and tripod from me.

"Everything okay?" he asked.

"Yep!" I chirped with perhaps a bit too much enthusiasm. Eager to distract him—and myself—I said, "Wait. Didn't you say you had a surprise for me?"

"I said, I had something I wanted to show you."

I arched a brow and gave his crotch a pointed look.

"Not that." He shook his head. "Though I'd be happy to show you that anytime."

"Mm." I licked my lips, my mind flashing to last night and the way I'd sucked him off.

Watching him lose control had been glorious, but I wanted more. I wanted something real. Telling him about my alopecia had been a good first step. And his reaction had been, well, everything.

But could he love me? For now, maybe it could be enough to know that he cared about me. Regardless of his feelings, our situation was complicated. So long as we were pretending to be a happily married couple, I wasn't sure I could distinguish what was real from what wasn't.

We walked to the edge of the *grand allée*, and Graham watched as I set up the camera. "Okay," I said. "Can you walk down the *grand allée* toward the château?"

"That's all you want me to do—walk?" He looked incredulous.

"For starters, yeah. I need to make sure the angle and framing are right, and then we can go from there."

I also wanted to start getting Graham comfortable in

front of the camera, but I didn't tell him that. The more relaxed and natural I could make this feel, the better.

I pressed the record button, and he walked up the *grand allée* toward the château with Queen V and Prince Albert. It was perfect. The lighting. His clothes. The framing. It made me giddy with excitement—my creative juices churning at the prospect of including Graham in my videos.

"Perfect," I called out. "Come back, and we'll do it again. Together."

He returned, and we retraced his steps, this time hand in hand. I smiled up at him, and he was silent. Stiff.

"What's up?" I asked, knowing the camera wouldn't pick up our voices without a microphone. Even if it did, I could edit out any conversation. "I feel like your ass cheeks are clenching so hard, you're going to shit diamonds."

He barked out a laugh. "You paint quite the image."

"Well, you are a billionaire. Maybe you do shit diamonds."

"I don't. But I have noticed that you rarely wear your ring." He gave me *a look.*

"I'd hate to damage it. You know how rough some of these projects can be."

"It's insured, but I appreciate your wanting to protect it."

I nodded.

"I should've asked sooner," he continued. "But is the style not to your liking?"

"Are you kidding?" I gaped at him. "It's beautiful."

Secretly, I loved it. And I loved wearing it—maybe a little too much. Not only because it was a beautiful piece of jewelry but because of what it symbolized.

Commitment. Family. Permanence.

I loved the idea of being his wife, but I had to remind myself this was temporary.

"Even so," he said, interrupting my thoughts. "If it's not you, then I get it. I'm happy to swap it out for something different if you'd prefer." He rubbed his thumb over my bare ring finger. I noticed he rarely took his wedding ring off, though it was a simple gold band. There were no stones to knock loose or damage.

We reached the château and stared up at it. "I'd hate for you to have to spend any more money on me than you already have." Just thinking about it gave me an ulcer.

The engagement ring was expensive. I wasn't sure I even wanted to know how expensive. But it seemed like a drop in the bucket compared to everything else he'd done. I was beginning to wonder if I'd gotten the better end of the bargain. And regardless of Graham's feelings for me, I vowed to do anything in my power to ensure that he succeeded with his plans for controlling the Huxley brand.

Graham stopped walking, and I slowed. When I turned to face him, I realized he was scowling.

"Not every decision is based on money." His eyes glinted with some emotion I couldn't place.

"Says the billionaire." I waved a hand through the air, wishing I could wave away my morose mood so easily. Why was I acting like this? I had everything I could've hoped for and so much more. And yet, I wanted more. I wanted Graham.

"Let's go back and get my camera, and then we'll take some other shots," I said.

He walked with me back down the *grand allée*. I stopped about halfway, turning and wrapping my arms around his neck.

"Kiss me," I murmured.

He peered down at me, placing his hands on my hips. "I don't like the idea of kissing you on-camera."

"Isn't that the whole point of this relationship?" I kept my voice low. "It's all for show."

God, Lil. Could you be more obvious or pathetic?

"I still don't like it," he said, and I wasn't sure what to make of his tone. I wasn't sure how to answer.

I was testing him, sort of. Did he feel this too? Was there any way he'd ever want this to be more than pretend?

Maybe I should've just told him what I was feeling, but I was scared. Scared he didn't feel the same way. Scared that I'd ruin something wonderful and turn it into something beyond awkward.

"You don't have to like it. But the more invested people are in our love story, the less attention they'll pay to stupid rumors."

He cupped my cheek, his touch a gentle claiming.

I clutched his shirt in my hands, wanting him closer—not just for the camera, but for me. "Do you want everyone to believe this is real or not?"

"I do, but—"

"Then kiss me," I said again, this time more forcefully.

He hesitated, smoothing my hair over my shoulder. And then he leaned in and pressed a kiss to my forehead.

"I can work with that," I said.

He grunted but said nothing more.

We filmed a few more scenes around the grounds, viewing the progress of various projects. Talking about what was coming up next.

"The sunflowers will be ready to harvest soon," Graham said as we passed through a field of them.

I glanced out over the colorful, happy field of flowers. I didn't think I could look at sunflowers without thinking of our wedding. Light suffused the air with a sort of golden quality that made it feel as if anything were possible. I wanted to capture this moment, live in it forever.

"Un tournesol," I mused. "To turn with the sun."

"Sunflowers can have numerous meanings, but my favorites are loyalty, strength, and resilience." He looked me straight in the eye, and it felt as if he was trying to tell me something more than what he was saying with his words.

Or maybe I was merely wanting to read more into it.

I tilted my head, watching Graham in the fading sun. "How do you know all that?"

"My gran."

He was quiet and so was I, giving him a minute to process his thoughts. I knew how important his grandparents were to him, even if he rarely mentioned their influence on his life outside the company.

"I used to pore over her books on botany and the hidden meaning of flowers. The Victorians attributed all sorts of symbolism to various plants and flowers. Often using flowers to send hidden messages to others."

"Like a secret code?" I asked.

"Sort of." The colors in the sky shifted, turning a beautiful pink. "My gran used to pick a fresh bouquet from her garden every week, always sending me messages of love with her flowers. It was something only the two of us shared. Our own little language."

"That's really sweet." I smiled, placing my hand on his arm. "I'm sure you miss her a lot."

"Like you wouldn't believe." He stared at the ground, a thoughtful expression on his face until his lips tipped into a smile.

"What?" I finally asked.

"It's funny. I haven't thought about her secret flower messages in years. Not until, well…you."

"Really?" I asked, surprised and delighted by his admission.

"Maybe it's because your name is a type of flower."

"Lily?" I asked, and he nodded. "And what does a lily symbolize?"

"Lilies can have many meanings, depending on the

culture or even the color of the flower itself. Everything from purity and innocence to fertility or even everlasting love."

But what did lilies mean to Graham? Especially where I was concerned.

"Mm. Interesting. And ferns?" I asked, hoping I wasn't being too obvious. Our wedding flowers had included lilies, ferns, sunflowers, and roses.

"Ferns are symbols of new beginnings and protection. That's why I chose them for our wedding."

Okay. Maybe not so subtle after all.

I blinked at him a few times. "*You* chose the flowers? I thought Carson took care of all the arrangements."

"He executed my plans, but all the selections were mine alone."

My jaw dropped, and I quickly turned away to mask my surprise. "*All* the selections?"

"The menu. The outdoor space. The flowers. Everything."

I jerked my head back. "Damn. You put a lot of thought and effort into a fake wedding."

"*Real* wedding," he gritted out.

"Yes. Yes. Fine." I waved a hand through the air, knowing this was a point of contention for him. "Real wedding."

I supposed I had the ring and the marriage certificate to prove it. But despite how legally binding our wedding had been, he hadn't married me for love. So in my mind, it would never be "real" in any meaningful sense of the word.

That day—as beautiful as it had been, and as *real* as it had felt to me in some ways—would always be overshadowed by our arrangement. By the fact that Graham needed a wife and I needed his money.

He grabbed me, pulling me to him. "You're mine."

But for how long?

I was already falling for my husband, and that scared the

shit out of me. His company had always been his first priority, and I knew that would never change. I'd never expect him to change. Heck, it was one of the things I loved most about him.

"We should head back," I said, worried that this honeymoon phase was just that—a phase.

A look of disappointment flashed through his eyes, and then it was gone. Prince Albert whined, ending further conversation on the matter.

The dogs were getting hungry and so were we, so we headed back to our living quarters. I set up the camera outside and got ready to film the tour.

"I thought we were done filming," Graham said.

"We are, but I'm not. My followers have been asking about my living situation, and I've been meaning to give them a tour."

He jerked his head back. "You what?"

"You know, a home tour."

He glowered. "Absolutely not."

I crossed my arms over my chest. "Excuse me?"

"It's a safety issue. People already have your address—there's no way to hide the location of the *Château de Bergeret*. But do you really need to give them a step-by-step plan to break in to our home?"

Our home. I liked the sound of that way too much.

But this wasn't our home. It was temporary. Everything about this was supposed to be temporary. Our living situation. Our marriage.

"It's common practice for vloggers," I said, trying not to betray my inner turmoil. "Besides, you had Hudson Security install surveillance cameras."

"I don't fucking care what other people do. They're not my wife." He practically growled the "my wife," and while it shouldn't have been hot, it was.

Hot, but also a reminder that he was protecting his interests because we were married. Because we had a deal. He didn't care about me, Liliana. He cared about "his wife." Talk about a reality check.

I gnashed my teeth. "I may be your wife, but I am still my own person."

He stepped closer. "I know you are." He placed his hands on my shoulders. "But I don't think you appreciate how much information you share with the world and what kinds of ideas and access that can give someone."

I frowned. "Now you're scaring me."

"I'm not trying to scare you. I'm trying to keep you safe."

"Isn't that what Willow's for?" I asked. "And where is she anyway? I haven't seen her at all since we've been here."

"She's been collaborating with the on-site residential team."

"For their assessment," I said, though it was more of a question.

"Initially, yes. But the team will provide twenty-four-seven surveillance whether we're here or not."

I blinked a few times, trying to process this new information. "For how long?"

"Indefinitely."

I stared at him, mouth agape. "Don't you think you should've mentioned that?" I mean, I'd seen the team around, but I'd figured their presence was part of their security assessment. Not something permanent.

Hell, our marriage was only supposed to last one to two years max. Did Graham intend to continue surveillance even after that? It seemed both expensive and intrusive.

He pinched the bridge of his nose and let out a heavy sigh. "You're right. I should've talked to you about it." He opened his eyes. "I'm sorry. With everything else going on, it wasn't a priority. But it should've been."

Mollified, I asked, "Is there a way I could do the tour without jeopardizing our safety?"

"If anyone would know, it's the team from Hudson."

"Okay. I'll talk to them," I said, knowing that his concern wasn't unwarranted. And my decisions didn't just affect me anymore; they affected Graham too.

"Tomorrow," he said. "First, I want to show you something. Close your eyes."

"Okay," I said, dragging out the word but ultimately complying.

He came to stand behind me, brushing my hair over my shoulder. He skimmed his hands over my shoulders, down my arms, finally taking one of my hands in his. I shivered at the contact.

He led me toward the entrance to our living quarters, and I was intrigued. "I hope you're not mad about this. I didn't tell you because I wanted it to be a surprise, but maybe that was a bad idea." The door creaked as it swung open, and I could feel his nerves.

I was apprehensive, excited. Nervous. But I could tell that he'd wanted to do something nice for me.

"You can open your eyes."

The living room slash kitchen looked about the same as it had this morning, though it had a new farmhouse sink as well as a new stove and oven. Nothing too over the top, but it felt like a luxury after cooking everything on a hot plate.

"Wow." I stood there, taking it all in. "This is nice."

"I'm glad you like it. There's more." He opened the door to an old utility closet to reveal a new, energy-efficient washer and dryer.

I nearly fainted. For the past year, I'd had to go to the laundromat in town to wash my clothes. This would save me so much time and energy.

"Come on." He tugged my hand, guiding me past the

bedroom, which looked the same at first glance. But then I froze.

"The new mattress arrived!"

He crossed his arms over his chest. "Looks good, doesn't it?"

He'd made the bed, so it looked like something straight out of a promo image for a Huxley Grand hotel. The new sheets I'd ordered had arrived, as had the comforter. They were freshly washed, and the bed looked so inviting.

"It looks amazing."

For a man who claimed not to be a cuddler, Graham had held me every night since we'd come to France. I'd gotten used to falling asleep in his arms, and I hoped that wouldn't change now that we had more space. Though, I noted that there was still only one bed. He must have gotten rid of my old mattress.

"One more thing," he said, pulling me toward the bathroom.

The top of the bathtub was obscured by a shower curtain that hung from an oval-shaped copper rod. *That's new.*

Graham pulled back the curtain to reveal a pole with a matching copper showerhead that looked as if it had always been there. "*Voilà!*"

"Wow." I stepped closer. "That's gorgeous."

"That's not even the best part." He grinned. He was too cute. Clearly, he'd put a lot of effort into this project, and he was proud of it.

I could imagine Graham as a little boy, showing off his hard work to his family. Seeking their approval, their praise. Who gave that to him now that his grandparents were gone? Who reminded him that he was doing a good job?

"What's the best part?" I asked, delighted both by the changes I'd witnessed in our home and in this man.

"We not only have a shower." He switched on the faucet,

and steam immediately rose into the air. "We have hot water."

I gasped. "No way." I stepped closer, placing my hand underneath the spray. Warm water cascaded over my hand, and it felt glorious. "Oh my god. I think I love you."

Shit. My eyes widened, and I quickly jumped to damage control, hoping Graham would brush off my admission as a joke.

I stepped closer, tugging on the hem of his shirt. *Distract. Divert.* "You want to try it out with me?"

"What about your wig?" This was new territory for us—showering together.

"I can shower with it, but I typically remove it. The wig will last longer if I only wash it once every few weeks. But I can keep it on if you'd prefer," I said with a twist of my belly.

He grasped my chin, bringing my gaze to his. "I want you to do whatever is most comfortable for you." The words were spoken in a slow, measured tone.

I nodded, and when I inhaled, my breath was shaky. He released me, and I took a step back, removing my baseball cap before setting it aside. Since I often got sweaty when working at the château, I'd opted to wear glueless wigs while we were in France. It still had a lace edge, to make it look more natural, but it was a lot more comfortable for my scalp.

With my heart in my throat, I removed my wig, baring myself to him completely.

"Lil," he said, his voice full of emotion. "Look at me."

I met his eyes, scared to see what I'd find there. But he greeted me with acceptance, his eyes glowing with warmth and affection.

"You—" he cupped my cheeks "—are stunning."

"You're not..." I glanced away. "Disgusted?"

"Disgusted?" He said the word like it tasted bad in his mouth. "Why would I be disgusted?"

"Most people are weirded out by the baldness." Some of the guys I'd dated in the past had been. So I'd always made sure to have my wig, eyebrows, and eyelashes on at all times.

"You're beautiful." He pressed a kiss to my forehead, to the bare skin there. *"Envoûtante."* I smiled, remembering him using that same word to describe me on our wedding day, and it meant enchanting or bewitching.

A tear streaked down my cheek. "Thank you," I whispered, feeling lighter.

"And if anyone ever says otherwise, they will regret it." Anger flashed in those green eyes like lightning.

I would've laughed, but his tone was so serious, so menacing. For me. I couldn't help but feel grateful. Loved.

CHAPTER TWENTY-SIX

Graham

I stared at Lily, marveling at the strong, confident, resilient woman who was my wife. My equal. My heart.

When she'd said, *I think I love you* earlier, I'd known she was making an offhand remark. And yet, I wanted to pretend she meant those words. That she loved me.

I am so screwed.

"Mm." She ran her hands up my chest. "I like you like this—all growly and protective. It's hot." She unbuttoned my shirt.

"You're hot," I said, yanking off my shirt as fast as possible.

I pulled her to me, crushing my lips against hers. There was nothing slow, methodical, or calculated about my movements. I was raw heat and passion ready to explode, and she matched my energy, my desperation. I couldn't touch enough of her fast enough.

"Everyone has it wrong about you," she said when we broke apart so I could peel off her clothes.

"What do you mean?" I tugged at her shirt, buttons flying in the process.

"Hey!" She scowled. "I liked that shirt."

"I'll buy you another one," I said between kisses. "I'll buy you as many as you want."

She rolled her eyes even as she pushed my shirt off over my shoulders. "You aren't cold or heartless. If anything, you have such a big heart that you feel too much."

I... How had she?

She placed her hand over my heart. "You're a good man, Graham Mackenzie."

"I—" I tried to swallow past the lump in my throat. "Thank you."

"Now, are you just going to stand there, or are you going to join me?" she teased, snapping me out of my thoughts. She was naked, and I reveled in the sight of her.

"Get in," I rumbled.

For once, she obeyed. I kicked off my pants and followed her into the tub. Warm water sprayed over my skin, and my body sighed in relief. *Damn.* It was glorious after too many days of cold baths. She was right; heating the water with the kettle was a pain in the ass, so I rarely did it for myself.

I closed the shower curtain and guided her foot to the edge of the tub. I went to my knees, gazing up at her like a supplicant before an altar. "Beautiful."

She peered down at me, so full of love and desire that it nearly stole the breath from my lungs.

I inhaled deeply, trying to steady myself. *"Laisse-moi te plaire."* I was commanding. I was pleading. *Let me please you.* Not just with my body but with my everything.

She cupped my cheek. "You do please me, *mon amour*."

The moment felt fragile and beautiful, like the first bloom of spring. It filled me with a sense of hope and excitement as I glimpsed a vision of our future. Of the life we could build together.

She clutched my shoulders, urging me closer. *"Please, Graham."*

I didn't have to be asked twice. I nuzzled her mound. Hot water cascaded down our skin, filling the bathroom with heat to rival our own. The more I lapped and licked her clit, the more her grip on my shoulders tightened.

"Yes," she panted. "Yes. Yes. Yes."

It turned into a chant, my name a benediction on her lips and music to my ears. Until her legs were shaking. Until she came undone, screaming my name.

I stood, gathering her into my arms and just holding her close. Letting her catch her breath, though my heart pounded just as fast as hers. Our bodies were slick, and our mouths were locked. Our kisses teasing. Tasting. Breathless. She was so goddamn perfect.

"I need you," I rasped, grabbing her ass and holding her even tighter. It was as close as I had come to admitting the truth.

I needed this woman in my arms, in my bed, in my life.

I worried about telling her. Worried she didn't feel the same. But then I'd remember the way Lily would look at me. The way she'd touch me. And I'd think it couldn't possibly all be an act.

Lately, I worried more about *not* telling her. My parents had died at such a young age. What if something happened to me? What if I'd never told her that I loved her? What if I missed my opportunity?

But then her words floated back to me.

If you're worried about me falling in love with you. Don't.

Followed by, *I know you don't do relationships.*

But what if I did?

Wasn't that what this was? A relationship? It may not have started off as "real" or anything more than a business arrangement, but even in the short time we'd been married, it had certainly transformed into something more—at least for me.

Qui ne risque rien, n'a rien. Or he who risks nothing, has nothing.

I took risks every day in my job. Did I really want to risk losing out on something amazing with Lily because I was scared?

If she could have the courage to tell me about her alopecia, to remove her wig and show me a side of her that she usually kept hidden, I could find the courage to tell her how I felt.

"You okay?" Lily asked, placing her palm to my cheek.

I nodded, enjoying the warm water and the comfort of her touch. My heart was in my throat, but I had to do this. I had to tell her the truth.

"*Je t'aime,*" I rasped, the words feeling both foreign and yet right.

She stilled, eyes searching mine. "You...*what?*" She was breathless.

"I—" I cupped the back of her neck. "Love. You," I said again, this time in English.

"Y-you do?" she stammered.

Had I really done such a shitty job of showing her how I felt? I'd figured it was so painfully obvious, even if it had taken me a little longer to realize it. To put a name to those feelings. Not just respect or admiration or lust, but love.

"Yes." I scanned her eyes, searching for an answer. Hoping she might feel the same or even might someday come to love me. "I didn't think I was capable of love. But you made me see that I am. That I always have been. I just had to believe it myself. And the only reason I do—" I kissed her gently. "Is because of you."

Water droplets rained down her face, her expression unreadable. "I—"

I placed a finger to her lips, stopping her from speaking. My heart was pounding a million miles a minute. "It's okay. You don't have to say it back. You don't have to say anything. I just..." I took a breath, feeling a rush of emotion. "Needed you to know."

"Are you done now?" she asked, all sass and sexiness.

I fought back a smile. "Yes."

"Good. Because..." She draped her arms around my neck, pressing that soft, supple body to mine. God, I loved her curves. Loved her. "I love you too."

Fuck. Yes.

I wanted to fist-pump the air. I wanted to run outside and shout it from the top of the château so everyone could hear it for miles. I wanted to—

"Kiss me," she said. "For real this time."

I trailed my finger over her cheekbone, down her jawline. She was so incredible. And she was mine. Not because of any agreement. Not because we'd signed a contract. But because she wanted to be with me. And I wanted to be hers.

"It's always been real for me," I whispered.

I kissed her cheek, just beside her lips. Her collarbone. Her shoulder. Anointing her with kisses, bathing her in affection and love.

She cupped my cheeks, meeting my eyes before kissing me with love and reverence. She might not have said the words aloud, but I felt them in her touch. In the way she looked at me.

I kissed the center of her chest, in the valley of her luscious breasts. *Mine.*

She laughed, making me realize I'd said the word aloud. "You're very possessive, husband."

"Only about the people and things I love."

Her gaze softened, turning molten. "If I'm yours, then you're mine."

It felt so good to be claimed. To be wanted.

"No more talk of expiration dates," I said.

"I'm yours as long as you'll have me."

"Forever isn't long enough," I said. "I want you to be mine longer than forever. *Sans cesse*." I kissed more of her skin. "*Toujours*."

"*À tout jamais*," she gasped as I moved my attention to her breasts, licking and sucking her nipples in a way that drove her wild. Her words drove me wild—a promise that emphasized the eternal nature of her desire.

"*Promets-moi?*" I asked.

"Promise." Her hand was on my cock, stroking, teasing.

"Not going to last long if you keep that up," I said, circling her clit. Making sure she was ready for me.

"Need you, Graham," she panted. "Need you inside me."

I lined myself up at her entrance, but then she screeched as the water turned cold. I switched off the shower and hopped out, grabbing towels for us before carrying her to the bed. I set her down on the mattress, crawling up her body, water droplets clinging to her skin.

My eyes were locked on hers as I pushed inside her. We groaned in unison, and I'd never felt more at ease. At home.

"*Mon cœur*," I whispered against her skin, pressing kisses to her forehead, over her ear. Trying to show her just how much I loved, accepted, and desired her just as she was.

I was honored that Lily had told me about her alopecia. I couldn't fathom the strength and vulnerability that it took to reveal something like that, but I could imagine the fear and pain she must have felt—it had been clear in her body language.

She wasn't used to being accepted, cherished, for who she was. And that made me intensely angry—at her family, at her friends, at the men she'd dated in the past. They were idiots, all of them.

Because she was incredible. Not just because of what she'd endured but because of who she was. Her work ethic. Her determination. Her resiliency.

It made me want to burn the world for her. It made me—

"Graham." She placed her hand to my cheek. "Stay here. With me."

I rested my forehead against hers, eyes locked. Her bottomless blue ones peered up at me with such trust and tenderness and love that it stole the air from my lungs.

I rolled us so she was on top, in control. "Ride me," I panted. "Take control. Take what you need from me."

She did, taking her pleasure and giving too. I kept one hand on her hip, the other on her clit, circling, building that pleasure. A flush crawled up her chest, over her cheeks. She was close.

"That's it, *mon cœur*. Come for me. Only me."

"Yes," she gasped, toying with her breasts, her nipples. Fuck me, she was sexy. I wanted to stay with her, like this, forever.

I'd never felt more like myself than I did when I was with Lily.

Pleasure coiled tight at the base of my spine, building, climbing, trying to escape. I gritted my teeth, desperate to hold out a little longer. I yanked her forward, tugging her nipple into my mouth. Swirling, sucking, biting.

She moved faster. Sliding up and down, neither of us in control of our movements any longer. For once, I didn't care.

I didn't feel the need to control everything, and I wanted her to see that. Wanted her to know that when it came to us —she held all the power. She had my heart in her hands.

She cupped my cheek, her eyes locked on mine. It was so intense, so raw, that I couldn't—wouldn't look away. We were connected in the most intimate and primal of ways, and I loved her.

Seconds later, she cried out, shattering on my cock as she fell apart. Unable to hold back any longer, I followed her over the edge into oblivion. Giving myself to her completely.

Later, as we lay in bed, cuddling and talking, I marveled at the space she'd carved out in my life.

"Tell me something about you. Something not many people know," she said, hand grazing the skin of my stomach, my chest, with just the right amount of pressure. I wondered if she even realized it. If she had to consciously think about the way she touched me. But she always made it seem so effortless.

In the past, other women had gotten annoyed with my... needs. When I'd ask them to touch me differently, they took it personally. They made it about them and not me. It was exhausting.

But being with Lily felt as natural as breathing. And not just in bed. All the time.

"I used to get in a lot of fights when I was younger."

"Really?" She tilted her head. She looked different without her wig on, but she also seemed more at ease. More herself. Regardless, she was always beautiful to me. I kissed the top of her head, wanting her to know that. To feel that. To feel nothing but love and acceptance. "But you're always so calm. So controlled."

I chuckled. "I wasn't always that way. It's part of the reason why Gran enrolled me in karate. She wanted to teach me discipline and control. That, and she probably knew that if I kept going the way I was—a tall, lanky, angry kid—I'd get the shit beaten out of me."

"I wish I could've met your gran. She sounds like a wise woman." Her tone was wistful.

"She was the best," I said, my heart aching even after all these years. Gran had been the glue, the one to hold us together after the loss of my parents and aunt and uncle in that tragic plane crash. "She would've liked you."

"Yeah?" I could hear the smile in Lily's voice.

"You're full of gumption, and you don't take shit from me or anyone."

She laughed. "You're right about that. But you're good for me too. You push me to think more strategically. But also to dream."

"I do?" I asked, nearly choking on the word. The strategic thinking wasn't a stretch. But the idea that I gave her freedom to dream? My heart soared at the prospect.

"You see things that other people don't. You take risks that others are too afraid to attempt. You make me want to push the boundaries. You make me believe anything is possible."

Wow. "Thank you," I said around the lump in my throat.

"Though, I'm curious, when did you have time to do all of this?"

I tucked my arm beneath my head. "All of what? It was a new oven and hot water."

"Oh my god. Seriously?" She pushed up so she was peering down at me. "You know it's so much more than that."

I reached out and cupped her cheek, pleased when she leaned into my touch. "I'm just glad you like it."

"I love it, but..."

"But what?" I asked, muscles tensing. *Shit.* Had I somehow screwed up?

"I'm just surprised you left it at that." She glanced down at the floor. "I figured, based on what you'd said, that you'd gut everything and build new."

I glanced around the room. "This place does have a certain charm. It didn't need a gut job, and that's not what you would've wanted."

It wasn't what I would've wanted either. During the time

we'd been here, I'd come to realize that I liked it as is. I liked our simple life. I liked the feeling of contentment that I'd found here, with Lily. It was the closest thing to normalcy—to a home—that I'd felt in longer than I could remember.

She opened her mouth, surprise lighting her features.

"See. I can listen," I teased. "And after living in the space as it was, I learned what the pain points were. Mostly, the kitchen and the bathroom. Though the new mattress and sheets are nice."

"Agreed." She nuzzled my chest, snuggling closer. "Very nice."

We lay there, just enjoying being together, touching, after a long day of hard work.

After a while, she said, "It's going to be weird to go back to LA after this."

"It is." Though I'd already been brainstorming ways to spend more time at the château. I hadn't told her that yet, though. I didn't want to get her hopes up. I didn't want to promise something I wasn't sure I could deliver.

"Did you mean what you said earlier?" she asked. Even though she was being vague, I knew exactly what she was referring to.

I pushed up on my elbow, peering down at her. "Yes." I cupped her cheek. "I meant every word. I love you, Lily."

It wasn't as terrifying to say it now as it had been the first time. Knowing my feelings were reciprocated definitely helped.

She smiled—a smile full of hope and relief. "I love you too, Graham."

As I fell asleep that night, Lily in my arms, I felt content. Hopeful, in a way I hadn't been in a long time.

CHAPTER TWENTY-SEVEN

Lily

"So, if I'm Mr. Darcy," Graham said. "Does that mean you admit you're obstinate and headstrong?"

"What?" I glanced up from my laptop. We were headed back to LA, and I was trying to get some edits done during the flight. I'd done my best to stockpile some content before we'd left so I'd be able to continue my release schedule for my YouStream channel, but I was realizing this was going to be a constant balancing act—living between two countries. Two worlds.

"Elizabeth Bennet," Graham said. "She's obstinate and headstrong."

I narrowed my eyes at him. "She thinks for herself, unlike many of the women of her time."

"I know. It's what I like about her. Though, she is awfully quick to judge Darcy's actions."

Wait. What? I jerked my head back. "Are we seriously discussing *Pride and Prejudice* right now?"

"Yeah. Keep up." There was a teasing glint in his eyes.

"I'm sorry. I thought you said, and I quote, 'I don't have time for pleasure reading, and I'm pretty sure that book wouldn't make the cut.'" I'd pitched my voice low in a poor attempt to mimic him.

"I listened to it on audiobook at two-times speed one of the days while I stripped the lead paint in the entry hall. And then I started *ACOTAR*, though Carson had to help me figure that one out."

I stared at him, mouth agape. "You what?"

"*ACOTAR. A Court of Thorns and Roses*. I didn't realize it was an acronym at first."

I furrowed my brow. "You listened to them?"

"The audiobooks, yeah. Some people claim it's not 'reading,' but I think that's bullshit." He pursed his lips. "It's also a bit ableist, to be honest."

"I…uh. Yeah." *Wow.*

"The book was better than I'd expected," he continued, oblivious.

"Which one?" I asked.

"Both."

I arched my brow. "Interesting."

"It was. And while I wouldn't want to go back to the time period of *Pride and Prejudice*—especially because of what it would mean for women's rights and equality generally—the idea of set social rules is appealing."

I smirked, setting my laptop aside. Of course that would appeal to him. Expectations. A societal code of conduct. Still, I couldn't believe he'd read *Pride and Prejudice*. *Why* had he read it?

"Because it's something you enjoy," he said, making me realize I'd asked the question aloud.

So sexy. He'd read a book because I'd mentioned how much I loved it? Talk about speaking my love language.

"Do you want to discuss it some more in private?" I arched my brow.

His brief confusion was quickly overcome with understanding. He stood, giving me a wolfish smile. "I'd love to."

CALIFORNIA SUNSHINE POURED THROUGH THE CURTAINS OF Graham's penthouse. The light was different here, harsher somehow than the mornings at the château. The bed was bigger, empty. But when I turned to check the time on my phone, I saw a fresh vase with an arrangement of sunflowers, white roses, and white lilies.

I smiled, thinking back on everything Graham had told me about his gran and the secret language of flowers. I wondered if he'd been trying to send me messages all along.

My mind drifted back to that evening in the field of sunflowers. When he'd told me that lilies could have many meanings, including everlasting love. And he valued sunflowers as symbols of loyalty, strength, and resilience. The next day, I'd downloaded a book on the symbolism of flowers, and I'd pored over it.

I didn't remember Graham saying anything about white roses. But according to my book, they symbolized anything from loyalty and respect to silence or even eternal love.

I stretched and grabbed my phone, typing out a quick message to thank him, including several red rose emojis to symbolize love, passion, romance, commitment, desire, and devotion. All the things I felt about him.

> Graham: Good morning, beautiful wife.

> Me: Thank you for the flowers. How early did you leave?

> Graham: Early. Needed to get a jump on some stuff before the board meeting. You were sleeping, and I didn't want to wake you. Have a good day, mon cœur.

> Me: You too, mon doudou.

I WAITED FOR HIS REACTION TO MY LATEST PET NAME. I'D basically called him the French equivalent of "pookie." He was going to hate it. *If only I could see his face right now.*

> Graham: Try again, mon petit poisson.

I LAUGHED TO MYSELF. NOW THAT I KNEW THE MEANING behind his pet name, it didn't bother me as much. It had taken me a while to get it out of him, but Graham admitted that he'd called me *mon petit poisson* in reference to our conversation about a chemistry test and the fact that Nate had likened kissing Cece Golden to kissing a dead fish.

Graham said that I was the opposite of that. And when he'd realized how much the nickname irked me, he couldn't help but needle me a little.

I typed out another message. He didn't like that? We'd see how he felt about being referred to as "doll."

> Me: Ma poupée

> Graham: Absolument pas.

A HUGE SMILE OVERTOOK MY FACE, AND I FLOPPED BACK ON the bed. I held up my left hand, admiring my wedding ring, thinking about my husband and how lucky I was. I had a spouse who shared my interests. Who was smart and generous and kindhearted and nurturing. A man who was fluent in French and loved to flirt with me in the language of love. A man who supported my dreams and did everything in his power to make sure they came true.

And to think it had all started because of a business arrangement.

I had some things to take care of for the château, but I wanted to see Graham. I needed to see him. We'd both been so busy since returning to LA last week, and he was supposed to play poker with his brothers and Pierce tonight. I'd been invited to hang out with Kendall, Emerson, and Emerson's twin, Astrid.

I was happy for him to enjoy time with family and friends. And I enjoyed spending time with Kendall and Emerson. But I found myself longing to return to the château. Not only to see the progress and work on projects but so I would have Graham all to myself.

I texted Willow my plan for the day then pushed out of bed and padded to the closet, grabbing a wig before heading to the bathroom to get ready. I'd just finished applying my brows, lashes, and wig when my phone rang. Jo's name flashed across the screen, along with a request to video chat.

I pressed the button to accept the call as I headed toward the closet.

"Ooh, girl. That wig is fire!"

"Thanks." I fluffed my hair, a new wig that Graham's

stylist Jay Crowe had helped me select. "I call her Genevieve." I did a sexy little shake.

"*Très* French," Jo said. "I approve." Her jaw dropped. "Wait. Is that a store? Where are you?"

"In my closet," I said, panning the phone around so she could see it. "Technically, Graham's and my closet at his penthouse." I indicated to his suits and shirts, all perfectly pressed and precisely spaced. I smiled.

"One of the many perks of marrying a billionaire, I suppose." She let out a wistful sigh.

"It is fun to dress up," I said. I'd always had hand-me-down clothes, never anything new. And certainly not anything that was in style or on-trend, let alone designer. "And look at all these wigs Graham got me."

"*Graham* got them for you?" She coughed. "You told him about your alopecia?"

I returned the camera to my face so I could see my best friend. "I did." I smiled. "And he was incredible about it. He's been so supportive and loving and…"

Her eyes widened. "Did you say loving? Did I hear that right?" She gawked at me.

I dipped my head, my cheeks flaming. "Yeah. I guess it's been a little while since we talked on the phone." She'd been hosting some retreats and had limited cell phone service. And I'd been so busy—traveling back and forth between LA and France. Focused on Graham and the restoration of the château and everything else. "And it wasn't really the kind of thing I was going to mention over text."

She leaned forward, eyes intent on the screen. "Tell me *everything*."

I launched into a summary of the past month and a half. When I finished, she asked, "So was I right?"

"About what?"

"Graham being a freak in the sheets."

I bit the inside of my cheek, doing my best to neither confirm nor deny it.

"That's a yes," she said, knowing me too well.

My cheeks heated. "No comment."

"Mm-hmm." She wagged her finger at me. "I knew there was something there. That kiss at your wedding—"

"You mean our first kiss?"

Her eyes bugged out. "*That* was your first kiss? The one at the altar?"

I tried not to laugh at her expression. "Yeah."

I thought back to the kiss at our wedding. To the way our bodies had come together, silencing my doubts, the world.

"Ballsy." She shook her head. "Anyway, I remember thinking I needed to fan myself because that was one hell of a kiss."

"I know," I sighed. "I remember you asking me later that day, 'Are you sure this is fake?'"

She laughed and so did I. It seemed like so much time had passed since then. So much had happened.

"I'm glad it's going so well. But—" She chewed on the end of her pen.

"But what?" I asked, bracing myself.

She sliced a hand through the air. "Nothing. Never mind."

I frowned. "What aren't you saying?"

"It's just…" She sighed. "The two of you had an *agreement*, right? And I understand that feelings change, but where does *that* fit in with all of *this*?" She circled the air with the end of her pen, likely drawing a ring around my face on her screen.

"I—" I opened my mouth then closed it. I didn't know what to say. Jo was right.

"Oh, Lil." She frowned. "I'm sorry. I don't want to burst your bubble. I just don't want you to get hurt. You deserve to be happy. You deserve someone supportive and loving. And if that's Graham, awesome. But you have to admit that the agreement muddies the waters a bit."

I didn't disagree, but I hadn't wanted to confront the truth of it.

A text came in from Willow, confirming the time I wanted to leave.

I blew out a breath. "I have to go. I'm meeting Graham for lunch."

"Lil." She frowned. "Don't—"

"I'm not mad at you. I'll think about what you said, but I have to go or I'll be late."

"Okay. For all I know, I could be wrong. Either way, I'm here for you. And we can always talk about it more over the phone or when I see you in a few weeks."

Right. I couldn't believe it was already almost time for *les Journées du patrimoine*.

"Thanks, Jo," I said before we ended the call.

I dressed quickly, choosing a dress with a floral design. My mind immediately started cataloguing the flowers and their meanings. Now that Graham had told me about the symbolism behind flowers, I saw them everywhere.

Willow and I headed to Graham's office. He had another board meeting today. I hadn't heard anything more about the board's thoughts on our "inappropriate relationship" or their attempts to invalidate the clause in the will, though I knew legal challenges took time.

For now, I was going to focus on being supportive. On showing Graham that I was there for him. And reminding the board that I wasn't going anywhere. Regardless of whatever bullshit they tried to pull, I was here to stay.

"Hey, Carson," I said, stopping at his desk.

"Mrs. Mackenzie." He jumped up. "I didn't realize—"

I waved him away. "It's fine. I already checked Graham's

calendar, and I know he doesn't have any meetings scheduled for lunch." The perks of being his former assistant.

"You're—" He shook his head, brow furrowed. "Yeah. You're right."

"Also, how many times do I have to ask you to call me Lily?" When he hesitated, I gave him a stern look.

"Yes. Of course. Mrs.... Lily."

I laughed as I knocked on the door to Graham's office. He glanced up from his computer, the corner of his mouth tilting into a grin. "Hey. This is a pleasant surprise."

I smiled, shutting the door behind me. "I know you have a busy afternoon, but I thought we could review some decisions for the château."

It was all a pretext. I didn't need his opinion on the château or even lunch, for that matter. I needed him. I needed to know that this was real. That our feelings, our relationship, would last.

He stood, rounding the desk to greet me, pressing a kiss to my cheek. "The château, huh?" Graham asked, brow arched. "What could you possibly need my help with?"

I palmed him over his pants. "I have some *hard* decisions to make. And you are very experienced with these types of matters." It was totally cheesy, but he didn't seem to mind.

He somehow maintained a straight face when he responded. "I am. I'm glad you're finally acknowledging the benefit of my knowledge. I would be happy to lend you my *experience.*" He angled his hips against mine, letting me feel his arousal as he slid his hand up to cup my breast.

"Good." I bit back a smile. "That's good. Because I could definitely," I gasped, "use it." I pressed against him, needing him closer.

"Yeah?" He kissed my neck, and I tried not to moan.

"Yes." My voice was breathy.

He twisted some of my hair around his fingers. "I like this one. Is she new?" he asked, referring to my wig.

I nodded, looping my arms around his neck. "It's one of the nicest wigs I've ever owned. Thank you."

"My pleasure. What's her name?"

"Genevieve."

"Elle est jolie, mais c'est toi la plus belle." *She's pretty, but you're the most beautiful.*

My cheeks heated at his compliment. *"Merci, mon préféré."*

"I'm your favorite?" he asked. "Your favorite what?"

"My favorite husband."

"I better be your *only* husband." He glared at me, clutching my hips.

I laughed. *So serious.* "Favorite and only, yes. My favorite, and only—" I kissed his jawline "—lover. My favorite person." I placed my hand over his heart.

His expression softened. "I'm your favorite person?"

I nodded.

"Okay." His tone turned teasing. "What do you want?"

I tilted my head. "What do I want?" I didn't understand.

"Yeah." He chuckled. "You're clearly buttering me up for something. What is it—more time at the château? Because I'm planning to speak with Jasper and Sloan about spending an extra week there for *les Journées du patrimoine*."

"You are?"

"I am," he said.

I smoothed my hands down his lapels. "You know I'd still love you even if you didn't do anything for me, right? This might sound ironic or even hypocritical, considering our arrangement, but I love you because of who you are. *Not* what you can do for me."

His stare was intense. So intense that I worried I'd pissed him off, but then his shoulders relaxed.

"Even so," he said. "I like helping."

I was beginning to suspect it was his love language—acts of service. Graham was always doing something for someone else. I wanted to show him that he was important. I wanted to make him feel as special as he'd made me feel.

"It's my turn to help you with something for a change," I said, backing him toward his chair. I was determined to prove that my love for him had nothing to do with our agreement or the twenty million dollars.

"Oh yeah?" He arched one eyebrow. "And what's that?"

"I know how stressed you've been lately," I said, smoothing my hands over his shoulders then unbuckling his belt. "Dealing with the board. Straddling two worlds."

"Mm." He dragged his thumb along his bottom lip, watching me. "I'll give you something to straddle."

"Later." I smirked, kneeling before him, freeing him from his trousers. His cock bobbed toward me. I'd never done anything like this, but the idea that we were in his office and I was going to suck him off beneath his desk sent a rush of desire straight to my core.

"Right now—" I kissed his tip, and he jerked in my hand "—is about you. You give and you give and you give. I want to give you something."

He cradled my chin in his hand, his hold firm yet full of tenderness. "I have everything I could ever want, *mon cœur*." His green eyes were darkened with lust but also love too. And warmth.

"Oh, so…" My eyes darted to his cock, the head hard and insistent, a drop of precome leaking from the tip. "You don't want me to suck you off?"

A muscle in his neck twitched. "I didn't say that, did I?"

I laughed, bending down to take him in my mouth, ignoring the trill of a phone ringing outside. He groaned, gripping the edges of his chair. "Fuck, Lil. Your mouth feels so good wrapped around my cock."

I kept going, teasing him with my mouth and my hands. Wanting to make him lose control. Wanting to give him a release.

"*Tu es tellement belle,*" he coaxed, telling me how beautiful I was. "On your knees for me." His touch was gentle despite the bite to his words.

"Mm." I took him deep, humming around him. My clit was aching, my core throbbing with need. I squirmed, desperately trying to rub my thighs together.

"Fuck," he rasped, deep and low. "Fuck," he hissed. "I love seeing you on your knees for me, but I want to come inside you." He grabbed my wrists and pulled me to a standing position.

"Yes," I gasped. "Yes. I want that too."

His eyes darkened. I knew we were being reckless, but I was desperate for him.

He stood and kissed me, turning me so my back was to him. Even now, even when we should be rushed, he was tender. Loving.

He lifted my skirt then groaned when he realized I wasn't wearing anything beneath it. He palmed my ass, his skin warm against mine.

"Mm. Is this a fantasy of yours?" he asked in a dark voice. "Having your boss bend you over his desk and fuck you?"

"I would say yes, but you're my husband." I smiled at him over my shoulder. "*Not* my boss."

"But you like it when I tell you what to do," he taunted, reaching around to tease my clit, his long, elegant fingers sliding through my folds.

I whimpered. *Oh god.* "*Oui.*"

This was insane. And yet, I'd never felt more alive.

Higher and higher, I climbed, until I was teetering on the edge. My desire was coiled tight, my body primed to explode.

"*Lâche-toi.*" His deep voice caressed me, telling me to let go. And I was powerless to resist, especially when he spoke in French.

It was as if I'd been waiting for his permission. His command.

After that, my orgasm came on quickly, barreling through me like a runaway train. Hard. Fast. Powerful. I was still feeling the aftershocks of it when he pulled out of me and gave my ass a slap.

"Turn around," he commanded. I turned to face him, and he picked me up and planted me on the desk. "Wrap your arms around my neck, and don't let go."

I marveled at the sight of him in his suit. So buttoned-up and yet so unrestrained. Such a man of contradictions and hidden facets.

"Was this your fantasy?" I grasped his tie, wrapping it gently around my wrist and pulling so that his lips met mine.

"You are my every fantasy," he said. *"Mon rêve. Mon amour. L'exception à toutes mes règles."*

His kisses, like his words, were a balm to my soul. I was his dream. His love. The exception to all his rules.

My heart swelled at his admission, at all the ways this man showed me he loved me. From flowers laden with symbolism to words of love and so many big and small acts of service that I'd lost count. I'd never felt more cherished or wanted.

"Je t'aime." I kissed him, wanting him to feel my love for him, my desire. *"Prends-moi. Je suis à toi." Take me. I'm yours.*

I released his tie and shifted a little, both of us watching as he eased himself inside me inch by glorious inch. When he was fully seated, I groaned. "This is so much better than any fantasy."

"Mm." He pulled aside my dress, kissing my collarbone. "Tell me more about your fantasies."

"Most of them involved marching in here and telling you what to do."

"And what—" he dragged his nose along my ear, my cheek, my jawline "—would you have told me to do?"

"This," I said, embracing the moment, dwelling in the fantasy. "This," I sighed as he continued to pump into me in slow, lazy thrusts. "Fill me. Take me. Make me yours."

"You are mine," he said, lifting our left hands, lacing his fingers with mine and showing off our wedding rings.

"And you're mine."

He grunted, picking up his pace. We were racing toward the finish line when I heard someone say, "Oh god. Oh shit."

Graham cupped the back of my head and pressed my forehead to his chest. My eyes widened. Jasper? Was that Jasper's voice?

Oh my god. He'd…

"Get out!" Graham bellowed with a murderous look in his eyes. "Get. The. Fuck. Out. Now!"

I cringed and dropped my head to his chest, beyond mortified. The orgasm I'd been chasing had evaporated faster than water in the desert. The door closed with a snick, and I wished the floor would open up and swallow me whole.

I righted my dress, contemplating the scene Jasper had walked in on. It could've been worse. I could've been facing the door while Graham fucked me from behind as he had earlier.

I groaned, looking at the floor. Nope. This was still completely mortifying.

"You okay?" Graham asked, tucking himself back into his pants.

"Your brother just walked in on us having sex in your office in the middle of the workday." I covered my face with my hands. "I'll never be able to face him again," I mumbled the words into my palms. There was only one solution. I was going to have to change my name and disappear.

"Carson should've stopped Jasper—or, at the very least, warned me." Graham moved as if to march toward the door.

I placed a hand on his arm. "Don't. It will only make things worse."

"I should fire him for this. I would fire my brother if I could."

"No, you wouldn't. Jasper is too big of an asset. And don't take it out on Carson. From what I can tell, he's a good assistant."

Graham grunted. "I suppose you're right."

"That said, this is not going to help the rumors about us."

"You're looking at this the wrong way," Graham said, rubbing my arms. "For anyone who had doubts about our relationship, we've now effectively dispatched them."

"Not. Helping," I ground out.

And while I knew he was joking, part of me worried that there was a kernel of truth in those words. Worried that even though Graham was teasing, he wasn't all that upset about being caught because it supported the narrative he was trying to build.

I didn't like that I was even questioning Graham's motives where I was concerned, but a lifetime of living with my family, coupled with Jo's comments earlier, had given me pause. I understood why she was concerned, and I appreciated that she was looking out for me. But Jo and I hadn't talked in weeks, and she didn't know my husband like I did.

Graham was merely trying to comfort me. Besides, I was the one who'd initiated this. He hadn't asked me to come to his office. He hadn't even known I was coming.

But deep down, I worried that Jo was right. And whether she was or she wasn't, I hated that I even had to consider the agreement and how it factored into our relationship.

CHAPTER TWENTY-EIGHT

Graham

Sloan leaned forward, peering at Jasper and me through the computer screen. "Why are you guys acting so weird?"

I ignored her question and kept my focus straight ahead. After Jasper had fled my office, Lily had gone back to the penthouse so she could work on the preparations for *les Journées du patrimoine*. My brother hadn't said anything about what he'd walked in on earlier, and neither had I.

"Can we please focus on the agenda for the board meeting?" I asked.

Sloan's eyes flicked from Jasper to me. "No. Not until we talk about whatever's going on. We need to present a united front to the board, and you guys are acting so strange."

The tension built in the silence, so thick it was ready to snap. I huffed. Jasper tapped his fingers on his thigh.

"I walked in on Lily and Graham having sex in his office," Jasper blurted.

I rolled my eyes. Sloan's mouth dropped open in shock.

"There!" Jasper threw his hands in the air. "Are you happy now?" He glared at her, still unwilling to look at me.

I groaned, dragging a hand down my face. "Jasper, seriously? Jesus."

"This is unexpected," Sloan said, clearly bemused. "But I'm glad."

"I'm not," Jasper grumbled. "I did *not* need to see that." He shuddered.

"Why are you glad?" I asked my sister.

"Promise not to get upset?" she asked.

"Why would I be upset?"

She glanced at Jasper, and they shared a look. What was that about?

"We thought your relationship with Lily was fake. We worried it was all a stunt to get the shares."

Well, shit. Had we been that obvious? Or did my siblings just know me that well?

"And now?" I asked, unwilling to give anything away.

They weren't wrong, but I wasn't going to admit the truth. There was still so much at stake. And besides, what Lily and I had now was real. It didn't matter that it had started as a lie.

"Now, we see how wrong we were," Sloan said.

"So wrong." Jasper screwed his eyes shut, and I gave him a playful shove.

"Though—" Sloan tapped a finger to her lips. "We should probably keep this to ourselves. We don't want to fuel the gossip about your 'inappropriate workplace affair.' If people find out you were having sex in your office, they may draw the conclusion that it's happened before."

"That rumor is bullshit," I scoffed. "Donahue must be getting desperate."

"Even so, perception matters. You don't want to throw away all the goodwill you've garnered since your marriage. Stock prices have been on the rise too."

I pounded my fist on the table. "This shouldn't even be an

issue. I'm married. Legally, those shares, and this company, are ours."

"I know," Sloan said in a placating tone. "We just need to play the game a little longer."

I blew out a harsh breath. "Fine."

"Jasper?" Sloan asked.

"Yeah. Of course," he agreed.

"How are you feeling?" I asked Sloan, wanting to leave the matter behind.

"Good. Baby is healthy, and I'm finally having less morning sickness."

"Good," I said. "I wanted to check in about my travel schedule. Lily has a big event coming up, and I need to stay in France a little longer."

"How much longer?" Jasper asked.

"An extra week. This event is important to Lily, but it's also important for the château and the community as a whole."

"When is it?" Sloan asked.

I gave them the dates and my proposed travel itinerary. Then I said, "Thanks for stepping up in my absence. Especially you, Jasper." I turned to him.

"It's fine." He shrugged it off. "You know I'm happy to help."

"I know, and you've done a good job. I appreciate it." I held his gaze. "I appreciate you."

"I…" He blinked a few times. Swallowed. "Yeah. Of course."

"You have good ideas, and I don't give you enough credit for all you do for the brand. And Sloan—" I turned to my sister, who quickly swiped away a tear. "Are you crying?"

"I—" She sniffled. "No. Dang pregnancy hormones."

My expression softened. "You are instrumental to the

success of our brand. And you're going to be such an amazing mom."

"He's right," Jasper chimed in. "I just wish you lived closer. I'm going to hate being an uncle from afar."

Her lips turned down. "I hate being so far from our families."

"I thought that's what you liked about London," I teased.

"I used to love it. And I still love this city. But when I moved here, I needed to get away. I needed space. And now..."

"And now?" I prompted.

"Now I hate the idea of being so far away from everyone. Jackson's mom offered to come stay for an extended time after the baby's born, but what about Greer and her kids. She's my best friend. Jackson's sister. Our kids will be cousins. And what about Brooklyn and..." She started crying again, covering her face with her hands. "I'm sorry."

"Do you want to move back to LA?" I asked, both surprised and not.

"It's not that I want to live in LA. I just don't want to be so far away from everyone."

"I could swap with you," I said. My brain hadn't even caught up with my mouth, but I knew this could be a good thing.

"What?" Jasper coughed.

"Actually, that would be perfect. You could be closer to everyone here. And it would make it easier for Lily and me to travel back and forth to the château without completely upending our schedules."

Jasper and Sloan shared another look.

"What?" I asked.

"You've never wanted to leave LA before," Sloan said. "You've always believed it was the hub of our operations and that you had to be there."

I lifted a shoulder. "And now I know that's not true. Even if it were, you and Jasper can more than handle the company."

Jasper reached out and placed a hand to my forehead. "Are you feeling okay?"

I batted away his hand. "I've never felt better."

And the more I considered this idea, the more excited I was. About leaving LA and all the board's bullshit behind. About a shorter commute between my office and the château. About less travel for Prince Albert and Queen V, who had been struggling with the long flights. But most of all, what it would mean to Lily.

"You're sure you want to proceed with this?" Sloan asked.

"I need to run it by Lily, but I don't see why she wouldn't be on board."

"And I'll have to talk to Jackson and Halle about it," Sloan said.

"Halle? What does Halle have to do with it?" Jasper asked.

Sloan frowned. "She's my assistant. I'd need to figure out if she'd want to come with me, which would be ideal. Or maybe we could arrange a swap," she said to me. "If Carson wants to stay in LA and Halle doesn't want to leave London."

"Can she leave London? What about her son?" Jasper asked.

Why was Jasper so concerned about Sloan's assistant and her ability to relocate? I knew they'd worked together when he'd gone to London to stand in for Sloan during her sailing trip. He cared about our employees; we all did. But he seemed more invested than usual.

"It's something I'll have to find out," Sloan said.

"Do you have any problems with this plan?" I asked Jasper.

"No. None," he said. "Though it would be weird to be here without you."

"True, but it could also be a good thing." I stood and clapped a hand on his shoulder. "You've thrived in my absence. And I love seeing you take the lead on new projects." I gave his shoulder a squeeze before releasing him.

"You're very complimentary today," Sloan said.

"Because he got laid," Jasper said.

I gave him a playful shove. "And here I was going to say that my praise was long overdue. I don't tell you two enough how much I appreciate and love you. I can't imagine running this company with anyone else."

Jasper peered up at me, and Sloan's smile was soft when she said, "Gran and Pops would be proud."

I nodded. "If only they could see us now."

When Knox opened the door to his house, I held up a bottle of whiskey.

"Welcome," Knox said, accepting it from me. "Thanks. Jasper's already here. Nate's running a little late but should be here soon."

I followed him into the house. "Can I get either of you a drink?"

"I'll take a whiskey," Jasper sighed, sharing a look with me.

The board meeting had started off well enough, all things considered. But then it had turned into a complete shitshow. Many of the board members were pushing back hard—on the validity of the clause in my grandfather's will. On the way my marriage to my former assistant would reflect on the brand in light of our other recent scandals.

I tried to let it roll over me, but their comments rankled.

They weren't pleased about my new schedule—alternating between France and LA. They questioned my commitment to the company. But when they tried to talk about Lily, I'd drawn the line.

"Graham?" Knox asked, saying my name as if it weren't the first time.

"Hm?"

"A drink?"

"I'll have the same, please." My phone buzzed, and I glanced at the screen. "Pierce is on his way too."

"Great." Knox clapped a hand on my shoulder, handing me a glass of whiskey with the other.

I pocketed my phone. "No Jude?"

Knox shook his head. "He's at a team function for the Leatherbacks."

"We could've rescheduled."

"It's fine." Knox poured Jasper a glass. "It's a smaller community outreach project, and it's good practice for him."

I tilted my head. "Why? Are you thinking of stepping down?"

I was teasing, mostly. Knox was in his late forties, and he was passionate about the pro soccer team he owned. But his priorities had shifted a lot now that he and Kendall were together.

"Not any time soon."

It wasn't long before Nate arrived, and Pierce along with him. Though Pierce seemed withdrawn, closed off.

"You good?" I asked.

He gave me a curt nod. "We'll talk after."

I frowned, hoping everything was okay.

Drinks were poured and cards were dealt.

Nate leaned over. "Hey. Did you hear about the Hawks?"

The Hollywood Hawks were the local NHL team, and

they'd recently hired Emerson's dad, Declan Cross, as the new head coach. I hoped he'd be able to turn the team around.

"Holden Hansley?" I asked. There'd been rumors of a trade, but it seemed too good to be true.

Nate nodded, confirming my hopes. "Declan's pretty excited."

"No shit. I'm excited." We might have a real chance at the play-offs for the first time in years. But then I frowned. If I moved to London, I wouldn't be able to attend as many home games. Nor would I get to enjoy poker nights with the guys.

"You okay?" Nate asked.

Before I could answer, Knox jumped in. "All right. Pierce, you're up first."

"Easy." Pierce leaned back in his chair. "I want a night at the new golden key penthouse."

"Golden key penthouse?" Nate's curiosity was piqued, as was Knox's. "What's that?"

"A new luxury experience that Jasper designed for the Huxley Grand LA."

"A five-figure-a-night luxury experience," Pierce piped in.

"Shit," Knox said. "Then it must be decadent."

"Like you wouldn't believe," Jasper said. He explained it in detail, growing excited, while we played. He was proud of what he'd created, and he should be.

Clients and celebrities were going to love this new offering. It was a huge suite with tons of unique features like a custom-designed Louis Vuitton ping-pong table, Hermès dopp kit, and YSL pajamas. Plus, it had tons of privacy.

Nate won the round, and Pierce seemed disappointed. I wondered who he'd planned to take to the penthouse. He hadn't dated in a while—at least not seriously. And I wasn't aware that he was seeing anyone, even casually.

"Nate?" Knox asked. "Name your prize."

He pursed his lips, considering. "I want to stay at Lily's château."

I tried to fight back my smile. "You sure about that?"

"When the restoration is finished, yes. Em said that it's a little rough still."

"Rough is an understatement." I sipped my whiskey. "When I first moved in, we didn't have any hot water."

Jasper's jaw dropped. "No hot water? No thanks."

"There wasn't a showerhead either, so I had to take cold baths every night. It sucked. I honestly don't know how Lily lived like that for over a year."

Pierce made a noise, and I couldn't get a read off him. What was that about?

"Sounds very rustic," Knox said.

"Very. But that's part of the allure. Life there is simpler. More authentic."

"Is that why you want to move there?" Jasper asked.

"Wait. What?" Knox asked, and everyone stilled.

Jesus. If only my little brother could keep his mouth shut. "We only just started discussing it, but Sloan and I might swap."

"Because of the château?" Nate asked.

I lifted a shoulder and tapped the table to indicate I'd like more cards. "That's a big part of it."

When I was there, I felt like my true self. I wasn't a billionaire or a CEO. I was just…me. Graham. And Lily loved me just as I was.

"And with the baby on the way, Sloan wants to be closer to family," I added.

"Wow." Knox arched an eyebrow. "That would be a big change."

"Brooklyn would be thrilled to have Sloan, Jackson, and

the new baby so close by," Nate said. "But you and Lily would certainly be missed."

"Thanks. We'd miss everyone too, but we'd visit. And it would make things a lot easier if we only had to commute from London instead of LA."

I said that, but I'd definitely miss my family. And Pierce, who was practically like family.

I glanced over at my best friend. He'd been silent through all of this. A muscle in his jaw ticked, and I knew him well enough to know he was agitated about something.

"You're making a lot of sacrifices for Lily." He gave me a knowing look.

"They're not sacrifices when you love someone," I said, laying down my cards. Putting it all on the table.

"Graham's right," Knox said. "Loving Kendall never feels like a sacrifice."

"I'm not saying that love's a sacrifice," Pierce said.

"Then what are you saying?" Jasper's tone was more curious than judgmental.

"I'm just wanting to make sure that Lily is as committed to you and your relationship as you are to her."

"Lily is committed," I gritted out. He was walking a fine line.

"Definitely committed." Jasper kept his eyes on his cards. "No doubt about that."

"Not a word." I glared at Jasper out of the corner of my eye. "Not. One. Word."

Knox and Nate glanced between us. "What's going on?" Knox asked.

"Yeah. What'd we miss?" Nate asked.

Jasper looked as if he might burst.

"Jasper," I chided. "Don't."

"Don't what?" He smirked. "Tell them I caught the two of you fucking in your office?"

I growled. "That was a private moment."

"Then I suggest you don't share a 'private moment' in a public place next time," Jasper said, raking the chips toward himself.

He'd won the round, and I rolled my eyes. He'd probably done all this to distract me so he could win.

We played a few more rounds, and then I followed Pierce out to his car while Jasper stayed behind to chat with Nate and Knox.

"What was that about?" I asked.

"I'm just trying to look out for you. We've been friends for a long time, and I don't even recognize you anymore."

I lifted a shoulder. "I'm happy. Why aren't you happy for me? Our plan is working, even better than we could've hoped."

"I just want to make sure she's not taking advantage of you."

"Where is this coming from?" I asked.

"You asked me to transfer the remaining ten million to the trust, and yet you haven't been married for two years, as required by the contract. Hell, you've barely been married two months."

I lifted a shoulder. "I'm passionate about the project, and I don't want Lily to stress about the funding. We're together, and I want her to have the money."

I also didn't want her to think our relationship was transactional or that my love was conditional. I wanted to love freely and without restriction, and I wanted her to do the same.

"And the will?" he asked.

I'd emailed Pierce earlier in the week to ask him to revise the terms of my will. He hadn't commented on it at the time, but I should've anticipated this conversation.

"She's my wife. I know she can take care of herself. But if

anything happens to me, I want to make sure she has what she needs."

"You could give her a million, and she'd be more than taken care of. Yet you want to grant her access to your fortune and your company? How would your family feel about that?"

"I like to think they'd be supportive. Regardless of what they'd think, those are my wishes. I shouldn't have to justify them to you or anyone."

He dragged a hand through his hair. "I think you're making a big mistake."

"I thought you liked Lily," I said.

I understood that he was trying to protect me, but did he truly believe that she was going to use me? She had no idea I'd asked him to transfer the remaining ten million. That had been all my idea.

"This isn't about Lily. You're my client and my best friend. It's my job to look out for you. And right now, I'm not sure you're getting your money's worth from this deal."

I clenched my fists at my sides, scarcely resisting the urge to punch him. "That's my wife you're talking about."

"Wife or not, you paid her for a job that isn't done. You gave her twenty million despite the fact that we still haven't secured the additional shares or hit the two-year mark."

"Pierce," I growled in warning.

"I know you don't want to hear it. I know you think you're in love. But if I don't look out for you, who will?"

"Are you speaking as my friend or my lawyer?"

"Either. Both."

"I don't *think* I'm in love. I *am* in love with her." And I'd had enough. I didn't need a babysitter on top of the board. "If you aren't willing to revise my will, I'll find someone else who will."

He scoffed. "Wow. Okay. I see how it is."

I reached out for him, regretting the words as soon as they'd left my mouth. "That's not what I meant."

"No. I think you said exactly what you meant." And then he turned and headed for his car.

Fuck.

CHAPTER TWENTY-NINE

Lily

"Damn, girl." Jo linked her arm with mine. "I still can't believe how much progress you've made since my last visit."

Sometimes I couldn't believe it myself. I followed her gaze up to the roof. Now that the zinc gutters had been removed, the roof was returning to its original shape. It wouldn't have been possible without Graham's help.

Jo and I hadn't discussed my relationship with Graham again since our talk about "muddying the waters." I knew Jo was concerned, but we kept our focus on preparing for *les Journées du patrimoine*. It was promising to be a beautiful fall day, and I was grateful for the sunshine after several days of rain.

"Do you think I forgot anything?" I asked.

"Not that I can tell. Run through it one more time, and we'll see."

I catalogued everything I could think of. Graham was chatting with the local vineyard while they finished setting up. The stonemasons had their tools ready for the demonstrations. I'd already checked on the local baker when he'd arrived earlier to start baking bread in the château's original oven. "And the gift shop—"

"I made sure all the displays looked perfect."

"You're the best." I gave her arm a squeeze. "Thank you."

The morning passed quickly in a blur of events and demonstrations. We had a great turnout, and everyone was so excited to see our progress. After how hard we'd worked to get to this point, it felt so good to revel in their praise.

Graham and I were answering some visitors' questions when a familiar figure approached. Graham and I turned to each other, our expressions ones of mirroring shock.

"Did you—" he asked.

"I had no idea," I said, though I was pleased.

"Jasper," Graham said, shaking his hand before pulling him into a hug. "What are you doing here?"

"I won a visit to the château," he said, and I assumed he was referring to their recent poker game. "So, we decided to surprise you." He winked at me over Graham's shoulder. "Hey, Lily. Hope it's okay we crashed your party."

"We?" Graham asked. And then the rest of his family joined us.

"Oh my god. I can't believe you're here," I said, hugging each of them in turn. My smile felt as if it might break my face.

"We've been watching your YouStream channel," Brooklyn said. "My best friend Sophia and her family are now obsessed with it."

"Wow. Thanks." I grinned, still trying to wrap my head around the fact that they were all here. For Graham. For me.

"No thanks necessary," Knox said. "You're family."

I tugged at the corner of my eye, trying not to cry.

"This is amazing," Sloan said, hugging me. "You should be proud of everything you've accomplished."

"I—" Wow. "I am. Thank you." I was just so overwhelmed by their love and support. "How are you feeling?"

"Good." She placed her hands over her stomach. "Baby is good."

"I'm happy to hear it," I said, doing my best to hold back tears.

"Oh my god," Emerson said, taking it all in. "This place is so amazing."

"Thanks." I was so proud of what I'd built, and it was nice to have others appreciate it. "I know it's far from done, but I'm glad you can see the vision."

"Oh, I can see the vision. You could have yoga classes on the lawn." She went on to rattle off a few other suggestions to appeal to guests who prioritized wellness. I listened intently, taking notes for later. She was full of great ideas.

"I can't wait for you to meet my best friend, Jo. She hosts these amazing retreats, and I think you two would really hit it off."

Graham's hand was on my lower back, and I smiled up at him, quickly swiping away a tear. I couldn't believe his family had done this. My own family had never shown up for me, even when I'd lived in the same town. Let alone flown across the world to surprise me.

It wasn't about the money; though, yes, that certainly made things easier. It was about the effort. It was about showing up for the people you loved and taking an interest in their passions.

Graham was lucky to have such a loving, supportive family. And I was lucky to be a part of it. The more I got to know his family, the more grateful I was to have married into it.

Our marriage might have started as a business agreement, but it had transformed into something real and beautiful. Even so, I couldn't stop thinking about what Jo had said.

I loved Graham, and we'd agreed that there would be no more talk of expiration dates, yet our agreement remained in place. Technically, money and services were still trading hands, and that was the opposite of unconditional love. Of the type of genuine and lasting relationship I wanted.

It was weighing on me, and I'd been trying to brainstorm some options. I needed to discuss it with Graham. I planned to, *after* we made it through *les Journées du patrimoine*.

Someone tapped me on the shoulder, and I turned, expecting it to be Jo or a journalist. But when I saw who it was, I froze and my smile fell. *What the...*

I felt as if I was having an out-of-body experience. Or maybe this was a nightmare. I subtly tried to pinch my arm, desperately hoping I'd wake up.

Wake up! I shouted in my head.

But I didn't. Because it wasn't a dream. My mom was standing in front of me, the rest of my family clustered behind her.

"Lil?" Graham asked in a low voice. "What's wrong?" just as Mom said, "Surprise!" with a bright smile.

"What are you doing here?" I blurted, so stunned to see her standing before me that I seemed to have momentarily lost my filter.

What were any of my family members doing here? Iris, her husband, all of them. All my siblings and their spouses.

"Now, is that any way to speak to your mother?" Mom asked in a sickly-sweet tone.

"Your mother?" Graham arched a brow, clearly as surprised to see my family as I was, even if his tone was level.

"Graham, these are my parents, Karen and Jeff."

"Mrs. Fontaine. Mr. Fontaine." Graham extended his hand to each of them in turn. "Nice to meet you. I'm Lily's husband, Graham."

"Husband?" Mom blinked a few times. "Did you just say husband?"

Iris decided to pipe up. "You're married?" She glanced at Graham. "To him?"

She said it like she couldn't quite believe that someone like Graham would be interested in someone like me. It was nothing new, but that didn't make it any less insulting.

I glanced up at the man in question, and his jaw was set in a firm line. I knew him well enough to know that he was angry, even if he was hiding it—and his surprise. He reached out to shake Iris's hand before introducing himself to the rest of my family with a poised calm that was unnerving.

"Their marriage came as a surprise to us as well," Sloan said, reminding me that Graham's entire family was there. Watching this awkward exchange. *Oh god. I think I'm going to throw up.*

"This is certainly a surprise," Dad huffed.

"We thought this would be a good excuse to celebrate the progress you've made on the château," Jasper said. "And to get the families together to meet."

I supposed that answered my question about how this fun little reunion had come to be. I appreciated that Jasper was trying to do something nice, but I really wished my family weren't here.

"Holy shit." Iris stepped forward, elbowing my dad in the process. "Look at that ring." She took my hand in hers, admiring my diamond. "Is that real?"

I resisted the urge to yank my hand from her grasp. Maybe the sun would glint off it, temporarily dazzling them so I could make my escape. But Graham's firm hold on my shoulder removed any thought of that. It was almost as if he'd turned into a statue, like one of the regal busts that graced the roof of the château.

"I'm so happy for you," Mom said in a loud voice before

pulling me into a hug. I bristled against her touch, knowing it was all for show. She spoke in a low tone, ensuring no one would overhear. "Why didn't you tell us?"

Was that hurt in her tone? More likely, accusation.

"We haven't exactly been talking lately," I murmured, smiling brightly to maintain the façade. We were just one big happy family.

"Now I'm even more glad we came," Mom said to Dad. Then she turned to Jasper. "Thank you so much for arranging this." Her tear-filled eyes weren't fooling me, but when I glanced around, everyone else seemed convinced of her sincerity.

Jasper waved a hand through the air. "It was no big deal."

"It is to us," Mom said, placing a hand on Jasper's arm and smiling up at him. "Liliana, your new family is so generous." I could practically see the dollar signs in her eyes.

I couldn't breathe. My chest felt so tight, like someone had tied a rope around it and was pulling it. Black spots danced in my vision.

Why did they always have to ruin everything?

"Lil," Jo called as she approached. Her eyes widened at the sight of my family, but she recovered quickly. "Marcel with the *Le Monde* needs to grab a quick shot of you and Graham for their article."

"Sure." I was eager to escape, but I was just as afraid to leave Graham's family alone with mine. That was certainly a chilling thought. I could only imagine what my family would say in our absence.

What were they thinking—coming here? What was Jasper thinking, inviting them here? Paying for their trip. Didn't they question why a complete stranger was offering them something so outrageous?

"Go," Jo whispered. "I'll handle this."

"I... *Merde*," I whispered, as the photographer indicated where to stand. "What are we—"

Graham shook his head and straightened, acting as if he were completely unbothered. "People are watching."

The bridge of my nose stung, but I stubbornly ignored it, pasting a smile on my face instead. I took a deep breath, trying to pretend I was happy, when I was stressed to the max.

An important event I'd spent countless hours planning and preparing for was well underway. *Les Journées du patrimoine* was crucial to showcase the projects and the restoration to the community and to everyone who had supported my journey thus far. Not only was it a condition of my funding from the DRAC, but it would also attract future funding. And while my financial situation was no longer so precarious, thanks to Graham, I still wanted to get as much of the project financed by the DRAC and other sources as I could, leaving me a bigger cushion with the trust, should I need it.

All the while, my family was probably wreaking havoc. For all I knew, they were ruining the effort I'd put into this event and into making my fake marriage seem legitimate. And Graham's statement had me reeling.

I'd never told him the reasons for my strained relationship. It didn't seem worth the energy. But Graham knew enough to understand how upset I'd be by their sudden appearance. And yet, he seemed more focused on the fact that people were watching.

I didn't want to believe that was true, but seeing my family had triggered my survival instincts. I was spiraling. Was it any wonder I was struggling to smile and act as if everything was fine without skipping a beat?

As soon as the photographer was finished, Graham wrapped his arm around my shoulder, ushering me to the *chai*. I was grateful the wine storage area was closed to the public until it could be restored. I couldn't breathe, let alone think, especially not with so many people around. Especially not when we were supposed to be putting on a show.

"This is a fucking mess," Graham said, beginning to pace. "We need to come up with a game plan. And fast." He dragged a hand through his hair.

His phone vibrated, and he pulled it out of his pocket. He glanced at the screen. "Pierce wants to talk to us about damage control."

Damage control?

I was barely holding it together, and Graham didn't even seem to notice. He was so focused on fixing the situation. On damage control.

I tried to remind myself of all the ways he'd shown me his love, but I was afraid. Afraid I'd misread the situation. Afraid that if it really came down to a choice between me and the Huxley brand, Graham would choose his company.

My phone buzzed multiple times, and I checked it, scared to see who the messages were from.

> Jo: Are you okay? I can't believe your family had the nerve to show up.

NO. I WAS NOT OKAY. IN FACT, I WAS FREAKING THE FUCK OUT. I planted my hands on my knees, crouching over in an attempt to catch my breath.

My chest was tight, my mind swirling with thoughts of my family, Graham, everything. I stood, interlocking my hands behind my head. But it didn't help. I bent back over again.

"Lil?" Graham rushed over to me. "What's going on?"

"I can't…breathe."

"Okay," he said. "Let's take a seat. Try to relax."

"I can't—" I felt a tear leak out, and I couldn't breathe. I couldn't. My chest was so tight, and my breaths were coming so fast. *Am I having a heart attack?*

When that didn't seem to help, he stood and pulled me to him, wrapping his arms around me. "Breathe, Lily. Deep breath in." He waited, counting down from four on the inhale, encouraging me to take a pause. And then let it out for seven. "That's it."

His hold was tight, and I felt safe in his arms. Secure. I couldn't think about anything else but the beat of his heart. And he just held me. Counting my breaths and giving me space until I'd calmed down.

"Thank you," I finally said, releasing a normal breath.

He loosened his hold, and I stepped back. I swiped my hair away from my face. "How'd you know to do that?"

He frowned at the ground. "After my parents' plane crash, I had a lot of panic attacks. My pops used to hold me like that until I calmed down."

"I—" I reached out and placed a hand on his arm. "I'm sorry, Graham."

"Jesus, Lil. Is this what your family does to you?" he asked, concern and anger and so many other emotions reflected in his features.

I rolled my lips between my teeth and shook my head, hoping he'd take the hint that I didn't want to talk about it. He studied me, and I avoided looking at him. I was afraid if I met his eyes, I'd break.

So instead, I straightened, steeling myself and turning for the door. "We should get back out there."

He moved as if to stop me. "Are you okay?"

No. "We have more pressing problems." I showed him the latest text from Jo.

> Jo: Where are you guys? Pierce and I are doing our best to run interference, but people are starting to notice.

"I GOT SOMETHING SIMILAR FROM PIERCE," GRAHAM SAID. "Do you want me to get rid of your family? We could have Hudson throw them off the grounds."

I barked out a laugh, surprising myself and feeling a little lighter somehow. Graham was on my side—I knew that. *I did.*

Auntie Jackie had always said that people showed you who they were through their actions, not their words. And Graham had always shown me—in ways both big and small—that he loved me. From fresh bouquets of flowers bursting with symbolism to helping out with anything and everything at the château, his acts of service were a testament to his love and commitment to me and our relationship.

"As amusing as that would be, it wouldn't be a good look for us."

He cupped my cheek, his expression full of tenderness and love. "It's good to see you smile."

I leaned into his touch, feeling a little calmer. More centered. Now that I wasn't freaking the fuck out, I could recognize that I'd been going to the worst-case scenario, when I needed to have faith in us and in our relationship.

"What are we going to do?" I asked, trying to focus on the problem at hand.

"What do you want to do?" Graham asked, dropping his hand from my cheek but continuing to touch me.

"What do I want to do?" I laughed. "I want to tell them to go fuck themselves."

"You could," he said. "But what if they came here genuinely wanting to make amends? It has to mean something that they traveled all this way."

At Graham's family's expense.

But I didn't point that out. He wouldn't understand. How could he, when his family had never treated him like mine had me?

My inclination was to continue to avoid my family, but Graham made a good point. They had come all this way. I wanted to believe that had to mean something. That they'd wanted to see me and not just get a free trip.

"Cutting off a relationship, especially with family, is a big deal. It might be worth hearing them out."

I wanted to keep an open mind, but if the past was anything to go on, I had a feeling I'd regret it.

CHAPTER THIRTY

Graham

"Why do you really want me to do this?" Lily asked. My phone buzzed in my pocket, and I ignored it. This was more important. *Lily* was more important.

I frowned. "Do what?"

"Talk to my family."

"I know I don't understand the circumstances behind the rift in your family, and that's fine. But I don't want you to have regrets."

I couldn't imagine not talking to my family. Sure, we'd had our differences. But they were my family. Cutting them out of my life would be like cutting off my own hand.

Even though Lily hadn't told me her reasons for ending communication with her family, I trusted that she'd made the best decision for herself. I was grateful I couldn't imagine a situation with my own where I wouldn't find a way to fix it.

"There's no other reason?"

Her question felt like a trap, and I wasn't exactly sure why. What was I missing? Where was this coming from?

Before I could ask, my phone vibrated again. When I glanced at the screen, Jasper's name flashed across it. I was tempted to ignore his call, send it to voice mail, but it was the second time in a span of minutes that he'd called. A niggling in my gut told me to answer it. As soon as I did, I could hear a siren in the background, and I realized how close it sounded.

"What's wrong?"

"Sloan," he rasped, and panic raced through my veins at that one word. At the tone of his voice. "Sloan collapsed, and she's being taken to the hospital."

"What?" I barked, trying not to freak the fuck out.

"Jackson is with her in the ambulance, and Pierce is driving me over now."

"I'll meet you there." I was headed for the door before I'd even ended the call.

"What's going on?" Lily asked. "Where are you going?"

"Sloan. Hospital. Now." I sounded like a caveman, but it was the best I could manage under the circumstances.

"I'll drive you," Lily said, racing ahead.

"No." I tried to snap myself out of it. Force myself into action. "You should stay here. What about the—"

"Graham." She glared at me. "I'm. Driving."

"Fine," I huffed, tossing her the keys. I knew I was too distracted to focus on driving safely. Lily used the talk-to-text feature on her phone to send a text to Luc and Jo, asking them to take over in her absence. *Oh god, les Journées du patrimoine.* We hurried to the car, and I called, "Thank you."

She said nothing, climbing behind the driver's seat. She'd thrown the car into reverse before I could even reach for my seat belt. She bypassed the main road, taking a shortcut through the forest I'd never noticed. The road—if you could even call it that—was bumpy. But it avoided all the cars coming up the main drive for the festival.

Lily tightened her grip on the steering wheel, twisting, her knuckles turning white. Even so, she was focused on the road, driving as fast as she safely could while navigating around all the potholes and rocks.

I braced myself, desperate for something to do. Worried about how Sloan was faring. If she was in pain. If she was okay. If the baby was okay.

I dragged a hand down my face, wishing we weren't in a small town in the French countryside. It was a great spot for vacationing, but I worried Sloan wouldn't receive the same quality of care here that she would in a big city like London. Could the team ready the private plane fast enough to get her to Paris? London? Could we hire a…

"Almost there," Lily said, pulling onto a paved road that led toward town. "I'll drop you off at the front, and then I'll go park."

I appreciated Lily's measured tone. Her planned approach. Because right now, I wasn't thinking clearly.

The car had barely stopped when I threw open my door and sprinted into the hospital. Pierce and Jasper were in the waiting room.

"What do we know?" I asked, hugging my brother. "What happened?"

When Jasper said nothing, Pierce jumped in. "Jackson's with Sloan. He said he'd update us as soon as he knew anything."

"Good."

Lily burst through the doors, scanning the room and then coming over to us. Lily gave Jasper a hug and then volunteered to get everyone coffee after we told her what we knew —which was basically nothing.

"Pierce?" she asked. "Would you mind giving me a hand?"

"Sure."

After they left, Jasper and I took a seat, and I tried to steel myself for the unknown.

Jasper bent forward to rest his elbows on his knees. "I just keep picturing the panic in Jackson's eyes. He's always so calm and cool, you know? And he was totally losing his shit."

A chasm opened up in my chest, but I tried not to let it show. "It's Sloan and the baby. Of course he was concerned. I'd be losing my shit too if something happened to Lily."

He gave me a funny look.

I grunted, the equivalent of asking, "What?"

"Why did Lily's family seem surprised to discover that you two were married?"

"Because…" I blew out a breath. "They have a strained relationship, and she hasn't spoken to them in months."

He cringed, squeezing his eyes shut briefly. "I wish I'd known. Now I feel like an ass for inviting them."

I patted his back. "It's not your fault."

"Does Lily hate me?" he asked.

"No. I'm sure it means a lot to her that you got everyone from our family to come for the festival."

"Yeah. And ruined everything. Lily. Sloan." He shook his head.

"Can you tell me what happened with Sloan?" I asked, even though I was scared to hear the answer.

Jasper seemed to curl in on himself. "One minute, she was fine, and then the next, she collapsed."

Hm. I rubbed a hand over my mouth. "Was she conscious when the ambulance came?"

"Yeah."

"That's good," I said, placing my hand on his back. "And she's here now. They can help her."

Jasper stood and started pacing. "I just keep thinking, how can we help her? Could we have done more to help prevent something like this?"

I wondered the same thing, though I still wasn't sure what had caused it.

"Did you have something in mind?"

He pressed the heels of his palms into his eyes.

"Jas?" I prodded. I knew my brother well enough to realize there was something he wasn't telling me.

He stopped pacing and locked his hands behind his neck. "All this drama with the board has been stressing her out."

I frowned. "Did she say that?"

"She didn't have to. I can tell it's weighing on her. Hell, it's weighing on me. Yes, the merger is tabled, for now." Voting was suspended until the situation with the additional shares was resolved. "But you know Donahue. He's not going to let this go, not without a fight."

"And you know me," I said. "I won't let him win."

"That's just it," Jasper said. "This battle isn't good for anyone. Not the company, not Sloan, not you. Aren't you sick of it? Isn't Lily sick of it? It's intrusive and disruptive and divisive."

"Yes, but that doesn't mean I'm simply going to roll over and let it go. This is our family's company. Our legacy."

"*We* are their legacy." Jasper jabbed his chest. "You and Sloan and me and Knox and Nate. Our family was what mattered most to them. Not profits. Not the brand. *Us. This family.*"

"I—"

"No," he cut me off. "I think you've lost sight of that. I think you've clung to the company because it's something tangible. Something you can control. But the company isn't all we have left of Gran and Pops. We have their love. We have one another."

"What are you suggesting?" I asked, grateful the waiting room was relatively empty and no one seemed to be paying us any attention.

"I don't know." He slumped in the chair. "I don't. But there has to be a better way."

Before we could discuss it further, Lily and Pierce returned, coffees in hand.

"Any updates?" Lily asked as she handed me one. I shook my head, grateful when she came to stand beside me and placed her hand on my back.

Jasper stepped forward. "I'm sorry if I overstepped by inviting your family. I just—" He swallowed. "I wanted to do something nice."

Lily glanced to me, and I gave her a subtle nod. It was crazy to me that we could communicate so easily without words. That we understood each other so well. And yet, she'd questioned my motives earlier for suggesting that she talk to her family.

Lily's shoulders relaxed. "I know." She gave his arm a squeeze. "It was really sweet of you."

I was constantly in awe of her. Even now, she calmed my brother and reassured him, all while facing her own problems.

Jasper's apology made me even more determined to clear the air with Pierce. While Lily and Jasper were talking, I pulled Pierce aside.

"Thanks for being here. I'm sorry about the other night," I said, referring to our disagreement after the poker game. "I know you were just trying to protect me, and I appreciate it."

He nodded, twisting the sleeve around his coffee cup. "I was, but I could've gone about it a better way."

My chest warmed at his admission, something inside me relaxing.

"I put you in a difficult position—asking you to be both my attorney and my friend. I'm sure it's not an easy line to walk."

"At times, it's tricky. Like now. How do you want me to approach this situation?" he asked. "As your attorney or your

THE EXCEPTION

friend?" There was no hurt in his tone. No anger. We'd said our piece, and we could move on.

"Both," I said. "I know it's not fair of me to ask, but I need you to be both. And right now, I just need you to be my friend."

"Okay. As your friend, how are you doing?"

"I'm a fucking mess." I dragged a hand down my face. "I know I should be thinking about how we're going to handle this situation with Lily's family, but all I care about is making sure Sloan is okay."

Hell, I should've told Lily to go back to the château. Back to *les Journées du patrimoine*. But I was selfish, and I needed her here—with me.

"If I'd known what Jasper was planning," Pierce said, "I would've tried to stop it. Or at the very least given you a heads-up."

"I appreciate that. Just like I appreciate you for being here for me, for my family."

"Of course I'm here." He placed a hand on my shoulder. "You're family."

"Yes. We are."

And that was what family did—show up. But not Lily's family. At least, not without significant inducement—a free trip. I understood that money might be a barrier, but there were other ways they could support Lily, even from afar. It didn't seem like that had been the case, and it made me even more determined to give Lily my love and support.

After Piece excused himself to make a call, Lily took his place. "Everything okay?"

I placed my hand on her thigh and nodded. "I was an ass, and I needed to apologize to Pierce."

I wrapped my arm around her shoulder, and she leaned her head against me. It was comforting—having her here. And I was grateful she'd volunteered to come. I would've never asked her to choose between the château and me, but I now knew that if it came down to it, she'd put our family first. And that helped center me, just knowing that Lily was with me.

We waited for what felt like forever. But every time I glanced at my watch, only five minutes had passed. Still no word from Sloan or Jackson, and I was growing more and more anxious by the minute.

Every time the door from the hospital opened, I looked up, hoping it was Jackson with good news. And in between, I found myself questioning everything. My grandparents' decision to put me in charge. My plan to marry Lily to gain control of the board.

All I'd ever wanted was to protect my family and our brand, but in my quest to do so, was I actually destroying everything I loved? And if so, how could I keep the company intact but end this fight?

I was so lost in my thoughts that I didn't realize Jackson had come through the doors until Jasper shot out of his seat. I tried to get a read on Jackson's expression.

"How is she?" Jasper asked.

"The doctor said Sloan will be fine," Jackson said, relief etched on his features. "Baby too. But they want to keep her overnight for observation."

We all sagged with relief.

"That's great news," Lily said, stepping forward to place a hand on Jackson's shoulder. "How are you hanging in there?"

"Exhausted. Relieved. Grateful," he said, summarizing my own feelings. I felt as if I'd aged a decade over the course of an afternoon.

"What can we do to help?" Jasper asked. "Does Sloan need anything from the hotel? Do you?"

This was exactly why Jasper was so good at his job. He

was always so thoughtful. Always thinking of what would make others feel more comfortable. More at home.

Jackson shook his head. "We'll be fine, but thanks."

"Can we see her?" I asked, needing to check on my baby sister. To see for myself that she was okay.

"Actually, can I—" He tugged on his collar then glanced between Lily and Pierce. "Can I speak to Jasper and Graham alone for a minute?"

My stomach plummeted, and I worried that something was wrong. Something he didn't want Pierce and Lily to know.

"Of course," Lily said, giving my hand a squeeze. "Absolutely." She smiled, and I appreciated everything she'd done. The way she'd been there for my family, for me, especially on one of the biggest days of the year for the château.

I held her hand, not ready to let her go. When she glanced back, I mouthed, "Thank you." She nodded, and I knew she understood.

"Sloan is okay, but the doctors have cautioned us that she needs to severely limit her stress for a while now. I keep telling her that she has to slow down. Has to off-load some tasks, and she has. But this situation with the board has been a major stressor."

Jasper shot me a look as if to say, "See!"

"We're also concerned the board will deny our request to relocate to LA and refuse to let Graham take over in London."

The board had been playing hardball on that, and I didn't see it changing in the near future. Donahue seemed determined to punish me for thwarting Moretti's merger offer. And until the judge lifted the temporary restraining order to grant me the additional ten percent of the shares I'd garnered by marrying Lily, we were at an impasse.

It was only Jasper, Sloan, and I who had these relocation

restrictions. No one else in the company. I understood why the policy had been put in place, even if it was frustrating.

"The last thing I want to do is add stress," I said, feeling responsible. I was the leader of our company. I was her older brother. And *I* was the one who'd been flying back and forth between LA and France—putting a strain on everyone. I was the one who'd been stirring up shit with the board. "She should be enjoying her pregnancy. Taking care of herself."

"Agree one hundred percent," Jasper said.

I didn't know what I was going to do about the situation with the board, but Lily's comments and Sloan's current predicament had definitely reminded me of my priorities.

It also showed me the importance of trusting others, of communicating your needs. I wanted the people in my life, the people I loved, to know they could come to me. But clearly, I was doing a shitty job of it. If Sloan had approached me sooner about managing her workload, she wouldn't be in the hospital right now. If I hadn't been fighting with the board, she—and Jasper—would be a lot less stressed.

"We'll keep working on a solution," Jasper said. "We know how important it is."

Jackson's shoulders relaxed. "Good. Thank you."

I called out to Lily and Pierce that we'd be back soon.

Jackson led us through the hallways of the hospital until we reached a room. He knocked softly on the door then opened it slowly. *"Hayati?"*

She said something I didn't catch, and then Jackson waved us in.

"Hey." I smiled at Sloan when I stepped through the doorway. It was a relief to see her awake and sitting up. This was good. "How are you feeling?"

"I'm fine." She smoothed her hands over her stomach. "Baby's good. I'm ready to get out of here."

Jackson had already told us as much. But even so, I knew

she had to be scared. I'd been terrified when I'd heard that she was being taken to the hospital, and I could only imagine how I'd have felt if it had been Lily. I didn't let myself go there, couldn't.

Jasper and I shared a look. Sloan might be able to put on a good front for everyone else, but we weren't buying it.

I needed to make some changes. I needed to show them that we were a team—my siblings and I. And Lily and I. That I would listen to them and work with them, not make decisions for them.

I stepped closer to the bed and took Sloan's hand in mine. "I'm glad you're okay."

Jasper took a seat on the bed next to her, and Jackson excused himself to take a phone call. "Me too, Sloaney Baloney."

Sloan rolled her eyes at the childhood nickname but laughed anyway. "You guys didn't have to come to the hospital."

"Of course we did," I said. "We're family. And as a family, we need to make some changes."

Sloan sighed, her hands resting on her stomach. "I know."

"You do?" Jasper and I shared a look.

"Yeah. I do. I thought I was handling stress, but clearly, my body doesn't agree. Landing in the hospital was a big wake-up call."

"Graham and I are here for you," Jasper said. "Just tell us what you need. Whatever you need. Do you need to take a hiatus? Work fewer hours? What would help you most?"

"I don't want to take a hiatus, but I want to work from home several days a week and try to take more breaks during the day."

"That sounds like a good plan," Jasper said. "Maybe hire a personal chef or some more help around the house."

She nodded. "I've been interviewing some candidates from the Hartwell Agency."

"Good," I said, feeling hopeful.

"And Jackson's been encouraging me to trust our employees."

"We have great staff and teams in place, and I don't think any of us have been fully utilizing their talents," Jasper said.

Sloan nodded. "Halle is a great asset, and I can definitely lean on her. And you're right, Graham. I need to learn to delegate more."

"Exactly," I said. "You don't have to do it all. Traveling back and forth to the château showed me that. Honestly, in some ways, it's helped me achieve a better work-life balance."

"I'm sure wanting to spend time with your wife helps," Jasper said.

"It does. So, what's going on with you, Sloan? Because I know you love spending time with Jackson."

She toyed with the edge of the blanket. "I do love spending time with Jackson. But I think I've been so focused on everything I have to accomplish before the baby comes that the due date has come to feel like a ticking time bomb."

"What do you mean by that?" Jasper asked. "What do you think is adding to that time pressure?"

"I guess I just don't know what to expect once the baby comes. And I feel this compulsion to finish as much as I can before then."

"Life won't stop just because you have a baby," I said. "It'll change, yes. But you'll still be you. And the company will still be here."

She nodded, and it felt like we were all learning a lesson in trusting our teams more. In taking time away from the company to pursue our passions or spend time with the people we loved.

"What about the board?" Sloan asked. "What if we can't

get the majority of the shares? What if they decline our relocation requests? Not to mention that this battle is hurting the company."

"Actually, I have an idea," I said, glancing from Sloan to Jasper. "And I think it will solve everything. But I'm going to need your help."

Jasper laid his hand over mine. It was something we'd always done as kids. Something we hadn't done in years. I smiled at the memory of the three of us, hands stacked one on top of the other, swearing our allegiance as the Three Musketeers.

It had always been us against the world. We'd always counted on one another. And while life had changed and the company—and our family—had grown, I knew I could always count on my siblings. I was done trying to control everything. If we were going to succeed, we needed to do this together.

CHAPTER THIRTY-ONE

Lily

My phone buzzed, and I glanced at the screen, silently willing Graham to send me an update. He and Jasper had gone back to visit with Sloan a while ago, and I hoped everything was okay. Jackson's words had been reassuring, but I knew Graham was scared for her and the baby.

> Jo: You okay?

In all the craziness, I couldn't believe I'd forgotten to update Jo. And what about my family?

> Me: They're going to keep Graham's sister overnight, but it sounds like she'll be okay.

> Jo: Oh my goodness. I'm sorry, Lil. Can I do anything?

> Me: No, but thanks. Sorry I ditched you to deal with Luc and les Journee du patrimonie.

> Jo: Family comes first. We've got everything under control here.

I was about to slide my phone back into my purse when another text message arrived.

> Mom: I hope you don't plan to ignore your family the rest of our visit.

I really didn't have the bandwidth to deal with this right now. I was tempted not to respond, but I was trying to keep an open mind, as Graham had suggested.

> Me: I'm not ignoring you. I'm at the hospital with Graham. His sister was brought here.

And then Iris chimed in.

> Iris: Lily thinks she's too good for us now that she's married to a billionaire.

I GNASHED MY TEETH. I COULD NOT BELIEVE THE AUDACITY OF my family. I'd wanted to view their presence here as an olive branch, but nothing had changed.

I thought about Graham's family and how they'd jumped into action when Sloan had gone to the hospital. I thought about the worry and the panic, but also the love. That was the type of family I wanted, and I was done being treated like crap by my parents and siblings.

I could no longer be silent. I could no longer ignore them and the way they'd treated me.

This wasn't a conversation I wanted to have at all, let alone via text. So I headed outside and pressed the button to connect the call. I sat on a bench and set the phone in my lap on speaker mode.

"Lily," Mom said. "I'm sorry to hear about Graham's sister. It'd be nice if you put forth the same amount of effort for your own family. Especially since we came all this way."

I wasn't even going to dignify that with a response. Was she seriously comparing flying over for a visit to being in the hospital?

"Did you come here to see me or because you wanted a free trip?" I asked.

"Can't it be both?"

"Like you'd pass up a free trip," Iris said from the background. "You're the queen of mooching off luxury-travel brands."

Mom shushed her. "Your husband's family seems nice."

"They are very nice," I said in a cool tone. Cool. Calm. Collected. That was me.

Was there a point to this conversation? I kept hoping Mom would apologize, ask how I was, something. But it all felt surface-level, as always.

"Honey, why didn't you tell us you were married?"

"Why do you think?" I asked. Did she truly not understand?

"Is this because of Auntie Jackie's money? Because that was a silly misunderstanding."

A silly misunderstanding?

"Really?" I asked. "So it was a *misunderstanding* when Iris called me selfish because I wouldn't lend her money? It was a *misunderstanding* when you told me to apologize? It was a *misunderstanding*—" my voice rose with every sentence "—when the whole family ganged up on me as if *I'd* done something wrong?"

"Well, your sister was disappointed. She'd fallen in love with that house. She was counting on you."

"I don't know what gave her the impression that I had

that kind of money or that she would be entitled to any of it." Because that was how she acted—entitled.

"Auntie Jackie left you more than enough to share with the rest of us. Because that's what families do. They help one another."

Wow. I didn't even know why I was surprised anymore.

"I'm done talking about this," I bit out. "The money is gone."

"Auntie Jackie's money, perhaps. But now, you're married to a billionaire. Just think of—"

"Let me stop you right there." I stood, more than ready to be done with this conversation. "Even if I had access to Graham's money—which I don't, because I signed a prenup. But even if I hadn't, I wouldn't give you a cent. Not. One. Single. Cent." Every word I said was punctuated with anger.

"Liliana, we're your family," Mom said. "I'm sure you could cuddle up to that handsome husband of yours and convince him to do whatever you'd like."

Unbelievable.

She didn't deserve anything from me, least of all an explanation. But I felt compelled to say, "I love Graham because of who he is. I would still love him even if he didn't have a penny to his name."

"Oh, please," Iris said. "Cut the crap, Lily. You married him for money, and he…" She paused. "I have no idea why he married you."

She kept talking, but I was done listening. Nothing had changed.

All I knew was that Jo and Graham and his siblings had been more of a family to me than any of them ever had. It was what gave me the strength to finally say, "I'm no longer interested in your version of being a 'family.' I'm done. Don't call me again. And don't you even dare think about speaking to Graham's family."

My hands were shaking so badly that I had to jab the disconnect button several times to end the call. But when I finally ended it, I knew that was it. It was done. Over.

I took a few deep breaths and tried to collect myself. I knew from my experience with restoration that sometimes things got worse before they could get better. But right now, it felt like everything was falling apart.

When I stood and turned to go back inside, Graham was standing a few feet away, his expression like a thundercloud. He was pissed, and it was a glorious sight to behold. Fury radiated from him, his hands fisted at his sides.

"Jesus, Lil. Is that how your family usually speaks to you?"

I dropped my head and blew out a breath. "Yes."

He typed something on his phone and then held it to his ear. Before I could ask him what he was doing, he said, "Please escort the entire Fontaine family from the property. They are not welcome at the château or any of our homes or hotels."

My jaw dropped open in shock, but then he was making another call.

"Carson," he said. "I need you to add the Fontaine family to the list of unwelcome guests."

Carson said something I couldn't make out. Then Graham said, "Call the hotel in the Loire Valley and tell them the Fontaines are checking out immediately. Arrange for transportation to the airport, and please tell the pilot to have the plane ready in an hour."

It wasn't long before he ended the call, and I continued to stare at Graham in shock. No one had ever gone to bat for me like that against my family, not since Auntie Jackie had died. And here he was, angry and protective on my behalf.

"Wow. That was...unexpected."

"And entirely necessary." His eyes flashed with anger—for me. "No one hurts you and gets away with it."

"What if the board finds out?"

"*If* the board finds out, then they should be pleased that I was protecting my wife." The words flowed off his tongue, smooth as silk.

He always found a way to spin the situation to his advantage. Was that what he was doing with me?

I pushed away that thought. Years of dealing with my family's bullshit made it difficult for me to trust anything. Believe in anything. But I wanted to trust Graham. I *did* trust Graham. And yet, I couldn't seem to move past my doubts and fears.

After the day we'd had—after the interactions with my family and worrying about Sloan—my logical reasoning skills were shot. Emotion was in the driver's seat, and she could be a reckless bitch.

"Protecting your wife or protecting me, Lily?" I asked, hating how insecure I sounded.

He furrowed his brow, and then he seemed to decide something. He stepped forward, cupping the back of my neck. He looked me in the eye. "In case I haven't made it clear, the board can go fuck themselves. You're my wife. *You're* my priority."

I sucked in a gasp. He'd never said anything like that. Yes, he'd said he loved me. And I knew he did, but the board and their expectations had always loomed over our relationship. It was a big reason why we'd married after all.

"I'm protective of you not because of our agreement. Or because you're married to me. But because you're *you*. Because I. Love. You, Lily."

My shoulders relaxed, and something inside me eased at his words. "I'm sorry. I know you love me. Interacting with my family just really fucks with my head."

"I can imagine," Graham said, rubbing my shoulders. "And I'm proud of you for standing up to them. I would've never suggested that you hear them out if I'd understood the extent of their toxic behavior. I'm sorry."

"You couldn't have known. I should've told you." I wished I had.

"I'm done letting people push my family around. I'm done letting the board control my life. I'm done letting them hurt the people I love."

"I get that, but until they concede the fact that you and your family own a majority share, nothing's going to change."

"I know. Which is why it's time for me to make a change." He took a deep breath then said, "I'm stepping down as CEO."

"What?" I jerked my head back. "You can't." I lifted my hands to my mouth. "Why would you do that? You can't do that."

"I can." He tucked my hair behind my ear. "And I am. I've already asked Pierce to draw up the papers to name Jasper as CEO."

"But, but—" I sputtered. Was he serious? He couldn't be serious.

This wasn't what he wanted. This wasn't what I wanted—him to give up the thing he held most dear.

He cupped my cheek. "For years, I adopted a certain persona because that's what I thought I had to do to survive. But loving you has made me remember who I am and that I'm worthy of so much more than just surviving."

I placed my hand over his heart, warmed by his admission. His revelation. "You are."

"And your insistence on communication, on vulnerability—"

"Emphasis," I teased.

"Mm. You have been pretty persistent." He gave me a knowing look.

"Persuasive." I bit back a smile, loving our banter.

"That's true." The corner of his mouth tilted upward. "What I'm trying to say is that working with you on the château, spending more time with my family, has made me realize what I want for the future. And as much as I've loved running the Huxley brand, I no longer want to feel shackled to the past. My grandparents wouldn't have wanted that for me either."

"Then what do you want?" I asked, scarcely able to breathe.

The idea of Graham stepping down as the CEO of Huxley was unthinkable.

"First step. We tear up our contract. The trust is fully funded, and I find that I no longer require a wife to achieve my goals."

My heart dropped.

"And while I may not *need* a wife, I want you in my life. On your terms. Because you want to be there, not because you're legally obligated to be at my side."

I laughed, relief and happiness washing over me. "Of course I want to be in your life. I love you."

But I also didn't want him to do something he'd later regret. I didn't want him to make such a drastic change that he'd come to resent me for.

I chewed on the inside of my cheek. "This brand, your grandparents' company, is your life. Your everything."

He shook his head, peering down at me with so much love and affection I felt as if my heart might burst. "*You* are my everything."

"And you're mine."

I grasped his shirt, pulling his lips down to mine. With our mouths pressed together, I felt whole. I felt seen and loved.

"I love you, and I will support whatever you decide," I said. "But I don't want you to give up your company for me."

"That's just it," he said, forehead pressed to mine. "It's not for you. Or at least, not just for you. It's for me. It's for my family. It's for the brand."

I frowned. "I'm not sure I understand." In my mind, there was no one better suited to run the Huxley Grand. No one more dedicated.

Not that Jasper wasn't qualified or couldn't do a good job. But he wasn't Graham. And I knew how much the company and his grandparents' legacy meant to my husband. If anyone understood the lengths he was willing to go to to protect it, it was me. The woman who'd entered into a marriage of convenience to help him do just that.

"The situation with the board is causing unnecessary stress to everyone. It's part of why Sloan ended up in the hospital."

I squeezed his bicep, silently lending my support. My encouragement.

"If Jasper takes over as CEO, it ushers in an era of new leadership. You know Jasper—he can make anyone fall for him. He will bring a warmth and playfulness to the role that's been missing. And, if I'm right, I think the board will be less focused on me gaining the additional ten percent of the shares because I would no longer be in control."

"Don't you worry that they'll suspect you're still pulling the strings, just working behind the scenes?"

"Not if I'm in a completely different role. And if I were no longer the CEO or an SVP, we could relocate here permanently. As soon as the change goes through."

"What?" I shrieked.

"I love the château, and I love our life here. It's fulfilling in a way that running the Huxley brand hasn't been for a long time. It was as if I was using my role as CEO and my quest to defend my grandparents' legacy to fill the void of losing them."

"Wow. That's..." I tried to ignore the sting of oncoming tears. "That's intense but powerful."

"It was. Both. And it helped me realize some other things as well."

And this was why I loved this man. I was so proud of him. He no longer held in his thoughts and his feelings; he shared them freely with me. He trusted me. We were partners in every sense of the word.

When I looked at him, I realized then how light he seemed. How unburdened. As if the weight of the world had been lifted from his shoulders.

"But they also wanted the company to evolve. They'd want me to evolve. New leadership brings fresh perspectives. And Jasper has always had great ideas."

"And Sloan?" I asked.

"She's not at a point that she would want to take on that role. Maybe someday, but right now, she wants to focus on her health and her growing family."

I found myself relaxing, secure in the knowledge that Graham was making the best decision for himself. Not just for us.

"I'm glad you love the château as much as I do. It's a big reason why I've been wanting to add your name to the deed."

His eyes flashed to mine. "You have?"

I nodded. "I spoke to Pierce about the legalities, and he assured me it was fine."

Graham knelt to the ground.

"What are you doing?" I asked, glancing around to see if anyone was watching, but the parking lot was empty.

"I have a proposal."

"Oh yeah?" I arched an eyebrow. "Let me guess. You want to help me. We'll help each other," I teased, paraphrasing his suggestion from that first night in Ixtapa when he'd asked me to marry him.

"Mm." He grinned, and it lit me up inside. "Something like that."

"This isn't a negotiation." I rolled my eyes, but it was playful.

"I know." His expression turned solemn. "It's a relationship. And in a relationship, there's give-and-take. And Lily—" he gripped my chin "—make no mistake. My love for you comes with no conditions or expectations. And I promise to spend every day for the rest of my life proving that to you. Will you be my wife? My partner? My friend?"

A tear streaked down my cheek. He didn't have to say it; I *knew* it in the very fabric of my soul.

Now, there was nothing but love between us. No contracts. No agreements.

I still couldn't quite believe he was stepping down as CEO. Moving to the château to help me fulfill my dreams—*our dreams*, I reminded myself. I had a feeling Auntie Jackie would've approved.

I leaned forward, wrapping my arms around his shoulders. "Of course I will. And you don't have anything to prove. I already know you love me."

"*Sans cesse.*" He kissed me gently, with great tenderness. "*Toujours.*"

"*À tout jamais,*" I said as he swiped a tear from my cheek.

My husband. I smiled to myself. Somehow, I'd known it all along. My heart had led me to him before my brain could catch up. But now, everything was on the same page. My mind, body, heart, and soul.

Graham and I were going to live life on our terms. And I couldn't wait to see what the future had in store for us. If the past few months were anything to go by, a lot of dust but also a lot of passion too. We were partners, and I couldn't imagine spending my life with anyone else.

CHAPTER THIRTY-TWO

Graham

Eight Months Later

"Can I get your advice on something?" Jasper asked.

He was sitting in his office in LA, my former office. And we were waiting for Sloan to join us on our video chat. She was still easing back into work, and I was glad she was taking time to recover and enjoy baby snuggles with the newest member of the family—Henry. He was adorable, and everyone was in love with him.

"Is it about the Thailand project?" I asked.

Jasper had taken over as CEO six months ago, and it had been a relatively smooth transition, all things considered. Once I'd explained my vision for my new role and reminded the board of all the reasons why Jasper would be an excellent leader for the brand, the vote had been overwhelmingly in favor of the plan.

The board had also stopped pushing back on my marriage to Lily, perhaps accepting that my decision to step down as CEO proved that my feelings—our marriage—were real. They'd dropped their lawsuit, and we'd come to a compromise—the ten percent of shares that I'd received from my marriage would be divided equally between me and my siblings. All ten percent would come from Donahue.

That escort scandal? The rumors had been started by him, and he'd continued to fuel them. He'd actively worked to bring down the company by spreading malicious lies about Huxley Grand locations filling its bars with escorts.

When the board discovered that—through an "anonymous tip," of course—they'd conducted an investigation. He had been stripped of his shares for trying to sabotage the company. Not long after that, Danika sold her shares. Nate had purchased them to solidify our family's stake in the company.

I had a strong feeling the takeover scheme had been Moretti's plan, but I had yet to discover a direct link. And honestly, I no longer cared.

"No. Closer to home, actually," Jasper said.

Occasionally, Jasper would ask my advice, but it wasn't a frequent occurrence. He was holding his own, and he was doing a phenomenal job. It was as if now that I'd taken myself out of the equation, he could truly find his voice.

He'd been hesitant to take on the role when I'd first suggested it, and it made me proud to see him succeed. He might not always do things the way I did, but he was staying true to the ethos of the Huxley brand while putting his own spin on it. I only wished Pops and Gran could've seen all that we'd accomplished—together.

"New York?" Atlas Blackwood was developing a new property there, and it was going to be a masterpiece.

Jasper glanced away and then back at the screen before leaning in. "Halle is driving me crazy."

I leaned back in my chair, fighting a smile. "Sounds like she's doing a good job."

He grumbled, and I chuckled some more.

"Don't worry. It's temporary. Sloan will be back in a few months, and then you won't have to work with Halle so closely."

Sloan's face appeared on the screen, baby Henry asleep on her chest in a wrap. "Were you two talking about me again?" she teased, looking tired but happy.

"We were talking about Halle," I said. "She and Jasper are having issues."

"That surprises me. I thought the two of you got on fine while you were in London during my sailing trip the summer before last."

Jasper said nothing, but his eye twitched. *Interesting.*

"Enough about me," Jasper said. "What's going on with the two of you?"

Sloan told us about Henry's latest developments. Jackson and Sloan were both on three months' paid leave, as was standard for our company after a baby was born or adopted.

Conversation turned to the château, though they were already pretty up-to-date, thanks to Lily's YouStream channel and our frequent chats. My relationship with them was so different now that I was no longer the boss. Now that I'd released myself from the need to control everything and protect everyone. It was freeing.

When I'd stepped down as CEO of the Huxley brand, I'd stepped into a new role with Fleur-de-Lis—a recently formed subsidiary. Lily and I were developing a line of Huxley Grand properties under that umbrella—smaller, boutique resorts at historically significant properties. It had been inspired by Lily's efforts to restore the château.

I wanted to breathe new life into older properties, restoring them while updating them with modern amenities and focusing on sustainability. For our first project, we'd selected a castle in Scotland. It was a mess, but it had so much potential. And the board had given us the green light.

Sloan, Jasper, and I discussed the new SVP, the upcoming board meeting, and then I hopped on a few more calls. By the end of the afternoon, I was impatient to be outside. It was a sunny day, and I'd much rather be working in the garden.

Finally, I signed off my last call and tugged on my boots. Prince Albert and Queen V followed me outside, sniffing the ground and exploring as we went off in search of Lily. They hung back with Luc when we crossed paths, and he told me where I could find my wife.

I leaned against the château and watched Lily from the shade of the tarp that had been erected over the roof like a canopy. Her boots were covered in dirt, and she wore a colorful scarf I'd given her for her birthday wrapped around her head. Her hat was sitting off to the side along with her water bottle, and I wondered how long she'd been at it.

We were nearing the finish line with the roof restoration, and I couldn't wait for the rest of the scaffolding to come down. In the meantime, Lily and I continued to work on other projects around the château and the grounds.

The garden was coming along nicely, and I only wished Gran were here to see it. She would've delighted in such a large space to plant, to grow. I certainly did. Lily and I had tried to recreate some of what the landscaping would've looked like when the château was constructed, but we'd also added our own contributions. We had a vegetable garden and were hoping to add some horses to the stables.

Every day, the château presented new discoveries and new challenges. But Lily and I took them in stride—together. Because we were partners.

Our latest project involved preparing the dry moat for restoration. Lily was currently working in one of the caves of the dry moat, cleaning away trash and debris. She used her whole body to attack the ground with her shovel, and I marveled at her strength. Her determination.

She caught sight of me and stilled, smiling. I rubbed at the pang in my chest, even as I smiled back. She was covered in mud and dirt, and she was beautiful.

Lily set down her shovel and removed her gloves before wiping her brow with the back of her forearm. "You just going to watch me, or are you going to help?"

I took a step closer to her, needing to touch her. "Maybe I'll do both."

She smirked. We both knew we were no longer discussing the work at the château. I gave her a quick peck on the lips. "Hi."

"Hey." She smiled up at me. "How was your call with the board?"

"Good," I said. Better than good.

Stepping down as the CEO of the Huxley brand had been the right move. For so long, I'd defined myself as the head of the company that I hadn't let myself consider anything else. Hadn't allowed myself to want anything else.

I'd clung so tightly to the brand and my control over it that I'd nearly destroyed everything I loved in the process. My relationships with my siblings. With Lily.

"Stock prices are way up, so the board should be happy."

"Mm." I placed my hands on her waist. "I love it when you talk dirty to me."

She smoothed her hands up my chest, my eyes snagging on her wedding band. She wore it every day, and I loved seeing it on her finger. "What else do you love?"

I leaned down, nipping at her earlobe. "That thing you do with your tongue…"

"The—" She bit her lip.

"Yes," I rasped, my cock already growing hard. "And I love how passionate you are about our projects."

"Oh." She palmed me through my pants. "Is that what you came here to discuss?" she teased. "Our projects?"

"Among other things." I couldn't help the guttural groan that escaped my lips.

She clutched my shirt, pulling me deeper into the cave with her. It was cooler in the shaded alcove, but my body was on fire for her.

I palmed her breast through her shirt, hating all the layers of fabric separating us. I slid my hand down to her waistband, prying it open, smoothing my hand beneath her underwear until I was cupping her mound.

"Oh god," she whimpered as I began to tease her clit. "Oh, Graham."

I covered her mouth with mine in an effort to silence her. I liked when she was loud, but her pleasure was mine and mine alone. With so many artisans and workers always on the property, we needed to be quiet. Though the constant background noise of construction did provide some cover.

"I need you," she panted. She was already close. "Need you inside me. Now."

I didn't withdraw my hand. I didn't change my pace. "You can have my dick after you've come on my fingers."

She moaned, her eyes rolling back in her head. She let out a string of unintelligible sounds, and I kissed her forehead, her cheekbones, her jawline. Anywhere I could reach.

All the while, she kept pumping my cock, and I was damn near ready to burst. I needed her to come—and soon. I needed to be inside her.

"Please. Please. Please," she chanted. I wasn't sure if she was begging to come or begging for me to be inside her. Maybe both. But on this, I would remain firm—I would always make sure she came first and often.

"Tell me what you need," I said. "Tell me what you like."

She held my wrist and guided me to where she wanted my touch. "There," she moaned. And then her face twisted with pleasure as she convulsed in my arms.

"Oh. Oh. Oh," she panted. "Oh god." She collapsed against me. "Oh my god." She giggled. "That was intense."

"Good." I kissed her forehead, holding her to me.

When my cock nudged her stomach, she asked, "Should we take care of this?"

I chuckled. "What did you have in mind?"

It wasn't the first time we'd had sex outside, but the other times, we'd had a picnic blanket to lie on. In this storage cave, our options were limited, as was the window of time before Luc or someone would inevitably come looking for us.

She shoved down her pants and turned her back to me. "Do me from behind."

Fuck. Yes.

She bent forward and braced herself against the wall. And her ass. My god, her ass was gorgeous. All of her was. I held my cock with one hand and palmed her ass with the other.

"What are you waiting for?" she asked. "Fuck me."

"Yes, ma'am," I teased, then plunged inside her.

She gasped and I groaned, our sounds a symphony of pleasure that echoed off the stone walls. I bent forward, curving myself around her, kissing her neck.

"You feel so good," I rasped. "Your cunt squeezing my cock, wanting to drain me."

I planted one hand on the wall to steady myself and wrapped the other around her waist, needing to be as close to her as possible.

"Harder," she begged, so I thrust inside her harder, faster, until sweat was dripping down my spine, and I didn't know how much longer I'd last.

With clumsy movements, I sought out her clit. I circled it until she was quivering in my arms once more. She was on the brink of her release, and I held on a moment longer before a jolt of energy shot up my spine and out my cock.

"Yes." She moved with me now. "*Yes.*" Her voice was higher pitched.

I sped up my pace, unleashing myself into her. Pouring all my love and desire, my hopes and dreams, into this woman. A woman who took it all and who saw me as I was. Accepted me as I was. Loved me as I was.

She sagged against the wall, and I rested my head on her back. As we were still catching our breath, she giggled.

"That was fun." She turned to face me, her smile bright.

"It was," I said, pulling up my pants and righting my clothes. I helped her do the same before giving her a quick peck on the lips.

She took a sip of water before offering me some. I thanked her with another kiss and guzzled some down.

"I want to hear more about your meetings. Any news on our offer to purchase the site?"

I tried to tamp down my enthusiasm. "We got it."

She wrapped her arms around my neck, pressing her breasts against my chest as she kissed me. "That's so exciting! I can't wait to get started on it."

I kissed her again, loving her enthusiasm.

Lily and I would oversee the restoration of the Scotland property, mostly from afar. And we'd continue scouting additional locations for the new line, while working to restore our château.

"Oh, I heard from Jo," Lily said. "She plans to come for *les Journées du patrimoine* again."

"Great. I'll ask Carson to have the jet stop in New York to fuel and pick up Jo."

Carson had relocated to France with us. He no longer worked for the Huxley brand; he worked directly for Lily and me. He was passionate about the château, and he lived in a small house in the village nearby with a French man he'd fallen in love with.

"Sloan and Jasper send their love," I said.

"Aw. I miss them. And I miss baby Henry and his cute little chubby cheeks."

I arched a brow. Did Lily want a baby? She'd mentioned possibly wanting children someday, but only if she found the right person. We'd been so busy with the château and everything else, we hadn't discussed it since.

"What?" she asked.

"Do you…" I wasn't sure how to ask this. I knew how I felt about it, but I found myself suddenly hesitant to ask. Afraid to hear her answer. "Do you want to have kids?"

She studied me a moment then nodded.

"Do you want to have kids with me?" I asked.

She nodded again. "Yeah. I mean…if that's what you want." It came out as more of a question, and I sensed she was nervous.

I took her hands in mine. "Even though we're not married for real," I teased.

Somehow, my grandparents had known exactly what I'd needed. And I liked to think that their marriage clause—as annoyed as I had been by it—was responsible for bringing Lily and me together.

Lily slapped my chest playfully. "Our marriage is real."

"Hey." I lifted my hands. "I'm merely repeating what you often said."

She narrowed her eyes at me.

"You're the one who said you might want to get married for real someday and have kids."

"Actually, I've been thinking about that."

I furrowed my brow. Where was she going with this?

"I know you don't like attention, but I feel like we should have a wedding redo. We could host it here, recite new vows that are more authentic to our relationship now. And invite your family."

"But still not yours," I said, and we shared a look.

Her family was still on my shit list for the way they'd treated her. Over the past few months, they'd called and texted a few times. Lily had yet to respond to their texts, even though they'd tried to apologize. Sadly, we both suspected it was a thinly veiled attempt to get back in her good graces so they could ask for money.

I hated it for her. And though I'd offered to do some hacking to make them pay, she said they weren't worth the effort. She was right. I was no longer pouring my energy into things that didn't matter.

"When?" I asked.

"Next summer."

I shook my head.

"Too soon?"

"Too far away," I said, pulling her to me. "I don't want to wait that long."

"To get married or…" She trailed off.

"Both," I said.

She jerked her head back. "Both? As in—" Her cheeks flushed. "As in, you want to have a baby?"

"As soon as you're ready, yes."

She threw herself at me, wrapping her arms around my neck. I caught her, hoisting her up so her legs were wrapped around my waist, her ass in my hands.

She held me tight, and it was only when her breath hitched that I realized she was crying. I loosened my grip, and she slid down my body to stand before me.

"What's wrong?" I asked.

She swiped away a tear, smiling as she did so. "Nothing. I'm just really happy."

I cupped her cheeks. "Me too. *Je t'aime, mon cœur.*" Because that's what she was—my heart. My love. My everything.

She grabbed her hat and water bottle. "Oh—" She held up her pointer finger. "Before I forget, I have a surprise for you."

"What kind of surprise?" I asked, intrigued.

"Close your eyes."

"Mm. Okay. I'll play along," I teased, adding a seductive lilt to my voice.

"Not *that*." She rolled her eyes. "Jeez. I mean, yes, I want kids. But I'm not sure I'm ready to start trying for a baby just yet. We already have so much on our plate."

"It's your decision," I said, meaning every word. "But just know that when the time comes…" I leaned in, my cock making its presence known against her hip as I rasped, "I will fill your pussy with my come until my seed is dripping out of you." She gasped, but I wasn't done. "And then I'll shove it back inside your greedy little cunt until you come again."

She shivered, and when I pulled back, her eyes were glazed over. "Okay. Um. Wow." She swallowed hard. "Maybe we should cut the day short and start trying now."

"What about wanting to wait?" I teased.

She smirked, running her hands up my chest. "Is it selfish that I want you all to myself just a little longer?"

I slanted my mouth against hers. "Not at all." In fact, I loved it. Loved that she wanted me all to herself.

I wrapped my arm around her shoulder. "Now, what's this about a surprise?"

"Oh. Right." She linked our hands together. "This way, please." She grinned and tugged me toward the entrance to our formal gardens.

There was a lawn overlooking them, and I paused when I noticed several metal benches that hadn't been there before. I'd seen them, but at the time, they'd been in one of the outbuildings. And they'd been in desperate need of some attention.

"These just got back from being restored." She pulled me closer. On each bench was a plaque.

I leaned forward, reading the inscription in the first one. When I realized she'd dedicated it to my parents, I was overcome with emotion.

"Thank you. That's beautiful," I said, touched by the gesture.

"And this one," she said.

The other was dedicated to my grandparents, and a bouquet of sunflowers rested on top. It felt as if they were there with us. Watching over us, in the home that we'd created. I grabbed the bouquet, and we sank down onto the bench. I wrapped my arm around Lily, kissing the top of her head.

"I love that you did this," I said, my throat clogged with emotion. "I love you."

"I love you." Lily turned her face to mine, our mouths connecting. "And *this*," Lily said as we looked out over the grounds, "is *our* legacy. A reflection of our past and a promise of the future we're building—together."

We stayed there for a while, reveling in all our hard work. In what we'd created. Of everything I'd done so far in my life, I was most proud of this. Of my relationship with Lily.

To think that I'd once been afraid of forever, when it was now all I wanted.

I kissed her again, and then she stood. "Come on. I want to show you one more thing."

"You're just full of surprises today, aren't you?" I chuckled.

She led me toward our vegetable garden, and I swore I heard the sound of clucking. A chicken coop came into view, and I glanced at her.

"Surprise!" She smiled. "I know how much you enjoyed caring for Lady Lorraine, and I just thought…"

"I love it," I said. "And I love you."

"I love you too." She pressed up on her toes, tilting her hat back to give me a kiss.

As I stood in the field of sunflowers with the love of my life, I knew this was exactly where I was meant to be. Lily and I had faced so many obstacles, and yet, we'd persevered. I pressed a kiss to her lips, and I was filled with nothing but hope.

Acknowledgements

When I was a kid, my family and I loved touring historic homes. I've always been fascinated by construction, and both my parents have held various jobs and volunteer positions in industries that involve building homes. Which was why researching the process of restoring a French château was so incredibly appealing to me. It's also why I can relate to Graham and his love of projects.

It feels good to create. To build something, whether it's a story constructed of words or a house built from wood. And I encourage you to find something you can create, whether it's a writing project, knitting, gardening, or building community; it feels good. The world can feel like a dark, isolating place, but building something positive can bring joy and hope.

Organize a trash clean-up. A book club. A protest. Do something! You'll feel better, I promise.

Ahem. Back to the story. I knew that Graham needed a push if he was going to fall in love. If he was going to believe himself capable of romantic love. A marriage of convenience was just the thing. It would force him to pretend to be in love and create a relationship he couldn't walk away from.

I've always enjoyed the fake relationship trope (see *Reputation* for example), but a marriage of convenience was tricky to me. I wanted their justifications to be believable. I wanted their relationship to be a partnership.

They had to overcome some obstacles, but I loved seeing Lily and Graham grow and communicate. And ultimately, fall in love.

Their story took longer than I expected but honestly, there was a lot going on in my life during the time I wrote their story. At times, writing was what kept me going.

I'm sad to leave them, but I'm also excited to see what's next for this family and this series. And don't worry...I'm sure there will be glimpses of Lily and Graham in future books. Just as we see of our favorite characters from earlier in the series in *The Exception*.

Thank you for going on this journey with me. I've been blown away by the response to the entire Tempt Series. And I am so so happy that so many of you love these characters as much as I do!

A HUGE thank you to all the readers who share your love for my stories. I could not do this without you.

Nor could I do this without my incredible team. Thank you to Angela for always being encouraging and supportive. For helping me with all the details, so I can focus on the big picture.

A huge thank you to my beta readers. Thank you for making me a stronger writer, for offering your unique insight and advice. You each bring something different to the table, and I'm always amazed and impressed by your suggestions. I'm so incredibly honored to have you on my team!

Thank you, Jade. You make me a stronger writer, and you challenge me on pacing. You are so clever and always provide great insight. I'm so grateful for your friendship, and our long chats! This story wouldn't be the same without you, and your help with all the French. Thank you for reading a million different versions of this story and always providing such valuable suggestions.

A huge thank you to Kristen for being such an amazing friend. I value your judgment and honesty, and I so appreciate your support. We've been through so much together, and I treasure your friendship and advice. Seriously, I cannot thank you enough for all that you do. You are my "hype girl." You always pump me up and make me feel fabulous.

Beth, thank you so much for your encouragement and support. I'm so delighted that we reconnected after all these years!

Thank you to Ellen, as always. Thank you for sharing your incredible eye for detail. Your comments are always priceless, and this book was no exception! I couldn't do it without you.

To my editor, Lisa with Silently Correcting Your Grammar. I so appreciate your attention to detail, and your patience with my questions. You always go above and beyond and this time was no exception. I value your insight and your friendship. While I hate that we've been experiencing some of the same trials, it's nice to have someone to talk to who truly understands.

A huge shout out to all my fellow authors. Sometimes this job can feel so solitary, but I know you're all out there. And we're all cheering each other on.

A big thank you to the Hartley's Hustlers and my Sweetharts. You rock! I cannot possibly tell you how much your support means to me! I appreciate everything you do to promote my books and to encourage me throughout my writing journey.

Thank you to my husband for always encouraging me. For always supporting my dreams and believing in me. You are better than any book boyfriend I could ever imagine. You constantly build me up, and I couldn't ask for a better partner.

And to my daughter, for always putting a smile on my face. You are spirited and independent, and I wouldn't have it any other way. Dream big, my darling.

Thank you to my parents for always being so encouraging. For reading my books. For being my biggest fans!

Dear reader, if this list of people shows you anything, it's that dreams are often the effort of many. I'm grateful to have such an awesome team. And I'm honored that you've taken the time to read my words.

About the Author

Jenna Hartley is *USA Today* bestselling author who writes feel-good forbidden romance, much like her own real-life love story. She's known for writing strong women and swoon-worthy men, as well as blending panty-melting and heart-warming moments.

When she's not reading or writing romance, Jenna can be found tending to her growing indoor plant collection (pun intended), organizing, and hiking. She lives in Texas with her family and loves nothing more than a good book and good chocolate, except a dance party with her daughter.

www.authorjennahartley.com

Also by Jenna Hartley

Love in LA Series
Inevitable
Unexpected
Irresistible
Undeniable
Unpredictable
Irreplaceable

Alondra Valley Series
Feels Like Love
Love Like No Other
A Love Like That

Tempt Series
Temptation
Reputation
Redemption
The Exception

For the most current list of Jenna's titles, please visit her website www.authorjennahartley.com.

Or scan the QR code on the following page to be taken to her author page on Amazon.com

ALSO BY JENNA HARTLEY

NOTES